John George Marks

# Life and Letters of Frederick Walker, A. R. A.

John George Marks

**Life and Letters of Frederick Walker, A. R. A.**

ISBN/EAN: 9783337017415

Printed in Europe, USA, Canada, Australia, Japan

Cover: Foto ©Raphael Reischuk / pixelio.de

More available books at **www.hansebooks.com**

Frederick Walker, A.R.A.

# LIFE AND LETTERS

OF

# FREDERICK WALKER, A.R.A.

BY

## JOHN GEORGE MARKS

Our business is not to wish the artist different, but to find out what he is, and to love him within the necessary limits of his sphere.—STOPFORD BROOKE.

*With Illustrations*

London

MACMILLAN AND CO., Ltd.

NEW YORK: THE MACMILLAN CO.

1896

*(The Right of Translation and Reproduction is Reserved)*

# PREFACE

ALTHOUGH in these days of book-making, no apology may be necessary for adding another to the number, I owe it to myself to state the reasons that have led me thus far to venture into unfamiliar paths. Chiefly they were these:—that the accident of my connection with Walker had placed in my hands a large number of his home letters, illustrative, as it seemed, of character ; and a belief that while his works endure, not only the present, but succeeding generations, will wish to know what manner of man he was who gave them birth.

These considerations, if offering sufficient excuse for a biography, did not in themselves point to me as the author of it. It was obvious that by placing the letters in properly qualified hands, more might be made of them from a literary point of view, than I could hope to arrive at. On the other hand, it appeared to be a necessity that any one making use of the letters should possess that intimate and continuous knowledge, not only of Walker but of his family, which would be likely to ensure due recognition of the points of character to be gathered from them, and sufficient explanation of their references to work. On the whole, in the opinion of my friends, it seemed best that I should attempt the task.

Thus much having been settled, the scope of the book fell naturally within certain well-defined lines. Whatever might have been the case had the letters been placed in other hands, it was no part of my duty to assume in any way the implied superiority of the critic. In no sense is the book a dissertation on Walker as a painter, or an attempt to estimate his place in the world of art. It is simply an endeavour, mainly by means of his own words, to give a picture of the man, and of the circumstances under which his works were produced. Such criticism by others as appears has been given for its historical value, as showing the manner in which he was received by his contemporaries.

In the letters themselves—many still in their envelopes as when opened by eager, loving hands; some still containing the dried and faded flower that once breathed of moor or hill-side—it has been thought best, for the convenience of the reader, to make some slight alterations. These consist chiefly of a more decided division into sentences [Walker having largely employed a dash instead of a full stop], and additions to the punctuation. Here and there an obviously missing word has been supplied, or a palpable error corrected, but in no case has the sense been in any way altered.

It has been a satisfaction to me, in dealing with such intimate letters, to come across evidence in Mrs. Walker's handwriting that she had in view the possibility of some such use as the present being made of them.

The assistance given me by others in the progress of the work has laid me under obligations which are poorly repaid by thanks. To my friend and neighbour, Miss Clementina Black, who has aided me by her skilled advice, as well as in more active ways; to Messrs. Thos. Agnew and Sons who have allowed me to reproduce those works in which they have an interest; to the owners whose names are given in the list of illustrations; and to those who have so greatly added to the value of the book by their notes; I tender my warmest acknowledgments. The manner in which the owners of the pictures and drawings have responded to my request for permission to reproduce them has been most gratifying, and has enabled me to bring together a collection in which but few important works of original subjects are missing. In this connection, I would especially thank Sir William Agnew, who not only has allowed the reproduction of the valuable works in his possession, and supplied me with an interesting note, but has personally procured for me the names of other owners.

Lastly, I would fain give fitting acknowledgment to my friend Mr. J. W. North, A. R. A., not only for the matter but the manner of his help. How much the book would have lost had his help been wanting, the reader will be able to judge. For me, the days I have spent with him when he piloted me over the historic ground of *The Old Gate*, *The Plough*, *The Right of Way*, must ever rank as the pleasantest part of my labours. In these times, and in the many letters which have passed between us, I have learned to know him better, and fully to enter into the regard in which Walker held him.

J. G. M.

BOSWELL HOUSE,
    SOUTH END,
        CROYDON.
            *September* 1896.

# CONTENTS

# CONTENTS

CHAPTER X

# LIST OF ILLUSTRATIONS

With the exception of those on pp. 22, 23, 254, and 313, all the illustrations are reproductions of Walker's own work. Those against which no owner's name appears have been supplied by the author.

## PLATES.



## ILLUSTRATIONS IN THE TEXT

# LIFE AND LETTERS

OF

# FREDERICK WALKER, A.R.A.

# LIFE AND LETTERS

OF

# FREDERICK WALKER, A.R.A.

## CHAPTER I

### EARLY YEARS

FREDERICK WALKER was born at 90, Great Titchfield Street, Marylebone, London, at half-past six o'clock in the evening of May 26, 1840, the elder of twins; his twin sister, Sarah, afterwards becoming the wife of the present writer. He was the fifth son, and seventh child, of William Henry Walker, and Ann (*neé* Powell) his wife; and his entrance into the world preceded that of his twin sister by a quarter of an hour. His father was a working jeweller in but a moderate way of business. As the family was a large one—ten children in all—it must have been no inconsiderable struggle to provide for and educate them.

There is a tradition (how far well-founded I do not know) that an ancestor of Walker's was the William Walker mentioned in Shakespeare's Will; and also that another ancestor fought as a lieutenant at Culloden. What is more to the purpose is that his grandfather, William Walker, was an artist, and is so described in the catalogue of the sale of his effects in 1812. To what extent William Walker had made a name for himself, I cannot say. There are, however, two portraits by him in existence, one of his wife, and the other of himself, which are certainly far above mediocrity. An uncle of Walker's, too, on his father's side, writing from America in the year 1835, speaks of engaging himself to Mr. Thomas Say, "the American Linnæus"; printing and engraving copper-plates for a work of Mr. Say's; so that we are not without evidence on which the curious in such matters can propound the theory of heredity in Walker's case. That he inherited from his mother a large amount of artistic perception, there is little doubt. No one who knew her intimately could fail to be struck by her expression of keenest enjoyment at the sight of anything beautiful in her surroundings. She had a little way of almost hugging herself as anything took her fancy—a pretty group of children, especially rustic children, the beauties of flowers, and trees, and grace of movement, and colour—and I have often thought the mother's influence is clearly traceable in much of her son's work, particularly in the more homely character of some of his earlier subjects. For what of loving care and watchful tenderness he was also indebted to her, we shall see as we go on.

Walker's father died about the year 1847, leaving eight children; and by a Will dated January 31, 1846, he left his business in the hands of trustees (his wife among them), to be carried on by them until his second son Henry came of age (which would be October 28, 1852), after which it was to pass absolutely to his wife, his eldest and second sons, to be carried on by them for the purpose of maintaining, supporting, and educating, themselves and the rest of the family. The income from the business, however, does not appear to have been sufficient for the purpose, even before the father's death; for at an early date Mrs. Walker was engaged in laying the foundations of a business as embroidress, which afterwards became for a time the family's chief support.

Of Walker's school days there is little to be said. It appears from a prize book that he was at " Cleveland Academy " (wherever that may have been) in 1851; though his principal schooling was at the North London Collegiate School, where he was during the latter half of 1853, but for how long before and after that date, I cannot say. A school copy pencil drawing, dated in that year, is in existence; and its possessor remembers seeing a drawing of the interior of the schoolroom with boys at work, done by Walker about the same time. In addition to his fondness for drawing, he was also very ingeniously and mechanically inclined; making cardboard models of hansom and four-wheeled cabs, an electrical machine, and similar things, as boys of a constructive turn of mind will. There are abundant evidences, both in his school days and at other times, that the passion for drawing was strong in him from his youth up. His earliest attempts at anything like systematic art training appear to have taken the form of copying wood engravings from the illustrated papers. An early letter, written from the sea-side in June 1854, asks for " the picture of ' The Turkish Coffee House ' which I was doing, and the Cassell's paper from which I copied it "; and the habit of making more or less use of wood engravings in the study of his art was kept up by him for some years later, and probably contributed not a little to his success as a draughtsman on wood. Many, if not most, of the drawings done in this way were in pen and ink; and he would also make original drawings of subjects that struck his fancy—a beggar in the street, a scene from a novel—and in the time of the Crimean War, many battle scenes; which last is a little unexpected, in view of what the late Mr. J. E. Hodgson, R.A., tells us (Cassell's *Magazine of Art*, Sept. 1889); that among his " strange whims " was " a hatred of soldiers."

He is described at this time as a very thoughtful and rather silent boy, fond of long solitary walks. In his holidays he would take some food with him, and be away all day long on a country ramble.

There are early indications of that nervous susceptibility which showed itself in various ways in his later years. When about twelve years of age he occasionally walked in his sleep, and was once so found opening a window with the idea of going to the Gymnasium at Primrose Hill. The letter above mentioned speaks of his not going to sleep for " I don't know how long " ; and a frequent inability to sleep was not confined to his earlier years. Among the drawings by Walker in the possession of my eldest brother, Mr. H. S. Marks, R.A., is one of himself huddled up in a blanket before the open bedroom window of his lodgings at Swanage (where he was with my brother in 1863), entitled, a little pathetically to those who knew the true meaning, *So Early in the Morning*.

Some time in 1855, when Walker was about fifteen years of age, he made his first start in life, being placed in the office of Mr. Baker, an architect of Gower Street. The ruling passion would, however, assert itself ; and if at any time there was an idea of this opening eventually leading to his following architecture as a profession, it was not long before such idea was abandoned. Mr. T. Harris, F.R.I.B.A., of 6, Southampton Street, who joined Mr. Baker for twelve months in 1856, and who had Walker constantly under his charge during that time, tells me that though no one could do an architectural drawing better than Walker when he gave his mind to it, he was always making drawings, on his own account, of things that he had seen in his daily walks. So clearly indeed was art his vocation, that he, Mr. Harris, encouraged rather than checked him in this unofficial work, and urged him to betake himself to serious study. Mr. Harris has several of the drawings done at this time, and evidently retains nothing but pleasant remembrances of Walker's simple, boyish ways while in his employ.

In all probability this placing the boy in Mr. Baker's office was more the outcome of necessity than choice. When he left the Collegiate School, the question of his following art as a profession had been under serious consideration, but the difficulty was how to manage this without his being a burden on his mother during the time of study. It was suggested that he should be apprenticed to a lithographer, with whom, it was thought, he might improve himself in drawing, and at the same time earn something towards his own living ; and though this suggestion was not carried out, his going to Mr. Baker's must be looked on rather as an attempt in another way to solve the difficulty, than as showing any abandonment of the idea of his becoming an artist, either on his own part, or on that of his advisers. So he went on drawing in a desultory way at home and at the office, and in the spring of 1856 appears to have submitted some of his drawings to the inspection of Mr. Maclise.

I have not been able definitely to fix the length of his sojourn with Messrs. Baker and Harris ; but it must have been somewhere between eighteen months and two years, as he continued in the office till the beginning of 1857 ; when, owing no doubt to the suggestions of Mr. Harris and others, he took a further step towards the attainment of his hopes.

It may well be thought what anxious consultations there were before it was finally decided that he was seriously to enter on the career of an artist.   His mother had enough to do to maintain those who were dependent on her, and must have looked forward to the time when this other son should, by his exertions, partly relieve her of her burden.   The pursuit of art, too, at that time, whatever it may have been since, was not looked on as offering much more than a bare livelihood, and there were all the long years of study before even this could be reached.   But the bent of the boy's genius was too strong to be withstood.   After much consideration, and not a few misgivings, the die was finally cast, he left the office with its lenient rule, began drawing at the British Museum, and

entered Mr. Leigh's studio in Newman Street.   The influence of these early studies at the British Museum was felt by Walker to the end of his life.

There are still many to whom the mention of " Leigh's studio" calls up affectionate remembrances of the master.   He was a grand old fellow, brusque in manner, but with the kindest of hearts ; sturdy and independent to a degree that often militated against his pecuniary interests, sternly repressive of anything like conceit, but full of kindly help to those who needed it, and who sought it in the right way.   It has been truly said that, in its time, his studio turned out more artists of mark than the Royal Academy itself ; and though he could be severely and epigrammatically satirical over their shortcomings, most of the students loved him, and looked with affection at the stalwart figure in the black velvet gown and skull-cap, as, with long clay pipe in hand, it paused among them at their work in the gas-lighted gallery.  There were few who knew him but felt they had lost a friend, when, a few years later than the time of which I write, he died after a painful illness borne heroically to the very end.

A few months after he joined Leigh's, Walker was seeking admission as a student at the Royal Academy.  In June of this year, 1857, he writes from North Cave in Yorkshire, where he had gone for a holiday, hoping that those at home would not forget to send in his Academy drawing.  He appears, too, to have again sought the advice of Mr. Maclise ; as, according to a letter from that painter, dated in pencil, in another hand, July 7, 1857, "Mr. Maclise will be glad to look at any drawings Mr. Frederick Walker may bring him on Friday morning next at 11 o'clock."  On the first occasion mentioned above, Maclise seems to have refrained from giving advice, though admitting that the drawings showed talent ; but there is no record of what his opinion may have been on this second occasion.

Walker still continued for some time drawing at the British Museum during the day, working at Leigh's in the evening.  It was at the latter place I, myself a student, first met him in the summer or autumn of this year.  I fancy I must have seen him occasionally for some time before we spoke, but I quite remember his coming up to me one evening, and speaking in the quick, eager way which those who did not know him so often attributed to conceit.  It was a mutual love of fishing more than art that led to the beginning of our friendship.  He was one evening telling me of some fishing excursion at West Drayton, and so it came about that we arranged to go there on an early day in December.  After a pleasant day's outing, at his invitation I accompanied him home to 7, Charles Street, Manchester Square (now merged in George Street), where he was then living, and there first saw his mother and sisters, among the latter her who afterwards became my wife.  Of her it is no part of the purpose of this book to speak.  No life of Walker would, however, be complete without full mention of his mother.  Though some idea of her character will, I trust, be gathered from the following pages, I may perhaps be permitted a few words here as to my own opinion of her worth.  She was one of those women whom it is a privilege to know ; one of those who raise one's estimate of humanity.  Through sorrow she had learnt a chastened wisdom ; to her, indeed, sweet were the uses of adversity, and not to her alone but, through her, to all who had the benefit of her guidance and counsels.  She was of a retiring nature, and only opened her heart to those she felt she might trust—mostly those of her home circle—and in the love, the devotion, the veneration, of that circle she found her best reward.

# CHAPTER II

## 1858—1859

Though it has been said by some that Walker was not a diligent student, it may be questioned whether he could fairly be called an idle one. It is true that he was never regular in his attendance either at Leigh's or afterwards at the Langham Chambers Society ; but at the same time he certainly, in one way or another, did a great deal of work that never met the eyes of his fellow-students. He could, moreover, almost without putting hand to paper, and merely by making use of his eyes, get as much good out of a cast or model as his less gifted fellows by their laboriously stippled drawings. Probably few artists who have attended any school have had less in the way of student work to show. But I believe it may be said that at this time, as was certainly the case later, his art was continually present to him during his waking hours, and he was ever learning in his own way, though with little outward result as yet. I fear he fell short of Mr. Leigh's ideal of a student. A letter from his eldest brother, early in 1858, speaks of his having incurred Leigh's disapprobation, and more than hints that the reason was to be found in his not having shown application and perseverance. There are besides, other letters with urgent exhortations to him to work ; and though this tends to support the charge of idleness, it may probably be accounted for by the anxiety of his family to see him begin to earn his own living, and the fear they had lest, in following art, he might possibly have made a false step on the road to that desirable end. That his mother was not altogether without anxiety as to his future at this time, there is no doubt. I remember her earnestly asking me, in the early days of our friendship, if I thought he would succeed ; and though there is no credit to be taken to one's self on such a score, it is a satisfaction to me now to think that I unhesitatingly gave my opinion in the affirmative.

On March 31, 1858, whether as a result of the drawing mentioned above or not, I cannot say, Walker was admitted as a student to the Royal Academy ; but of what he did there I have no personal knowledge. I believe he was no more a regular attendant there than at Leigh's. Mr. Tom Taylor, in his preface to the Catalogue of the Exhibition of Walker's works at Mr. Deschamps' Gallery in 1876, says he never even reached the Life classes, and this is very probably the fact. He drew from the life at Leigh's, but in the same fitful way as from the antique ; and indeed, it does not seem that he owed much to any

school training.  But in the autumn of the year of his admission to the
Royal Academy, he was contemplating a step that was fraught with
benefit to him ; both as inducing a more settled habit of work, and as
affording that practice in black and white which has proved of such
inestimable value to many artists.  After a good deal of consideration
and much seeking of advice, he was, on November 10, 1858, apprenticed
to Mr. J. W. Whymper, the wood engraver, of No. 20, Canterbury
Place, Lambeth, and worked there three days a week for two years.

Here he began to acquire that art of drawing on wood, to the advance-
ment of which, it may fairly be said, he contributed not a little.  It was
here, too, he met Mr. J. W. North, A.R.A. (his junior by some eighteen
months), with whom he was afterwards in close companionship while
painting several important, and many minor, works.  Mr. Charles
Green, R.I., was another of his fellow-workers.

Of the drawings he made at Mr. Whymper's, there is probably now
no trace.  Those that were done for publication have all been used or

have disappeared long since. Mr. Edward Whymper, of Alpine fame, tells me he has nothing in his possession that Walker drew at this time. Such sketches as he made for his drawings—preliminary designs, &c.— he invariably used to tear up, and all efforts to get possession of them beforehand were unavailing. They would, of course, only be interesting as showing his progress ; and for that purpose there are enough early drawings to be found in the pages of *Once a Week* for the year 1860, and later.

Walker was now regularly employed for three days in the week, having the rest of the week at his own disposal. Some time before his apprenticeship to Mr. Whymper, he seems to have taken to oil colours, for early in 1858 he writes : "I go in for painting at Leigh's, and I may fairly say it diddles me completely." Even earlier than this he had been gradually feeling his way in water colours, though the greater part of his home work now, and for the next year or so, was with the pen or pencil. There are drawings still in existence, of a period a little later than that at which we have arrived, showing much careful work, and great delicacy of touch. In some of them the influence upon him of other men's work is clearly apparent. I have one that strongly recalls Sir John Tenniel, and another appears to have been inspired by Sir John Gilbert. But there was never anything like a slavish following of the methods of others, nor indeed any perceptible following at all for more than a limited period. He seems to have been able just to take what he wanted from any particular source, and then having made it his own, and added something to his stock of knowledge, to go on working without trace in his work of the source whence this added knowledge was derived.

It was this habit of his of watching for and taking hold of everything and anything that might be useful to him in his art, that appears to me to largely qualify the notion that he was wanting in industry. As an instance of his power of turning things to account, a circumstance may be mentioned that occurred some three or four years later. Among a series of wood drawings which he did for Messrs. Dalziel Bros. after he had left Mr. Whymper's, there is one of a fishmonger, at the door of a cottage, receiving payment from a little boy ; and on one side of the drawing there is a clump of jasmine growing up the front of the house. The original of this jasmine Walker had seen in Mr. Whymper's back yard in Canterbury Place, during his apprenticeship ; and though it must have been fully two years since, in all probability, he had set eyes on it, he remembered it when making this drawing, and went expressly, block in hand, to draw it—a dirty old bit of jasmine in a London back yard.

It is impossible, at this distance of time, to trace every step by which Walker was fitting himself for his after work. It must, however, have been somewhere about the year 1859, that he began making those drawings in Indian ink which were the forerunners of his serious efforts in water colour. That he deliberately adopted this method as best

THE FISHMONGER.

calculated to impart facility with the brush cannot be affirmed, but it would appear to be more than probable.  He was regularly working with the pencil in black and white on the wood ; and it may well have seemed advisable to him, while still retaining the practice in light and shade which such work afforded, to add thereto the use of the brush, apart from the distractions of colour.  If this were his idea, it was more than justified by the exquisite delicacy of his subsequent water colours.

THE SECRET—(Langham Sketch).

Some time in 1859, he left Leigh's and joined the Artists' Society in Langham Chambers (commonly called "The Langham"), and there met many of those who were amongst his warmest admirers and truest well-wishers in after years.  The Langham at that time, but for the absence of teachers, stood in something the same relation to Leigh's that the universities do to the schools ; and study there formed a regular part of the curriculum of many of Leigh's old students.  Those, too, who had got beyond their student days, and were beginning to make a name for themselves, would often revisit their old haunts ; and so acquaintances were made, and friendships formed, and much pleasant talk of the distinctly "shoppy" order went on, not altogether without profit.  It was, and I believe still is, a society of artists and amateurs formed chiefly for study from the life. There were, too, nights at regular intervals when sketches were made by the members from subjects given out at the preceding sketching meeting, the time for the production of these sketches being limited to two hours. At the end of this time, the drawings and paintings of those who cared to show them were collected, and a little exhibition held of the results of the two hours' work. At these meetings Walker was a pretty regular attendant, and his quiet, homely way of treating the subjects, as well as his method of work, must still be in the remembrance of many. Some of these sketches formed the subjects of his earliest finished water colours, for it was his habit to make all the use of his ideas he could ; and having given time and thought to the composition of a subject, he did not care, if a good one, to throw it aside, but would carry it as far as his skill at the time allowed.

STUDY FOR BLACKBERRYING.

There had been somewhat similar sketching evenings at Leigh's, preceded sometimes by a lesson in perspective. Of one of these evenings Walker writes :—" To-morrow is the sketching night, but I cannot go till past 8 by reason of the perspective. What fearful meaning is in that little word."

In October of this year, for the greater convenience of his work when not at Whymper's, he joined a fellow-student in taking a room as a studio in Great Portland Street, staying there, however, only till the following summer. In December, he was sent by Mr. Whymper to make sketches at the house of Mr. Assheton Smith, Tedworth, Hamp-

shire, which were engraved for the biography of Mr. Smith published by
Murray.   In a letter from Tedworth, he speaks of working at what he
calls "that infernal hunting picture."   He also mentions having done
*The Wreck*, on wood (a boy, with clasped hands, kneeling on a sea-
washed deck), to show the *Once a Week* people, and says the Langhamites
were very pleased with the drawing when he took it to show them.
So at this time he was beginning to set about getting work on his own
account, and was so far successful that *The Wreck*, under another title,
appeared in the number of *Once a Week* for February 25, 1860.   There
was method, too, in his plans for the future, for the same letter says :—
"I am busy now, and shall be ; and for the future shall look to making
more by wood drawing than painting, till I have advanced in practice to
that extent, that I can rely on painting with safety."   And thus, with
many difficulties overcome, and a fair prospect of further conquests, the
year 1859 closed for him.

THE BROOK—(Langham Sketch).

# CHAPTER III

WHATEVER doubts there may have been as to the wisdom of
Walker's choice of a profession, they must by this time have been set at
rest ; for, from the year 1860 onward, his progress, if not phenomenally
rapid, was steady and secure. Though he continued occasionally to draw
on wood for some years after 1864, the five years from the beginning of
1860 to the end of 1864 may broadly be stated as the time during which
he worked for the wood engraver, and won a name as one among the first,
if not himself the very first, of our illustrators of books. Of his work
in this kind as shown at the exhibition held in January, 1876, after his
death, it was said by a brother artist, " There is enough here to make any
man's fame " ; and though, to some, this may seem too high praise,
I believe a careful study of the wood drawings of the time will result in
a true appreciation of Walker's influence on the art, and show the
observation to have been just.

Mr. Joseph Swain, the wood engraver, who engraved the greater part
of Walker's wood drawings, and to whom and to whose paper on Walker
in the number of *Good Words* for July, 1888, I am indebted for some
interesting details, tells me that towards the end of 1859, when he (Mr.
Swain) was engaged upon and had the management of the illustrations
for *Once a Week*, Walker called on him seeking employment as a
draughtsman on wood. Mr. Swain saw at once that he was capable of
doing good work ; and either at that interview, or shortly afterwards, gave
him the poem of *The Wreck* to illustrate ; the drawing for which, as
mentioned in the last chapter, Walker speaks of having done to show the
*Once a Week* people. Mr. Samuel Lucas, the then editor, was pleased
with the drawing, and on February 18, 1860, under the title of *Peasant
Proprietorship*, there appeared the first of a long series of drawings by the
young artist's hand—*The Wreck*, under the title of *God help our Men at
Sea*, appearing in the number for the week following, as has been said.
Walker's very first illustrations, consequent on his visit to Mr. Swain, had
appeared a little before this ; one in the number of *Everybody's Journal*
for January 14, 1860, and another in *The Leisure Hour* about the same
time. Of a figure from the illustration for *Everybody's Journal*. Mr

Swain gives an engraving in the number of *Good Words* referred to above,
and speaks of it as containing indications of some of those excellences
which afterwards made Walker famous.

At Mr. Whymper's, where Walker had now been employed rather more
than a year, he was engaged in copying and making small designs, many of
which appeared in the publications of the Christian Knowledge Society.
Apart from his natural desire to improve his position, it must have been
a great relief to him to find in *Once a Week* a larger field for the exercise

THE FIRE—(Langham Sketch).

of those powers which were growing stronger in him day by day.
Millais, Tenniel, John Leech, Charles Keene, and many other of our
best artists, were drawing for that journal, and it was no slight thing for
Walker to have gained a footing amongst them.   That he made good use
of his opportunities, the pages of *Once a Week* will show.   In them may
be traced his steady progress and gradual mastery over the difficulties of
the art, though his highest achievements in this line must be sought for
later in the *Cornhill Magazine*.   *Once a Week* from February, 1860, to
September 1863, with one drawing—*The Vagrants*—in January, 1866 ;

*Good Words* for March, June, and November, 1862, and from January
to August, 1864 ; the *Cornhill Magazine* from February, 1861, to June,
1864, again from July, 1866, till November, 1868, with one drawing in
July, 1869 ; and some drawings done specially for Messrs. Dalziel Bros.,
which will presently be referred to, will show nearly all the work he did
for the wood engraver.

OLD AGE.—(Langham Sketch).

Many of the early drawings show no very special power, and bear
traces moreover of a want of sympathy with the subject, or of having
been done against time ; Walker not being altogether free from the sin
of a careless ordering of his work, which caused him no little trouble,
and brought many an anxious pang to the breasts of the expectant wood
engraver and publisher. But it is interesting to note the difference in
other drawings where his fancy had freer play, or where the greater importance of the tale gave a keener zest to his efforts. As Mr. J. Comyns
Carr has well observed in his *Essays on Art* :—" Here and there, in a
drawing of only modest pretensions, the eye is suddenly arrested by some
passage of subtle beauty : the expression of a childish face, the turn of a
head, or some fortunate choice of gesture which seems new in art though

familiar enough in nature,—these are the slight indications that already give notice of the existence in Walker of a special power of drawing from reality some secret of beauty that escapes common observation."

After the appearance of his first drawing in *Once a Week*, Walker was regularly employed as one of the illustrators of that periodical. For nearly twelve months, apart from his engagement with Mr. Whymper, his drawings on wood were confined to its pages. In the spring of this year there was a £100 prize competition for drawings illustrating Tennyson's *Idylls of the King*, and into this competition Walker was very strongly urged to enter. Probably from want of time, he does not appear to have thrown much heart into the affair, as after making sketches, and finishing one drawing, the idea was abandoned. He was now, too, receiving little commissions for water colour drawings at moderate prices ; and, considering the limited time that he could call his own, it is not surprising to learn from a letter of his in May of this year :— " I am deluged with work now, and must put the steam on in earnest." Of the water colour drawings executed in this year, I have been able to trace : *The Fight, Blackberrying, The Cottage Door, The Cosy Couple, The Peep Show* (from a sketch made at the Langham), *The New Boy*, and *The Angler's Return* (also from a Langham sketch) ; this last selling for the respectable sum, for Walker at that time, of forty guineas.

THE ANGLER'S RETURN—(Langham Sketch.)

The term of his apprenticeship to Mr. Whymper was now, in the autumn of 1860, drawing to a close. In November, amid the good wishes of his fellow-workers, he was free to employ his time in his own way. His two years at Canterbury Place, though doubtless to one of his temperament irksome enough in their regular and business-like demands on his application, had been of great service to him ; and formed for him the nearest approach to that close and continuous training, which less gifted mortals find essential to the development of their powers.

THE PEEP SHOW—(Langham Sketch).

With his talent, Walker, in all probability, would have arrived at the same result, had he been left to his own devices ; but, however this may be, the fact remains that the end of his term found him with his progress established on a firm and enduring basis. He had entered Mr. Whymper's a mere student, he had now become an apt exponent of his craft. He had acquired the means of earning his own living, and, what I doubt not he valued more, the means of lightening his mother's burden, and smoothing her path in life. In other ways, too, he was a joy to her ; and, an exception to the general rule, was not without honour in his own country, and in his own house. In the letters of the home circle at this time there occur such sentences as these :—" It is pleasant to see that he seems to keep his friends, and that every one likes him. Well it would be odd if it were not so, as he certainly is as good as he is clever " ; and again : " What a blessing Fred is ; everything connected with him seems perfectly satisfactory." " He has only to go on so and he must be famous, if that is so very desirable. What is better still, he will be honoured and respected." Though I believe the truest estimate of his character will be formed by the perusal of his own letters in the following pages, it is perhaps not out of place here to give these evidences of the regard in which he was held by those who knew him best.

Soon after leaving Mr. Whymper's—towards the end of 1860—Walker and Thackeray first met, and their acquaintance afterwards ripened into a friendship that was perhaps more highly valued by Walker than any that he ever formed. Thackeray was at this time engaged in the preparation of his novel, *The Adventures of Philip on his Way through the World*, the first instalment of which was to appear in the *Cornhill Magazine* for January, 1861 ; and, in accordance with his usual custom, was illustrating the story with his own hand. The small designs—initial letters, &c.—Thackeray would put on the wood himself. For the large illustrations, he used to send sketches on paper to Mr. Swain, who employed different artists to draw them on the wood, and make such little improvements in the drawing as Thackeray, who was very jealous of any alteration of his sketches, would allow. It occurred to Mr. Swain to suggest that Walker should do some of this copying. Walker accordingly (though, as afterwards appears, more with the hope of getting original work) called at the office of the *Cornhill Magazine*, with some of his drawings. Mr. George Smith, of Messrs. Smith, Elder, and Co., has kindly given me an account of his meeting with Walker, and the subsequent introduction to Thackeray, as follows :—

" At that period my time was very fully occupied, and in order to prevent interruption, my room at 65, Cornhill was carefully guarded from intrusion. On one occasion, when leaving my room, I saw a young gentleman quitting the outer office, whose appearance attracted my attention; I inquired who he was, and was told by the clerk, who acted the part of Dragon, that he was a young artist of the name of Walker, who wished to draw for the *Cornhill Magazine*, and who had called before with specimens of his drawings. 'He is a mere boy,' said the clerk ; 'I told him you were engaged, as I did not think it would be of any use for you to see him.' I said I would see him if he called again. About this time Mr. Thackeray was beginning to find it troublesome to draw on the wood the illustrations for *The Adventures of Philip*, which was then passing through the Magazine, and two or three of the drawings had been made on paper, and afterwards redrawn on wood, but not to Mr. Thackeray's satisfaction.

"When Mr. Walker paid another visit to Cornhill, and I saw his drawings, it occurred to me that here was the artist who would redraw Mr. Thackeray's designs satisfactorily. I mentioned the subject to Mr. Walker, and understood him to accept the idea; but his nervous agitation was almost painful, and although I did my best to set him at his ease, he left 65, Cornhill without my being sure whether my suggestion, that he should make drawings from Mr. Thackeray's designs, was acceptable to him or not.

"I mentioned the subject to Mr. Thackeray, who said, 'Bring him here, and we shall soon see whether he can draw.' An arrangement was afterwards made for me to call for Mr. Walker, and drive him to Mr. Thackeray's house in Onslow Square, early one morning, towards the end of 1860. The drive was a silent one, Mr. Walker's agitation being very marked. When we went up to Mr. Thackeray, he saw at once how nervous and distressed the young artist was, and addressed himself in the kindest manner to remove his shyness. After a little time he said, 'Can you draw? Mr. Smith says you can.' 'Y-e-e-s, I think so,' said the young man who was, within a few years, to excite the admiration of the whole world by the excellence of his drawings. 'I'm going to shave,' said Mr. Thackeray, 'would you mind drawing my back?' Mr. Thackeray went to his toilet table and commenced the operation, while Mr. Walker took a sheet of paper and began his drawing; I looking out of the window in order that he might not feel that he was being watched. I think Mr. Thackeray's idea of turning his back towards him was as ingenious as it was kind; for I believe that if Mr. Walker had been asked to draw his face instead of his back, he would hardly have been able to hold his pencil."

It is interesting to read the following note of Thackeray's account of this interview, which Mrs. Richmond Ritchie (Miss Thackeray) has kindly given me. "My father told me one day, with interest, that a very clever young fellow had been to see him, offering to draw for the *Cornhill Magazine.* My father had asked him whether he could draw, and when Mr. Walker modestly said 'Yes, he could draw,' my father, who was dressing at the time up in his own room, said, 'Well, draw my back,' and turned round to the glass over the chimney and began to shave, and so the drawing was done."

Of the merits of the drawing made under these rather trying circumstances, and indeed of the drawing itself, Mr. Smith has no recollection. The result was presumably satisfactory to Thackeray, as he soon afterwards asked Walker to make a second drawing of his back, as a study for the initial letter of *Roundabout Papers*, No. 10, in the *Cornhill Magazine* for February, 1861; the design for the illustration being supplied by Thackeray in a rough sketch on an envelope. This second drawing remains in the possession of Mrs. Richmond Ritchie. Of it she says:—
"It is wonderfully like him—I sometimes think more like than anything else I have ever seen." The completed woodcut is the first of Walker's which appeared in the *Cornhill Magazine;* and it may be noted in

passing that in an article in *Scribner's Magazine* for June, 1880, on *Thackeray as a Draughtsman*, it is wrongly attributed to Thackeray, and spoken of as probably his last portrait of himself.

As has been said, the first instalment of *Philip* appeared in January, 1861, and the large illustrations for that month and the next, though evidently from Thackeray's sketches, show traces here and there of a more practised hand, and may have been put on the wood by Walker. That this was the case with the large illustration for March—*The Old Fogies*—there is no question ; the drawing itself proves it beyond a doubt. It is to this drawing that the following letter from Thackeray, though not wholly in his handwriting, refers :—

> "36 Onslow Square, S.W.
> "*Jan.* 21, 1861.

"Dear Sir, — Can you copy the faces on this block as accurately as may be on to another block, improve the drawing of the figures, furniture, and make me a presentable design for wood engraving ?

> "Faithfully yours,
> "W. M. Thackeray.

"The less work the better. The two tumblers touching each other—the old man red-nosed and a wig. The young man, light hair, large whiskers, moustache."

But this was not the kind of work that suited Walker, nor that which he had in view in submitting his drawings to Mr. Smith. Accordingly we find Thackeray writing on February 11, by the hand of his secretary :—

"Dear Sir,—The Blocks you have executed for the *Cornhill Magazine* have given so much satisfaction that I hope we may look for more from the same hand. You told me that the early days of the week were most convenient for you, and accordingly I sent last Monday, or Tuesday, a

couple of designs which, as you would not do them, I was obliged to
confide to an older, and I grieve to own, much inferior artist.  Pray
let me know if I may count upon you for my large cut for March.

> "Believe me, very faithfully yours,
>
> "W. M. THACKERAY."

To this letter Walker made the following reply, as I find by a copy
in his mother's handwriting :—

> "7 CHARLES ST.
> "*Feb.* 13, 1861.

"SIR,—When I submitted designs for your inspection, I was in
great hopes of obtaining some original work for the *Cornhill Magazine*,
and although I am gratified to hear that the sketches I rendered on
the wood are satisfactory, I confess such work is distasteful to me,
and I think not calculated to really benefit me.  I therefore respectfully
solicit that whatever directions you may favour me with, they may be
consonant to the wish I had in originally applying to you.

> "I beg to remain,
>
> "Yours most obediently,
>
> "F. WALKER."

Those who knew Walker can well imagine what a turmoil there must
have been before this letter was written.  It will be noticed that
Thackeray's question as to the "large cut for March" remains unanswered, and there is, moreover, an awkwardness about the letter
generally, indicative of the struggle between his wish not to offend one
whom he greatly respected, and his feeling of what was due to himself.
In his difficulty, he betook himself to Mr. Smith, whose account of the
interview is as follows :—

"He afterwards came to me, apparently under some excitement, and
said at once, without a word of introduction, 'I am not going to do any
more of this work.'  I naturally inquired what was the matter, and
asked if he was dissatisfied with the payment he received.  'No, he was
quite satisfied, but it was not original work, and his friends told him he
could do original work, and that he ought to do it, and not copy other
people's designs, which any fool could do who could draw.'  I said
I would speak to Mr. Thackeray on the subject, if it were clearly understood that he would be willing to make the illustrations from proofs of
the story, and that he would listen to verbal suggestions from Mr.
Thackeray as to the subjects to be illustrated and their treatment.  I
felt it necessary to expatiate on the fact that this would in no way
derogate from the originality of his drawings.  Mr. Thackeray, who
had by this time conceived a high opinion of Mr. Walker's ability as
an artist, was glad to accept this arrangement ; but the illustration for

the next part of *Philip*, published in April, 1861, was not drawn by Walker."

Throughout these negotiations, one cannot but remark the kindness—I may say gentleness—with which the great novelist, in the height of his world-wide reputation, treated the young and almost unknown artist. It is small wonder that Walker's attachment to Thackeray became as ardent as it did. Nor was his kindness confined to words;

for, from this time forward, Thackeray took the greatest interest in Walker, introduced him to many of his friends, and received him constantly at his house.

The large illustration to *Philip* for April is clearly from the hand of the " older, and I grieve to own, much inferior artist " (who, the reader will have guessed, was Thackeray himself); but all difficulties having

A QUARREL.

now been arranged, that for May—*Nurse and Doctor*—duly appeared signed with the familiar FW, and to the end of the series (August, 1862) Thackeray was content merely to indicate, by slight sketches, and a few explanatory words, his idea of the form the illustrations should take.

These suggestions of Thackeray's are full of interest, both in themselves, and as showing the terms on which author and artist worked together. The first I have relates to the July, 1861, illustration—*Good Samaritans*—which Thackeray is satisfied to leave in Walker's hands, with no more guidance (beyond the proofs of the story) than a very slight pen and ink sketch with the words, "Then you must be hungry, and shall have my piece of cake," and a note :—"Dear Mr. Walker, I think this will make as good a subject as another. The three or four children *ad libitum*, Mrs. Pendennis, Bandeaux, Madonna ; Mr. P. round face, no moustache ; Mrs. Pendennis making breakfast, two or three children. Pendennis reading the newspaper. Philip just come into breakfast-room." For the illustration for October—*A Quarrel*—on half a sheet of note-paper bearing the stamp of the Brighton and Sussex Club, and headed, " For Mr. Walker " ; there is a small pencil-sketch of Lord Ringwood, with the words : " Lord Ringwood dressed in an old-fashioned tail coat of 1824 date. High stock and collar " ; a note : " Lord Ringwood on his sofa in the gout. Philip puts on his hat and makes him a bow" ; while underneath, in a rough pen and ink sketch, Thackeray gives his idea of the general design. For the illustration for March, 1862—*A Letter from New York*—Thackeray has written out, on one side of a sheet of note-paper, about twenty lines of the end of Chapter 31 ; and on the other, made a slight sketch, underneath which is written :—"Children laughing at school-room door. Philip and Charlotte reading the letter." With regard to the ending of this Chapter 31, it may be said in passing that both in the manuscript I have mentioned, and as printed in the magazine, the concluding words are :—"There was a pretty group for the children to see, and for Mr. Walker to draw " ; a pleasing proof of Thackeray's kindly wish to give Walker a helping hand. I have noticed with regret that in some subsequent editions, published after Thackeray's death, this has been altered to : " and for an artist to draw."

Another of these suggestions refers to the illustration for April, 1862 —*Mugford's Favourite*—and represents : " Old gentleman in thick shoes scratching a pig's back over a pig-stye railing in his garden. Philip disgusted. Background, trees, cottages, villas, Hampstead Heath," and headed : " Dear Mr. Walker, Will this do ? "

But the most interesting of all is a letter, unaccompanied by any sketch, relating to the beautiful drawing of Philip in Church ; which, under the title of *Thanksgiving*, ended the series in August, 1862. The letter is here reproduced, and will appropriately close this chapter.

Palace Green,
Kensington. W.
June 15

Dear Mr. Walker

For ~~July~~ August I mean.

Philip . the little Sister , and the little Children saying their prayers in an old fashioned church pew not Gothic .

The church is the one in Queen Square Bloomsbury, if you are curious to be exact .

The motto

PRO CONCESSIS BENEFICIIS.

And that will bring the story to an end. I am sorry it is over. and you?

Always yours

W.M.T.

# CHAPTER IV

## 1861—1863

For the sake of clearness I have continued the account of Walker's connection with *Philip* to the end of the story, but must now go back a little and pick up such threads as have been missed.

First of all, in order that those who did not know him may attach some kind of individuality to the mere name of Walker, I will endeavour to give an idea of his personal appearance. He was considerably under the average height—I believe not more than 5 feet $1\frac{1}{2}$ or 5 feet 2 inches—but of an exceedingly well-proportioned figure : good square shoulders, narrow hips, straight legs, and so well set up altogether that his want of height was not as noticeable as it otherwise would have been. An instance of the way in which his appearance struck one is given by Mr. G. D. Leslie, R.A., in his book *Our River*, where he tells us that an old fisherman at Cookham, who knew Walker well, exclaimed on hearing of his death, "What, not the little model !"

His head, which was of rather a remarkable shape, having a peculiar flatness on the top, and considerable development at the back, was well placed on his shoulders ; the eyes blue, with an earnest, thoughtful, far-seeing look about them ; a broad forehead, with the thick brown hair growing rather low down and having a knack of falling over it ; a well-shaped, straight nose with great breadth between the eyebrows ; the mouth and chin showing firmness and decision ; the possession of which qualities was still further indicated by the massive squareness of the jaw. He was left-handed ; in fact, in some pursuits may be said to have been ambidextrous. Later on than the time of which we are speaking, he wore a moustache, and for the last year or so of his life a full beard as a protection against cold. His figure never lost its slimness, and his keen sight never required any artificial aid. His voice was soft and musical, his speech quick, eager and emphatic ; and though he himself said, " I haven't the gift of the gab," he would talk well when roused or interested in his subject, though but seldom about his art.

It was in the year 1860 that Walker began those visits to his sister and me in our new home at Croydon, that were full of pleasure to us, and of some little advantage to him, inasmuch as, the town at that time not being the overgrown place it has since become, he could readily find countrified little bits useful to him in his work. Many were the pleasant walks we had together, mostly on Sundays. On these walks "the little woodpecker," as he was often called, would frequently have with him an unfinished wood block which he had brought for the purpose of putting in, or noting, something he was in want of at the time. He had a most inveterate habit of biting his nails, and would stop and stand with his fingers to his mouth, looking intently at anything that struck his fancy ; and then perhaps the wood block would be brought out and some additions made to it, though as often as not he had taken in all he wanted in that keen and earnest gaze. On one of these occasions, I remember, he took back with him to town the branch of bramble which figures in the foreground of his first oil picture, *The Lost Path*, exhibited at the Royal Academy in 1863.

A note I find of his having gone early in 1861 to draw some graves in Beddington churchyard, reminds me what a favourite subject that of a boy looking at a man digging a grave was with him, though one which he never carried to completion. There were no fewer than three sketches of this subject in the exhibition held after his death, at Mr. Deschamps' Gallery in New Bond Street, in January–February, 1876 (which exhibition I will in future refer to as that of 1876) ; and I have in my possession a discarded water colour, 18 by 22 inches, which he had brought to a considerable state of forwardness. A branch of the large yew tree in Beddington churchyard and part of the old church are put in with great care ; and though the figures themselves have been nearly obliterated, their positions can still be seen.

One evening when he came to see us, I happened to have a cow-boy in a smock-frock standing to me for a little water colour I was doing. Walker took his colours and a piece of paper, and did a good evening's work ; putting in the whole of the figure with the exception of the bottom of the smock-frock and the feet, and making a thoroughly William Hunt-like study. I think he worked a little on the drawing afterwards, but it remained unfinished for some years ; when one day he cut it out of the frame in which I had placed it, added the feet and a dead bird, and left it in the state in which it was etched by Mons. Rajon. Later on, as will be seen, he did a good deal of other work in the neighbourhood of Croydon.

Notwithstanding the fact that since leaving Mr. Whymper he could call his time his own, Walker had not much opportunity for idling.

An Old Boy's Tale. (*Once a Week*, April 27, 1861.)

In addition to being fairly launched on the monthly drawings for
the *Cornhill Magazine*, he did in 1861, 29 wood drawings for *Once a
Week* besides a few others for Messrs. Dalziel Bros., which appeared in
various publications, and several water colour drawings. Of these I have
been able to trace : *The Fisherman's Wife, Mushroom Gatherers, The
Wet Day, The Picture Book*, a small portrait group of the wife and three
children of Mr. Geo. Smith ; and others mentioned merely as " study " or
" sketch." Reference is also made to a drawing of a fisherman and his son
finding a drowned sailor on the beach ; but though a sketch in black and
white of the fisherman and his son is in existence, I cannot find that the
entire composition was ever carried out in colours. This in itself may
not seem a very large amount of work ; but, in view of what has been
said of Walker's want of method, it is not surprising to come across
despairing inquiries as to when drawings would be sent in, complaints of
letters remaining unanswered, &c., and to read a playful allusion to the
havoc wrought on him by reason of " a certain long seedy man from
Dalziel's who lies in wait for me in the passage."

 But, in spite of all such drawbacks, the quality of his work was
constantly improving. Every now and then would come a wood drawing
like that for *The Magnolia for London with Cotton*, in *Once a Week* for
March 2, 1861, or for *An Old Boy's Tale* in the same journal for April

27 (both afterwards reproduced in water colours), which showed what advance was being made. As has been said, his full strength in wood drawing was reserved for the *Cornhill Magazine*; but the illustrations to the serial stories, *The Settlers of Long Arrow*, and *The Prodigal Son*, in *Once a Week*, and the eight illustrations to *Oswald Cray*, in *Good Words*, do not, perhaps, fall far short of his best work. As one instance among many of the curious way in which an idea would stay by him, lying dormant as it were, until an opportunity arose of giving it fuller expression, it may be mentioned that the first drawing for *The Settlers of Long Arrow*—a boy, dripping wet, coming up the beach, having swum ashore from a boat—was in his mind when projecting the large oil picture which he never lived to complete, called *The Unknown Land*; and the number of *Once a Week* containing the drawing was on his studio table at the time of his death, nearly fourteen years after the drawing was made. Those conversant with his after work, too, will notice that we have already a *Mushroom Gatherers*, and *The Wet Day*, subjects to be more fully developed later.

THE SETTLERS OF LONG ARROW. (*Once a Week*, October 12, 1861.)

Apart from his work, there is little to be said of Walker's life at this time. His circle of friends and acquaintance was widening, there were visits to various places in connection with his work, sketching nights at the Langham and the houses of artist friends, but nothing that need detain us. I will, however, just mention that on May 26, 1861, Walker came of age ; and at Christmas of this year I find a characteristic little note of his having made a garland of evergreens with initials in the centre, in honour of my little son's first Christmas.

In 1862, in addition to 20 wood drawings for *Once a Week*, there were 10 for the *Cornhill Magazine*, 3 for *Good Words*, 1 for *London Society*, and some of a series of independent drawings for Messrs. Dalziel Bros., to which reference has already been made. The choice of the subjects of these independent drawings was to be left to Walker, and it is interesting to see how most of them were of that homely character which marked his earlier work when free to choose his own subject. The titles of the entire series were :—*Charity, The Shower, The Mystery of the Bellows, Winter, Spring, The Fishmonger, Summer, The Village School, Autumn, The Bouquet*, and one other ; and the drawings first appeared in some publications of Messrs. G. Routledge & Sons called *Wayside Posies*, and *A Round of Days*.

*The Fishmonger* [1] and *Summer* are especially worthy of notice—the former as containing the germ of the idea of the water colour, *A Fishmonger's Shop*, and the latter that of the oil picture of *Bathers*.

Of these drawings, Walker reproduced in water colours, either the same size or enlarged, no less than six, viz. :—*Spring, Autumn, The Bouquet, Charity, The Village School*, and *The Shower ;* and the original wood blocks of five :—*Autumn, The Bouquet, The Village School, Summer*, and *The Fishmonger*, were exhibited by Messrs. Dalziel Bros. in the exhibition of 1876. Where the wood block of *The Bouquet* now is, I do not know ; but in the Print Room of the British Museum may be found *The Village School* and *Autumn*, and at South Kensington Museum, *Summer* (engraved) and *The Fishmonger*.

Messrs. Dalziel Bros. were among the first to recognise Walker's talent, not only as a wood draughtsman, but as a water colour painter. It was for them his first important composition in water colours—*Strange Faces*—was executed towards the end of 1862. For this drawing, his mother, eldest sister, and an uncle, stood to him ; and not only at this time, but for a good many years later, his models were frequently taken from the home circle. Indeed, no man could have received more willing help in everything connected with his work than Walker did from his mother and sisters. It was a labour of love in a double sense— love for him, and love for the art that found expression at his hands. No trouble was too great for them, that would help him to attain his ends. This willing service was accepted by him as freely as it was offered ; accepted not as a personal tribute, but for his art's sake. Later on, when

---

[1] See page 9.

SUMMER.

he was living at Bayswater, his mother would think nothing of a journey
to Soho Square to fetch him a tube of colour or anything he might be in
want of, this being but one little instance of what went on continually ;
and though perhaps there may be some who would see in this acceptance
of help a want of consideration bordering on selfishness, it did not so
strike those who knew him best, and knew, too, how his own life
was given up to the claims of his art.

It will be remembered that the story of *Philip* came to an end in
August, 1862, and in November of that year appeared the first of those
illustrations to Miss Thackeray's stories in the *Cornhill*, which gave

STRANGE FACES.

us some of Walker's best work.  This first illustration was to *The Story
of Elizabeth*.  It was followed by two others, and later on by a frontispiece ;
this last—a charming girlish figure standing in front of a rustic porch,
and carrying her hat filled with flowers—appearing when the story was
published in book form.  The combination of the work of authoress and
artist thus begun proved a most happy one.  It was continued for some
years after Walker had ceased to draw for others, and in it his work on
wood reached, I believe, its highest point of development.

After the year 1862 Walker worked much less for the wood
engraver.  Although it will be necessary to refer again to some of the

drawings, it may perhaps be convenient to give here a list of the remainder of his illustrations for the magazines. In 1863, there were two for *Once a Week*, and five for the *Cornhill ;* in 1864, eight for *Good*

Out among the Wild Flowers. (*Good Words*, November, 1862.)

*Words* (*Oswald Cray*), and four for the *Cornhill ;* in 1865, none; in 1866, one for *Once a Week* (*The Vagrants*), and six for the *Cornhill ;* in 1867, four for the *Cornhill ;* in 1868, three for the same magazine ;

D

and in 1869, one—afterwards reproduced in water colour—for a short story in the *Cornhill* called *Sola*.   The above list only refers to the large illustrations, and not to initial letters.   There were also a drawing of Hogarth and the drummer girl, for a posthumous edition of Thackeray's *English Humourists*, and two drawings for *Punch*; one, *The New Bathing Company (Limited)*, in the Almanack for 1865, and *Captain Jinks of the " Selfish " and his Friends enjoying themselves on the River*, which appeared on August 21, 1869.

Mr. Swain tells me Walker was one of the first to introduce brush-work into his wood drawing, using the spreading of the brush to give texture, and also producing the same effect by the peculiarity of his lines. He was exceedingly particular as to the way in which the blocks were cut.   Mr. Swain has many letters of his, in which, on receiving proofs of the drawings, he has noted by means of pen and ink sketches, such alterations as he required.   This cutting of the blocks was a source of constant anxiety, notwithstanding the care that was always given to his work ; and it was with a certain flutter of excitement in the home circle that the proofs were generally received.   Some member of the family— more Papist than the Pope—would give vent to his or her disappoint-ment at the loss the drawing had suffered in the process of cutting ; while Walker himself, knowing no doubt the extreme difficulty of rendering with perfect exactitude all the delicacy of his work, would put the proof from him with a smile in which deprecation of his family's partiality, and a sense of his own disappointment were curiously mingled.

Of smaller water colours about this time, I can only trace the *Charity* mentioned above, which was painted towards the end of 1862 or beginning of 1863.

Hitherto Walker had been known to the public only by his wood drawings.   The year 1863, however, gave us his first exhibited oil picture, and may be said generally to have been a year of preparation for his public appearance as a water colourist.   After a week or so of preliminary cartoons, he, on February 26, began on canvas his oil picture of *The Lost Path*—the " snow picture " as he calls it in a little diary he kept for about a year at this time—the subject of which had first appeared as an illustration to a poem, *Love in Death*, in the March, 1862, number of *Good Words*.   His youngest sister, Mary, stood to him for the figure in this picture, as she did for so many others ; and snow, as a rule, not being available here in March, he made use of salt as a substitute.   He also refreshed his memory by photographs, which fact accounts for an entry in the diary when the picture was practically finished : " feel anxious to begin carefully and from nature."   There is a note of his having gone to Croydon " to look at fir trees for snow picture " ; but apparently he did not consider them an improvement, as they do not appear in the finished work.   On April 4—the Saturday before sending-in day to the Royal Academy—the picture was shown at the evening meeting of the Langham, where, he says, " it seemed to be admired."   Some three weeks later he learnt that the picture was accepted, but hung high up. On May 4 he writes :—" Very fatiguing day— opening of Royal Academy, met Marks, Calderon, Yeames, Hodgson,

THE LOST PATH.
*(By permission of Messrs. THOS. AGNEW AND SONS, owners of the copyright.*

Leslie, &c. Met all kind friends—general sympathy as to picture, &c." Notwithstanding its position, the picture attracted attention. Mr. Tom Taylor, in the preface to the catalogue of the exhibition of 1876, says of it :—" I still remember how deeply it impressed me, hung as it was in an undistinguished place in the North Room. I still think it one of his most pathetic pictures." It was sold, after the close of the Royal Academy, for the modest sum of £90, and has been etched by Mr. C. Waltner.

THE DEADLY AFFINITY. (*Once a Week*, October 25, 1862.)

Shortly after *The Lost Path* was sent in to the Royal Academy, Walker paid his first visit to Paris. Of this visit Mr. P. H. Calderon, R.A., has kindly given me the following particulars :—

" I had had a rather serious bout of illness in the spring of 1863, and it was decided that as soon as my picture was sent in to the Royal Academy, my wife and I should go to Paris for change of air. The sending-in day was Tuesday, April 7th ; Walker spent the evening of that day with us, and *almost* decided to join us in Paris. I say ' almost,' because he always had the greatest difficulty in making up his mind, and seemed incapable of keeping to an engagement when made. I started on the 8th, spent some days at Boulogne, and reached Paris on the 13th. Walker joined us at midnight on the 14th."

After mentioning the various places of interest to which he took Walker, and the difficulty he experienced in interpreting for Walker's benefit the jokes and puns of an Opera Bouffe, Mr. Calderon continues :—

"As far as I could judge, the Louvre left him quite unmoved. I do not remember his remaining entranced before any picture there—nor did he ever say anything about any of them. (If I am not mistaken, much the same was said by friends of his visit to Venice later on.) At the Luxembourg he passed rapidly over the usual lions there—the big Couture, the big Müller, even the Delacroix, but fastened upon the Jules Breton *La fin de la journée*—this he looked at intently, evidently the picture went home to him.

"At Versailles the miles of historical and battle pieces left Walker very indifferent, until he came to the *Sacre de l'impératrice Joséphine*. This he studied from corner to corner; and when, after a long pause in that room, we moved on to the next, Walker slipped away from us, and I had to go back to fetch him away. He never spoke of the picture afterwards, and I am in doubt to this day as to whether it was admiration of the grace of the female figures which bewitched him, or whether he had a sudden revelation of the possibilities of the short-waisted 'Empire' dress. He certainly showed great affection for that costume afterwards."

It may be as well here to give the remainder of Mr. Calderon's note, though it has no special relation to this Paris trip:—

"It is unsafe to speak of Walker's silence on pictures or other subjects, however, and to conclude therefrom that he had no opinion favourable or the reverse. Walker never expressed an opinion about anything, or joined in any discussion whatsoever. He sat with us, either sketching or doing something with his clever little fingers; possibly listened (very often not) whilst we argued, and laughed at our excitement when we had done. How fond he was of jokes and fun, you know full well.

"The mention of his 'clever little fingers' reminds me that he found me one evening modelling a small bust of my wife in wax. He was quite excited over the process, pounced upon some wax and modelling tools, and immediately began a tiny head of me, much caricatured but wonderfully like. This new 'fad' so fascinated him, that we got well into the small hours before I could induce him to go home. This was his first attempt at modelling, and, as far as I know, his last."

Considering this was the first time Walker had been out of England, his letters from Paris are singularly devoid of interest. Although, naturally, there was much that impressed him, he refers only in the most general terms to what he saw. One characteristic quotation, however, may be given:—"The difference of everything is overpowering, and though this trip is doing me a world of good, yet if I thought that I was *not* going back in a short time to some pets of mine near Spanish Place" (he was still living in Charles Street), "to work (like a demon) upon one or two things we've laid out for ourself—you know, dear old Mummy—I should be miserable indeed."

While still engaged on the "snow picture," Walker began the water
colour drawing, from *Jane Eyre*, of Rochester, Jane Eyre, and Adèle in
the garden, which was a commission from Mr. Geo. Smith, in whose
possession it still is.   Mr. Smith tells me that the only instance within
his knowledge of Walker having failed in illustrating anything he
attempted was in the case of *Jane Eyre*.   In the course of an after
dinner conversation, when Walker was staying with Mr. Smith at his
house in the country, he said he had been reading *Jane Eyre*, and
should like to illustrate it.   Mr. Smith said it was a difficult book to

ROCHESTER SHOWING HIS MAD WIFE.   (*Jane Eyre*.)

illustrate, and he was afraid it would be difficult even for "the great
F. W." to satisfy him.   Ultimately it was arranged that Walker should
accept a commission for a water colour drawing of any subject he liked
to choose from *Jane Eyre*; and that after the drawing was made, they
should talk of the matter again.   The drawing was completed, and Mr.
Smith adds :—" It need hardly be said that it is a beautiful drawing, but
Walker's 'Rochester' is not Charlotte Brontë's 'Rochester' and
Walker's 'Jane Eyre' is not Charlotte Brontë's 'Jane Eyre.'"   The
subject of the illustration of the book was never referred to again.

Whether Walker was discouraged by what Mr. Smith had said, or
was over anxious to prove Mr. Smith's estimate of his powers a wrong
one, I cannot say.   It is certain, however, that this drawing gave him an
immensity of trouble which he does not seem to have experienced when
working in a less familiar medium on the *The Lost Path*.   Begun in

March, it was laid aside for a couple of months, taken to again, and again laid aside ; and it was not till the beginning of October that it was finished.    The greatest difficulty seems to have been with the figure of Rochester, which was wholly or partially rubbed out no less than four times.    The entries in the diary respecting the drawing are at times full of despondency.    " Very dissatisfied with it "—" Cannot get on with J. Eyre, and much troubled about it "—" Miserable about J. Eyre and afraid it will never be done "—are some of the references he makes to it, and show something of the travail of soul with which the drawing was produced.    However, it was at length finished, taken to Mr. Smith, who was " very pleased " with it, and a graceful little entry in the diary, " very sensible of Smith's kindness," brings the record to a close.    It may be mentioned that the wall in front of which Rochester is seated, was painted from that enclosing part of the grounds of the old home of the Carews at Beddington, now the Female Orphan Asylum.

I have not been able accurately to fix the date of the well-known etching of the *Blind Man and Boy*, but believe it was early in 1863. It is worth noticing that though the oil picture of *Wayfarers*, of which the etching was the forerunner, was not exhibited till some three years later, Walker was at Haslemere twice in the course of this year, looking for a suitable background for the picture ; and was engaged for nearly a month on preparatory sketches, from an old soldier he had found in Oxford Street, selling pocket books.

At Midsummer of this year, Walker removed from Charles Street to No. 3, St. Petersburgh Place, Bayswater—the house he occupied till his death.    I also had, about a month before, moved from Croydon to a cottage at Beddington, standing by itself in the fields ; and as the place was

easy of access from town, and at the same time quite in the country, it formed a convenient base of operations for Walker of which he availed himself for some time to come. The first work he did there was a little water colour called *Refreshment*, the design for which had originally appeared in the June, 1862, number of *Good Words*, in illustration of a poem entitled *The Summer Woods*.[1] This little drawing was among his first four exhibited water colours, and has been etched by W. Boucher.

Contrary to his practice in later years, Walker would at this time frequently seek advice, outside his home, on matters relating to his work —as price, accepting commissions, and so on—and in this way, being in difficulties over a *Cornhill* drawing, he once went to see Sir John Millais, and, as he says, found him in bed and talked to him there. He would also consult my brother and Mr. Calderon, and on one occasion at least was himself able to offer advice; for calling one day on Mr. Calderon, he found him out of spirits about his picture of *The Burial of Hampden*, and advised that the picture should be put aside until after Mr. Calderon's return from a contemplated visit with my brother to the Continent. One result of this incident was the accompanying caricature ; about which it is only necessary to say, by way of explanation, that Mr. Calderon was at that time usually spoken of by his intimates as " The Doge."

" *Up a Tree, or, The Doge and His Troubles.*"

Mr. Calderon's difficulty with his picture added point to another caricature, in which he figures as a poodle with a saucepan labelled

---

[1] See page 46.

"Hampden" tied to his tail—the caricature and a sham medal being presented to the voyagers on their return from this visit to the Continent by a mock deputation, as related by my brother in his book *Pen and Pencil sketches.*

It will have been noticed that Mr. Calderon speaks of Walker as having been fond of fun, and so he was. Many of his letters are full of boyish playfulness, and though he was not wont to indulge in boisterous outbursts of laughter, he had a keen sense of the ridiculous, and a quiet fund of humour, which found vent pictorially in his many caricatures. Of these my brother has reproduced several in his book above mentioned, some of them owing their origin to the visit to Swanage, referred to on page 3, which took place towards the end of August of this year. My brother had written from Swanage urging Walker to throw aside wood blocks and water colours for awhile, and come and have an idle time ; and Walker had gone, accompanied by his eldest sister, Mr. and Mrs. Calderon joining the party shortly afterwards. At Swanage Walker spent, as he says, "a most delightful holiday" ; and having, while there, received a cheque for his picture of *The Lost Path*, he sent it on to his mother with the words :—"and the reason I send it to you, dear, is that you should break into it as soon as you like."

No allusion has as yet been made to Walker's connection with the little band of St. John's Wood artists, known as "The Clique" ; but as some of its members were among his most intimate friends, and he himself was elected an honorary member about this time, some mention of the subject may here be made. The original members were : P. H. Calderon, G. D. Leslie, J. E. Hodgson, W. F. Yeames, G. A. Storey, D. W. Wynfield, and my brother—it has been seen that Walker speaks of having met five of the number on the opening day of the Royal Academy—and honest and searching criticism of one another's work was the main object of the brotherhood. The badge was a gridiron, with the motto, "Ever on thee ; " a die of this badge was made for the members' notepaper, and a small brass gridiron was worn suspended from the button-hole on certain ceremonial occasions. There were meetings on Sunday mornings at the studio of one or other of the members, outings in the country after the pictures had been sent in to the Royal Academy, and in all their sayings and doings there existed a thorough bond of cordial goodfellowship.

During this and the next few years, Walker saw a great deal of the Clique, both collectively and individually ; and though, as time went on and his circle of friends widened, the intimacy somewhat declined, there was no loss of friendliness on either side. Ten years later—in the winter of 1873—when Walker was about to leave for Algiers for the benefit of his health, it was the Clique he gathered round him at a farewell dinner at the United Arts Club, of which he was an original member, and their letters of reply to his invitation, carefully put together, are among the papers that have come into my hands.

The atmosphere of the Clique must, I think, have been rather a robust one for Walker. The honest and searching criticism was not altogether confined to a member's work, and the peculiarities, physical or otherwise, of the man himself, sometimes came in for a share. Walker's extreme sensitiveness, and a readiness to imagine a slight when none was meant (which developed almost painfully in later years), rendered him peculiarly open to attack ; and I fancy some of the shafts which were aimed at him must have sunk a little deeper than was intended. As I write, I have before me three unfinished caricatures, all of the same subject, and in that which has been carried furthest towards completion the seven members of the Clique are seen walking off arm-in-arm, some looking back, some in attitudes of derision, while in the foreground Walker shows himself slowly moving away, with bent head and dejected air, apparently hard hit. But though in the friendly war of words, Walker might be unable to hold his own, he could reply with good effect when he betook himself to caricature, and in this characteristic manner would often manage to have the last laugh.

After his return from Swanage, Walker was chiefly engaged, for a couple of months or so, on work that has been already referred to, and in November he began the beautiful water colour drawing of *Philip in Church*, on which he worked pretty constantly, though not exclusively, for the remainder of the year. The drawing was a tolerably long time on hand, but though he once or twice speaks of being dissatisfied with it, and had some trouble with Philip's head—which, satisfactory in itself, was wrongly placed, and was eventually cut bodily out of the paper and its position altered—there are none of those groanings in spirit which marked the progress of *Jane Eyre*. For the background, Walker several times visited the church in Queen Square, Bloomsbury, to which it will be remembered Thackeray referred him, "if you are curious to be exact." It may interest some to know that in the face of the elderly lady in a light bonnet, seen in the background below the base of the pillar, is to be found a very recognisable likeness of Walker's mother.

While working on one subject, Walker would frequently have another in hand. Of the smaller water colours executed in this way, and, as nearly as can be ascertained, during this year, he completed *The Young Patient*, *The Shower*, *The Village School*, and one from his illustration to a short story of Miss Thackeray (entitled *Out of the World*) in the September, 1863, number of the *Cornhill*. I fear these bald lists of less important water colours may have somewhat wearied the reader ; but, without pretending that the catalogue is exhaustive, I have been anxious to make it as complete as possible, for the reason that it is generally to these earlier years that any spurious drawings are attributed. After the year 1863, Walker's works were not only more widely known, but bore in themselves such evidences of their origin, that imposition is easily detected ; though even as regards later years, there have been instances where an unfinished study has been added to by some unscrupulous person, and disposed of as Walker's own—a deception rendered the more possible from the fact that so many unfinished studies were dispersed

PHILIP IN CHURCH.

after his death. The one or two cases in which unfinished work of his has been openly and honourably touched on by other hands, will be referred to in their proper places.

It was at Christmas of this year that many a home in England, and Walker's not the least among them, was saddened by the news of Thackeray's death. It so happened that I was with Walker when he first heard the news. On the evening of Thursday, December 24, we had been having a game of billiards at some Billiard Rooms, and on taking a cab for Bayswater, Walker, who was a little anxious, told the cabman to drive first to Thackeray's house in Palace Gardens, where he learnt that his friend had passed away that day. It was a silent drive back to St. Petersburgh Place. On reaching home Walker went upstairs, and left to me the task of breaking the news to his family. The entry for this day in the little diary—only two words, " Thackeray died "— is touching in its simplicity. Mrs. Richmond Ritchie tells me :—" When my father died, I remember being touched and affected by hearing some one say that Mr. Walker had come running to the house, and that one of the household met him wandering about the stairs in tears." Though at first it was not Mrs. Ritchie's wish that this should appear in print, I have since obtained her permission to record an incident that is honourable alike to him who could inspire such affection, and to him who was capable of feeling it. Walker attended Thackeray's funeral on December 30, and returned home, as he says, quite worn out and still unwell, and " much impressed with the morning's event." Much impressed, and not a little sad ; for, in common with all who were privileged to know him as he was, Walker had learnt to love and reverence the great and kindly man.

On moving to St. Petersburgh Place, and for some two or three years before, Walker's household consisted of his mother, his sisters Fanny and Mary, and his brother John, and the number was now to be reduced by the marriage of his sister Mary, on January 2, 1864. In his diary, after briefly chronicling the day's doings, he adds :—" Consider this the end of the year."

# CHAPTER V

## 1864

The year 1864, at which we have now arrived, marks an important epoch in Walker's life, and may almost be said to form for him a dividing line between comparative obscurity and renown. Among the numerous misstatements that have clustered round his name, it has been said that Walker's talent was recognised only after his death, but this is far from having been the case. From the first, his powers had met with the most ready recognition from his brother artists ; on his now approaching public appearance as a water colourist, and henceforward, the critics were mostly lenient with him, sometimes indeed vying with each other in a chorus of praise ; his works were eagerly sought after ; and the estimate of their value afforded by that popular criterion of merit, the money test, could not be deemed other than satisfactory.

The Royal Academy had perhaps done him but scant justice in dealing with *The Lost Path*, but the Society of Painters in Water Colours (now bearing the prefix of Royal, but known then as now by the more familiar title of the Old Water Colour Society) was soon to throw its doors wide open to him, and receive him with open arms ; and from this time forward, success followed success, almost without a check. A few months before, he had been urged by two members of the Society—first of all by Mr. A. D. Fripp, and shortly after by Mr. Carl Haag—to become a candidate for election as Associate, and it was with this object that he was now— January, 1864—bringing the drawing of *Philip* to completion. The regulations were, and I believe are, that a candidate must submit three finished drawings as specimens of his ability ; and the three submitted by Walker were the scene from *Jane Eyre*, *Refreshment*, and *Philip*. The latter received the finishing touches on January 25, and it was then taken to "dear old William Hunt," as Mr. Ruskin calls him, who "seemed greatly pleased with it, and gratified me very much." The old man was then nearing the end of his career. In little more than a fortnight his hand was still, and Walker wrote :—

"I thought of writing this afternoon, and if I had, should not have had to give you a bit of bad news which I have just heard at the Club.

W. Hunt is dead—took cold on Sunday on going down to the Gallery
to see the competition drawings—the good old man is gone, dropped off
like the ripe fruit he painted.   A long and happy life I should say, and
surely one passed in giving the purest pleasure . . . . I feel great
pleasure in knowing that one of the last things W. Hunt did, was to send
his vote for me."

The election took place on February 8, and Walker was elected an
Associate by a unanimous vote—an honour that falls to the lot of very

THE SUMMER WOODS. (*Good Words*, June, 1862.)

few.   It was even suggested by some that he should not be subjected to
the ballot ; and the following extract from a letter of a brother artist
will show something of the warmth of welcome he received.   Mr. F. W.
Topham, writing on the day of the election says :—" I went to the Gallery
the other day, and I cannot help telling you how entirely charmed I was
with the exquisitely refined and touching work you have sent.   A more
lovely drawing than your ' Philip ' *I have never seen*, and I envy the
possessor of such a gem.   I do not know who is to have the honour of
proposing you, but wish it had been mine to do so."   It is strange that,

with this drawing of *Philip* on the walls at the exhibition of 1876, Mr. Ruskin should have written :—" There is no evidence in the entire Walker exhibition that he had ever heard of such a thing as prayer."

Though so far this year Walker had been engaged principally on *Philip*, wood drawing was also claiming a share of his attention. In the previous November he had undertaken (with considerable reluctance) the illustrations to Mrs. Henry Wood's story of *Oswald Cray*, the first part of which appeared in *Good Words* for January; and Mr. Smith had lately proposed that he should contribute the illustrations to Thackeray's unfinished story of *Denis Duval*. This too he had agreed to, not without some consideration, for though without doubt he fully appreciated a further association with Thackeray's writings, wood drawing had now become irksome to him, and took up time that he felt might be more advantageously employed. The drawings to *Denis Duval* appeared in the *Cornhill* in March, April, May, and June; and, though not, I believe, as a consequence of the considerations just mentioned, they have not been classed among his happiest efforts. It may be that he was hampered by the costume, or, as possibly was the case with the scene from *Jane Eyre*, over anxiety to do justice to his subject was the cause of any shortcoming; for the care that has evidently been bestowed on the drawings seems somewhat to have detracted from their spontaneity, and rendered them a trifle laboured. The first illustration—*Little Denis dances and sings before the Navy Gentlemen*—was redrawn by Walker from a water colour drawing by Thackeray in the possession of Mr. Smith, to which Walker refers as the last drawing from Thackeray's hand. Of the four illustrations, Walker reproduced two in water colour, viz. : *Evidence for the Defence*, and *Denis's Valet*.

The incentive to work afforded by the personal nature of the connection between author and artist in the case of *Denis Duval*, was wanting as regards the illustrations to *Oswald Cray*; and though the drawings themselves did not suffer on that account, the labour attending them, and the necessity, as in all such work, of having them ready by a certain time, were more keenly felt. The story had not been long on its way when Walker wrote :—

" I begin to think it was a mistake to take those 'Good Words' things, and the beastliness of wood drawing is full upon me—support me in the resolution to take NO MORE as these things get finished. I am utterly tired of it—yes utterly. There is not a single reason that I can see *now* for doing them, certainly not on the score of money." And again a little later :—" I asked Swain if he thought I could get off doing any more 'Good Words' drawings—in fact give 'em to some one else. He seemed shut up and said he thought not. Strahan's away—at Jerusalem—for three months, so I must bear that burden."

Soon after the three months, however, the burden was cast aside. The eighth illustration—that for August—brought Walker's connection with the story, and also with *Good Words*, to an end ; and for some time to come he possessed his soul in peace, unharassed by the myrmidons of the wood engraver.

On the day of his election to the Old Water Colour Society, Walker wrote :—" I've begun at the blind man on the large canvas and will work hard, but sha'n't send in if I'm obliged to scamp it." This is of interest as showing that, whatever disappointment he may have felt at the failure of *The Lost Path* to secure a better position the year before at the Royal Academy, the fact that he did not again exhibit there till the year 1867, was due to other causes than mere pique. It was, however, to be many a month yet before the picture of the blind man was completed. On March 11 he wrote :—" As for the blind man, as it's impossible to get done for the R.A., I shall take time and slap at the primrosy Spring, and send it in with the rest—shall just have time if I work hard—only a single figure." " The primrosy Spring " was the fourth drawing of the quartette with which Walker made his public appearance at the Summer Exhibition of the Old Water Colour Society ; the other three being those which had secured his election. The landscape was taken from the copses near the cottage at Beddington, in which he often strolled, and where he hailed with pleasure, as a sign of coming spring, the " tender green primrose leaves just peeping up."

This drawing of *Spring* was the first of the many important works of Walker's which passed through the hands of Messrs. Thomas Agnew and Sons ; but was not, as has been stated, the means of bringing together Walker and Mr. (now Sir. William) Agnew. The latter had come to Walker in the month of February, before the drawing was begun, with a letter of introduction from Mr. Calderon ; and had subsequently secured the drawing by a cheque on account, nearly a month before the private view of the Old Water Colour Exhibition. It is a thankless task to spoil a good story ; but the statement that the drawing of *Spring* was purchased by Mr. Agnew at the private view, and the account of Walker's emotion at the purchase, hardly seem consistent with the facts just stated. Mr. Agnew's recognition of Walker's talent was, however, in any case, immediate and complete. A friendship was formed which quickly passed the narrow bounds of business, and was continued to the end of Walker's life. The genuine delight that Mr. Agnew took in Walker's works, coming as it did from one so well qualified to judge, must have been very gratifying. That the large and open-handed methods which marked Mr. Agnew's conduct of affairs, afforded Walker frequent relief from anxiety, is evident from many expressions in his letters.

The date of the private view—April 23—was a memorable one to Walker, and I regret that among his letters there are none bearing on this day. The critics were loud in his praise. It was affirmed that he had risen to the height of his profession at a single bound ; the Society was said to have made the most valuable addition to its figure painters that it could have made ; his work was most favourably compared with that of

Spring

By permission of Mess.rs Thos. Agnew & Sons, Proprietors of the Copyright.

the lately lost William Hunt ; and its grace, beauty, and delicacy, both in treatment of subject and in execution, were freely acknowledged. Some exception was indeed taken to the drawing of the scene from *Jane Eyre* (which by the advice of Mr. Smith had been sent in with the simple title of *Garden Scene*), but where so much was praise, this was a small matter. It may easily be thought what joy this success brought to the household of St. Petersburgh Place. Thenceforth Walker was recognised as a master in water colours, and his drawings were among the first looked for at the Exhibitions of the Society.

In recognition of the merits of his four exhibits, Walker was this year awarded the silver medal of the Society for the Encouragement of the Fine Arts. At the sale of the collection of the late Mr. William Leech, *Spring* was purchased by Sir William Agnew for the sum of £2,000.

*Philip in Church* has been etched by Professor H. Herkomer, R. A., and *Spring* by Mr. R. W. Macbeth, A. R. A.

On looking down the list of Walker's exhibited works, it will be noticed that, so far as production for exhibition was concerned, his first success in water colours was followed by a period of comparative inaction. There were but two more drawings in 1864, and two only in the following year. It must be borne in mind, however, that Walker had no notion of confining himself to water colours, but was desirous of becoming known as a painter in oils. As will have been seen by the references to the blind man picture, he was already working with that object. The paucity of exhibited drawings just mentioned, was due, I believe, to the fact that he was endeavouring thoroughly to prepare himself before again appearing as an oil painter ; and the searching self-criticism and fastidiousness which were always with him made this a matter of time. He must, too, have realised the importance of avoiding anything approaching a falling short in oils of the standard he had established for himself in water colours, and was not likely to imperil his success by hasty or premature effort. To these considerations, special to this time, must be added the fact that Walker was throughout incapable of regular and methodical work. This alone might lead many to suppose that he was wanting in industry generally. That it was the opinion formed of him by Mr. Hodgson, is evident from what he says in the article in the *Magazine of Art* already referred to :—" nor was he in any danger from over-industry and application." If, too, Mr. Hodgson's account of the difficulty Walker experienced in production, be taken as representing his normal state, the wonder would seem to be that any completed picture ever saw the light. Mr. Hodgson says :—" Never did artist groan as he did in the throes of production. It was painful to see him ; he would sit for hours over a sheet of paper, biting his nails, of which there was very little left on either hand ; his brows would knit, and the muscles of his jaw, which was square and prominent, would twitch convulsively like one in pain. And at the end, all that could be discerned were a few faint pencil sketches, the dim outline of a female figure perhaps, but beautiful as a dream, full of grace, loveliness, and vitality." That Mr. Hodgson wrote of what he saw, there is no question. His statement cannot, however, be accepted without considerable qualification. As Walker was not in the habit of working before others, it may fairly be assumed that the scene which Mr. Hodgson describes took place at some sketching meeting ; where, having so to speak, to produce something to order in a given time, it may well have been that, if the fit were not on him, Walker's ideas were slow in coming. That he did not, when alone, sit for hours in the manner described, is clear for the simple reason that, when not in the mood, he would not attempt to work at all. When he had thoroughly thought out what he intended to do, or when making a simple transcript from nature, he worked quickly and with ease, laying down his foundations and building upon them with a precision that would have been impossible, unless he had had from the beginning a clear idea of the effect he intended to produce. Nevertheless there are instances—one will be mentioned directly— where it can hardly be said that Mr. Hodgson's statement is overdrawn ; though the quantity and quality of the works shown at the exhibition of 1876 prove, I think, that the sterility spoken of by him could only have been present at certain times and under certain circumstances.

The two other finished drawings of this year, referred to above, were those exhibited at the Winter Exhibition of the Old Water Colour Society, viz. : *Denis's Valet*, painted for Mr. Geo. Smith, and a postman delivering a letter at a gate, which, though exhibited with the simple title of *Sketch*, is named *My Front Garden* in one of Walker's papers, and was taken from his house at St. Petersburgh Place. Among the other work on hand was the drawing of *Autumn*, the instance just mentioned as tending to support Mr. Hodgson's statement. This drawing, though begun in June, and so far finished as to be exhibited at the Summer Exhibition of the Old Water Colour Society in 1865, was not finally out of hand till December of that year ; this too, as far as can be ascertained, without the need for any of those radical alterations, brought about by the further development of his idea of the subject, which so often led Walker to discard work that seemed to others to be progressing satisfactorily. Several other drawings were begun and finished during the time that *Autumn* was on hand, and possibly the difficulty Walker experienced in bringing this drawing to completion was again due to over anxiety. The favourable manner in which his first exhibits had been received would in itself spur him on to greater exertions ; while the knowledge that *Autumn*, if only from its title, would assuredly be compared with *Spring*, must have made him anxious that the later work should not suffer by the comparison. The following extracts show the spirit in which he was working :—" I sha'n't hurry it, and will do *all* I know." " I've improved the head, and am working conscientiously as I began." To a certain point he was apparently satisfied with the result, as towards the close of the year he writes :—" I carry my chin higher than I have done for some time. I know the picture *now* is a good one." Here, for the present, it must be left.

"*E.N.E. Wind.*"

In August, Walker went with the family to Ilfracombe, but does not appear to have done any work there. In November, he received a visit from Mr. Mark Lemon, the then editor of *Punch*, who solicited an occasional contribution to that journal, and particularly wished for a drawing for the Almanack for the coming year. This latter Walker undertook, and speaks appreciatively of the kindness and consideration shown by Mr. Mark Lemon during the negotiations as to choice of subject, &c. The drawing was entitled : *New Bathing Company (Limited) —specimens of Costumes to be worn by the Shareholders.* As has been remarked by Mr. J. L. Roget in his *History of the Old Water Colour Society*, it is " more distinguished by graceful fancy than by comicality of humour." As usual, not too much time was left for the wood engraver, and on receiving the proof of the drawing Walker writes :—" It gave me the usual 'turn,' but I must not grumble, considering the short time they had for the cutting."

About this time, too, Walker had a communication from the authorities of the South Kensington Museum, inquiring whether he would be willing to undertake a design for a full-length figure of Flaxman as a sculptor, but though, at the time, he appeared anxious to accept the commission, and wrote :—" I have great hopes that it refers to one of the frescoes—portraits of great men round the new and rather splendid gallery," the project was not carried out. A letter from the Museum, dated December 10, 1867 (the authorities appear to have been very long-suffering), states that, in the event of no design having been begun, the commission will be given to some one else.

The only other work of this year of which the letters speak, is the first of those invitation cards to the musical evenings of the Moray Minstrels, which Walker executed for his friend, Mr Arthur J. Lewis, at whose house these gatherings were held. Of this Walker writes :—" A. Lewis has asked me as a favour to do 'a sketch' for his music ticket of this season. Of course I will, and take pains too for such a good fellow, and will do more than the 'sketch.'" The result showed that he kept his word ; and, from a copy of a letter to Mr. Lewis, it would appear that the card was undertaken as a labour of love and in acknowledgment of many kindnesses received. The card was drawn on the wood, and engraved by **Mr. W. H. Hooper**, of whose work Walker justly had a very high opinion. A letter to Mr. Hooper, dated January 12, 1865, shows not only this, but also the care with which Walker scrutinised the work of the engraver :—

"I have to thank you very much for the truly capital way in which this block is being cut ; that of the 'Minstrels' themselves *seems to me quite perfect.* I see I made a decided mistake in putting that man's face in at the corner ; he is a regular *brute*, and must, I think, be altered at any sacrifice. Could you change him into a back view, like the rest? I have put a touch or two of dark in altering with the white, which makes me fear you will say you cannot alter him without plugging. He was considerably too dark

moreover. The lady's face would be better for a little attention ; rather too much line on the pupils of her eyes—her precious eyes—the line round the outside of the foot rather too thick, which makes the foot itself look a *leetle* wide ; the lines on the toes hardly tender enough. I wish I'd hardly shown so much of her leg too ; you might make the line of drapery rather more distinct—tenderly though. I am vexed to suggest so annoying an alteration as the man's head. If it be necessary to use a plug (and I hope it is not), let me know directly, that I may draw it while the messenger waits."

Walker had, some time before, been taking riding lessons—he speaks of going out riding with John Leech in November, 1863, while on a short visit to Mr. George Smith, at Brighton—and Mr. Lewis frequently gave him a mount, and took him out hunting. In various other ways, too, Mr. Lewis had shown him kindness, freely placing his house at Walker's disposal for backgrounds to his drawings—the phaeton in the first illustration to *Oswald Cray* was drawn from Mr. Lewis's phaeton. The statement of Mr. Claude Phillips in the *Portfolio* for June, 1894, that Walker had been in the employment of Mr. Lewis's firms, is, however, incorrect.

So much has been written of Walker's frailness, delicacy, timidity, and so on, that the above reference to his hunting may possibly come as a surprise to some. Without, however, being an athlete, he was by no means wanting in manliness. He was a good rider and swimmer ; had at one time belonged to a rowing club ; would walk five or six hours at a stretch ; and from his youth up was an ardent fisherman, rising later to that highest branch of the gentle art, salmon fishing. Nor would he tamely submit to anything approaching an affront, and indeed, as has been said, was often too ready to take offence where none was meant. Like most "anglers and very honest men," Walker was a smoker.

The year, which in its earlier months had been marked by such success, was, towards its close, to usher in a period of trial and anxiety caused by the state of health of Walker's youngest brother, John. This brother, having his share of the artistic feeling of the family, had been apprenticed to Mr. Strong, the wood carver, some four years before ; and, had he lived, it is probable he would have become favourably known in this branch of art. He had, however, never been very strong, and at the beginning of October, symptoms of probable lung-trouble were so apparent, that it was considered necessary for him to give up work, at any rate for a time, and pass the winter away from London. The place first selected was Shanklin, in the Isle of Wight, and he went there early in October accompanied by his mother, whose devotion to him, as to all her children, was extreme. It was weary watching for her, dear lady, with its alternations of trembling hope and sickening fear ; and though her care delayed the end, it came at last some three years later. Many were the letters that passed between Walker and his mother during the times of her banishment from home, of which this was the beginning, and nowhere are the relations that existed between mother and son more clearly shown than in this correspondence. Not to take too high ground, it may well be imagined that to Walker, standing as he did, as yet, barely on the threshold of pecuniary success, the expense attending these wanderings must have been a matter of serious moment ; yet in all his letters there is not one word of impatience or complaint on this score, but, on the contrary, repeated inquiries as to what he could send " the poor exiles," as as he calls them, in money or otherwise, to add in any way to their comfort.  Such expressions as these :—" You think too much about the money—if it only has the desired effect, never was money better spent," " Tell me what to send down," " Do let me know if I can send down anything," " And if I hear of your stinting yourself while you are there I shall be angry," recur like the burden of a song ; while his letters throughout, and especially the evidence they afford of the unselfishness with which he took upon himself all the cares of the head of a family, show how Walker's sterling qualities were brought out in this time of trial. And his mother's letters, with their gentle resignation, their wise counsel, their tender solicitude, their absolute trust !  No wonder Walker's love for her was what it was.

# CHAPTER VI

1865

In the early days of 1865, Mrs. Walker and her invalid son left Shanklin, and took up their quarters at Torquay. It was to the latter place the letter containing the following reference to *Wayfarers* was addressed. Writing to his mother from Croydon, while on a short visit to his youngest sister and her husband, Walker says :—

" I am preparing myself for the 'great go'—the Academy picture, while here, and am getting into the *devout* (!) spirit which my little worries were beginning to eclipse, and without which no picture (of the character my ambition proposes for this) ought to be commenced." In the same letter he gives this advice to his brother :—"Tell him to always have his time employed, to make this his first object ; and of an evening write a romantic and thrilling history of a young man in search of the lovely, during a winter in Torquay ; and done in a style of writing as though he were going in for a Government situation, and by the way, who knows what might turn up in case it should turn out not expedient to let him go back to Strong's ? I write this because want of occupation is such an unwholesome thing, such a foul thing."

A few days later—January 25—he writes :—

" You'll want to know what I'm doing in the way of work. Well, I have begun a sketch for the blind man, as I must considerably alter the ' compo ' of the figures, and in a few days I hope to have the little water colour of Smith's done. As for ' Autumn,' the little that it requires may stand over for the present." " The little water colour " referred to was the reproduction of the subject of the wood drawing for *Denis Duval—Evidence for the Defence*. It was painted for Mr. George Smith, and was first exhibited at the exhibition of 1876.

Walker so evidently intended *Wayfarers* for the Royal Academy, that his account of a meeting with Mr. Gambart, in whose gallery the picture was eventually exhibited, may here be given, as tending to throw some light on the change of plan. This meeting took place at Mr. Lewis's on the first night of the season of the Moray Minstrels— January 28. After speaking of the congratulations he received on the success of the invitation card, Walker says :—" I'd only got a short distance into the room at first, when Gambart *got at me* (that is the only way I can describe it), and with greeting most tender insisted upon coming to see me, and said, ' I'll come to-morrow morning.' I told him he couldn't see anything but an unfinished water colour of Agnew's. ' Never mind, we'll talk over what you are going to do for me.' "

Mr. Gambart's persistence triumphed in the end, so far as *Wayfarers* was concerned.

It will be remembered that in 1863, Walker went to Haslemere to find a background for this picture. He had also been looking for something suitable in the neighbourhood of Addington Hills, near Croydon ; the line of these hills having formed the background in the etching. The place eventually fixed on, however, was an out-of-the-way spot in the fields, near the Beddington cottage, which he thus describes in a letter to his mother dated February 9 :—

"I am happy to tell you I have got regularly into the bowels of my picture. Yesterday was a capital day. I worked with a *will*, after great trouble in getting the canvas (no trifle), easel and things on to the spot, which is on the swell of a hill beyond the copse where I did 'Spring,' and looking over some ploughed land towards old Croydon, and indeed I shall just indicate the church ; so instead of having the *stupendous* ridge I originally intended for the background, there will be the modest line of hills and feathery trees I have got to appreciate from seeing so often ; and in front, quite to the right, I have slapped in an old pollard willow stump, of which there is a

fine ivy-grown specimen in John's own place. I thought I never should have got the things up to the place, for the wind was high, and I had to cross a lot of heavy land, and a ploughed field where I nearly stuck fast, but I did not mind, I had snowboots over my own, and I preferred going that way to crossing Steadman's violet field, and suffering the grins and probably the company of his 'hands.' I sincerely hope it may go on well, for I give myself credit for having *begun* it in the right spirit."

Steadman's violet field was itself to be pressed into Walker's service a couple of years or so later.

Though begun in the right spirit, the picture had yet many difficulties to encounter. Before long arises the bitter cry of the London artist in his fog-girt home :—

"I've been trying to work this morning through a kind of light as though the sky had a mixture of beer and dirt, and in the end I dismissed the model in disgust ; and as I hear they are skating, I shall just put my skates in a pocket of my pea-jacket, and go and have a look. I cannot tell how sick I am of this cold. The sun is just beginning (now that I've knocked off work) to break out in a sickly way, the first time since I left Croydon, I'm sure." Shortly after he wrote to his mother :—" I have not yet finished Smith's water colour, but then I am making it rather more important than I thought I should. I fear that for this year's Academy it is all up with my picture. I shall see in a few days if it is as I fear. I shall anyhow be going on with it, and at the same time have another picture for the Water Colour Gallery. I feel that I am up to my neck in promises to let people have my work, but then I do it *so* slowly. . . . . My longing for Spring and warm clean weather is fast becoming intolerable, I have never felt anything like it. . . . . Write continually to me—remember the post is a speaking-tube of only a few hours length. Tell that Jack to, as well—never mind what scraps they may be."

By the beginning of March, all idea of finishing the picture in time for the Royal Academy was abandoned, and his thoughts turned again to *Autumn*. On March 8 he wrote :—

" 'Tis well I gave up the R.A. picture. I took 'Autumn' out and had a look at it on Sunday, and with a fresh eye *I saw that it was good*, and I shall have it appreciated too." *March* 13 :—" I have come to the determination of only sending one large water colour, the 'Autumn,' to the Exhibition, and finishing it very carefully, as I am pleased with it."

March 15, to myself :—

" I shall be with you again soon, for I have to finish 'Autumn' this month. I am in a rather depressed state about my work. My Academy picture cannot possibly be done, so I have set it aside ; and a subject I meant to work Polly into, I find does not look inviting on closer acquaintance. I have done a small one for Smith, however, and shall fill up the time in doing more of them in your locality, for I find I have agreed to do no end, and they certainly do bring in the cash. I am tired of yearning for a day or

two of something that might be dignified by the name of *weather*.   I
never was so utterly sick of this sort of thing—it takes the bread out of
one's mouth too, for I am actually waiting to work in the open air.   I
go into the garden daily, in hopes of seeing something refreshing, but
with the exception of one or two wretched crocuses, that look as though
they'd made a mistake, it might be the end of November.  The two poor
things at Torquay are getting tired of their banishment, but they
mustn't return till we are quite into next month. . . . .  I think I must
go to Torquay next week, mother has been begging me to for some time."

He accordingly went to Torquay, and while there painted the little
*Moss Bank*, which was exhibited this year at the Winter Exhibition of
the Old Water Colour Society.  He brought the drawing back with him,
and writes on his return :—" I've had a look at the ' Moss Bank ' this
morning, and am happy to say it looks very well in London light."
The drawing of *A Vision of the Clique*, from which Walker's own
figure is here given, was produced on the occasion of this visit to
Torquay.

Monday, April 10, was the date on which *Autumn* had to be sent in, and
Walker was at Beddington, working on the drawing, on that day.  On the
13th he wrote to his mother :—

"I have indeed been bothered by the picture, especially as I found
on coming home that the sending-in day was last Monday.  I shall
get it again on Saturday morning, so you see I shall work on it
up to the last moment, and certainly I never spent so much time and

trouble over anything before. I don't ask people's opinions on it, because they are sure to say something that is meant to be comforting, whether they feel it or no. I fear it will not be liked so much as 'Spring,' and altogether I am very anxious about it—time will show however."

To this his mother replied :—" Do not fear about the success of 'Autumn.' Of course there will be difference of opinion, but there will be enough to commend and appreciate to satisfy you, and us for you, I am certain. Even should the reverse be the case, why cheer up ; there is a long life before you, my boy, only take care, and your ultimate success and fortune are certain." Walker himself took a more hopeful view on getting the drawing back from the Gallery for a little more work before the opening day, for he writes :—" As for ' Autumn,' it came back from the Gallery to-day, and I am really pleased with it ; and if it has not a proper place at the Gallery, and is well received, it will be a shame."

Walker's forebodings as to the reception of the drawing were not without warrant ; though, happily, other criticisms upon it were not in the same vein as that of the then art-critic of the *Athenæum*, who wrote that it " lacks solidity and even truth of colour " ; that the shadows were painted " from feeling, not from nature " ; and that the girl's figure is " audaciously reckless or childishly ignorant." In justice to this critic it should be stated that the drawing, as then seen, was not in the state in which it finally left Walker's hands.

So many allusions to his flute playing occur about this time in Walker's letters, that it may be convenient here to make some reference to the subject. He was exceedingly fond of music, and his efforts as a musician began very early on the despised penny whistle. From this he advanced to a small flute ; and now, for some months past, had been taking lessons of Mr. R. S. Pratten, the flautist. He had, too, lately

" The Last Rose of Summer."

become the possessor of a really good instrument, which he cherished
with great care. He speaks of it as follows in a letter about this time :—
" I had another lesson of Pratten, and my flute has had a polish up and
the keys looked to. If it was lovely before, guess the blaze of delight
now ; I'm almost afraid to open the case." Walker played with much
grace and delicacy, paying particular attention to tone, and endeavouring
to bring out the sweet reediness of which the instrument is capable. His
flute was his constant companion in his journeyings, and the joy of making
music brought rest to many an hour.

" *Andante and Rondo à la Polka.*"

Towards the end of April, the exiles returned from Torquay, and,
after staying a few weeks in London, went down to Cookham for the
summer. In this way began the connection with the little village,
which has caused it and the name of Walker to be inseparably associated.
The cottage where they lodged was a rather tall, flint-built one, situated,
as Mr. Leslie says in *Our River*, " about half-way up the main street,
on the right-hand side as you go up from the river to the railway
station " ; and from the front windows could be seen the picturesque
old cottages (now no longer existing), which later were to form the
background of *The Street, Cookham*. A consideration assuredly not lost
sight of by Walker in fixing on a river-side place, was that his brother
John was as keen a fisherman as he was himself ; and here was an
opportunity for the invalid to indulge in his favourite sport to his
heart's content. Here, too, would probably be found the necessary
landscape for a picture of which the idea was already simmering in
Walker's brain. Soon after her arrival at Cookham, Mrs. Walker
wrote :—" This is a very lovely place, Fred would be delighted ; and
for a summer picture of boys bathing, there cannot be its equal, at

least in my experience." So here, with *Wayfarers* still unfinished, *Bathers* was to be begun.

About this time, there is mention of a water colour drawing, called indifferently *A Farm Yard* and *The Poultry Yard*; and I regret to be unable to state with certainty to what drawing these titles refer. My impression is that it was a drawing done at Beddington, of a man opening the half door of a stable, and letting out some stately Cochin-China fowls, which drawing at the time, Walker intended to call *The New Arrivals*; but as there is subsequent mention of the introduction of two figures into the drawing of *The Poultry Yard*, and I have never again seen the drawing done at Beddington, so as to ascertain if there were any alteration in the first idea, I cannot say whether my impression is correct.[1]

It was during this summer, too, that Walker painted *The Bouquet*— a gardener giving a bunch of flowers to two children in black—which was the reproduction, with considerable alterations, of the original design executed on wood for Messrs. Dalziel Bros. For the background, Walker made large use of an old red-brick house standing on the left by the cross roads, about a quarter of a mile out of Croydon along the Mitcham Road ; and, though of no general interest, I may perhaps be pardoned for mentioning that the dog in the drawing was painted from my dear old bull-terrier, "Smudge," who from puppyhood to old age lived his faithful life with me and mine.

To return to *Bathers*. On August 10, Walker, who was with his brother at Cookham, wrote :—

" Jack seems pretty well I think. He coughs a little in the night, and as I do not quite shut the door of my room, I always hear him ; but he sleeps well, and in other respects is all right, and in good spirits. I have just taken him up a cup of coffee, as I have done the last few mornings, as I know it is a comforting thing. I shall be glad to see Fan or some one, because as I have just got to work with the river bank, I shall necessarily be irregular. As I told her, beginning a picture is like taking a wife ; one must cleave to it, leaving one's relations and everything, to work when one can."

There is no record of the amount of work given to the picture during the next two months ; but at the end of that time a change of scene and an enlarged canvas were determined on. Early in October, Walker wrote from Bayswater to his brother, after a flying visit to the river :—

" You'll all say that wonders will never cease. I have just come home, having gone away by the 8 train last evening. I have come up to-night for the big canvas and my easel. I shall go back early to-morrow. I have had a most wondrous day. Had a good breakfast and went down to

---

[1] Since the above has been in type I have ascertained that *The Poultry Yard* and *The New Arrivals* are one and the same drawing.

Poulton's, took one of the little boats and rowed to Marlow ; then I was driven in a little pony gig to Mill End, where I had some bread and cheese, and started to go back on foot (6 miles) ; and I think I never had a more fetching walk—all along the banks, over great meadows, quite made my legs twitch to think how I could have cantered over them, and at last came to a place having for a background that which will *top everything* for the picture, instead of Cliefden, though I shall keep the nearer trees, also the meadows and rushes, just the same. I got so excited that I saw the whole thing done from beginning to end ; and a little further on was the lock house where the Coopers once stayed. I have taken a room there from next Thursday, and before I come back I'll have done *something* you'll see. When I saw this loveliness to-day, the whole picture came before me in such a way, that I decided upon commencing on the big canvas at once. I got into my boat at Marlow in an ecstatic state, and was only cooled down by the time I got back to Poulton's, feeling horribly hungry."

The lock house was that at Hurley, and a week later Walker wrote from there to his sister Mary :—

"Haven't I been primitive for the last week, that's all—eating steak and onions with such a relish, and everything like an ogre— I never knew myself to eat so much, and with an iron spoon too —this last *must* shock you ! But I get on with the picture, that's one little comfort ; and when I think that it may be a real good success, I feel inclined to cuddle myself, though, my dear, it's fetching work—such tramping over fields with the horrid great canvas—it's all warped, having been wetted through once or twice. I pull up in a boat to the scene of action, and then have to take all the things across a great meadow ; and a mob of long-faced horses have once or twice become so excited, rushing about in circles and kicking each other, then stopping close to look at me, and I let one come quite close, and sniff the canvas. You see, as I have to cook the composition up, taking a bit here and a bit there, I have to drag the canvas to all manner of places, and nearly put a hole in it getting it over a hedge this evening ; my poor nail-less fingers were numbed. I've got a pair of splendid shooting boots, and leather gaiters up to the knee, and my riding breeches with the little pearl buttons at the side, and a velveteen hat of a dark cinnamon colour, and look as much like a countryman as I can, but it won't do ; the few people I have met are frightfully respectful, and *will* wish me 'good day.' I've got my tackle here, but have only caught two perch ; however, I shall try for a jack to-morrow before work. This is a funny little house, and the boats pass through the lock under the windows ; and there is a parrot here that laughs the most horrible sardonic laugh, like a wicked old woman, and talks like one. The lock keeper is a butcher as well, and has a shop at the side of the cottage, about a yard and a half wide. He is fond of music, and has a bass viol hanging up that he used to play in church. I have been tootling to him, and gave him 'Romance' to-night; he knew 'Rose Softly Blooming' quite well."

The following will appeal to some brother of the angle :—

"Tell that Jack that I caught two of his namesakes to-day. I began at midday, or near one, after a long morning's work, and very soon had a small one; and not very long after, I *saw* a regular monster rush out of the weeds and gobble down my bait (I was trolling), and then he seemed to give great gulps as though he liked it; so I thought it time to give him gruel, and struck. He dashed right down the stream, bending my rod like a reed, and whirring the line out like old boots, when he sulked under some weeds. I stopped a little time, and then I thought he'd better come out of that, so I gave a bit of a tug. Then he made a great dash on the surface of the water, and spewed up the hooks and bait all mangled—guess my frame of mind when I saw he'd vanished, my language was quite shocking. However, just before dusk this evening, I got another; not so big, but still decent. I shall try again to-morrow—my work is close to the bank."

After a run up to town from Saturday till Monday, Walker wrote to his mother, October 16 :—

"I got here in time to do a good hour's work, and now I've just come in to have some tea and to send off a scribble to the poor, old, careworn dear. I had plenty of time to think of you on my journey down, and wished I could have left you all in better case. My walk from Taplow was very solitary, and exceedingly lovely, not a breath of wind stirring, and indeed a sort of afternoon to make one *think*, if ever one may take credit for such a proceeding. I got here feeling slightly tired, and was not sorry to hear the Poll parrot's voice echoing across the water before I came in sight of the little place. I did not go away, but sat down to copy some rushes nearly opposite the house. I have begun my tea, and it's beginning to rain, I'm grieved to say, but perhaps it won't be much. . . . I've been outside to see a boat full of people, forming a wedding party—one of the Marlow fishermen— they were all singing, and had a cornet player with them; the bride with a white bonnet on, which will be spoilt I'm afraid. . . . . Endure the coming discomforts as well as possible, and think of the blessed spring beyond. For my own part I am exceedingly happy, and am *only* con- cerned about these matters which must take time to remove, and which you are helping and doing your very best to remove—so bravely in my opinion, that let me here declare, I am filled with admiration at your unselfish sacrifice."

The "coming discomforts" referred to in the foregoing extract were those attendant on another term of banishment soon to be begun; the place chosen being once more Torquay. It is worth notice, too, that part of the letter was written while at a meal. This was quite a habit with Walker, many of the letters having been written under similar circumstances ; for the reason, as he says in one of them, that " I don't like being idle."

*November* 2.—" I was just imprecating the name of Eatwell for not sending two tubes of colour, and I find them laid on the table, so now I shall have a very hard day's work ; the last, I hope, for I intend going away for good to-morrow. I did a considerable bit yesterday, and much improved it ; taking out a pollard willow, and putting a large nut bush (?) in its place, and during the afternoon flinging anything into the water, anything I could get hold of, to make circles, &c. It's astonishing how much I have rubbed out in order to keep it *simple ;* for if I don't, I know by bitter experience how it will be when I get in the figures. The first two days' work went out at one lick. . . . . Adieu, I go to my work. This will be a fetcher after all, I know ; and oils too ! "

In connection with this study of circles in the water, it may be mentioned that Walker, while painting *Bathers,* took suggestions as to the play of colour in the water, from a handful of opals he had for the purpose in his studio at the time.

On November 3, Walker returned to London. In a letter to his mother written on the following day, he describes the difficulty he had in getting the picture and his belongings to the railway station, and continues :—

" I had another episode at Paddington. I had in my possession a letter saying that if I desired it, I could have the money for a ticket which I didn't use, and as it was 4s. 1d. I did desire it, so went, *in my rustic attire,* into an office to inquire for the superintendent, and there stood a group of young clerks at a sort of counter, and one whom I addressed civilly, instead of answering, grinned at the others ; whereupon I brought my fist down on the counter with a *bang,* exclaiming '—— it, sir, don't *grin,* but *answer* me.' The effect was electrical over the whole office, which was full of functionaries. The superintendent, I may add, who was in the next office, was wise enough to treat me with great courtesy. . . . . What a lovely day, so was yesterday ; and I had a little heart-ache in leaving the beauteous Hurley, everything was bathed in gold. But no matter, I am in our castle once more, and have turned up my sleeves for months of real hard work."

While at Hurley, Walker had begun the water colour portrait of himself, in my possession, which forms the frontispiece of this book. It is an excellent likeness. Soon after his return, he began another portrait thus described in a letter to his mother :—

" I know you'll like just a line to say I'm all right, and at work on my portrait, although not the one you saw. It's a standing figure, and will be more of a study and less of a portrait, though I shall be quite faithful as to dress and feature, with

AUTUMN.
*(By permission of* Messrs. Thos. Agnew and Sons, *owners of the copyright.)*

perhaps a little softening of my defects here and there. The figure is standing, as I observed, and is holding up to the spectator a jack, and I shall have proper accessories, and then call it, 'Study—an Angler.' The fish will be a caution, and will be held up by a string or something passed through the gills." The drawing, however, was never completed ; and no trace of it exists.

Hitherto Walker had used as a studio one of the rooms of his house at St. Petersburgh Place. The studio he built at the bottom of the garden was now in course of construction, and the letter just quoted from says :—" The painting room is quite lovely. . . . and I could not resist going down with a candle last evening, to see how it looked by that light."

On getting home _Bathers_ from Hurley, Walker was, as he says, "more than satisfied with it." It was, however, to be laid aside for a time, in order that _Autumn_ (now received from the Old Water Colour Society) might at last be completed. On November 11, he wrote :—

"I am hard at work on 'Autumn,' having thrown over the 'Study' at Agnew's request, and my own desire. . . . How glad I am that I never allowed 'Autumn' to leave me, it's ever so much better already." _November_ 15 :—" There is no news ; the weather is dark and dreary, and makes me feel very disinclined for work. Still the 'Autumn' is going on, and is, in my opinion, much improved." _November_ 22 :—" I expect Agnew in town by Friday, and then he'll see how tremendously I've fetched up 'Autumn'. . . I shall have the 'Moss Bank' in the Exhibition which opens on Saturday." _November_ 27 :—" I am depressed in my work, and can _not_ get the brutal 'Autumn' off my hands, do all I will. . . I have begun another card for Lewis, greatly to his delight." _December_ 2 :—" I am quite well, and am just on the point of finishing—what I need not say—I'm sick of the very name." _December_ 4 :—" I am all serene, and have been working well ; so well that Agnew will take the beastly thing with him to Manchester after all, for he is still in town. . . I am quite yearning to get at the big picture. Fan will tell you the opinion of a good and clever man named Mason, who saw it yesterday." With the remark that it has been etched by Mr. Macbeth, _Autumn_ may now be finally left.

Unfortunately, the letter referred to above, in which was recorded George Mason's opinion of the big picture (presumably _Bathers_), has been destroyed. There is, however, no doubt that Mason held Walker in very high esteem. One evening, Mr. Leslie and my brother had been dining at Mason's house, and, as Mr. Leslie is good enough to tell me :— " We had been talking over the merits and demerits of a number of our contemporary brother brushes, and at last Mason said, 'Well, who do you think is the biggest genius of the present day?' and then he said, 'Freddy Walker' ; to which Marks and I simultaneously assented."

It was in this month of December that Walker insured his life, and

though much has been said of his bearing about him "the germs of in-
sidious disease," he not only passed, but passed well.  Writing to his
brother, in great spirits, on the day on which he had seen the doctor, he
says :—"I'm all hunks, I'm going to see the Clique to-night and feel
equal to anything ; 'cos why.  I went to the insurance doctor this
morning, and he complimented me on my chest and circulation, there !
So the insurance goes on all serene.  I dined with Lewis yesterday ; his
ticket will be quite a success."

This invitation card—a beautiful design of Minerva and Apollo,
seated one on either side of a wreathed and massive pedestal, crowned
by a shallow vase—was etched on copper.  The comic mask lying at
Apollo's feet is one of Walker's many caricatures of my brother.

During the autumn of this year, Mr. Agnew, having become interested in the firm of Messrs. Bradbury and Evans, had asked Walker,
as a favour, to contribute a drawing to the Christmas number of *Once a
Week*, of which periodical the firm were the proprietors.  Walker agreed,
and though the drawing was not ready in time for that number, he was
working on it at the latter end of the year.  The subject chosen was
that which was to be the first idea of the oil picture of *Vagrants* ; indeed,
the drawing appeared under that title in *Once a Week* for January 27, 1866.
There is also reference to his being engaged on the drawing of Hogarth
painting from a model beating a drum, of which mention has been
made on page 34.  In addition to these, Walker had again taken up
the picture of *Wayfarers*, and speaks of having been at work on it
on Christmas Day ; when, let us hope, his circulation, on which the
insurance doctor complimented him, stood him in good stead.

# CHAPTER VII

## 1866

" My dear, I have begun this year with an earnest—well, prayer—
that I may do my duty as regards *work*. I will do my best, yes I will
do my best, even though I am more alone than I was two years ago.
Never mind, I know I can still rely upon the good help of some one
who has always had for me a word of genuine comfort, &c. Bother,
I am getting sentimental, and as I live it's nearly one o'clock." Thus
wrote Walker to his sister Mary, on January 3, 1866—the day after
the second anniversary of her marriage.

The wood drawing of *Vagrants* was now finished, and the same
letter says :—" Yes, the O. A. W. block is done, and I took it down
on Monday to Swain's in a cab, quite like old times. I call it *Vagrants*
or *Wanderers*. . . I expect to be elected into the Garrick in less than
a fortnight, and shall then be able to buttonhole one or two R.A's
quietly—*after dinner*! . . . I've just perpetrated myself as I shall appear
to-morrow. It's very bad, but what can you expect at 1 a.m."

*" To-morrow ½ p. 8 p.m."*

Though *Wayfarers* had been taken up again, it was soon put aside for *Bathers*. On January 16, Walker wrote to his mother that he was making charcoal sketches for the latter, and two days later says :—

"We seem to be going on the excellent plan of writing every day; much the best, even if only just one line. . . Congratulate me; this is the first day I have used my studio, as up to this I have been quite able to dispense with it. I have designed the whole of the 'Bathers'—there. Took one design to Poll last night, and brought away a song of Haydn's called ' Recollection,' which is so beautiful, that as I have blown it to-day, I have felt, you know what, quite affected. I am full of hope as to my work." A little later :—" My work is yielding to my endeavours, and is rewarding me already. I have been getting on famously."

Walker was duly elected to the Garrick on Jan. 20. A day or two after, when, as he says, he was expecting Charles Keene "to smoke a quiet dottle," he writes :—

"Jolly, my getting into the Garrick. I am bent upon slowly working a certain line which has R.A. at the end, and this is a part of my scheme. I shall always be dignified there. . . Lewis's ticket is already getting talked about—old Keene thinks it 'beautiful.'" *Jan.* 29 :—" Lewis's was a great affair, and I seem to be tremendously popular somehow. I was welcomed by a lot of 'Garricks.' . . . Tell Fan that her chief occupation must be keeping me up to the fight. I must go to bed early, and be at work by daylight. She will have to do it with a strong hand, and we shall both have to make sacrifices."

By this time it had been arranged that Walker was to contribute the drawings for Miss Thackeray's story of *The Village on the Cliff*, in the *Cornhill Magazine*. Although in the following extract he speaks of the story beginning next month, its publication was delayed till July, when the first instalment appeared together with Walker's illustration, *The Two Catherines*. *Jan.* 30 :—" The beautiful little pathetic story in the *Cornhill*, called 'To Esther,' is by Annie Thackeray. The story I am to make drawings for commences next month, and as the time is so short, there will be no drawing for the first number."

During the month of January, John Walker's illness took an unfavourable turn, and for some time his state was the cause of very grave anxiety.

On Feb. 2, Walker writes :—

"I wish I could, my good mother, send down a phial of elixir that should do all we desire for the poor old chap. Asking him to bear up is almost stale, and yet he must. I was going to say, beg him to look forward as hopefully as he may. I hope he has been getting out if it has been such a day as we have had, with lovely clear air, and banks of rosy clouds. I have been working well, and feel the comfort of having done my duty, or at least of having striven. . . . . I do think I shall finish *both* pictures, and shall show one to G. on Sunday."—" G." was of course Mr. Gambart. By this time it was settled that he was to have the offer of " the blind man."

*Feb.* 5 :—" Thank goodness my work is going on well. John was here yesterday—spent the day with me, and he seemed much struck with ' the bathers,' as far as it has gone, and with the other too. As long as I am all right *there*, I fear nothing." *Feb.* 6 :—" I have better news as regards my work. Gambart came yesterday, and was pleased enough with the blind man. I told him I really could not name the value till it was more advanced. . . I told him that no one had seen the blind man, and that, until some of the family had done so, I could say nothing as to price, as I invariably took their opinion."

Walker's statement that none of the family had as yet seen " the blind man " must not be taken literally, as what he probably meant was, either that it had not been seen by them in its then state, or that the question of price had not been discussed. That he did take their advice as to the prices of his pictures, is a matter of fact.

On Feb. 9, Walker wrote to his brother John :—

" I have felt the great comfort of steadily working, and am very hopeful, although I feel the strain sometimes ; and you know I am never so well as when I have lots of exercise, which I can't possibly take now. And this weather too, it's really too much, but Heavens ! if I only do finish these pictures, how I shall be comforted, even though I be ever so seedy in the end. . . I said just now that I'm never so well as with exercise, but I am really *very* well. What I mean is, that I have the irritable, nervous, snappish feeling, which must be resisted, or it grows into something monstrous for those about me, and the only antidote is a walk ; hence my bitter complaint of the wet. . . I wish I could give you advice, but *you* know how much rests in your own hands as to trifles—no one better—and you must be sick of advice ; but do try and keep a brave heart."

Feb. 13, also to his brother :—

" Of course I didn't know you were so bad when I sent my last. . . I only wish I could do more than sympathise with you, my boy, and you know I'd see everything else at the deuce, although I am surprising myself with my work. I have put in one boy that will *do it, I think*, the classic fellow standing up and throwing off his shirt—will require fetching up bit by bit, though he's *all there* now. Then I've got one chap in the left corner in front, who is rushing in bellowing, and tearing off his coat ; besides the back view of two fellows who are running towards the water, one of them throwing up his arms. These are on the other side of the picture ; and I've put in a boy in his shirt only, who is helping another out of the water, and another leaning on his arms with only his hat on, à la Mercury ; and when I tell you that it's seven feet long, you will understand that I mean it this time. The other, the blind man, has simply to be trickled off. I dined at the Garrick last night with Marcus Stone, 'twas an old arrangement. . . After dinner we rushed to the R. Academy to hear a lecture on painting by O'Neil, A.R.A. (who spoke up for me on the Garrick Committee), and a capital lecture it was. I saw one or two students who were there with me, and who are students still !. . . A lot of my tunes, at least one or two, almost make me *feel* last year at Torquay ; they remind me so strongly of the time when I used to blow at 'em of an evening. Fan is playing the accompaniment of one now, called 'Si la Stanchezza.' Do you remember the white violets at Cockington, and sitting on that gate looking across that deep valley at the plantation ? I have that stay very deeply printed in my mind. I trust you will be ready to hold up your head with the best, by the time I am free, for it is my work that has stopped my being with you before this."

A day or two after the above letter was written, Mr. Agnew first saw the *Bathers*, and his emphatic approval of the picture was the cause of great rejoicing at St. Petersburgh Place. On this occasion Mr. Agnew gave so many reasons against sending the two pictures to the Royal Academy that Walker decided to give up all idea of finishing *Wayfarers* in time for the Exhibition, and devote his energies to *Bathers*.

On February 19 he wrote to his mother : —

"All right, picture going on swimming. . . . . I don't work unless I feel at my strongest." *February* 24 :—"I haven't anything to write about, save that I have come to one or two hitches in my work. I have overcome one, and of course made it all the better afterwards, and now I'm wallowing in a regular big 'un, no less than an uncertainty as to the size of certain figures. But it is sure to come right. . . . . Should I break down in my work, I'll come to you if only for a day." *February* 26 :—'The Bathers' is going on capitally, for I have got over the trouble I mentioned. I slapped in a figure yesterday, which I am very pleased with, and another this morning. I rather expect a visit from J. Philip the Academician, this afternoon, and shall know what *he* thinks, at all events. I should not show it to him, but he goes to Rome in a few days, and will *talk about it* to the others. . . . . I was at Lewis's evening on Saturday ; like all the rest it was immensely jolly. Every one was there, lots of people want to come and see my picture. A Mr. Graham, an M.P., told me he thought my 'Spring' the most beautiful thing of its kind 'in the English language'! He thinks I shall never beat it, however he wants to see my present one, and I've promised he shall." It is well known that Mr. William Graham afterwards became the possessor of *Bathers*.

Mr. J. Philip, R.A., did come to see the picture, and though very pleased with it, made several suggestions, about which Walker decided to ask the advice of Sir John Millais, on whose opinion he placed great reliance.

On March 4 Walker wrote to his brother :—

" If I do not proceed more rapidly with my work, I shall cut it and make my appearance at Torquay on Wednesday or Thursday." . . . . . The next day to his mother :—" I am greatly bothered about my work, but do not like to think of leaving it so long as I think I may get over it without going away. . . . . The time is so dreadfully short that I really don't know what's to be done. I shall send you a line to-morrow telling you how I get on ; if I don't find an improvement, I shall certainly cut it for a few days.''

Walker's visit to Torquay was, however, to be hastened by an altogether unexpected event : the death in London, on March 6, of his second surviving brother, Harry, after only a few days' illness. The dark cloud of anxiety which hung over her charge at Torquay, had barely lifted for a time, when Mrs. Walker was called upon to face this new sorrow. Small wonder that one so well remembers the way in which she would pause in her work, and looking over her glasses, wistfully scan the faces of those who remained to her. Walker at once went down to Torquay to break the news to her, and wrote a long letter to his sisters to say how the news had been received. From this letter there is no need to quote ; it will suffice to give his mother's words to him on his return, to show how he had fulfilled his mission. On March 11 she wrote :— " How can I thank you enough for your thoughtful loving kindness in this time of trouble to us ? I can tell you the trial has been so much lessened by your gentle consideration and thoughtful goodness. Ah, what should I do without you, my Fred ? I can only thank and pray God to bless you, for all your goodness to your grateful Mother."

Walker came back to work, still hoping to finish the *Bathers*. On the day the above words were written, he had, as he says, " arranged for a tremendous day's work to-morrow." A couple of days later, he went, as intended, to see Sir John Millais, and makes mention of a pretty little incident there, which I trust all concerned will pardon me for printing. After dinner, the second little girl came in to say good-night, and Walker says :—" When she came round to me she said, ' Effie ' (her sister) ' says that you are little Walker,' and this dot of a thing asked me if my picture was getting on ! "

On March 15 Walker wrote to his brother :—

" I am working like a nigger at the picture, and am beginning to funk not getting it done for the R.A. I funk it because I find very little will be done with a rush as I want it. Those parts that I have slapped in, thinking all was right, have had to come out again. I shall have models at 7 o'clock, and work from that till 'my eyelids will no longer wag,' before I yield to the notion of not having it ready. I shall see the Clique to-night at Hodgson's sketching class, but somehow I cannot sketch lately." The concluding paragraph of the foregoing extract is worthy of notice, as bearing on the subject of Mr. Hodgson's estimate of Walker's productive powers, already referred to.

March 19, also to his brother :—

" I am going to give a day out to the Clique when the pictures are sent in. I should like to hire an omnibus for the day, and call for them all, I acting as conductor with a great gridironical badge and a large neckcloth. . . . My picture at last begins to reward me for my hard work, and I feel pretty sure of getting it finished enough to send in."

March 21, still to his brother :—

" This is to ask you to get for your own reading, a book called ' The Water Babies,' by Charles Kingsley—the most wonderful book. I have got it, and if you cannot borrow it, I'll send it down. ' The Water Babies ' seems a stupid title, but that is because it is really a child's book ; but it is so splendid that you will be quite fetched, both by the poetical ideas, and the gentle satire and philosophy. No news ; picture going on clipping. My model can scarcely keep the pose for a cough that almost lifts him off his feet at times."

March 24, to his mother :—

" I am rapidly coming to the conclusion that to finish my picture is simply impossible, although I shall of course work very hard.

Agnew begged me not to hurry, as he felt sure that it would be much more famous if time were given to it, and I cannot but agree with him ; for though the intention and idea of the subject are all there, there are parts of the drawing involving so much study, that to rattle it off strikes me at this moment as sheer madness. I have let two men see it to-day, and they think it on the eve of being so fine, that it would be a thousand pities, &c. I am going round to Millais—he will have nothing ready I hear—and shall try and bring him round, and his opinion will be final. . . . I am half distracted about this picture. No one seems to be able to judge truly, for I have done so much work in the last fortnight, that now and then I almost feel equal to anything, but to-day I am quite off work."

*March* 28 :—"I am afraid my last was an absurdly gloomy letter, although it was scarcely to be wondered at. I am now perfectly happy as regards the picture, I see that it would be more than miraculous to get it done. I shall keep to it steadily, as though it were certainly going in. Yesterday was so lovely that I cut work, and went by 10.25 to Boyne Hill and walked to Hurley to see how things were going on. The place was looking very tranquil and beautiful, and after having dinner with the old people, I took a stroll about, and then started along by the river to Marlow, walked on, passed 'Gibraltar,' and Marlow Road to Cookham, had a refreshing cup of tea at Ford's, and then, the sun getting rather low, I started for Taplow and just caught my train. I thought of writing a long letter to Jack describing everything I saw, but I saw enough for a book. You see I walked quite 14 miles, and got into town quite fresh, and am all the better for it to-day. I have arranged to go next week to paint the water in my picture. I shall take one of my boy models with me, who will sleep in Lane's cottage, outside my bedroom, on a large landing—this is because I wish to ascertain the truth of some of my flesh tones, and because I cannot manage a seven foot canvas without constant help. Yes, I think I shall give Jack a letter describing yesterday—I thought of last summer and of him all day. You seem to have secured the deepest respect at Cookham, old lady, as you are sure to do wherever you go." The intended letter to his brother does not appear to have been written. This is to be regretted, as Walker never wrote in happier vein than when filled with some such quiet beauties as he found by the river's bank.

Notwithstanding what he wrote in the letter just quoted from, all idea of finishing the picture was not yet given up. In a letter of his sister's, dated March 30, he sends a message to his mother that, "as sure as he is alive and in health, the picture will be in the Academy after all." The next letter, dated from Hurley April 3, hardly, however, bears out this confident tone :—

"Here I am all snug, and just having tea comfortably—shall return on Friday I think. I am expecting my model and servant ; he

could not get away in time to come down with me.  I  have  laid
out  my  plans  for  a  jolly  day's  work  to-morrow, everything is lovely
and  I  have  a  boat  in  readiness. . . . I am  quite  happy  about  the
picture, and know that it will have the desired effect whenever it  may be
seen."—*April* 4 :—" Just having tea.   It  has  been  rather  an  aggra-
vating  day,  so  showery,  and  rather  cold too.   However I have done
my poor old picture good, so that's a comfort, although the canvas has
got wet.   If the wind would but get into the west, how thankful I
should feel.   I wear my thick coat, and sealskin waistcoat, and leather
gaiters, and my shooting boots well greased.   The boy I have with me
turned  out this morning to have boots that were not weather proof, so I
sent him into the village to buy a thick clod-hopping pair—he says they
are more comfortable than any he has had.   The birds here are wonderful,
the song is a continuous one, rain or sunshine.   Jolly old blackbirds that
seem so fond of soliloquy, and Mrs. Lane's parrot imitates the rooks in a
sneering tone.   Alas, I look out and see the water covered with  dimples
of every size : I sha'n't get any more work to-day, I fear, as it's now
¼ to 6.   I brought my flute with me, and Fan popped my Shakespeare
into my trunk. . . . I am going to write to George Leslie, who has
shown true sympathy, and who has the generosity to express admiration
where he feels it, and has shown an absence of *self*, by making comparisons
(before others) to his own disadvantage, in trying to express that admiration.   I don't know if I explain myself, but he has shown lovable qualities
that you (who have generally seen him masked under a kind of flippancy)
would scarcely credit.   I know he will be glad to have a line to say how
I am getting on. . . . The rain has left off, and I think I might do
half an hour's work."

THE HURLEY BIRD

Mr. Leslie will, I trust, forgive me for printing the above reference to him. It is a pleasure to know that Walker fully reciprocated the kindly feelings to which Mr. Leslie has given expression in *Our River*. The letter to him, which probably contained the drawing of *The Hurley Bird*, here reproduced, was as follows :—

*April* 4.—" I know you will like to hear how we—the picture and myself—get on, and we're very well, thank you, in spite of the abominable cold wind. I came down yesterday afternoon. The case was of course too big to go on a cab, so the man who sees to the garden at St. P. Place undertook to send it to Paddington, and it went there *in a brick cart* [that had just brought a load of gravel] and I followed in the Hansom of our daily life. At Maidenhead, a *dog-cart* was made to bear the precious load, greatly to the astonishment of the chaw-bacons on the road. I don't know how it was managed—it appeared to me to stick out yards behind, and the whole thing rocked from side to side in a most exciting way. However, we got here safely, and after a cup of tea, I took a walk to my pollard willow—and saw that it was good—then started to meet and to bully the wretched boy who was to have accompanied me—and didn't. He had followed in the next train, and I met him at a chalk cutting in the twilight, looking so fetched at the novelty of the situation, that I e'en forebore.—Well, this morning I got into my boat [like R. Crusoe] and pulled in [the boy becomes hopelessly idiotic directly he steps into the boat] to the place, and had just got into that jolly state over the thing which makes one oblivious of time, when splash, down comes the rain, and we had to go as hard as we could pelt to the little Medmenham public, where I looked out and blessed the rain for an hour. Then we got back again to work, but it came down again such a drencher that my poor bathers had a taste of the real thing, and my canvas is like a drum. But I warn't to be beat, for at 6 it cleared up, and I popped out again and fetched it a nasty one that time—as you'd say."

The next day Walker wrote from Hurley to his eldest sister :—

" I shall endeavour to get home to-morrow, but it must depend upon weather &c. I have been rather depressed to-day about the work. The morning was frightful ; horrible cold wind, black sky, and raining hard, it seemed striving against impossibilities. However it has cleared up, and all right but for the eternal east wind. When *will* it lose its bitterness ? But really I, even I, was astonished at the blackness of this morning's sky. Old Lane said ' Well a don't know as ever I see sich a thing afore.' " There were now but three or four days to " sending-in day," and on his return to London, Walker finally abandoned the idea of having the picture ready in time.

The " day out to the Clique" duly came off on April 11, and next day Walker wrote the following account for his brother's benefit :—

" I flatter myself I gave them as good a dinner at Richmond as I ever tasted. We took the 'bus from the Norfolk Hotel near the Great Western, and I conducted 'em. We passed this house, and Fan had put an enormous silver gridiron on the window, and they cheered as we caught sight of Fan and the sacred emblem. I arranged to dine at the Castle, Richmond, with lawn, &c., going down to the river. We met at half-past 10, drove straight to Richmond, left hats, &c., at the Castle, sherry and bitters all round, and then drove off to Hampton, walked through the gardens of the Court, and lunched at a little boating public famed for its good cheer. We should have dined there, but that I found out the day before (when I went down to arrange) that there were no billiards or skittles to be had anywhere if it came on wet, which it did in right good style ; so we all got into the 'bus, and got back to Richmond at half-past 4, had a cup of jolly tea and a wash, and settled down to pool seriously. Cleared up, with beautiful sky at sunset, we walked about the lawn and enjoyed the river, and got very peckish, did a little jumping, and sat down to dinner 20 to 7, beginning with oysters and sauterne. The champagne was stunning, and the wine altogether so good, that although we didn't stint ourselves, I am as fresh as a daisy this morning. Du Maurier, who is an hon. member, sang capitally, we sat down a dozen, and *all got up again*. Calderon was at the table end, and I made my speech like a man ; and at 10 we were thinking of moving, after coffee and swizzle. We all went home singing lovely, and in charity with all men. I think they will all remember the day with pleasure. . . . . Leslie completely stopped all art talk, from beginning to end—said that it wasn't to be done." Hitherto, it had been the practice to conduct these outings on a much more modest scale ; and Walker's munificence, though surely not arising from ostentation, was, my brother says in his book already referred to, the cause of their being discontinued.

On April 17 Walker wrote to his mother :—

"I have been calling myself all kinds of names for not writing to you or to Jack (for one seems to answer for the other), but I've been to Beddington and Croydon. Began a little water colour (slight) until next week, when I hope to be in full fig to return to my 'iles.' . . . . I sent off the picture to the Water Colour yesterday."

This picture—*The Bouquet*—was Walker's sole contribution to the Summer Exhibition of the Old Water Colour Society of 1866. The " little water colour " was that shown at the Winter Exhibition of the Society in this year—No. 413 in the catalogue—and though sent in without title, has always been known in the family as *The Spring of Life*. It has, however, been lately exhibited at the Guildhall Art Gallery under the title of *In an Orchard*. Walker went to Beddington, as he says, and found the little cherry-tree, which gave rise to the drawing, in full blossom. His sister and two of our children supplied the human interest, and the lamb, borrowed for the occasion, completed the composition. This beautiful drawing, with its flood of sunlight, was but a short time on hand, and has been considered by some to

THE SPRING OF LIFE.

be one of the most successful of Walker's minor works.   It was fortunate enough to secure Mr. Ruskin's approval as having "right sunshine in it."

Early in May, Walker, accompanied by Mr. Agnew and another friend, paid a second short visit to Paris, and again there is little to record in the letters he wrote from there.   Nothing can be found indeed of any interest beyond the following :—"We have been to see the lovely Gérôme, and are crushed by the splendour of his place.   Such artistic perfection, and such a brick of a man !"   It must not, however, be supposed that Walker was insensible to the charms of Paris, for in a former letter to his brother he had written :—"I have been thinking all the morning of Paris.   I recollect saying once as we sat in the jolly sunny gardens after a wonderful French breakfast, that surely it must be one of the few favoured loafing grounds on the earth's surface.   I always find pleasure in recollecting the scenes at Paris."

The following letter is characteristic.   It was written in reply to a complaint that a join in the paper of a water colour drawing, "running as it does right through the centre of the face and figure of the man-servant, is too distinctly seen" :—

"My Dear Sir,

In answer to your letter, I cannot help thinking that you are over anxious as to the join in the paper.   Those who wish for my work will not (or ought not to) be deterred by so small a matter.   In the light in which the little picture was painted, the join was not percep-tible, and in such a light it should be seen, join or no join : nor can I ever undertake to paint pictures that look their best in every light. Any alteration that may be necessary to the artistic merit of my work, I am ever ready to make while pictures are in my hands, and in certain instances, after they have left my hands ; but a suggestion to repaint a figure which I am satisfied with, in order that the surface may be more perfect, I fear I must decline to take.   Trusting that these reasons will appear to you just,

"I am, my dear Sir,<br>
"Very truly yours,<br>
"Frederick Walker."

I regret that, even with the clue afforded by the mention of the man-servant in the letter of complaint, I have been unable to identify the drawing referred to.   Indeed, from Walker's habit of alluding to these minor designs merely as "the little water colour," (or as he mostly wrote it, "the little w. colour,") it is frequently a matter of difficulty to ascertain on what particular drawing he was engaged.

About the time of Walker's return from Paris, Mrs. Walker and her son came back to London, and shortly afterwards went again to Cookham for the summer.   Walker remained behind for some time, as

he was engaged on the first illustration for *The Village on the Cliff*, and was also making a final effort to get the *Wayfarers* off his hands. On June 15, he writes :—

" I am doing my best to finish the blind man, and have just sent off a proof of the Cornhill drawing to Miss Thackeray. Swain has cut it capitally, I think."

*June* 18 :—"Shall stick to the picture now ; the boy's head is far better I think—of a higher kind. . . . I have a fire in my painting room, and shall finish the picture straight off now . . . I shall come to you next Sunday, I think, if not before—all depends on the picture."

A week or so later, the picture was at length out of hand—rather more than three years from the time when Walker first went to Haslemere in search of a suitable background. It was exhibited at Mr. Gambart's Gallery in Pall Mall, in November of this year, and has been etched by Mr. C. Waltner.

At the end of June, Walker went to Cookham, taking the *Bathers* and all his materials with him. It was, I believe, during this visit that the drawing of *The Street, Cookham,* was begun. He also worked a good deal on the *Bathers*, apparently to his satisfaction. He returned to London at the end of July, before going on a visit to his friend Mr. R. Ansdell, R.A., who rented some salmon fishing on the river Spean, at Corrichoillie, near Kingussie, Inverness-shire. This was the first of several visits Walker paid to Mr. Ansdell's hospitable home in the Highlands, where he spent some most delightful days. It was on this first visit that he was initiated into the mysteries of salmon fishing. On July 28, he wrote from town to his brother, in great spirits, giving some rough drawings of himself in his ordinary river-side working dress, and in Highland costume, headed " before " and " after " ; and says in the letter :—

" . . . All the Hyde Park railings were pulled up by the British workmen last Monday to show that they deserve the franchise. Such a row, military called out I hear ; while we were peacefully doing nothing by the whispering reeds—grand idea ! Ho for Scotland."

On the day of his departure from town—July 30—he wrote to his youngest sister :—

" Just a line before starting. . . . I have been fetching up the Bathers to rights, I can tell you—you'll never know it for the same picture ; and far from wearying of it, I long to be at it again, and on Saturday I did a capital day's work from a naked small boy, who dodged behind a bush each time a boat passed. Ansdell has been catching lots of salmon. One 36 lbs., after an hour and a half's hard fighting."

Walker reached Corrichoillie in the evening of July 31. On August 1, he wrote to his mother :—

"Here I am after a good night's rest and a breakfast, quite restored and prepared to go in vigorously for everything. It's most lovely and gigantic, but must give particulars in the next, for Ansdell is just going out for the day. Ben Nevis is behind the house, with streaks and plains of snow on its summit. Strawberries are not yet ripe, and they are just thinking of cutting the hay."

Sunday, *August* 5.—"At last I can sit down and quietly write without fear of being told that some one or some meal is being kept waiting. We daren't fish to-day. . . . Truly this is a life that I had no idea of—the grandeur of the place is beyond belief. The last day or two has been windy and occasional heavy rain, enormous banks and rifts of cloud have partly hid the hills, and now and then a gleam of sunshine would show, high up, a glorious far off peak, with perhaps a silver thread or two, that one knew to be a cascade, destined to swell the noble river that rushes within sound and sight of the house. I have been quite unable to see a single weed in the stream, such as fills the Thames—the river is too swift—nothing but rock and great round stones, made round by the everlasting tumble and riot. Some of the rocks are of quartz, just like marble, with black streaks. At night one might be at Hastings, opposite the sea, for the wind and river make just the same noise. We have breakfast at 8.30, being already fully dressed (and I find my dress is mere nonsense. Ansdell haas pair of macintosh coverings for the feet and legs ; these go over socks and trousers, then outside these a pair of rough wool socks to prevent the friction of the india-rubber against the shoes, which are buckled across the feet, and have nails like ship rivets). Our man is meanwhile smoking his morning pipe outside, and putting the tackle together. The sandwiches and flasks of whisky being ready, we sally forth ; and from that time to 8 p.m. we are doing every kind of violent exercise, the hardest being throwing the fly. I have made very poor work of it, and as I have been unable to wade, like Ansdell and the man, I have been unable to get at the good pools. . . . The man who accompanies us does not trouble himself with macintosh, but wades all day across falls or any other

place, up to his middle. He is a frightfully 'cute chap, and loves fishing with a frightful intensity. The way he gaffs a salmon is won-derful—waiting at the bank, in or out of water as the case may be—and directly the fish comes within reach, down goes the hook bang into Mr. Salmon, through his back or anywhere, and with a heave, pitches him clean on to dry land. He does not speak English very well ; but, like the few of the natives about here, very grammatically. They learn it as a Frenchman would, in order to understand the few English swells who visit them. They invariably talk Gaelic among themselves. . . . . I do wish I could give you some idea of the wild weird beauty of this stream, as it rushes over the rocks through one of the deep glens that it has made itself, and then over a fall, with a deafening row, where the salmon leap up like bars of silver. And then, one perhaps looks up, and over the pines one sees a dark indigo hill (if the clouds permit), with its solemn outline. I picked the enclosed harebells and heartsease among the grass, they grow thick as clover—the bells sometimes eight on one stalk. I placed them among the leaves of my cheque-book, but their glory has departed—they were double the size too. I need not say that we are ready for dinner by 8, and jolly it is, and always salmon or sea-trout during the fish course, and winding up with the soft smoke and grog hour, so forgive me if I haven't written to my dear family—I have talked of it, and thought of it. I am glad Jack is not here ; for I do think that, at present, the day's routine far too rough to be really beneficial ; but I think I see a picture of future happiness here (if we are spared), which is the truest kind of country pleasure, because the simplest, only it requires money. My present experience is useful, as it shows me that money is worth getting, to enjoy such as this. I was saying so to Ansdell, and he answered, ' Ah ! you have it all before you ; I am getting an old man, and must make the most of my time here.' . . . . In the dining-room are all Leech's enlarged woodcuts of Mr. Briggs's fishing experiences, hanging on the walls. Agnew gave the set to Ansdell, and I am going to write for a set to be sent to Cookham. They are strained and varnished, and I expect they are very cheap. God bless you, my dear mother. Be sure and send word if I can do anything or send anything. I shall have received great benefit from this delightful change, I'm sure, and hope that you will see a healthier and better edition of your own Fred."

The illustration to *The Village on the Cliff* for August—*Beamish and Catherine*—had been finished early in July ; but, owing to some delay in the arrival of the MS., there was no time for a large illustration for September. The only drawing for the story, for that month, was an initial letter, done at Corrichoillie, of a girl standing on a croquet ground. It was of this subject Walker made the sketch referred to in the following extract.

*August* 9 :—" I have just finished the Cornhill initial letter, and so feel inclined to get out. Have made a little water colour sketch of the Cornhill subject for Miss Ansdell, who has been sitting very kindly, and they are all kindness itself. We had dancing last night, and the servants and men came in and did reels and flings. Ansdell sent in just now a splendid salmon, by two of the small boys who witnessed the fight."

August 12, to his brother. After giving a long account of his success among the trout—the first salmon was yet to come—Walker wrote :—

" The head keeper lives in a cottage behind the house, and is a tall well-made fellow ; always wears rough knickerbocks. He has two boys, the elder with a face perfectly beautiful—would be on a girl's shoulders. He is very tall, and always goes about in a kilt, without shoes and stockings, as all boys and girls do. . . . . You know I went trout fishing one day with one of Mr. Blair's keepers, 'Sandie.' It was very wet, and we took refuge in a shepherd's hut while waiting for the coach. Sandie and the shepherd were soon deep in Gaelic, while the half-naked children, and two or three great sheep dogs, regarded us with great interest ; the latter evidently as intruders. Sandie sat in a recess which formed the family bedstead, the wife of course had an infant at the breast. The dogs rushed out in a body at our approach, as they always do, and a pet lamb made up the picture."

Soon after this, Walker killed his first salmon. On August 19, he wrote :—

" You will be glad to hear that yesterday I caught and killed two salmon ; one $9\frac{1}{2}$ lbs., and a young fellow of 5 lbs., so now I shall go on all right, I hope. I have sent all particulars to Jack, and if you are interested, he will tell you all about it."

The letter in which Walker gives the details of this crowning experience of an angler's life is not forthcoming ; but Mr. Hodgson, in his already mentioned paper in the *Magazine of Art*, quotes the commentary of an eye-witness of the fight as follows :—" I can recollect the words of old Green, the fisherman on the Spean : ' It's a nice gentleman, is Mr. Walker ; when he was catching the first salmon, och ! I never saw any man so pleased whateffer ; he wad be making me drink whisky, and the fish drink whisky too.' "    Mr. Hodgson gives this as an instance of the way in which Walker would be " childishly elated."    The making the fish drink whisky may possibly seem to point that way.    Green, in spite of the extraordinary nature of the proceeding as regards himself, probably rose to the occasion without much difficulty.

On August 24, Walker wrote:—

" I have begun a study of the head-keeper's handsome boy, which if finished will form a comforting ' pill ' on my departure, viz. by paying expenses."

*August* 26 :—"I'm doing a little water colour sketch of Mrs. Morley, for Mrs. Ansdell, but I regret to say that the study of the boy I began has fallen through—quite a failure somehow."

Walker had intended to return to London at the end of the month, to prepare the October illustration for *The Village on the Cliff—Let us Drink to the Health of the Absent.*  He was, however, not only loath to end his holiday, but particularly wished to do some work in water colour before leaving.  He accordingly decided on attempting the illustration at Corrichoillie.   On August 31 he wrote :—

" The panels and your letter came last night, and I commence work after to-day, which is the last day Ansdell has one of the two ' beats.' I have written to Pall Mall for the Cornhill slips.  Every one has volunteered to sit, or do anything to help me, but I shall immediately come to town if the subjects cannot well be worked here."

*September* 1 :—" I am going to raise a good thing out of the ashes of the one I mulled, and shall hope to have it seeable when W. Agnew appears in a day or two."

This " good thing " was the drawing *Fisherman and Boy*, exhibited at the Summer Exhibition of the Old Water Colour Society, in 1867. Mr. Hodgson speaks of it as an " exquisite drawing," and a " gem."

*September* 4 :—" Pray send at once the book ' La Normandie,' I have been looking out for it ever since I had the letter.  Both were from Miss Thackeray, and the book contains the dress that Reine wears.  I am hard at work, too, with the water colour.  W. Agnew is coming on Saturday or Sunday."

*September* 5 :—" Just a line.  All going on well.  Agnew comes on Saturday, and I shall finish the water colour before leaving.  I am to-day doing an initial letter for the Cornhill ; the whole of the proof sheets have not yet arrived, but I shall be able to do the large one here, I think.  I had a long letter from Miss Thackeray.  Have not been fishing at all."

FISHERMAN AND BOY.

On September 6, in a letter to his brother, after the usual fishing talk that went on between them, Walker wrote :—

"And now I may as well tell you why I work here. I lost £15 somehow, while wading I think, but two notes one for £10, and one for £5, came out of my waistcoat pocket somehow. This occurred about a week after I came down ; so I resolved to take it out of the place somehow, and I *am*. . . . Pray accept the ' Briggs ' prints, my boy, with my good wishes ; they have been a great comfort to us all here. The more one looks, the more absurdly true they seem ; the boats and rocks I can almost identify."

*September* 13 :—"I sent off the Cornhill drawing yesterday, after a tremendous struggle, and I hope it will be well cut, for I took pains with it. So now I have only to finish the water colour—that is, as nearly as possible here."

September 16, to his sister Fanny :—"Agnew seems delighted with my water colour, as far as it goes. I shall be able, I think, to leave this on Thursday. By that time I shall have done all that's necessary here. The Cornhill drawings went off quite satisfactorily, but very late ; and then only because Minnie Thackeray sent me a lot of MS. I chose a subject where Reine, Catherine, and some children, dine together in Normandy. The girls sat like bricks."

September 17, to his mother :—

"Well, my dear, I am homesick at last—tremendously so this morning—and shall certainly do my best to leave early on Thursday morning, so as to be with you (if you are at the 'Burgh) on Friday night . . . I am afraid you have been exerting yourself a good deal, now that you have so many visitors. Pray do take care of yourself, that you may keep your health, and long be my comfort (as you are to all you have to do with). I mean to work very hard when I get back. I must be a few days in town to finish this water colour, and arrange one or two matters, such as making my studio comfortable for the winter."

Walker returned to London at the time he mentions, and after a flying visit to his mother and brother at Cookham, was soon hard at work. One of the drawings he was engaged on was *The Street, Cookham*, which he intended for the Winter Exhibition of the Old Water Colour Society. In order that he might carefully study the geese, which form so prominent a feature in the drawing, he had three of the birds sent to London from Cookham, and housed them at St. Petersburgh Place. During October, he finished the Scotch drawing of the *Fisherman and Boy*, practically finished *The Street, Cookham*, prepared the November illustration for *The Village on the Cliff—Dick and Reine*—and once more

Let Us Drink to The Health of the Absent.

took up *Bathers*. The geese—two geese and a gander—after their unusual experiences in London, were sent down to the cottage at Beddington, to be added to the already numerous live stock there ; and duly increased and multiplied.

At the end of October, Mrs. Walker and the invalid (who had left Cookham early in the month) began another term of banishment. They went first to Shanklin ; soon, however, making a move to Hastings, on account of its greater accessibility and liveliness. The picture of *Wayfarers* was now about to be exhibited at Mr. Gambart's.

On November 4, Walker wrote to his brother as follows :—

"I cannot tell what the verdict is on my picture ' Wayfarers ' at Gambart's, for the crush was so hateful, and everything so distasteful to me, that I merely nodded to people, and got out as quickly as possible, looking very sulky, I fear. On our arrival there, I stopped behind to pay for the cab, and a great animal of a policeman was bullying the cabby for not ' moving on ' quicker, so I stopped him ; for cabby was giving me change. Mr. Bobby said, ' But here's a carriage waiting,' and sure enough there was, and a very gorgeous one ; but I said, ' I can't help that, *I'm* of more importance than a carriage.' The poor peeler's jaw almost dropped, he caved so completely ; and then I walked majestically in. I have taken out the two figures on the right hand of the ' Bathers ' and put them in again smaller, and somewhat differently ; the improvement is very striking I think, and so does Fan. They are more like this

I mean the bigger boy's leg to be right off the ground, and his face *not* turned towards the small boy, and the latter's head not thrown back. I shall have another figure just entering at the side, but I have not arranged it yet."

The press verdict on *Wayfarers* was not one of unmixed approval. Whilst the originality of the picture, its power, and the way it holds the memory " by qualities peculiar to itself," were fully recognised ; exception was taken to the execution, which was described as " peculiar," " spotty and rough," " coarse yet unsubstantial," and even " slovenly." As against

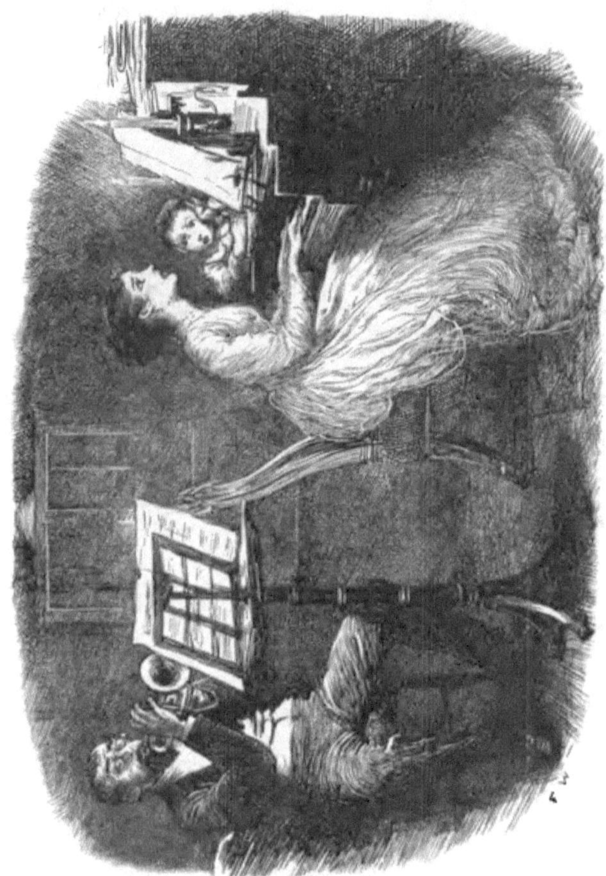

A VACARME.

this, Mr. North's opinion is that, for mere painting, Walker never did anything finer than the landscape in this picture. His impression is that from the painting being less "tight" in execution than the majority of the pictures by eminent men of that day, such as Gérôme, Meissonier, Holman Hunt, or even the earlier works of Millais, the critics did not understand it. He remembers Walker telling him that he had painted the whole of the landscape part of the picture—that is, the surface painting over that which was already on the canvas—in one day. Walker worked again on the figures in 1869, after the picture had come into Mr. Agnew's possession.

On November 9, Walker, then at work on the sixth drawing for *The Village on the Cliff—A Vacarme*—wrote to his mother :—

"Just a line with the enclosed, for I'm sure you must be getting short of cash. I began a letter last night, but as I had been working rather hard (and badly as it proved this morning) on the Cornhill block, I was too tired to go on. You go into the *old* town of Hastings for lodgings, and get a comfortable meal at such a place as 'The Ship,' before looking for them."

*November* 22 :—" I've just come in from a jolly ride, and feel much more fit to write than I may have done last time, or many other times. . . . I am very much comforted about my big picture." (*Bathers.*) "Ah, my dear good mother, there's the root of everything. If I feel I've gained a point during the day, you may see me looking tired perhaps, but it doesn't require much watching to see that I'm not unhappy. The dark boy is to my mind better than anything I've done yet, and I feel that it is getting into 'focus' as it were, altogether."

At the Winter Exhibition of the Old Water Colour Society this year, Walker exhibited four drawings—*The Street, Cookham, The Spring of Life, The Introduction* (a reproduction in water colours of a wood drawing for *Once a Week* for April 27, 1861)[1] and one other ; the first named being the only one that bore a title. The subject of the fourth drawing —No. 385—which could not be ascertained when the list of exhibited works was prepared for the exhibition of 1876, was a woman seated near a window, sewing ; and was either the portrait of Mrs. Morley, done at Corrichoillie, or another version of the same subject. These four drawings met with unqualified praise. Of *The Street, Cookham*, it was said :—" All these geese have character, and various character too," " We never saw the bird more efficiently represented," " The village street is as good as a page of George Eliot," the figures "are all real people, not conventional artist's figures." *The Spring of Life* was said to be " tenderly and poetically treated," and the woman sewing was pronounced " a gem of beautiful colour." On November 30, Walker was elected a full member of the Old Water Colour Society. *The Street, Cookham*, has been etched by Mr. Birket Foster.

See page 28.

The Street, Cookham.

On November 26, Walker wrote to his brother :—

" . . . . My small works at the Old Water Colour seem to be a success, from all I hear.  Wait a bit, I *am* going it at the 'Bathers '— been doing more to the dark boy to-day.  Tell Fan that I have begun the little water colour for the Yankee at New York, 'tis the last Cornhill subject you know."  (*Let us Drink to the Health of the Absent.*)

Though painted at this time, this subject was not exhibited till the year 1870.

November 27, to his mother :—

" Just a line to say I shall probably be with you next Sunday, and stay over Monday.  Miss Thackeray has been here this afternoon, and there is to be a sea subject for next Cornhill, which I shall bring down with me, as it's wanted very early ; and it's the *last*, thank goodness.  I have been doing the little water colour to-day.  Mrs. Morley with nurse and small boy came to-day, and I nobbled the kid for the water colour."

*November* 28 : —" . . . . I know you are always pleased to see anything favourable in the way of criticisms on your son's work, no matter how worthless they are.  In my opinion they are worse than useless very often, for they are read by people before the work is seen, and then their judgment is influenced unfairly."

Walker went down to Hastings with the wood block, and on his return wrote :—

" . . . I was greatly disappointed with the work I did just before leaving—the boy with the shirt I mean.  However, I have given him a regular hot'un to-day, and no mistake ; and I'm very much deceived if I haven't done it this time.  I cannot tell till to-morrow for certain, but I have found out the reason of its looking hitherto slightly strained.  Everything is all right here, and very snug.  The cats gave me a welcome, and the servants seemed glad . . . . The fellows " (at the Arts Club) " were congratulating me upon my things at the Water Colour Gallery.  I am surprised at the effect they seem to have."

*December* 7 : —" Just a line, for I'm right in the middle of the Cornhill which must be done to-night or not at all ; and a pretty hard day I've had of it—three models standing at once."

*December* 17 : —" . . . . Worked hard at 'Bathers ' all yesterday, and have got the two boys at the right the thing at last . . . B——called and bored me, and then I got out and called on the Thackerays, where, perhaps, I should have bored them, but they were out. . . . . No news to-day.  I've been working on little water colour, and shall go at it

from the two Ansdell kids to-morrow (Alice and Harold). My cats.
have been plaguing my life out—a perfect nuisance."

This letter contains a sketch of the two boys on the right, in which
the positions are the same as those of the sketch of November 4. The
finished picture shows, however, that the smaller boy had yet to undergo
considerable alteration.

After much anxious debate as to the advisability of the journey, John
Walker and his mother came up from Hastings for Christmas—the last
but one that all four were to spend together. The wood block of which
Walker speaks in the letter of December 7 was that entitled, *Out of the
Valley of the Shadow of Death*; and in the face of Dick, as he lies on
the beach, there is a strong likeness to Walker himself. As this closed
the series, it will be well to give here Mrs. Richmond Ritchie's estimate
of the drawings, and of Walker, for which I am indebted to her :—

" When I was writing *The Village on the Cliff*, I was very nervous
about it, and quite at an end of my ideas and resources, when one day
came the first proofs of the lovely drawings. They were so completely
everything that I had ever hoped or imagined, that the sight of them
gave me a fresh start, and I have always said *he* wrote the book not I,
for the figures were to me almost miraculous realisations of what I tried
to imagine the people might become. As a curious instance of a sort
of brain wave, I had a nightmare one night, and saw the figure of Reine,

very bright, coming *down* upon me, and when the little letter piece came next month, there was the identical figure I had dreamed of, with a basket, descending ; no longer a nervous terror, but a delightful reality. I have always thought M. le Maire playing the cornet was the keystone of the little story. My sister and I walked through a fog one evening to the studio, and he showed it to us on the block. I was dreadfully disappointed, I remember, when he said he could not spare time to illustrate *Old Kensington*. I wrote him a vehement letter, which I meant as a joke—I have always been grieved when I remember that he thought I could be in earnest. The day before my sister married, he came to see us, and said he should like to give her a drawing for a wedding present, and at her request, then and there he sat down and made a most charming, delicate, little pencil sketch of our little adopted niece, a child then—now a woman and married, and to whose husband I have given the sweet little picture. We had a delightful three days' visit from him once at Freshwater, and I remember his pleasure in the place, and how each morning he went up the beacon hill before breakfast, coming down with a drawing. There was one lovely summer's day too, which I remember, when we were on the river—young people picnicking —and Mr. Walker met us in a punt and brought us to the Cliefden woods, where a kettle was boiling, and a sylvan tea spread out to greet us. Everything he did had a sort of grace of its own. He had a true heart as well as a true genius, and all who ever have known him must have felt the reality of both in their intercourse with him, and do not forget it."

# CHAPTER VIII

## 1867

WHEN John Walker returned to Hastings early in January, 1867, he was accompanied by his eldest sister ; and Mrs. Walker remained in town till the middle of the month. Walker was now engaged on the third of the invitation cards for Mr. Arthur Lewis—a group of musicians and dancers, " parodying," as Mr. Claude Phillips says in the *Portfolio*, " but ever so slightly, some Anacreontic scene from a red-on-black vase." The following letter on the subject, was addressed to Mr. W. H. Hooper :—

" I have been for some time wanting to write and ask you if you would care to undertake the engraving of a card for A. Lewis's evenings, which are a month later this year. I am just about to do something very simple, and fancy figures on a black ground, similar to those on an old Etruscan vase ; and in that case it would be well to have the card of a dull red, the figures and writing showing red, the rest of course being black. I went to-day to the British Museum, and think that something done on this plan would be novel."

H

January 11, to his brother and sister :—

" Why do you want letters from me that have no news that has not
been already given you by the Mrs. ? I can only give you detail. You
will be glad to know that I worked very well to-day, that is, in the
morning. . . On Monday I had a jolly and almost touching letter from
Arthur, who fancied on Sunday night (because I suddenly grew and felt
a sort of dark grey) that he had said something that had hurt me, and
saying that he should never forgive himself if any interruption of friendship took place, &c. Of course I answered from my heart, and called
on him next day, and told him I'd go next Sunday. He has just sent
me a ticket for the next Wanderers and Morays combined, at Lord
Gerald's. . . I took Mamma and Poll to the British Museum in grand
style. It being a private day, we wandered among all the glories by
ourselves, not even with the gallant Holmes. Since you, Fan, went,
there has been a most lovely and large collection of ancient jewellery
and gems placed in the little room with the Portland Vase. I did as
well as I could in these vile times with L. Colls as to the little water
colours. Both will be finished to-morrow or next day ; the candle light
one is, already. . . How did you like news of Old—poor Old Croydon
Church being burnt through carelessness ? "

This candle-light drawing was the water colour of *A Vacarme*—" M.
le Maire playing the cornet "—from *The Village on the Cliff*. It was
exhibited at the Summer Exhibition of the Old Water Colour Society of
this year, together with the *Fisherman and Boy* done at Corrichoillie.
The other drawing was presumably *Let us Drink to the Health of the
Absent* ; which, though begun for the " Yankee at New York," does not,
as far as can be ascertained, appear to have been sold to him.

On January 16 Walker wrote to his mother, who had then returned
to Hastings :—

" It seemed rather hard duty I thought, my dear, going away into
the beastly cold as you did yesterday, and I only hope that to-day
you are not having it as we are *here*. I assure you it is simply
intolerable. I have been out, and defy any one to be more than just
*miserable*. Every one looks it, and with my cold I hated the sight of
them all. The wind is blustering, and the dust and dirty snow bang in
one's eyes continually—everything looks dirty to-day. I have been to
the Museum, and have been making sketches for Arthur's card. . . . . .
You'll want to know all about last night, I know. Well, I got to
Millais' pretty punctual, and only the two Lewis's had arrived. I was
warmly received, and needed it, for I felt perished. Mrs. M. made me
sit in front of every one with my feet on the fender. . . . . . Sir E.
Landseer was presently announced, and Lucas, the builder, &c., &c., and
Arthur Sullivan, the musical writer, and one or two others. After dinner,
when we adjourned to the studio for cards and smoke, Sir Edwin was

jolly, and not having caught the name of your son in the general introduction in the drawing-room, I saw him put a whispered inquiry to
Arthur after dinner, and then he came up and said some very pleasant
things, Arthur putting in a word or two, and his big brother standing
behind me. . . . . Tell me, dear, if I can send anything to you. Love
to poor old Jack, he must live upon that which is to come. There be
many *chub* I trow, under the ice, and a little rod that I know of, and a
sun that will soon be getting warmer. I shall not be in time for post, I
fear. Fan is a brick to do the dutiful so. This is ever a miserable time
with us, and must just be *lived through*."

In the next extract, under the title of *Wanderers*, the reader will
recognise the picture of *Vagrants* now in the National Gallery.

*January* 17 :—" . . . I have decided upon doing, as quickly as possible,
an oil picture (small) of the 'Wanderers,' a thing I did at the beginning
of the year " (1866) "for Once a Week. I have forgotten how stunning a
subject it is, and indeed could not lay my hand on the book containing
my proofs, &c., but I found it this morning, and I find there is a little
mine of wealth as far as subject is concerned—two or three I mean to
rattle off, directly this of Lewis's is done. *It's all right, my dear*, we shall
go on well now I think, and the lengthening afternoon gives me a feeling
of hope that I have not experienced for a long time. The frost here
continues, and so no rides ; however, it can't last long. . . . . Ask old
Jack if there's anything I can possibly do for him—anything I can send
down—and the same to Fan. Anything of that kind is much easier done
than writing this letter, for it takes more time on account of no one
being able to *help* one to write. Farewell all of you. Try and be as
comfortable as you can. You will not, I fear, unless you *try*, for the
time is as wretched as can be, I think. We ought not to have been born
in so cold a climate."

*January* 18 :—" Just a line to say that I did not get home this afternoon (having gone to the Museum on account of Arthur's card) until
past 5. . . . . I began the picture of ' Wanderers ' this morning, and shall
get on with it as fast as I can—shall disregard 'the Bathers' till I *feel
inclined* to take it up again. The concert last night was quite stunning,
and the number of familiar and kind faces most refreshing. . . . .
There's no news. I cannot help feeling rather solitary sometimes, now
that you have gone ; but am all right, and my cold has nearly
vanished."

*January* 19 :—" . . . No news. I am at work on Lewis's card, and
on the beginning of the picture, which will be a success, I think. I
suppose your letters have been delayed, for up to this time none have
come to-day."

*January* 21 :—" . . . . Poll has been standing to me for the

' Wanderers '—the standing woman. I have been getting on beautifully, and Poll is delighted. As for the card, it created a *furore* at Arthur's last night."

January 22, to his brother :—

" Just a few lines to say that the Missus has arrived, greatly to my satisfaction, and we've just had a cup of tea together. Poll came this morning and stood to me for a short time. . . . The weather is still intolerable, though I don't think quite so cold this afternoon, for the wind is a little more S. When I'm to have another ride, Heaven only knows. Bother skating, I haven't been on once ; am not at all bitten with it this year, for I think my skull is rather more sensitive than it used to be, and there's a good deal of *black mud* at the bottom of all the park waters. They are not the waters that chub or trout delight in, so I love them not. I wish I could see some of my broad-nosed or spotted friends in their snug winter quarters. Arthur will give three regular nights this season only, the fourth will be a special one ; and as it is in May, you may perhaps be in the way of going, before settling into your summer residence. . . . The picture I'm at will fetch you—it is 4 feet long. The snow here is gradually shrinking away— drying away as it were—and what is left is a fine dirty grey."

February 4, from Beddington, to Mr. Hooper :—

" As I expected, Lewis was quite delighted with the result of our labours, and only expressed a hope that the printing might be good, and that they would be done in good time, to make it a *perfect success.* As for me, I sat with it before me in the carriage the whole way to Croydon, and looked at it longer than I ever did at any engraving done for me before ! In short, it made me feel happier, and helped me to get through a splendid afternoon's work. More than I shall do to-day, for the rain has begun to come down in deluges, and all my energy in getting down by an early train brought to nought. I suppose you will insist on the printer getting a crumbly look with Lewis's card. I think certainly that the ink should be anything but dark or glossy. I am burning to see it printed ; let them even be sent to Lewis in small quantities as they are done, for I know that, even now, he is waiting to issue his invitations."

February 5, to his mother, who had returned to Hastings :—

" No news, no letters, none from you this morning. I have just returned from Beddington, quite sick with struggling ineffectually against difficulties and vile weather. I've brought the picture home with me, and shall go at it here for a day or two. Sarah knows of some gipsies who are evidently brought into this world to sit for my picture, they are so suited ! "

As will be gathered from the above, Beddington supplied the background for *Vagrants*. In these searchings after suitable spots, Walker must have roamed about the fields a good deal ; for this place again was quite out of the beaten track, though not so far from the cottage as the site chosen for *Wayfarers*.

About this time, Walker seems to have been depressed and out of health—the weather, of which he complains so bitterly, may have had something to do with it—and work was interrupted. On February 25, he writes to his mother :—

"I regret having sent you so depressing a note on Saturday. I have been much better since, indeed I have. . . . I have been working all right again. George Leslie came yesterday, and said he thought it splendid."

*February* 27 :—". . . . I am really better I assure you, and have been working quite hard. The picture is going on capitally, and is now in the frame."

"*Romance for you Two.*"[1]

John Walker had come up to London for a little change, and on his return to Hastings, Walker wrote, February 28 :—

". . . . I'm very glad you got down all right. It's *awful* here, the cold seems *too* great and miserable for frost or snow. I've had to leave off work every now and then, both yesterday and to-day. The sky becomes not dark but dirty. It may be cold where you are, but it cannot be so perfectly cheerless. . . . My love, my best love, to the dear old 'un. Her presence will be a comfort whenever she comes, but don't send her especially on my account. I am much more comfortable than I was, and work better. . . . Can I send you anything, any food for mind or body ?"

[1] The figure on the right is a representation of John Walker.

March 2, to his mother :—

" I have been doing a very good day's work on the ' Bathers,' and do think to have it and the other finished if I go at it very hard."

*March* 7 :—" Been snowing and very dreadful. I've written to Agnew about the ' Bathers,' and have offered him the other picture. . . There has been a wonderfully flattering critique on me in last Saturday Review."

*March* 8 :—" I had a letter from Agnew this morning ; he will be here on Sunday or Monday, so that's all right, I suppose. This weather is indeed enough to finish one without anything else—one must endure it that's all. . . . The ' Bathers ' are going on all right, I am thankful to say. I have worked with all my might sometimes. Did not do much yesterday, for I felt depressed and seedy—better to-day. I am going to dine with Poll, and then am going to see the Clique. . . . Hope Jack will be himself directly the wind changes, if it ever means to. Give him my love, and I wish I could pop round and have a game of bills with him at dusk always."

*March* 9 :—" I am glad you are coming up, and only wish old Jack could come with you, but suppose it must not be thought of. . . . I think the continuance of this miserable weather well nigh intolerable. There has been nothing but dirty grey sky here for nearly a fortnight. . . . . I have not been getting on quite so well with my work this morning, but hope to do better this afternoon."

Shortly after this, Mrs. Walker returned to London, followed in a few days by the invalid and his sister ; and the consequent break in the letters deprives us of any further record of Walker's struggles with *Bathers* before sending the picture to the Royal Academy. As will be seen, he was afterwards very doubtful of the wisdom of having exhibited the picture this year. It was far from finished ; was returned to him at the close of the Exhibition to be further worked on ; and was not in Mr. Agnew's hands until May, 1868. Even then, the picture was not finally completed, for Walker worked on it again about the end of the year 1869, some time after it had come into the possession of Mr. Graham. In its finished state, *Bathers* has been considered by many to be Walker's masterpiece. However this may be, it was undoubtedly one of his most important works ; and though I will not weary the reader with any lengthened criticisms, a few extracts from press notices of the picture, when shown at the exhibition of 1876, may be of interest :— " Certainly one of the finest and best works that was ever lifted from an English painter's easel." " One of the finest of Walker's compositions, and one of the noblest pictures of the English school. . . . It would indeed be hard to find an artist in any school who has more truly combined a feeling for colour with delight in the beauty of form, or

Bathers.

one whose triumphs in either direction are more surely based upon simple nature." "The composition from one end to the other is complete and altogether excellent, even if measured by the highest standard of excellence we know—the sculptures of Phidias. . . . I hardly know how to put into any form of words the praise I feel towards this picture." "Perhaps the most perfect and delightful example in the collection is the *Bathers*, a group of nude forms upon the banks of an English river." "No painter in England has ever produced a picture more worthy immortality."

At the sale of Mr. Graham's collection, in April, 1886, *Bathers* realised the sum of 2,500 guineas. At the time of the sale, it was believed to be a question whether this picture or *Vagrants*, from the same collection, would be secured for the National Gallery ; but the choice fell upon the latter, at a cost of 1,770 guineas. *Bathers* is now (1896) in the possession of W. Cuthbert Quilter, Esq., M.P., and has been etched by Mr. Macbeth.

The drawing of *Philip in Church* had been sent to the Paris Exhibition of 1867 ; and Walker went to Paris in April, accompanied by his friend Mr. W. C. Phillips. On April 23, he wrote from there to his eldest sister :—

"I am breakfasting by myself, as Willie and his old school-fellow have gone to a place called Enghein, I think. . . . My thoughts often enough fly quicker than the telegraph to all that I have left behind me, and my

work too. Somehow or other my poor 'Bathers' make me unhappy when I think of them. *N'importe*, I shall come back and do better work ; and even since I have been here I have had one or two

thoughts on a certain something that, D. V., I will work out while we
are at Cookham. I will tell you of a little adventure we had the night
afore last, which began while we were dining at a certain café, like a large
conservatory, and full of people. At a table near us were seated an old
lady and gentleman, and a young lady, who at once attracted my attention, there was something rather strange and *English* about her, and she
evidently looked upon me with some interest (Heaven knows I say it
without conceit, and Will's back was to the party). Now this went on
for some time, and the more I looked upon the girl the more I liked her,
and Will said he heard some English words uttered that could only have
come from her, as all others near were unmistakably French to the back-

*" Coffee for Two—s'il vous plaît."*

bone. The old lady had a little beast of a white toy dog, which was
attracting the attention of every one, and at last was the medium through
which I addressed the old lady, when the young one bent forward, and in
a nice winning way talked to me in good English. It ended in our
taking our coffee at their table, and the talk going on to Shakespeare,
&c., by the time we left the café, the familiar face explained itself, for it
belonged to no other than Stella Colas, who some time ago created such
a *furore*, as Juliet. We sauntered down the Boulevards in their company,
and later in the evening left a bouquet with both our names at their
hotel, and next morning I left a card with 'Garrick Club' on it. She
goes to-day to the South of France, and two months hence will visit

London. She has been in Russia all the winter, and has been working very hard, and with great success, in St. Petersburgh. She has been ordered a good long rest by the doctor."

On the same date, to his mother :—

" I have been dreadfully backward in writing, but not so much as others, for I have only received one letter of any kind, and that was from your own dear self. I am impatient for news. . . . Went to the Exhibition on Monday, and saw 'Philip,' which is prettily hung in a nice light ; but on the whole the English school is very badly represented. Our time is simply taken up in gadding about, so there is very little to be written about, but much to be said when I return, which will be on Saturday, I think. I often wish you were all with me— Jack would enjoy much of it, I know, though he is quite right in not being here now ; for the fatigue and excitement of sightseeing would soon knock him up, I feel sure."

Undated :—" We have been to the Exhibition to-day, and have seen all the jolly pictures—most of them I have seen before. . . . I think of you all very often, and shall, I hope, return to the fight with fresh strength."

The drawing here given—*Doing Paris : The Last Day*—owes its origin, I believe, to this visit to Paris.

After a little more than a week's stay in Paris, Walker returned to London. On May 8, he wrote to his brother (who had gone to Cookham earlier in the month) as follows :—

"I did hope to have shown up before this, but I cannot finish my confounded Cornhill drawing, so must content myself with writing, and I have something to write about. I heard news yesterday (and I am now going out to get it fully corroborated) which is news indeed, although it almost seems too good to be true, and it is this. *The French have awarded me the English medal for water colour.* This is more important than it seems at first. The ceremony of awarding them will be very brilliant in Paris, and will be done by the Emperor. Calderon, who carries off the other (for oils), and who was one of them to tell me the news at the Academy yesterday, says he certainly will go over to be invested: he was in tremendous spirits. Marks, who was with Leslie and Poynter, was the first to tell me, but they would not believe that I had not already heard. I thought they were trying to fetch me at first, till old Marks said, 'Then I am devilish glad to have been the first to tell you.' Frith afterwards congratulated me, so I suppose it's all right. I must tell you that it is considered a very great honour, and that a small sum of money goes with the medal, which is of gold, and worth about £30. It will be an awful sell if it isn't true, and there seems to be no official notification of it as yet. However, Calderon was repeating a conversation of one of the Lord Commissioners, who said that he 'didn't even know who Walker was,' or something of the kind ; and now, my boy, you know about as much as I do. If it turns out true, the old Missus shall go to Paris to see her boy's triumph. . . . The 'Bathers' looks capital, and people were congratulating me—it looks quite a small picture at the Academy though, among all the rest. . . . I must rush off now to get at the truth of this medal news, for it's driving me mad."

As a matter of fact, Walker had been awarded a medal for his drawing of *Philip*, but of the second class ; and as only first class medallists received their medals at the hands of the Emperor, the scene depicted above did not take place.

During May, Walker was engaged on the frontispiece to *The Story of Elizabeth*, already referred to, and on an illustration to *Beauty and the Beast*—one of the series of Miss Thackeray's stories, founded on fairy tales, which appeared in the *Cornhill*. It must almost have been about this time that he began the beautiful water colour drawing of *The First Swallow*, (now in the possession of Professor Herkomer, R.A.) which

was shown at the Summer Exhibition of the Old Water Colour Society, the next year. Walker was at Cookham a good deal during this month, and probably it was there he painted the hawthorn-tree that figures in the drawing. Owing, however, to the absence of letters, in consequence of the family being together, there is no record of the progress of the work.

Another drawing belonging to this time, was the *Boys and Lamb*, painted from three of my boys, and a pet lamb which had lately been added to the animal population of the Beddington cottage. Though offered to others, the drawing was sold to the agent of a gentleman in America, and has never been exhibited in this country. It is to this drawing Walker refers, under the usual title of "the little water colour," in the following letters to his mother.

*June* 4 :—"I have decided upon going with my 'Wanderers' to Beddington, and there finishing it, as the gipsy boy has shown up. I am off now. The little water colour is finished—it is too good for the American, so I telegraphed to Morson (who has been waiting for a very long time), and he is coming to see it between 4 and 5 to-morrow. . . . It will be a very good thing for me to finish the 'Wanderers.' I saw directly what it wanted. Two of the figures must come out—the boy and girl—they spoil the standing figure, which is, by itself, quite satisfactory. I am very anxious to get it done, and can, I think, do it quickly, and feel sure it will be a success."

*June* 8 :—". . . I have sold (or as good as sold) the little water colour to Morson—he was much pleased with it. I asked £70, and he asked if he might come to-day to see it again, as one corner was a little unfinished, but I have had a telegram to say he cannot get to me and will write ; so I suppose I must wait for a day or two, which is provoking as I wished to conclude the matter to-day, and cannot now very well sell it to any one else. I am just going to get it photographed. I do not know what to think about being with you to-morrow, as it depends upon what I hear to-day about the gipsy people. I have not seen any of them yet."

*June* 12 :—"I write to let you know that all's well, and that I shall not leave my picture for anything else until I finish it. I wrote to Quilter, of Norwood, as to the little drawing, and have not yet received an answer. If he does not come up to the scratch, I must let it go to the American (whose letter I have found in one of my coat pockets, after rummaging, as you know, all through my entire wardrobe), for I cannot bother any more. . . . . . The picture looks the better for the alteration already, and I hope to go ahead this week. The vile gipsies had 'struck camp' by the time I got there yesterday, so now I give them up, and go at my own models here. The fools ! to let money slip through their fingers."

*June* 19 :—"Just a line to say that the agent (to whom I wrote about the little water colour for the American), writes that he is quite prepared to hand over £50, and wishes to know when he may call. I have written to say to-morrow, so that's a comfort. I am all jolly, and am going in for a bit of work now. Love to my old dear ; I shall probably be back on Friday evening."

*June* 20 :—" The American's agent came this morning, paid me in notes, and took away the water colour ; so that's all right.    As for the big picture, it's going on very well."

*June* 24 :—" I feared you would be troubled by my gloomy looks, although, believe me, they meant little enough.    You know one sometimes feels cast down without the least cause ; at any rate I do.    I did not like going away, it always makes me feel uncomfortable, although I wanted to get to town so very much. . . . . Come to me if you like, and feel that you can leave Jack for a day or two.    Of course you will conduce to my happiness, for you know so well where all my discomforts lie, and have mind enough to look generously on my faults."

After sending photographs of the *Boys and Lamb* to his sister at Beddington, Walker wrote to her on July 2 :—

" I did not send a line with the photos, as I thought it unnecessary, and was in a great hurry.    I do not think them at all good, but if you

BOYS AND LAMB.

have them handy when next time I come, I will touch them up as much as I can, and sign them. . . . Tell John I have a Paris medal after all, but of what kind I do not know, and have a suspicion that I have been unfairly treated by the S. Kensington authorities, in not receiving official notice from them.    I do not know if I have not missed being presented with it by the Emperor, but shall soon know.   Adieu, dear, I have finished my 4 o'clock tea, and must do some more work.   Calderon is indeed lucky ; he has gone to Paris for his medal."

Notwithstanding all the care that had been lavished on him, John Walker gradually grew worse, and the anxiety about him deepened as the year wore on.   Walker, ever thinking of what could be done for him, was anxious that he should winter in Algiers ; but when the time came, the idea had to be abandoned.   On July 4, Walker wrote to his mother :—

". . . Shall I send you some money ?   That is all I can think of, unless it be some tit bit for Jack to eat.   We must stick to the Algerine scheme—the more I think of it the better I like it.   The change will of course be such as you have no conception of.   We must not mind what —— says, unless it be an unconditional 'no' ; and even then, other advice ought to be taken.   I am quite satisfied with my picture," (*Vagrants*) "it's going on capitally. . . . Love to old Jack ; am sincerely sorry he is not the thing.   This soft warm wind will do him no harm.   Tell him to let me know at once if I can get him anything—if there is any eatable he has a notion of."

*July* 16 :—". . . . I have just been to Dr. ——.   The interview was all that I expected it would be as to Algiers, and should therefore be an additional incentive on all our parts to care and industry.   He thinks, with me, that after the last 3 or 4 years of work, the change to me will be of the greatest benefit.   He thinks that the project may with more wisdom be entertained now, than before, especially as we shall all be together.   However, there is plenty of time, and this prospect will be an additional reason for care on Jack's part."

*July* 23 :—"I have had a very good day's work, and the picture is much better.   I am feeling very well, and pretty jolly. . . . I am feeling very confident about the picture, and am now going in for half an hour's work from the cart."

*July* 24 :—"You will be relieved to hear that Agnew was very much pleased with the picture, and that he has bought it, not as I hoped for £600, but for £550.   This £50 I regard as the cost of certain recent events, and I will endeavour to explain to you what I mean.   I have come to the conclusion that two very great—well perhaps not *mistakes*, because I could not avoid matters at the time, very well—but two pictures have had at my hands rather bad generalship since last year.   I have come to the conclusion that the 'Bathers' would have done me much more good if I could have managed to keep it, and (occasionally working on it) have sent it to the R. A. next year ; and I have come to the conclusion that I ought to have kept the blind man for the Academy, instead of letting Gambart have it for his winter exhibition.   You know that after all, from bad position, &c.,

I only regard the 'Bathers' as a partial success ; when it might, under happier circumstances, have been a very great and complete one. It is not as yet off Agnew's hands ; and he says that Gambart offered to let him have the blind man for less than I received for it. . . . . He says that in his opinion, I shall find I cannot finish this picture to its fullest, in the few days I propose, and that if I will go, as soon as possible, for my holiday, and busy myself with some water colour while there, he will take it of me (or more than one if I manage to do 'em) before I leave, and will make a point of meeting me there. . . . . So now I can do no better than be off, and quietly finish it when I return, for I feel at present pretty well fagged. . . . . I left off for dinner, and now, dear, I will take it to the Gt. Western Ry., so that you may get it to-night. Tell me what you think, and whether I have done well. I do not feel ill, but must confess to feeling a great wish to get away. You have had a nasty fagging time too, lately, but be comforted, dear, there will be a good time for us yet I hope."

On the same day, Walker had written to his sister at Beddington :—

"Will you let me have the little water colour that I began before I went to Paris—you know, the view of 'Merridge's Farm.' I am going to Scotland, and may manage to finish it there. I have not been to you, dear, for an age, nor have I been to Cookham much, for I have been hard at work here on the oil picture, which I have at last made into an important affair. I have had to take the group of the boy and girl &c. out—I found when I came from Paris, as I told you, that it was all wrong ; and I have, as it were, made another picture of it. I am this day expecting Agnew to come and see it—have been in a state of suspense ever since ½ past 10, when he was to have been here. I shall be glad to get away, for I sometimes feel almost pumped dry."

" Merridge's Farm " was the Croydon irrigation farm, then kept by a Mr. Marriage ; and the buildings could be seen, some distance away, from the front windows of the Beddington cottage. The view was made use of in the water colour of *The Violet Field*—a woman and boy gathering violets—which was exhibited this year at the Winter Exhibition of the Old Water Colour Society. The drawing was not finished in Scotland, but at Beddington, after Walker's return.

July 29, also to his sister Sarah :—" In haste I just write to thank you for sending the drawing so kindly. . . . I shall see you very soon after my return, as I ought to spend an afternoon more over the background of the ' Vagrants,' which I thought to have finished before starting. I must work too, while I am away, but these will be water colours. I start by 10 train to-morrow."

Walker's second visit to Scotland was again to the house of his friend Mr. Ansdell. He reached Corrichoillie on the evening of July 31, and next day wrote to his mother :—

" Here I am all right, and you will know that I am so, on Saturday morning. . . . . I think I have already arranged, or rather selected, a spot for a good water colour, and rather near this. All seems here just the same, but I don't think my stay will be so very long. I shall do my best to keep well, and prepare for all that is to come. Give me all news, either trifling or otherwise."

*August* 5 :—" Your most welcome letter came last night. I am glad to hear the ' Bathers ' came all right, and I hope to polish all off directly I get back. . . . . I wish I could pop upon you whenever I wish. However, we shall soon be as much together as you could ever wish for." The same date to his brother :—" This is just to tell you that I drew first blood this morning in the shape of a $6\frac{1}{2}$ lbs. fish—no very great weight, but very pretty, and the first salmon I have seen killed this year, for I have never been with Ansdell during his little successes. It was in the second pool I fished. In the first I had a good rise, but he never touched ; and in the second (which is about the most beautifully picturesque on the river, and where Ansdell took the 36 pounder), I had taken three or four casts in the rough water, when there came a very subtle kind of jerk under the surface, and I struck, and at once my rod went

He only made one rush of any consequence, and—the rod being a new one—the rings being a little stiff, did all the rest. The head keeper, who was with me, neatly gaffed him, and then out came the flask. Half a mile or so further on, we came to a deep but clear pool ; and looking from the rocky height on to the river, we could see three or four wagging their tails in one spot. The sight was too much for the keeper—though the throw was a very difficult one, across a lot of stones and sharp edges just above the water—so he carefully stole down among the rocks, and as the sun kept going in and out, he changed three flies in as many throws, but on the fourth or fifth he had a rise—I saw him come up, and there he was. I clambered down after him, took the rod, and killed him in a deep pool just above. He was smaller than the other, only 5½lbs., but both pretty fish, and fresh from the sea, by their deep indigo backs. After that we had no other rise, though they were jumping everywhere, and the keeper said we should scarcely have time to save our jackets from getting wet through, and sure enough as we returned, Ben Nevis became enveloped in lead-coloured cloud, and now it is coming down like fun, greatly to my joy, for the river is nowhere. We go out again at 5 o'clock, and if I do not get a bigger fish, I send both these to you at Cookham on Mrs. A.'s suggestion.'

August 11, also to his brother :—

" I wish I had some good news of the fishing to give you, but I seem to have been just on the wrong beat always. What do you think ? Yesterday, Ansdell and his friend went to the Mucomer pool, and took five, in the morning—they were rising right and left, and the largest weighed over 17lbs. . . . . There is a whole lot of poultry about the place, and among them a lot of youthful cocks, who make the place absurd by their attempts at crowing. I saw one, a very young one, that kept lifting his head and opening his mouth at intervals, perfectly satisfied, though no sound came forth. One or two of the tribe submit to having their necks wrung every day, because we are obliged to feed upon our resources—no butcher or butterman coming round with a swell cart—our very mutton is browsing among the heather, near the house. Some very young broad beans have made their appearance at dinner lately, and some currants are reported to be ripe, though the peas will not ripen this year. . . . . I often think of the peaceful meadows and gigantic shady trees about Cookham (even though I have been away so short a time) and compare the scene with this. No language of mine can draw the difference. Both sometimes, especially in the evening, have the same peaceful effect, though this is usually of an evening *most melancholy*—at least it suggests it to me, especially on the finest evenings. Several times, all the hills have been shut out by low clouds, and sometimes one sees a beautiful luminous cloud quite low down, almost on a level with one it seems, and the whole mountain stretching up above it. Thank you, my boy, I do not want anything. I sent to Farlow for some casting lines and a book, and I have a collection of flies of my own ; indeed am well set up for life as regards salmon tackle. I sent also to Eatwell for some brushes, &c., which came by post. I do hope the fish I sent you arrived safely ; I took a tracing of the one I hooked. May the day come when you and I can act as fisherman and gillie to each other in turns, on this or some other water.  We must do our best—you to get well, and I to get the wherewithal."

August 15, to his mother :—

"I sit down to answer yours, as first among the batch that came last night ; and Heaven knows how welcome they were, for there has been a scarcity of them lately, and in my vexation I declared to myself that I wouldn't write till I was written to. . . . . You'll be glad to know I've begun work—a small water colour about the size of that 'moss bank' I did at Torquay.  It is a pool, and there will be a young girl on the bank.  There is a golden-haired lass that I noticed last year, who lives at one of the huts or 'bothies' near this, who will do splendidly, if she will only sit ; and this evening, or to-morrow, I go down to inquire. . . . I expect to do two water colours while here ; the second, bigger than the one I am now about, and more important.  As soon as this one is forward, I write to Agnew to know when he arrives here."

The smaller water colour was the *Stream in Inverness-shire*—a girl bringing linen to wash—exhibited at the Summer Exhibition of the Old Water Colour Society in 1868.  The larger one, the subject of which Walker does not mention, was not carried out.

*August* 18 :—"I fear this will be a dull day for you, whether you are at Cookham or the Burgh ; with all the brood dispersed.  Your letter, which came last night, made me feel a little depressed, especially that referring to poor Jack.  I cling to the idea of his going to Algiers, for his sake, and for mine, and for yours.  I do not see what else is to be done, and only trust that the heat has made him seem less well. . . . I am getting on pretty well with one of the water colours, and have written for a fresh panel for the other, as none I have here are of the right shape.  One of the Agnews will be coming at the end of next week, but I don't know if it is W. Agnew or no. . . . God bless you, my dear mother.  I often feel a very great desire to see your dear old face again, and think of you in the most strange moments—while fishing, &c.,—and believe me that my present absence, will, I think, knit me more closely to you."

*August* 24 :—". . . . The Agnews—W. and his brother—were, with their wives, to have been here to-day, but their visit is postponed on account of one of the latter being ill.  I am not sorry, for although my work is going on pretty well, it is backward, and will be even better if I send it to them.  The girl I mentioned is expected every minute, and the eyes and opera glasses of the establishment are all directed across the valley, from the little lawn in front."

August 25, to his eldest sister :—

". . . . The letter of Smith's enclosed a little story of Annie

Stream in Inverness-shire.

Thackeray's—'Little Red Riding Hood'—with a request that I would do a drawing and initial. I think I shall do it. . . . There is a bull belonging to a gentleman farmer on the next estate, next this on the road towards Spean Bridge, that every one has to pass, and which has always shown more or less signs of savagery, and yesterday he made a rush down the slope on to the road, at the head keeper's two boys (one of them I painted, you know), and they only just saved themselves by getting up a tree, and had to remain there, with Mr. Bull underneath, until the shepherd and his dogs came—nice, isn't it? I'm going to write to Mr. Wallace, the owner, because next week I shall want to go that way to a bank where I shall be working, and don't choose to risk being ripped up. . . . Two Scotch lasses came here yesterday, for me to look at. One, who was very splendid last year, with bare feet, and a shock-head of light and beautiful hair, I thought would do for my water colour, and Rosalie rode over and negotiated with her people ; but Heaven help us ! when they came, you never saw such swells—such crinolines, such cotton gloves, such hats and feathers—looking like servant gals going out on the spree. Of course, I explained through one of the servants here (for they could only speak Gaelic), that I would most likely go over to them and draw from them in their week day dress ; but I shall not, for one of the wenches over here will even do better."

August 28, to his mother :—

" . . . You will be glad to hear, dear, that the work I have been doing is quite satisfactory, and in comparatively a forward state ; and I am only waiting to hear from the Agnews, and finish up here, before you see me again, which will be as early as possible next week. I thought of you much, as being alone, my dear, and knew that you must be lonely either at Bayswater or Cookham, and sincerely hope that it will be a long time before you are again placed in such a position—it shall not be if I can help it. . . I know that work is awaiting me, and I know that I shall get into harness again, and perhaps with none the less advantage for being 'out to grass' for so long. If my health be spared, I have the best years yet before me, and will show you that all promise that I may have given, shall be fulfilled. God bless you for all your loving care and anxiety for us. Look forward to a possibly much happier future. You will have time to answer this—let me know all news, especially as to our Jack. I had a long letter from him last night ; I could wish that the Worthing trip had been more improving to him. Tell me all—all that you think ; and when we meet next week, we will have a quiet talk over things."

*September* 1 :—" . . . I mentioned the Cornhill drawing. I have not done it yet, and blame myself for not having done more work, while here, than the one drawing, but perhaps I should not have been so well as I am now, if I'd stuck too hard at it ; and when fishing and shooting are going on all round one, the temptation to loaf is very strong.

I went out on Friday, with Eden Ansdell, and Lord Abinger's keeper, grouse shooting on the moor behind this house, and we shot some game of a kind we little expected. You know I mentioned a bull belonging to a gentleman on the next estate, and that he was proving very savage, and that the owner would not believe it. Well, we were quietly crossing the moor, and going towards a stream—the Cour, where we fish for trout—and when within half a mile of the Cour, I just espied Mr. Bull running down the opposite bank. I felt very uneasy, and told my fears to the others, who pooh-poohed the idea. Of course Mr. Bull had disappeared, but I could hear him bellowing dreadfully, and getting louder every minute ; the beggar was actually crossing the stream, and a few minutes after, his ugly head appeared above the bank on this side, and he came at us, and we knew we were in for it. The row he made was hideous, and when 15 or 20 yards from us, put down his head to charge ; and then the keeper, who had quietly put into his gun a double charge of shot, levelled and fired, hitting him well. He staggered, and then to my relief, sullenly passed us, and joined a herd of cattle on the side of the mountain. Goodness only knows what the result had been if the keeper had missed, or we had been without guns at all. I wrote an indignant letter to the owner of the animal, and had a stupid incredulous reply ; and it is in this way that horrible things happen. I shall send a line either to Cookham or Bayswater before starting. If you are at Cookham, do not put yourself, or selves, out of the way, or think of tiring yourself by going to Bayswater. I can manage well enough, and can easily get to you next day."

After his return to London, Walker was engaged in finishing the *Stream in Inverness-shire*, and in preparing the wood drawing for *Little Red Riding Hood*, which appeared in the *Cornhill* for October. He was also again at work on *Vagrants*. Of the latter he says in the letter to his mother dated September 16, and addressed to Henley, to which place Mrs. Walker and her invalid son had gone for a few days :—

" I cannot help feeling some pride in my ' Vagrants ' as I look at them, and know the picture will be considered successful. I work on the smallest child to-morrow, which is the most unfinished of the figures."

A little later, Walker took a short trip with his friend Mr. Phillips, and writes from Salisbury, September 24 :—

" . . . We have been this morning to the most beautiful place I think I ever was in, I mean for a private place—Sidney Herbert's (Lord Herbert of Lea that is), and in time to come I will describe it to you. We went into the dear old Cathedral again this morning, and sat about, listening to the solemn music, and glorious boys' voices. There are plenty of old tombs, with Knights and Bishops on them, and I have found it resting to mind and body, to leisurely sit and think.

One finds one's self making good resolves too, though Heaven knows whether they are destined to be kept."

On September 27, he wrote to his brother :—

". . . I enclose one of the envelopes from that theatre-ridden, or I should say stage-struck Will. He came a week ago to me, asking if I could tell Miss Oliver the best way of getting an advertising envelope done, and I thought the best way would be to sketch one myself, which I did on wood, and here it is—Black-eyed Sue, and the gallant Crosstree."

For the remainder of the year, Walker was mostly with his mother and brother, either at Cookham or Bayswater. Part of October they spent in town, and early in November, the weather being mild, John Walker went to Cookham for the last time, returning about the middle of the month. His youngest sister, then living at Cookham, remembers the look on his face as he turned away from the river he was never to see again.

In November, Walker was at work on the illustrations to Miss Thackeray's story of *Jack the Giant Killer*; the first drawings—*The Fates*, and an initial letter of a *Weeping Cupid*—appearing in the *Cornhill* for December ; and the second—*Waiting for Papa*, and an initial—in January, 1868. A water colour of *The Fates*, of which Mr. George Smith became the possessor, was also executed in November. Walker subsequently reproduced in water colour both *Waiting for Papa*, with the title of *The Chaplain's Daughter*, and the *Weeping Cupid*. In

THE FATES.

November too, he completed *The Violet Field*, to which drawing the following extract refers.

November 20, to his sister at Beddington :—

" Look out for me on Friday, and if you have time to see about a screen opposite the cabbages, I shall be thankful. I am just off (8 a.m.) to the Water Colour Gallery, to the sweet task of hanging the things—went early yesterday, and didn't leave until past eight last night. . . Oh, and I wish, dear, you could send to Steadman's field, and ask if Mr. Steadman can come and speak to you, then tell him about the violets—tell him I am likely to want lots, some really fine bouquets if he will supply me at a rate that will pay him. And ask if he can lend one of those cans that the boys strap round them when they gather the violets. Tell him I am painting some violet pickers, and that I would like to sit in his field, if I could be sure of not being interrupted."

November 25, also to Beddington :—

" . . . I am afraid you'll think me a sad worry, but could you get Steadman to send me a bouquet of violets about the size of a dinner plate. I dare say you will not be much puzzled as to where it is to go afterwards. . . . This is a little matter in which you can really help me, so I don't hesitate, dear."

Walker was never married, but in the above passage the breath of violets comes across the years, telling us he knew of love.

A little incident occurred about this time in connection with the *Vagrants*, which may be worth mentioning. One Sunday afternoon, Walker was at work at Beddington, on the background of the picture, when I went to take him some refreshment. As I stood near him afterwards, a robin came and perched on a bush a little way off. I called his attention to it. "By Jove," he said, "I'll put him in"; and in a few touches there was the robin as he now appears, towards the top left hand corner of the picture.

The last letter of this year was also addressed to his sister Sarah. The child mentioned was his little niece, who stood for the "little fashionable wretch," as Mr. Ruskin calls her, in the wood drawing of *Waiting for Papa*. After speaking of the important matter of the violets, Walker writes :—

"I was at Cookham on Friday, sketching Poll's kid, and lovely the river looked, in spite of the cold : a beautiful golden light shone on the banks. I went out with old Wilder to try for a jack, but though one got on, he got off again. I attended an important meeting at the Water Colour Gallery last night, and, confound it, I'm on the next hanging committee, and this is how they did it."

# CHAPTER IX

## 1868

T HE year 1868 opened but sadly for the household at St. Petersburgh Place. John Walker's health had been rapidly declining for some time past, and all now felt that the end was not far off. He died at Bayswater on January 27th, at the age of twenty-two. As has been said, his sister Mary was then staying at Cookham, and it was to the house where she and her husband were living, that he was taken the day before the funeral —the first of four who were to be laid in the old churchyard. He was borne to the grave by riverside men and fishermen, to all of whom his tall thin figure had been a familiar object on the river for three summers past. The simple stone which still marks the grave was erected by Walker as in keeping with the surroundings.

Soon after his brother's death, Walker went with his mother and eldest sister to Brighton. From there he wrote to Mr. North, as follows :—

"Your letter forwarded this morning finds us staying here after a recent great sorrow. I have lost the dear brother whom we were permitted for so long to nurse and help comfort—he died on the 27th of last month.

"I went to town on Monday for the election, and did intend writing you on the subject, and to express my concern that you were not successful, as you truly deserved to be, in my opinion ; and I am requested by Burton to convey to you his regrets. John Gilbert, too, did his best in the matter, both for you and Pinwell ; and I fancy that the reason you (so narrowly) missed going in was a certain opinion some of the members expressed, that there was want of finish in parts of your work—which opinion I am not at all sure I share. Let me beg you not to let this in any way interfere with your trying hard next time. I feel very sure that your perseverance will be rewarded.

"Yes, come and see me. I have done very little work for some time, but I return to the mill during the middle of next week, and shall be glad to see you at any time."

February 4, from Brighton, to Mr. Phillips :—

" Here we are, and I think all the better for the change and bright weather, though subject to times of gloom, heavy enough Heaven knows ; but the bright sun and crisp sparkling sea help one vastly. I brought down the little water colour with me, and will complete it and send it you if you like. . . . The little picture ought to bring me the nimble ninepence while I am here, so if you are ready for it, my dear fellow, it will be a pleasure to once more resume work in this way. No chance of seeing you, I suppose. They say the season is over here, but there seem to be mobs of people—and all happy ! I took a long solitary walk yesterday about Lewes, Glynde, and Berwick (if you know the locality), and came home with a fine appetite, rather a wonder of late."

SCENE FROM " MEG'S DIVERSION."

Soon after this, Walker paid a visit to Mr. Birket Foster at Witley, where he had previously spent a short time, though no mention of his having done so appears in the letters. On February 17, he wrote to his mother :—

" I've just returned from a long drive, which we, B. F., Mrs. F., and Miss Brown (F.'s niece), have had, to see Mr. Hook, R.A. *This is a paradise.* If I had but some money ! I am half mad with envy and other feelings. There is a beautiful little cottage within a stone's throw of the house Hook has left, with a studio and four or five bedrooms, which I would, this day buy if I had money enough (it is £1,200). The situation is perfectly romantic—such a sweep of glorious country ! Alas, I could sell *myself* to be doing what I might do here. The cottage has two acres of ground, with beautiful heather, &c., stretching down from it, and altogether I do not think you have any conception of the wondrous beauty of this place. As for the house Hook has left, it is simply splendid ; but like the cottage—which he built as a kind of retreat—it is to be sold, not let. I shall stay here as long as I can, and work as much as I can. B. Foster says : 'My dear boy, why don't you paint a picture, and buy it ?'—meaning the cottage ! He is most kind, and begs me to stay here and work. Gambart is coming to-morrow or Wednesday, and I think I have a subject already. I am very glad I came, and trust that, with Heaven's help, I may now have turned the corner. How you would revel in this place ! "

In expectation that his mother and sister might have returned from Brighton, Walker ran up to town, and left a letter dated February 19, from which I extract the following :—

" My dears, in case this finds you here to-morrow, know by it that I came up hoping to find you both here, and jolly ; and lo, the place is desolate, as you will find it I fear ; but no matter, only a few minutes could I spend with you, in any case, for now it is 8, and the last train leaves Waterloo at 9, and the Fosters' carriage has to then meet me at Godalming. However, I cannot help feeling sorry not to meet you once more in the old crib, but let this represent me. . . . This morning was too lovely at the Fosters'. I am doing my own wonderful bedroom window there, with the stained glass, and comfortable recess with cushioned seats—that Fan recollects no doubt—and a figure. The ' nigger ' is on my shoulder welcoming me, and I have only just time to get back."

*February* 23 :—" I suppose you have at last returned, and have found my letter and explanation. . . . . No news ; I am well and happy, and getting well on with my work. It will be finished next week, as early as possible, and another begun, so I can't say anything about coming home, but will come up to see your old face and show you mine if you like —only say when, and I'll be with you."

*February* 24 :—" . . . B. Foster wants me to finish the little subject of the workhouse children for him, and at some later time to do an important work for him, for he believes in your boy's work, and has much comforted me in the unconscious signs of *respect* he shows. . . . . My room here is not the one I occupied before : it is the chief room for visitors, and from it I see the Brighton downs, and ' Devil's Dyke,' 30 miles off, so you know the kind of prospect there is above the beauteous fir trees that enclose the grounds. But I hope you will see it, for I do think you ought to fetch me home from so lovely a place. I have worked pretty hard to-day, and successfully. . . . . Birket Foster and I went for a beautiful walk yesterday morning, finishing up by visiting a little church. In the churchyard they laid poor Lindsay Watson, who first came with the news of my election into the Water Colour Society, and which I remembered as I stood there yesterday."

*February* 26 :—" Just a line to say I received both yours this morning, with Smith's which I enclose, and intend answering to-day. I am glad, dear, that you are pretty comfortable, both of you, and this weather will help Fan surely. To-day here is a fine spring one, the downs in the far horizon tinted with gold by the setting sun at this moment. F. and one of the little girls are on the charming lawn playing at bowls, and the birds are going it like mad. My work is nearly finished."

The letter from Mr. Smith, above mentioned, related to a proposal that Walker should illustrate Thackeray's *Esmond*. The idea, however, was never carried out, though Mr. Hooper tells me that Walker completed one drawing.

On February 29, Walker wrote to his sister Mary :—

" I have just received your nice long letter, and the neckerchief, which I have put on and mean to wear all the evening. This has been an awful day, rain and wind no end—very different from the lovely days ever since I've been here. We have just had dinner, and coffee has been brought in ; and though I mean to touch upon the water colour (which is all but finished) I look upon the evening, and indeed all the evenings here, as leisure time, for I have worked very well since coming here, resisting many a temptation to take a jolly walk. I wish I could tell you how dainty this place is, from the delightful little drawing-room we're now in, with its walls covered with water colours—little gems by old Hunt, Millais, &c., &c.—to the bedroom I occupy, and in which I paint, for the subject is the window, which is in a large recess, with stained glass and diamond-shaped panes, and I am doing a woman brushing her hair. It is just the house you would revel in, my Poll. Part of the garden is a gentle slope, with its shrubs and bushes covering the beautiful lawn, on which the blackbirds promenade in the sun of a morning. There are two smaller flat lawns, on which we play bowls or croquet ; and above, and around down below, plantations of firs and pines, and so many evergreens, that one forgets that it is the leafless season ; and from my bedroom, as I sit on the cushions in the recess, I can see across to the Brighton downs, and ' Devil's Dyke,' 30 miles off. Foster is very jolly and kind, with a great sense of humour in a quiet sort of way. He makes me very comfortable, and I know he likes my being here, and he admires my work much ; and, by the way, has asked me to finish the workhouse kids and your kid for him, so you will have me down upon you again. . . . . You know, my dear, what a fearful time it has been for me. I realise it most awfully sometimes while here, and my heart aches—God knows how much—when I suddenly find myself thinking of poor Jack, and how complete a companion he might always have been for me. On Thursday evening, I went up to town, as I dare say you know, and took the Missus by surprise, and we had a little bit of dinner together—we three—and then I came back by the last train, the carriage waiting comfortably outside Godalming station for me, as the last train does not go on to Witley. The Missus was cheered by my visit, I know ; and we agreed to work like fun, and stick by each other this year. . . . . Thank you, my dear, for the tobacco-box. It's sure to be good, and I'm afraid I have almost a child's pleasure in receiving a gift. . . . . I shall be sorry to leave this place. As you say, there are lots of new ideas ; and if I could, I'd stay here until the summer. Old Keene shares a cottage with another man named Bridger, close by this. He comes down now and then, and there is a dog at the cottage with a short tail that reminds one of old dottles himself. . . . . Foster is glaring at my picture, which I brought into the room at dusk."

The following undated letter was addressed to Mr. Phillips :—

"I am staying with Birket Foster ever since Sunday week, and shall, I expect, remain a week longer, for I am at work, and am happier here than I have been for a long time. . . . This place is the most lovely and snug that I ever stayed at ; all the horrors of winter, and all discomfort of every kind, seem done away with. I can see 30 miles from my bed-room window, across the most beautiful part of Surrey. The house (which B. F. built himself) is the most perfect ; the eye is continually refreshed by good colour."

March 5, to his mother :—

"I shall in all probability be in town to-morrow evening, or Sunday morning, and spend Sunday with you, though I think I had best return here to finish up. Gambart came yesterday, and carried off the work I have done, and I only wished that the other had been ready—so did he. . . . . Thank you, my dear, for the little wallflower, it is as good as anything can be, and makes me feel that the same sun that gilds this place so wonderfully, does not forget to look upon the place you are in. . . . . I like the idea of ' Esmond ' very much."

Before leaving Witley, Walker visited Knole in connection with the illustrations to *Esmond.* On March 12, he wrote to his mother from the Royal Crown Hotel, Sevenoaks :—

"We've just come back from the visit to Knole, and I am doubled up with wonder and delight—such tapestry and lovely old furniture. We went into the room in which Millais painted the ' Eve of St. Agnes,' a room that is furnished with old massy silver ; and remains— cabinets, chairs, and everything, even the silver toilet service—just as it was prepared for the reception of James I. Millais painted the moonlight subject in it. The housekeeper says that if I write to Lady De La Warr she is sure to give me every facility ; so now I am only waiting for Smith's letter, which I suppose I shall have to-morrow morning, and sincerely hope it will be favourable. You would be delighted with this place, and this hotel has a most glorious old garden, with quaint alleys, &c., and high box hedges. We shall dine this evening at Charing Cross or somewhere, for it is easier to get to Witley from this by going to town ; so for once and away I shall be in town without seeing my mother there. . . . . I shall do my best in every case now, and shall return to town much benefited by all this change. Best love to my Fan. She'll have to help me with ' Esmond ' no end—every one will. Shall have to borrow lots of costume, and shall have to work like blazes."

Soon after this, Walker left Witley. While there, in addition to *The Bedroom Window*, he had painted *Well-Sinkers*—a lady and little girl looking down a well in course of construction, and three labourers standing near—a subject taken from work actually in progress in Mr. Birket Foster's grounds, at the time. He also makes mention of beginning other work at Witley, which, however, does not seem to have been carried very far.

Early in April, Walker received a letter from Mr. North, inviting him to spend a few days at Halsway Court, Crowcombe, Somersetshire, where Mr. North was staying for the purposes of his work. Later in the year, the invitation was accepted ; and so began those visits to Somersetshire in which Walker and Mr. North were so much together. On April 19, Walker wrote in reply :—

" I have been so pressed for time this last week as to have been scarcely fit for letter writing—from morning till night at the Gallery, hanging our water colours, till I have hated the very thought of pictures ! I fear I shall not be able to join you for some time. So soon as I can get away, I am inclined, and persuaded by my folks here, to go right away, perhaps up the Mediterranean to Venice ; for I am feeling overdone, and longing for sea air and entirely fresh scenes. If I go, I hope to return to a careful picture for next Academy, before this summer is well on. I shall be glad to know how you are going on with yours. . . . I am trying to finish up the things for our Gallery, so excuse haste.

" P.S.—Have given over ' Esmond,' for it is useless and a shame to attempt such a thing against time."

" The things for our Gallery " consisted of the *Stream in Inverness-shire*, *The First Swallow*, *The Bedroom Window*, *Well-Sinkers*, *The Fates*, and *The Chaplain's Daughter*, and formed a goodly show. Indeed, so far as exhibited work was concerned, this was Walker's most prolific year. He sent three more drawings to the Winter Exhibition of the Old Water Colour Society, and moreover had the *Vagrants* on the Royal Academy's walls at this year's Exhibition. All the above-mentioned drawings, and also the *Vagrants*, were well received ; but the latter does not seem to have roused any particular enthusiasm on this its first appearance. It may be noticed here, that in the Academy catalogue, the

WELL-SINKERS.

title was erroneously given as *In the Glen, Rathfarnham Park*. Mr. Waltner's etching of the picture is well known, as are also those of *The First Swallow* and *The Chaplain's Daughter*, by Mr. E. Gaujean.

His friends' persuasion, backed by his own inclination, induced Walker to visit Venice this year. It was at Witley that the subject had first been broached. Mr. W. Q. Orchardson, R.A., of whom Walker had seen a good deal while staying at Witley, was thinking of going to Venice with Mr. Birket Foster, in the late spring, and Walker had been urged to accompany them. For the sake of the voyage, however, he wished to go by sea, and it was finally arranged that he should do so, and meet the others in Venice. He accordingly took passage in the s.s. *Kedar*, trading between Liverpool and Alexandria, and calling at Genoa and some intermediate ports on the way out. On Saturday, May 2, Walker went to Liverpool, accompanied by his mother. The next day he wrote to his sister Fanny, from the Waterloo Hotel :—

" . . . . There is something always rather depressing in first coming to a strange place of this kind ; evidences of commonplace squalor and worrying business, and yet all new to the eye. I left the Missus at the station, as you know, and proceeded at once in a cab to Burns and McIver's office—a place something like a bank—and in my mind I resented the tone of the man who was called forward to speak with me. He had a broad Lancashire accent, and spoke of *his* doing everything in the matter—the speaking to Captain Muir, &c.—and rather giving me to understand that *he* had power to make me comfortable. This depressed me. I have since come to the conclusion that he was a conceited ape, and I don't suppose has influence with anybody. We had a a sight of the vessel, as you know, and this morning I went again— took a cab this time, there being no 'busses—and found that the ' Kedar ' had been moved altogether from her position yesterday, which gave me a walk of nearly a mile. However, I eventually found her, and did indeed go on board—everything sadly in confusion, but giving promise of comfort, and being all that I could expect. She is, to my unpractised eye, a large vessel, though not nearly the size of some belonging to the same people. The noble captain was of course invisible, and she seemed quite in charge of the dock people, who commence putting her cargo into her to-night, and I think there's no doubt that she goes first thing on Wednesday morning ; so whether it will be advisable for the Missus to stay over Tuesday night, I don't know. If I go aboard then, why I think she'd better slope. I think she will only be depressed by the ' last look ' at me from *terra firma*."

May 5, to his mother, who had returned to London :—

" I've just returned from Speke Hall and all its grandeur, to find your dear old telegram, like a whisper from your very mouth—20 past 10 —so if you sent it from Euston, they've done it pretty well this time. The night is fair and bright, and I am happy ; for all has been done

THE FIRST SWALLOW.

*By permission of Messrs. Thos. Agnew and Sons, owners of the copyright.)*

that can well be, and I can quietly say that I am simply of the same opinion as from the first, that for my future this is the one thing that will do me most good, and that my mind most eagerly turns to. When I left you, I walked back here, as there was a moment to spare, looked about and found there was nothing more to do, and went forth, found Miller and Leyland, and with the latter went partly by rail, and partly in his phaeton, to the wonderful old Hall, where I have spent a very comfortable quiet time—the vehicle and servant waiting to carry me back to the omnibus that stops at this door; so now you have the whole event. Of course the place was superb. . . . Well, a few hours will see me leaving it all for the present. I shall often think of our little scrambling stay here, and of your constant wish to be 'doing something' for me, though Heaven knows what more you could have done, and Heaven will reward you for all. . . . On getting up I shall add a few lines to this; and, if possible, will scrawl a line from the steamer before starting, but if I don't, you'll know that the bustle is too great. . . .

"$\frac{1}{4}$ to 8. All right and jolly, my dears; a lovely morning, and I am feeling quite well—just sitting down to breakfast."

In the envelope containing the above letter, there is still the hurried line from the steamer—in pencil on half a sheet of note paper. It may as well be given :—

"9 o'clock.—I write this in my cabin, which I have secured all right. Hope they will have posted the letter I left at the hotel.
9. 30.—We're just about off, I think, and for fear of missing the man who takes this, I shut up. All right, God bless you."

"Sunday, May 10, 1868. Steamship 'Kedar,' somewhere off the coast of Portugal.
"My Dearest Mother,—Of course this will be a much looked for letter, and so I cannot do better than begin at once, although I can only carry it up to this day, and double the distance, almost, has to be done, before it can get to the post. After I sent off that last scrap—which was taken ashore by one of the Captain's children who had come to bid him good-bye—we slowly began to work our way, inch at a time, out of dock, and it was not until about 12 that we passed New Brighton, and the first day was uneventful enough. It was fine, though exceedingly cold towards evening, the crew were busy getting rid of some of the dreadful confusion of ropes, &c., and I did not 'turn in' until past 10; and as you may suppose, the strange noises, the scuffling tramp of feet, the crackings and throbbings of the engines, kept one from sleeping for a long time. All this I need scarcely say affects me little enough now, and I believe that in time one might sleep sweetly on a runaway horse—with plenty of room for him. The next morning was beautiful, but with a long tremendous sort of swell from the Atlantic, and the only other passenger (who is a young

Liverpool man, and an invalid) soon became very ill, and disappeared. The crew were by this time preparing to get 'some of the dirt off,' as the Captain said, and soon there was nothing but sluicing and scrubbing. I was very hungry, and have had all since a famous appetite. At 2 o'clock, we were passing the Scilly Islands (see map). In the evening, the poor passenger was much worse, though he struggled on deck for a time. One of the officers asked me how it was that I was not ill—on which point I could not enlighten him. We were now entering the Bay of Biscay, and had long since lost sight of land. The roof of the saloon, and passenger cabins, &c., form a deck or promenade which you did not see, and chiefly on this I take my daily exercise, and on that evening walked with Captain M. until late, in the moonlight. My rest was afterwards disturbed by the great motion of the ship, which rolled tremendously in the swell. Friday morning was very wet and cheerless, but I was not going to remain below, and put on the wonderful macintosh suit, for which I have since been much chaffed by the Captain, who said I was got up like a Liverpool pilot. However, I didn't care, and if there'd ensued a week's wet, the laugh would have been considerably on my side ; and by the way, the Captain is a very dry caustic fellow, and can say rather severe things without seeming to mean it. In the afternoon, the rain cleared off, though by this time it was preciously rough, which was only to be expected as it was blowing S.W. and we were in the Bay. However, yesterday morning it was warmer, and we saw Cape Finisterre dreamily and beautifully in the far distance ; and knowing that I was looking at Spain, felt that we had really made some way, and the wonder was that we did not feel the difference in temperature more, but towards evening we felt it, and the air was miraculously clear, the stars most wonderful—Venus appearing like a little moon behind the light clouds, and casting a bright sheen on the big waves. I thought, as it grew darker, that the crests on the waves looked very light, and the Captain told me that if I went 'aft,' and looked at the ship's wake, I should see more light ; and on going, I saw the most beautiful sight, the great stream of water churned up by the propeller, was perfectly luminous, like the tail of a comet, and among it, appearing and disappearing, were bright globules of light. Such a sight, in the solitude, has a strange impressive effect on one."

"Monday night, about 70 miles from Gibraltar. Here I am in the Mediterranean. I did intend going on with this yesterday, but somehow I could not write. The day, which had been tremendously warm, ended with a strong, and anything but warm, wind, driving us, up to this time at a wonderful rate, right from behind. When breakfast was over yesterday, and the crew all in white ducks and ribbons, the Captain came up to me and made a request that rather collapsed me—it was no less than that I would *act as clerk* during service, which was to be held in the saloon. Of course I at once endeavoured to excuse myself, for alas, I felt unworthy and incompetent, but he would receive no excuse, and as as there was no *actual* impediment, I was silenced ; but I can honestly say that I then, in the time left me, did do my best to make myself fit for it, and when the time came, took the part with sincerity at at least.   At one o'clock, we were off the rock of Lisbon—the town being hid.   There were great shoals of porpoises, gambolling about, and shooting underneath—their great brown bodies going like rockets—and after passing the Cape of St. Vincent, off which the battle was fought, and seeing the poor old moon rise, I turned in.   The great event of passing Gibraltar came off at 3 this afternoon, and certainly the sight, as we passed between Europe and Africa, was as impressive as the idea. I made an attempt to do Gibraltar ; and as a background to a little

subject I have thought workable, it may do.   Since sunset (there is no twilight here) I have walked and talked with Captain M., who improves on closer acquaintance, and I fancy he rather likes the way I take and answer his chaff.   He commanded the vessel in which Thackeray went to New York.   And now I'll go above, for it is a true Mediterranean night, soft and warm."

" Thursday night.   I'm afraid, my dear, that this rum letter will read stupidly, and in a disconnected sort of way, but you won't mind I know. We are getting by this time towards Genoa, and I hope we shall be in the harbour by about 10, to-morrow.   It has set in a regular wet night, I fear—very calm since the morning, but since 4, gradually getting overcast, and now there is a smart wind springing up, and a splashing disagreeable rain.   Monday night was wonderful.   After I left off writing, I went up, and the whole sea seemed covered with *slabs* of phosphorus, the crest of every wave being perfectly luminous—so much so as to make a very sharp look out necessary for any ship's light being quite mixed up with it.   On Tuesday evening, there was a good deal of lightning, and since then we have seen whales, sharks, and porpoises, no end.   While I was making a little pencil sketch of the second officer's head, at his urgent request, a shoal of about twenty whales was all about the ship. I must tell you that I have earned the Captain's eternal gratitude, by doing a small water colour of him. He turns out very appreciative, and a thorough good fellow, and we now quite understand each other. He has told me that should ever I be in Liverpool again, with the same object as last, he will be very glad to lodge me at his house, before going aboard ; and that leads me to declare that I consider this such a success, that I certainly would hope, if I live, and all's well next spring, to come this way again, in this same vessel ; and then if we prosper, perhaps I need not be by myself. My appetite is very good, and I am always ready for breakfast ; and these last two mornings I've had a sea sponge bath, though yesterday it was a difficult matter, on account of the ship's motion. It is quite uncertain whether I leave this vessel to-morrow, or go on to Leghorn. If there is any changing of carriages, or that kind of thing, I certainly mean to do the latter, although in that case, I do not reach Leghorn until Sunday next, as we stay here until Saturday to discharge the cargo. However, Captain M. and I go to their agents at once to-morrow, and ascertain which will be the better plan. I rather expect the Fosters will be at Venice by the 20th, and though I'm bent upon being at another hotel to theirs, it will be nice to have them at hand. I have been reading a charming little book by Leigh Hunt—it is a gossiping little volume about Kensington —all that has happened in it historically, all about Holland House, and Kensington Palace, and the people that have lived thereabouts. It is called ' The old Court Suburb.' I am going to have a *herring* for supper. Supper is not laid out ; we have breakfast 8.30, dinner at 1, tea at 6, and if anything is wanted after that, it has to be called for. There is a kind of rack put round the table to keep the things from shooting into one's lap. I saw the steward once make a snatch at a soup

tureen, just in time to save it. I made a rough sketch of our dinner table, but fear it ain't good. Ah dear ! I wish I could tell you of the wonderful effects and sensations during such a little experience as this.

I certainly have the greatest admiration for the way in which this little vessel is managed. It is a kind of little kingdom—perfect obedience and order—one officer is always on duty night and day, and the great rough men all seem to work with a will. I often think (how often it would be difficult to say) of my dears at home, and all the troubles and ambitious little schemes that I seem to have left behind for a few weeks ; and goodness knows that I shall be glad enough to get back to it all. I wonder if our passing Gibraltar was telegraphed, and if you read of it. That man Duncan (Burns and McIver's clerk) came on board just as we were leaving dock, and he said he would give you the intelligence, in case you missed seeing it. I will not close this to-night, in case I have more to add before post leaves to-morrow ; but good night, with all love and blessings on you two and the others, from your own boy."

" Friday, one o'clock. We are in Genoa harbour, and I think I shall go on to Leghorn by this vessel, or at any rate, not start for Venice to-day. The Italian Royal Family are here. All the harbour is decorated, and there are to be grand doings for the next day or two— regattas, illuminations, &c. The agent's clerk will give me all information as to trains, this afternoon. The Italian fleet is here, and everything looks very pretty, and I only wish *you* were here to see it all. It's awfully hot now we are out of the sea breeze. I am going ashore after dinner, with Captain M., when I shall post this ; so best love to my dears, and farewell for a day or two, when I'll write again, and am always your own loving Fred."

The *fêtes* of which Walker makes mention in the next letter, and also in his letters from Venice, were in honour of the marriage of the Crown Prince Humbert of Italy with the Princess Margaret.

May 16, from Genoa harbour :—

" As I am leaving this 'ere wessel on Monday morning very early (the train leaves at 5.15, and with 2 hours' rest at Milan, gets to Venice at 8.15 p.m.), I shall scarcely be ready for letter writing when I get there, and so sit down for a little communication with my sister, who, by the way, is just about 2,500 miles from me. I cannot say how often I have wished that you, or all of my own people, were with me. The reality of such an experience as this is so far beyond any imagination, that description seems almost useless—at least I felt so as I rambled by myself this morning through the glorious, sunny, picturesque, old town. When I think that in poor old London, one cannot place one's self or one's belongings out of doors, without getting *dirty*, it seems so strange. There is a queer, almost theatrical, Masaniello-like effect about the groups of figures, and the queer buildings, all in good, beautiful, colour ; from the side of a house, to the unconscious way in which an old woman matches her head covering with her dress. I sat on a stone bench for an hour, near the theatre, and seemed to feed on the wonderful novelty ; and at such a time, most strangely I find myself face to face—now and then almost painfully—with all that I left, a little fortnight ago. By that I mean, one's thoughts are so wilful, that they fly from the object before one's bodily eye, to the possible present a long way off. . . . . Last night, I went ashore with the first officer, who is a red-whiskered, and rather genial, fellow, and with the passenger, who is very young, and not very interesting (poor fellow, he is much better already), to see the illuminations, and until last night, I had *never seen any*. The town was given up to it, and the dreamy, artistic effect was something marvellous, helped by flowing tapestries, and a thousand things that you'd imagine only enthusiasm and unbounded wealth could manage, and yet there seems to be a very moderate share of the latter, according to our standard of it. We mixed with the thick (and even in that light, picturesque) crowd, and a gentle, good-natured crowd it was ; and afterwards we turned into a café or wine shop, in a narrow, yet sparkling, turning, where we continued our cigars, and where you might have sat with us ; and indeed there were matrons, national guards, young girls, and little boys, all seeming to my eyes ladies and gentlemen, drinking iced water and sugar, or lemonade coloured with fruit. As for us, we drank our glasses of marsala, then strolled down again to the rows of boats at the harbour side, and quietly paddled over the cool water, twinkling with thousands of lights, past the silent, black ships, to our own. We are in the middle of the harbour, and to-morrow is to be the grand day. After the regatta (before the Royal folks), the town, the harbour, the fleet, even our own 'Kedar,' and the high hills that surround the city, will burst into coloured lights ; and as we are placed, we must see the best of it all. It seems odd to be talking of a mere light-up in this way, but if you only knew the headlong and perfect manner in which the thing is done, you could not help enjoying it. This reminds me that my epistle must be posted to-morrow morning, and it is my intention to take it ashore, and engage my cab and my boat for the railway station early on the morrow, for if I don't manage it quite soon in the morning, it will be impossible in the afternoon, I am certain. The people on the vessel seem sorry that I am going on Monday morning, instead of going to Leghorn with them, but money is an object (though I forget it often enough), and the sooner I get to Venice, the better. I have done no work yet—the confusion or something being against it—and this won't do, you know ; yet I do not feel as though I had been idle, as I should have been in the same time at home. I wonder how that red may-tree looks, by the way, and whether the blossoms on the other things fulfil their promise. . . . Well, dear, it is late, and I know the poor steward's mate is only waiting to put out the light."

Walker reached Venice on Monday, May 18, and was much disappointed to find no letters awaiting him. In a letter to his mother, written the same evening, from the Grand Hôtel de l'Europe, he says :—

" . . . . Why on earth haven't you written? I have asked, but there are no letters from the Burgh. It would have just made my slumbers a little sweeter, but I suppose they'll come all in a bunch.

I made a mistake in my letter to Fan. I meant that I had travelled 2,500 miles ; of course I am not that distance from you now. I did think of going round to the hotel where the Fosters must be by this time, but the storm and my aching limbs forbid. This is a wonderful old place, but more of it in my next."

*May* 20 : — " I cannot help beginning this by asking *how it is that no letters have reached me.* I did expect to find some on my arrival, and now two days have elapsed, and I don't know what to think. You see I am still my poor self, and cannot get on without knowing that all's going on well, and I cannot tell you how I have hungered for news from you or Fan, and to-day have sometimes felt quite unhappy, for fear that something has gone wrong. *I am alone*, and feel none the less so for this. I know you took the address, and of course, had they been unable to lodge me here, they would yet have received my letters. I had just as soon return at once, if I am to be kept in suspense ; do pray write, or all my comfort is gone. I look to having a letter in the morning, and then all will be well. I have seen very little besides the usual thing, by sauntering or taking a gondola. The Fosters have not arrived, nor can I tell what has possessed them, for they were to have left by the 15th at latest. If I thought they and their courier weren't coming, and could only have a few lines from you, I would engage a ' valet de place ' and begin work at once. The gentleman to whom Mrs. Millais' letter was addressed, was kindness itself, but can do very little for me, I fear. I am afraid this is a depressing note ; but if, on its receipt, you know that I have received a letter from you, it need not be depressing. I am quite well in body, thank goodness—eat and sleep well—and when I see the well-known hand on a letter shall be quite comfortable, and will then send you long, prosy letters. . . . I have walked and smoked on the wonderful square of St. Mark, listening to the band, until I am quite tired."

*May* 22 :—" At last I can say that your letter has arrived, and so with pipe in mouth, and slippers on, I sit down to answer. I really do think that if I'd not heard from you to-day, I should have been telegraphing, or doing something extravagant. The letter was brought to my room, for they knew I was anxious, and I read it while at my coffee and roll, which I take in bed, having no breakfast till 12 or 1, and then making it luncheon, with half a bottle of claret. And so I'm all right ; but you've no idea how many notions got into my head as I tried to review things, fancying that some bad news must surely reach me, and almost wishing I hadn't come so far. I am beginning work at last, and pretty high time too, I think. You see I've been so very unsettled—in a whirl of things that I might do—but then could not make myself understood ; no Fosters with their courier to apply to (what's gone with them, goodness only knows), and so at last, to-day, I've fixed upon a gondola subject, and the next thing is to carry it out. And, with the aid of Mr. Rawdon Brown, I've hired a man (who can speak enough

English to get on with), a lad, and last not least, a gondola, for very little more than I, as a swell, am expected to pay for a day's gondola alone. You'd be surprised at the difficulty in getting at men who speak English, just at this time, they're so snatched at ; I mean the ' valet de place ' kind of animal, who is after all a mere servant or interpreter, and a precious expensive one too, for very often they feather their own nests, and keep well with the natives at the same time, of course at ' Signor's ' cost.

" I never told you of my experience in getting from Genoa to this. I had, like an idiot, placed trust in the agent's clerk at Genoa—an amiable sort of foreigner in tight trousers—he was always on board superintending the unloading, and managed to have all his tribe on board last Sunday night, to see the display. Well, he undertook to have a boat ready at 4.30, Monday morning, and a cab at the harbour side. The boat was there sure enough, and the young fellow passenger, who wanted for some unknown reason to ' see me off,' and I, jumped in ; but at the harbour side, when my baggage had been searched, there was no cab ; so after waiting, and looking like a fool, I made two Genoese shoulder the things, and of course, as an Italian wouldn't hurry, to save his skin, my train had gone. But the fun is, that though I waited until 7.12, and then went by another route, I arrived here at just the same time—8.20 in the evening—and jolly glad I was to leave the train, too, and in my hurry I stepped into 6 inches of clear water—took one step too many in fact—trying to get into the gondola, and when in, I sat in the wrong place ! ! ! Yesterday, I went to an island called Lido. It is a longish strip of land that divides the shallow waters of Venice from the Adriatic ; and which, as a thin, wooded line, I can see from this window. It was a favourite place of Byron's—he used to walk and ride, and intended being buried, there, and Shelley the poet gives a very beautiful description of it—and from a little deserted cemetery one gets a very good view of Venice, seen between the melancholy trees—I think of doing it. On leaving my boat, I walked straight across the island to where the Adriatic seems lightly to plash on beautiful ridges of sand. There is no tide, you know, and the canals and sea rise and fall only a few inches. And this strangely melancholy island is covered with shells —one can see them among the drawable weeds and flowers, towards the shore—and towards the water-mark, there are seams of shells, some quite beautiful. I walked back inside the island, among the vines, and there are those trees with the shivering leaves, like the little ones opposite the Burgh ; and among the banks and straw fences are beautiful little lizards at every turn. I must do something there, and have been again this afternoon. R. Brown seems somewhat surprised that I am not copying ' old masters ' instead, but I thought the place looked interesting when I first saw it. However, R. B. is kindness itself, and lent me the volume of Shelley—the island is mentioned in the poem called ' Julian and Maddalo.' At R. B's advice, I bought a small, white sunshade or umbrella, the usual thing here ; for a ' coup de soleil ' is by no means an impossibility, without some little precaution. I shall be awfully glad of dear Fan's letter. How often I wish she were here, for my sake and for hers. . . . This place is no end gay ; the enormous Square of St. Mark is always full, of an evening, and the Prince and his bride show themselves at one of the windows. I am disappointed with the music—the military band, I mean—they play beautifully, but nothing but the sprightly dance business. Well, I have almost pumped out all I had to say for to-night ; shall have more no doubt when Fan's letter comes."

May 23, to his sister Mary :—

" I feel that I must send you a line or two, just to keep you from grumbling, you know ; but what I have to say, is the difficulty, for in writing to the missus, I've pumped myself dry of news, and I expect she will be retailing all I tell her. I've just had dinner at the *table d'hôte*, and as it's ½ past 7, I am writing this on the rough marble window sill of my room, for it's nearly dark, and the evenings don't 'draw out' and 'close in,' as in our poor dear England, that I snarl about so when I'm there. Between ourselves, I often wish I had a companion while here—some genial spirit, such as I could so easily make out of different bits taken from the fellows I know—or (blest thought) a little woman with my ring on her finger, and her heart given to me to take care of. I'm afraid such a thing will never be my good fortune, however ; or if it is to be so, why not while I can so fully appreciate the gift ? Others find all they want, and seem to take it as a matter of course ; and having now so much time to think, as I have so little chance of talking, I do confess to feeling sometimes *solitary*. Some men and boys have just begun to sing a glee in a canal at the front, and the great tower of St. Mark is booming out, as usual without any apparent object. It's an enormous tower—the gold angel at the top said to be over 30 feet high—and now I can hear, mingling with the other sounds, the military band in the great Square. I'm almost tired of their distant trumpeting and drumming, for I find they play little more than dance music—they played 'Bella Figlia' the other evening while I was strolling there, however. I've begun a water colour at last ; a gondola in front coming towards one down a narrow canal, with the green sea-weed clinging to the marble steps and walls. I've hired a man who can talk English a bit, and better still, can understand *me*, when I speak ; and he has a lad and a gondola, and I'm to have all three at about 7*s*. 6*d*. or rather 8*s*. a day. I take them by the day, as I would models—and indeed they'll have to act as such—reserving to myself the right of telling them I don't want 'em, whenever I choose. A gondola alone costs 5 francs a day, so as work is the object, this other arrangement will do for the present. It's not the easiest thing in the world beginning work, when you have to do without talking almost entirely. When my present gondolier knew I intended sketching, he inquired if I knew 'Monsieur Ruskin de

Londres,' and he turned out to have been his gondolier. . . . In this man's gondola there is always an engaging kind of poodle dog, with a stump of a tail—his hair is short, but he *doesn't shave*—and his chief object in life seems to be how to get in the shade ; all this afternoon he was in the little cabin of the gondola. I hope the new man's boat will be as good. The motion is very soothing, and gives one a luxurious feeling. They seem very elegant in line, and most of them have a good deal of carving. The way the men handle them, in and out among the others, is a miracle."

The same date, to his mother :—

" Just a line before I go to bed. I've begun work, and to-morrow I begin with my man who speaks English, and with him I hope to get on all serene. To-day has been occupied in putting in a gondola, which I find anything but easy to draw ; however, it's all right now, I think. Awfully warm it is, especially in the evening. After dinner I wrote a note to our Poll ; since then I've been to see if there were any news of the Fosters—Oh no, of course not. I want them to come, because I don't wish to see the grand pictures by myself, as it would take a great deal of extra time in finding them out, &c., and you see they have a courier, and I expect would set aside a part of each day to picture seeing ; and the rest, with me, would be picture making. A good deal of thunder and lightning before dinner, and indeed a little of it every day almost, from the direction of the Alps—keeps the air clear, I fancy, though. Shall hope for a second letter to-morrow morning."

I interrupt the course of the letters for a moment, to draw attention to the above reference to the pictures ; not on account of anything noteworthy in itself, but because this is literally the only time the pictures are mentioned in these Venice letters. The reader, however, must not conclude that Walker was wanting in appreciation of the masterpieces to be seen in Venice and elsewhere. From whatever cause his reticence arose, it was certainly not due to this. On one occasion, I remember his saying to me with extraordinary emphasis—I believe in reference to the picture by Titian, *Portrait of a Doge*, lent by Mr. Ruskin to the Exhibition of the Works of Old Masters at Burlington House, in 1870— " Titian must have been *brim full* of art when he painted that."

May 24, to his mother :—

" You see I can't help sending something just before going to bed, though before doing so I'm going to have a bit of supper, for I had no dinner. The heat was great, and I was in a working fit, so I came home, and while they were going it at the *table d'hôte*, I had tea and bread and butter while my boat was waiting, then out again, and altogether I've got on very well. The new boat and the men are a success, and I am very comfortable in the knowledge that I am making a bit more money. I have found a splendid bit of old stuff for the background—I won't describe it—to-morrow morning I go on with the gondola itself, which is moored some little way off, while I sit on some steps ; and in the afternoon—the sun being then off the place—I go on with the background. Since work (and I managed to go on till near 8), I have been for a sharp trot, warm as it is ; and I find that, once knowing the way, one may walk almost all over Venice. Just as I got past the canal where the Bridge of Sighs is, I turned round and saw the beauteous moon—it was a new moon, but the air was so clear that the rest of her was perfectly luminous—and now I suppose there will be a new splendour to this most wonderful place. Blessed work ! I am quite content to go on with that only, until I get back to you. I do not care for other company, now I am at it, until I leave the place ; and I know where to find my nooks and corners when I do return. Never fear if I am not back by the 10th of June—I have done enough for the present at Pall Mall—but you will see me, if I live, on some day in that sweet month, with every resolve to do my best. I sent a letter to Captain Muir at Naples, as he wished it much, telling him of my arrival ; and this morning, after reading over your letter and Fan's, I thought I might see if it were possible to go back with him on the return passage—we discussed it at Genoa, but he could tell me nothing, as all was uncertainty until after leaving Naples— so this morning I sent a telegram to the ' Kedar ' at Naples, asking if I could join him in returning ; but, alas, the vessel had gone, the answer said.

" Antonio is my new man's name ; he is very quick and obliging. He addresses me, not as 'Sir,' but 'gentleman.' He undertakes to procure me any native as model, such as I may require ; taking them to the place, as I may want them, in the gondola, then returning for me—I am going to have a pair of children on the stone steps in my new water colour—he seems to have a most refreshing instinct as regards the picturesque. The little cabin of the gondola forms a miniature room, with a sliding window on each side, cushioned and easy, and I feel sure that I shall do some creditable work now. Do not fail to write, because you think there's nothing to write about, there's *always* enough to interest me ; the words, ' no news, all right,' are worth the sending to solitary me, and a few lines will always help me to contentment for the day. God bless you both. Am suddenly feeling sleepy, since the bit of supper which I've eaten over this."

From the description given in the above letter, the reader who is familiar with Walker's work, will recognise the drawing of *The Gondola*, now in the possession of the Right Hon. Joseph Chamberlain, M.P.

*May* 26 : " No letter from you for two days, but I write just to say all's right. I am going on well with my work, though it's preciously hot, and requires all one's energy to get on. The Fosters and Orchardson are here in this very hotel. Yesterday morning, I was coming in to lunch, when I found the whole party on the steps. They had arrived on

Sunday night without my knowing anything of it ; the other hotel they intended putting up at was full. The telegram I sent to Naples has been attended to. I have received two since Sunday, and it appears that the ' Kedar ' will return to Naples early next month, I almost fear too soon for me to get back by her, but shall know more in a day or two, I think. The F's are very jolly and kind, and all's going on first rate. I have been out with them in the cool air, and have been with them since."

*May* 27 :—" I've just come in from the water, where I've been with the Fosters, enjoying another pageant that came off this evening, viz. the serenade of the Royal party down the Grand Canal. All the nobility were out, their fairy-like gilded gondolas forming a sort of a wall or passage in the middle of the Canal, all the gondoliers, &c., being in mediæval costume. These, with the enormous crowd of ordinary boats, and the great car, containing the performers waiting patiently until the Royal boats appeared from the Palace, and the whole floating city escorting them along,—the effect was thrilling and grand to a degree. Description is useless, and ah ! how often I wished you were with me. I must tell you that the heat is something tremendous, though I still go on with work, and my picture is going on very well, I think—I haven't let the F's see it. I bought a white felt broad-brimmed hat this morning, round which I wrap my white crape ; and I've ordered a cheap holland suit, such as is worn here, to be done by Friday. To-day I wrote to Naples on the chance that I may still go back by the ' Kedar ' ; I asked for particulars, and the date if possible. The F's go back *via* Switzerland and the Alps. Three days, and no letter. Well, I won't blame you, poor dears, for I know you must have plenty on hand ; but I confess to feeling disappointed this morning at having to get up without a letter, for when they do come, I always read them in bed over coffee. The heat seems to have driven some of the visitors away. This hotel is not so full as it was, but it is very comfortable. I have been reading ' Pickwick ' which I take out in my boat, and in the afternoon some seltzer to refresh me with, as I am rowed to and fro. By the way, that little book of Ruskin's is very good. I hear he was admiring my ' Well-diggers ' at the Gallery very much—this is from Foster. . . . I have slept very well lately. The boatmen used to wake me by their singing. There is a sort of boat station by the hotel side, such as would be a cab-rank in London, and the fellows are rather fond of glees at two or three in the morning. Well, I've disappeared without saying good night to the F's, so must go down and do a little cool drink, and so to bed, hoping that I shall see your handwriting or Fan's in the morning."

May 31, to his sister Mary :—

" I've just concluded the dreadful process of dressing, and now having struggled into my hollands and fortified myself with iced seltzer, I answer your letter, received this morning. And before I go further, I'd better tell you that this is the second letter I've had from you, and before receiving the other, I sent you a long one with a rough sketch of St. Mark's Tower in it ; and as you do not mention the letter, and question me as to my daily living, &c., I conclude that you never received it. I directed it to Braceley Cottage ; and I can only say that the bother and anxiety I've suffered as regards letters and their non-arrival, have tended more to keep me from being comfortable, than anything. My being 'savage' at not finding a letter here on my arrival, is scarcely the word. The last promise the Missus gave me was that letters should surely be waiting for me ; and if ever you go so great a distance as this, into a country where you don't know a word of the language, and by yourself, are kept in suspense for four days, as I was, you will know that it is no light matter. I could take by the throat any one I found keeping my letters back. After receiving your first, *nearly a week* elapsed without a line from Bayswater, and Mamma will show you the envelope containing the letter that reached me at length yesterday morning, and the way in which I secured it after all—that is, if it ever reaches her. I am afraid I cannot stay here much longer, on account of the heat, which is quite tropical. A funny little incident took place yesterday. An Englishman called a gondola near the Opera House, but the man wouldn't stir—it was mid-day, and I suppose as usual he was lying in the bottom of his boat—he called to another, and then to some more, but no, they wouldn't move. The Englishman just spoke to a gendarme officer who came down upon them, and said as they did not care to work, they shouldn't ; and all yesterday there were twenty unhappy gondoliers in their boats all of a row, not allowed to move the whole rest of the day. Talking of the Opera House, we all went last night, and though it was awfully hot, I enjoyed it immensely. It was 'La Favorita,' and 'Ange si pur' sounded beautiful. The Royal folks were there, and we were in a box—it's not considered the thing for ladies to be in the stalls. Great numbers of the gentlemen had fans, and used them all the evening like the ladies. . . . This hotel was once a palace, and it's most picturesque ; the outside from the Grand Canal is simply splendid. The Royal folks usually go about in a plain little gondola with four rowers ; men and boat being trimmed with blue, and a silver crown rising at the back of the seat. We went the other night to a *fête* at the Public Gardens. We were supplied with tickets for the aristocratic part by the proprietor of the hotel, which enabled us to mingle with the Royalty and nobility. The Princess is quite beautiful, and seems a very great favourite."

June 1, to his mother :—

" Your letter of Thursday came this morning, but I did not receive it until an hour ago, because I left with Foster and Mrs. Brown early this morning before post time, to go by steamer to a place called Chioggia—a town inhabited entirely by fishing people, and very picturesque—about twenty miles away in the Adriatic. We came back to dinner, and of course before sitting down I ran into my room for letters, and found yours, which I now answer, having finished dinner. . . . I expect this will be my last week here. The Fosters go at the end of this week, and I think by that time I shall be almost ready to leave. I haven't had a letter yet from Naples about the ' Kedar,' but may do so to-morrow. I read about the Derby yesterday, and am not sorry to have missed that, anyhow. . . . The reason the Fosters were so long in coming was, that at the last moment they arranged to drive from Marseilles to Genoa, which took up time. . . . The Fosters are going to take it easy, going home through Switzerland. I'd like to do it with them very well, but cannot afford it ; and, if possible, would after all prefer the ' Kedar,' for it would do me more good, I think. I cannot tell you how very often I think of home and its contents, and what we have gone through—its joys and sorrows. Ah, well, I hope you will soon be seeing me again now, and then we will talk of this as among the past. Bitter as some of our sorrows have been, we can, I hope, feel comfort in knowing that to the best of our limited powers, we tried to do our most—at least you did, at any rate."

*June* 2 :—" Just at this last moment before going to bed, I write to say that I sent another telegram to Naples, and the answer is that the ' Kedar ' does not return to Naples, but goes direct to Liverpool from Alexandria ; so it's all up with the idea of going home by her. And now I hear that the Fosters are leaving this on Thursday, and it's just possible that I may leave with them, going as far as Verona or some other place with them, and there leaving them, and getting home as fast as I can. I am almost finished with this place. I mean that I am tired of its very beauties, and longing to get back, and as usual I am in an uncertain state as to finances. All right, I think, as to getting back, but I want to begin afresh at home. So don't send any more letters on receipt of this ; I shall leave proper directions for letters being sent on, in case any arrive after I've left. As usual I feel that I haven't done a quarter the work I ought to have done, but it can't be helped. I've been to Lido to-day to begin a something else, and shall go there to-morrow, but the heat and other things prevent one doing the work that I'd like to do. I shall try to give you all account of my movements on getting home, but if you don't hear from me, you'll know it's all right. I am very well, and only want to be in old quarters again."

June 6, from the Hotel Cavour, Milan :—

" You see by the heading of this, that at last I am on my return, though the return will be a long one rather, for I have resolutely set my face against wilfully knocking myself up by a lot of night travelling. I left Venice early yesterday morning with the Fosters, and went with them to Verona. We got there at about two, and spent the afternoon in quietly driving about the place, and a wonderful old town it is, most beautifully lying at the tail end of the Alps. There is a stone amphi-theatre where the old gladiators fought, and fellows sat in their togas looking on. The Fosters had telegraphed for rooms, and we were made very comfortable. In leaving Venice with them, I avoided a world of discomfort, for the getting away is notoriously dreadful ; the confusion and bother quite maddening at the station, where they are awfully strict in searching all luggage, &c., and though I left the hotel with them I had my own gondola, for poor Antonio would insist upon my being served by himself and the lad, up to the last, although I had settled our little matters the night before. So I followed the Fosters up the canals, and tipped the lad through the curtains of the boat. Of course their courier managed everything at the station, and so my departure from Venice was a very different affair from what it might have been, had I left the place alone. We left Verona this morning, and I took leave of them finally at a place called Bergamo, where they had to change carriages, for they were going to the Lakes, and cross the Alps at St. Gothard, and finish up with the Rhine. They were all very sorry to lose me, I think, and I am sure I was to leave them, for they have been most jolly. Well, I arrived here at about half-past four, and there was the usual turning over of the baggage at the station, and I fancy the functionary thought he'd got a prize, for he literally turned over everything—all my shirts and things. My poor old flute was wrapped in one, and he even looked suspiciously at the end of it, till I said ' flauto ' ; and an old lanthorn that belonged to a gondola, which I am bringing home, was wrapped up in shavings so like tobacco, that he took out a pinch and sniffed at it ! However, he at last lifted his shako and thanked me, and I was soon driven here, and after dinner at the *table d'hôte*, I took a long walk, finishing up with the jolly public gardens that are near this hotel. I fear I must admit feeling a little solitary and home-sick in those gardens—so good and so prettily laid out, yet so very unlike ours—and then the little children seem so odd, with their small upturned faces lisping Italian. Ah, I shall indeed not be sorry to get back, and to do so I propose leaving this to-morrow, and sleeping to-morrow night at Turin, and on Monday I hope to cross the Alps at Mont Cenis. And I shall, I think, be among the very first of the public doing so by rail, for though it has been open for other purposes for some little time, it has not been available to the public as yet. The Duke of Sutherland was the first passenger about a fortnight ago, and he was chairman or something at the opening ceremony. The railway goes through the pass, side by side with the old carriage road, and of course, should I find after all that the railway is not opened on Monday, I cross in the usual way by diligence, and that takes ten hours, the other only four. At Turin, I sleep at the Hotel Feder, and next night shall be at Macon ; from Macon to Paris ; sleep there on Tuesday night—at Meurice's, I think—and may possibly get to town on Wednesday or Thursday. I cannot quite say which, but shall have time to send you another letter. So now, my dear, I've told you all of it in outline. I did think to write you a very long letter with lots in it, but somehow I am sleepy, and can't do justice to a long letter. They promised at

Venice to send on any letters arriving after my departure, and I suppose they'll *pour* in now I'm gone. In any case I sha'n't be very long after my letters."

The Mont Cenis railway at this time could only have been partially available for traffic of any kind, as the tunnel was not formally opened till some three years later. Walker crossed by diligence; wrote again from St. Michel; and arrived in London on June 11, after a holiday full of new experiences.

In the following week, he and his mother went to Goring for about a month; staying, by arrangement, in Mr. Heywood Hardy's house near the bridge. It was here he began the water colour, *Lilies*—a lady watering a border of flowers, where the old white lily is the conspicuous feature—and made a sketch for a large oil picture, to which reference will be made later on. From Goring he paid a flying visit to Crowcombe, in expectation of finding Mr. North there; but in this he was disappointed. Before long, however, another visit was arranged, and on August 3, he wrote to Mr. North :—

"With your letter this morning, there came one from the friend whom I mentioned. He went off to Boulogne on Saturday, as I told him I could not on any account leave town before Tuesday, when we were to meet at Paddington. He tells me that he finds Boulogne so jolly, and himself so much better, as to wish to remain there. Perhaps it is as well, for he is no angler; and sketching, to the mere spectator, is not exciting. Now I am bent upon going to you, but I certainly, in doing so, rely upon getting a little trout-fishing; and perhaps, as there is no necessity for starting on my friend's account, and as I must be back on Saturday in order to keep a promised visit with my sister to Birket Foster, it would be better to arrange, say, for next week. I know that good fishing is not easily had, unless you know the owners; and perhaps a little time and care would secure me that which I could not get by rushing down at once, with rod and fly-book. If by chance a letter were to come from you to-morrow morning, saying that you'd managed it, I might rush off at once, and in that case would telegraph from Paddington. But after all, as there is much for me to get through this week, perhaps a little delay would be better. So, like a good fellow, think over any of the jolly little bits that one might put on paper when you've shown them, and tell me if my writing to any one would help me to the fishing."

From the above it will be seen, that in going to Somersetshire, Walker had fishing, quite as much as work, in view. It was only when the place grew on him, that he decided to take up his quarters there for a time, and begin serious work. In a subsequent letter to Sir John Millais, he wrote :—

"I came here, as I thought, on a 'flying visit,' but the place is so completely lovely, and there's so much paintable material, that I expect to remain until quite the end of the month."

After a day or two spent at Mr. W. Agnew's house at Pendleton, near Manchester, he went to Crowcombe on August 13, and next day wrote to his mother as follows :—

"Here I am, and feeling well and happy. But, as usual, my arrival was unfortunate ; for though I had telegraphed from Bristol, there was no one at the little railway station here, to bring the message up, so on my arrival I found the telegram I'd sent, but no North to receive me ; and as I was then tired of my journey, and as it was just dark, I was by no means pleased, and expressed myself pretty strongly to the fellow at the station, who actually wished to know if I would take the telegram up with me—make myself the receiver as well as the sender of it ! I mean to have a little talk with the stationmaster, who had no right to leave the station with only one man there. However, I left my portmanteau there, and secured a man to guide me through the dark lanes. Of course poor North was very disgusted. He had not received the letter I wrote from Manchester [it came this morning], but he had been down to meet all the likely trains, as he expected I might arrive yesterday. I got here while a 'harvest home' was in full swing ; and after supper, took my cigar and glass into the old kitchen. Of course the singing and dancing were primitive enough ; and though they kept it up till past one, I never heard them, for the old place is large, and I slept like a top. To-day is lovely: fresh as early spring. N. and I took a stroll after breakfast, to see the beautiful bits close at hand ; and then we took ponies and rode to Sir W. Trevelyan's agent, who said all that was necessary, and ratified Sir W.'s permission ; but, alas, the stream is a mere brook, and though there are fish, they are small, and throwing the fly would be a mere farce. I am very savage ; but we are going directly to inquire if it be possible to get permission for the river Exe, which is sixteen or seventeen miles off, and which is notoriously good, but strictly preserved. If our intelligence is satisfactory, we shall go on Sunday, and perhaps North may leave me there ; but if we find it impossible, I perhaps will leave for town on Monday. I shall do a bit of work before I leave, and must go at it hard when I get back to my old dears ; but a week here would do me no harm, I'm sure, and old North is glad to have me. . . . You would like this place, dear. It stands very high, and the breeze is most strangely fresh, giving one that strange half sad feeling of having felt it before, in some more blissful state. The heather is very beautiful, and some of the foxgloves are not yet gone."

*August* 16.—"North and I have just come from a ride over the wonderful hills, and have just had a cup of tea. He reminded me that it would be no saving of time to write yesterday, so I do it now. I have been half wavering in my mind as to going home, or staying and working here until next month—I mean until we go to Scotland. The place is full of beautiful bits, and seems to agree with me perfectly. We are going this evening to see something very jolly. There is a wonderful little church, and a strange old cross in the churchyard [which might do for the background of that picture, if I lose no time], which we are going to see to-day. The fishing is a perfect failure ; I have given up the idea. We went for an hour or two last evening, but the brook—for it is nothing more, though we were told that, much lower down than where we went, we should find it much better—the brook is so buried in bushes and things, as to make throwing the fly an impossibility. I took one trout, however, that was not worth while carrying home, so put him back again. As for the other river I mentioned, it is too far off, and rather too late in the season for this part of the world. So now, if I stay—and North persuades me strongly—it will be only for work. This morning I did a little to the bee-hive subject ; a woman came with a baby, and is coming to-morrow. Indeed, it is easy enough to get models, for North is known to them all. What do you say ? Shall I stay and do my best here, or get back to you as soon as possible ? I sometimes want very much to get back ; and an hour afterwards, I see something that might be done, and feel it a sin to leave the place. This evening will decide me rather more I think ; anyhow I shall not leave to-morrow. . . . . Write, dear, to-morrow, and tell me if you'd rather have me return—that is, if you think I'll do more good by returning or remaining. If the latter, pack up the oil colours and brushes I had at Goring ; they are in a rush basket, are they not ? But I'll write again to-morrow, for I know what you'll say, ' only I can decide ' ; and a few days will suffice, I think, for whatever background I do in oils."

The bee-hive subject—a woman with a child in her arms, and a boy standing by, looking at some bee-hives—was begun at Beddington earlier in the year : the bee-hives were, in fact, altogether taken from those at the cottage. This was one of Walker's unexhibited works, and was shown for the first time at the exhibition of 1876. Reference will be made later on to the subject of the oil picture of which he speaks.

*August* 18 :—" Will you at once send all the colours and brushes, together with some benzole and turpentine ?—the latter is in a bottle on my studio mantelpiece, but the benzole you will have to buy. I am going to have a go at the background of the picture, as soon as it gets fine again. This has been an awful day ; it has not ceased raining since yesterday morning ; and you will be disgusted to hear that the parcel containing the thick boots and macintoshes has not arrived . . . . I have arranged with Mrs. Thorne, the farmer-*ess*, to stay on here in the same way as North. She said that of course she would be very happy, if I would but take things ' in the rough,' so that's all right, and I think it as well to stay on, for I shall do more work here. I have been working indoors on the bee-hive subject, from the figures, and am all agog for other work, directly the weather clears up, and just now it seems inclined that way ; the distant landscape from these windows shows itself for the first time to-day. My bedroom is as big as a chapel, with a sort of vaulted ceiling, and whitewashed rafters ; and though the rats scuttle about overhead, I sleep soundly enough, and have a good appetite, and manage a good breakfast even. . . . Old North is very nice—quiet and considerate *in small things ;* which is to me very refreshing. There is a feeling of repose about this place, which I enjoy after the eternal ' doing the civil ' of late."

*August* 19 :—" Another soaking day—never left off once ! Never mind, I'm getting on with the bee-hives, and am now going to write to Agnew about it. . . . The paints and other things have arrived safely ; many thanks for the thoughtful kindness. I see that dear Fan addressed it, so suppose you both had a hand in it. . . . I'm only afraid this rain will produce great floods in Scotland, and drive the salmon down into the sea. North and I went out this afternoon for a sharp walk, well wrapped up, and with his great sketching umbrella. The stupid little

trout stream is now quite a river. We picked some beautiful mushrooms coming back, which I carried home in my cap. I am taking great care of myself, especially changing my boots, &c. North would make me, if I didn't of my own accord."

August 21, to his sister Fanny :—

" Just had a cup of tea, and before going out again, write a line, for I sha'n't be back until dusk. I am just beginning the ' Mushroom Gatherers,' a little subject I've long thought of doing ; and when I've got it well under way, I go at the background of the picture [the canvas of which has arrived], and you'll be surprised to know that the subject is not the Stoke one, but the subject that Mummy has on her bedroom mantelpiece.

It is to my mind a better subject than the other ; rather less morbid, and with all the best part of it—I mean all the solemnity that such a thing well carried out could have. North has a proof of it, and he thinks it beyond comparison better than the other. The canvas is 3 feet 8 inches high. I've made one or two little mistakes since I've been here. A little water colour I began yesterday, I was obliged to destroy, because the paper was so impossibly bad."

The Stoke subject was, I believe, the old one of a boy looking at a man digging a grave, which was destined to crop up again still later, and yet was never carried out. The "less morbid" subject consisted of three figures in Puritan costume—an old clergyman holding a boy's hand, and offering words of comfort to him, and to the little sister who clings to his arm ; the scene being laid in a churchyard—and was taken from a wood drawing done some time before for Mr. Whymper, which appeared in a publication of The Religious Tract Society, called *English Sacred Poetry of the Olden Time*. Both these subjects, however, had to make way for *The Old Gate*, soon to be begun. The mention of the "impossibly bad" paper is worthy of notice. Mr. North tells me that, at this time, he and Walker often discussed the possibility of some plan whereby water-colour painters could obtain a paper that should be practically imperishable, and in every way fit for their work ; and that the scheme, having this for its object, which he has lately been engaged in perfecting, owes its inception to these conversations.

August 23, to his mother :—

" I began a little letter to you last evening, forgetting that it was Saturday, and that you could not get it until to-morrow, so I threw it in the fire, for there was but time to write the merest scribble. First I must tell you that the parcel has been recovered ! North and I yesterday made up our minds to go to Taunton, for two reasons ; to give the station people a passing bully, and then to buy some thick boots ; but on getting down to our little station, North came on the platform with the startling intelligence. Of course I was very glad, for it made a fresh pair of boots unnecessary, knowing that my jolly thick ones were in the parcel ; but I went on to Taunton with North, who bought his. We came back at about three ; and by that time, the rain, which had been falling all the morning, and the wind gradually rising, had increased to a perfect hurricane ; and to top all, when we got back to Stogumber station, there was no vehicle to carry us up. So I undid the parcel in the station, and donned my complete suit of waterproof, put on the boots, and defied the elements. How glad I was to have the things ! Poor North, of course, got drenched through in no time, and some of the steep narrow lanes, when it does come down as it has lately, are converted into rapid streams ; but I arrived here 'dry as a toast,' though at one time we had to go through water almost over the tops of our boots. I wanted North to share some of my waterproof, or wear my fishing stockings, but he wouldn't. He was very angry at the mistake of the people here not sending the cart or something ; however, we had some tea with a 'teaspoonful of brandy' in it, and were soon jolly again, and I began a little study of some mushrooms on some moss [*à la* Hunt], which I have nearly finished, and the evening concluded with flute, smoke, and talk. . . . This morning was truly lovely ; fresh and bright. We went for a ramble through some of the glorious sloping meadows, to get two or three more mushrooms to go on with. I feel mush-

MUSHROOMS AND FUNGI.

room mad. Some of them are lovely, and at dusk they gleam among the dark grass like stars. We propose getting up at dawn to-morrow, in order that I may get on with my ' Mushroom Gatherers,' which I think will be a success. I have had a sketching umbrella sent from town. I think I have been rather too apt to rough it in my open air work ; painting through difficulties, to my disadvantage."

The mushroom study was the well-known *Mushrooms and Fungi*, of which Mr. Ruskin wrote :—" It entirely beats my dear old William Hunt in the simplicity of its execution, and rivals him in the subtlest truth."

Mr. North tells me that Walker "almost worshipped the beautiful colour and texture of the mushroom. Many evenings in the 'dimse,' we have been out in the pouring rain, in macintoshes and fishing boots, getting hats full. I well remember the exact spot where we collected the other fungi [not the mushrooms] which he painted in that perfect water colour study."

*August* 26 :—" . . . Some time to-morrow, a small cartload of mushrooms will arrive in a basket or hamper. Some, and indeed the best, plucked by our own Royal hands, some by Lord North's, and the rest by our retainers. I think there will be a change in the weather ; everything in the distance is very distinct, and the wind is changing. North thinks my ' Mushroom Gatherers ' promises to be a great success— thinks the compo., &c., original ; so that's all right. I've nearly finished the little study of mushrooms, too, which I suppose Agnew or Gambart will have. I had hoped to finish the bee-hives, before this, but have had to alter parts. However, it's almost done now. The meadows look a most lovely green, and everything looks most jolly. I cannot tell when any time passed more smoothly, and if my work requires it, shall return here immediately on coming from Scotland."

*September* 1 :—" . . . At ' letter writing time ' yesterday, North and I went to that little stream. A long walk to get to it, but there was much bustle and noise here, in consequence of the farm being ' valued,' so work was pretty well interrupted. So we thought we'd ' loaf ' ; though North made a sketch when we got there, and I managed to take three small trout, which we have just eaten for breakfast. We walked back in the splendid moonlight, and I felt half sorry that I must so soon leave ; but no doubt I ought to come here immediately after my holiday, and get on with the oil picture."

The same date, to his sister Mary :—

" I shall be leaving this to-morrow, and so though late, I keep to my word about writing to you. I don't know how it is, but I seem to have done a most awful lot of writing ; always to some one or other in the afternoon, after a great stuffy dinner, to which I usually do justice I can tell you. . . .

"The above is a faithful representation of this dear old house, only I cannot give you its jolly old crumbly, aged look. It nestles on a hill side that on the top is covered with heather, and from which you can see the sea. The man who really owns the place . . . . takes possession at Christmas, and I suppose if he ever gets enough money to do it, he will proceed to make it into a ' modern residence.' There are queer old gargoyles at the corners of the towers ; one is a devil holding a man under him, and apparently biting off the back of his head. There is of course a lawn in front, and then lower, a large neglected garden that once contained fishponds ; and then again, the remains of the big gate—the stone sides, with what were once crests on the top. A cardinal once lived in it ; Beaufort, I think. My bedroom is that with the large bow window, and is about the size of a smallish chapel. No end of live stock ; three dogs who very soon made friends with me, and one of them, a sandy one with a wiry coat, always ' drops in ' at meal times, and the others very often. Three little pigs, too, roam the place in perfect happiness, the happiness that each day's work well done [stuffing without ceasing from morn till eve] can give. This morning on the lawn, one of the dogs was crunching some nameless mess or other, and the pigs soon heard the delightful sound, and came running up, and without exaggeration stood just as I've drawn 'em, watching for

" *Rose's Breakfast.*"

any accidental bit ; the dog every now and then giving a snap at them. . . . As for my work, I finished, and to-day send off, the 'Bee-hives ' ; have commenced a large water colour of ' Mushroom Gatherers ' ; nearly finished a small study [*à la* Hunt] of mushrooms, &c. ; and have laid all in train for going on with my oil picture when I come back. . . . Write to me soon, dear, and I'll reply. I hope you appreciate my sending the sketch. Those pigs are so tame, they run to me as I sit on the step, and take pieces of apple from my hand."

From the above description of the place, the reader will rightly conjecture that Walker was indebted to Halsway Court for the idea of *The Old Gate*. His forebodings as to the future of the house were to some extent realised, as the house has since been largely altered, and the gate is gone.

A few days after his return to town, Walker, his mother, and sister Fanny left for Scotland, where they were the guests of Mr. Ansdell, at Corrichoillie. During his stay there, Walker went for a short visit to Mr. W. Graham, at Pitlochrie, Perthshire, for some fishing. Writing from there on September 13, he first mentions Stobhall, which was next year to be the scene of the water colour drawing of *A Lady in a Garden, Perthshire*, of which Mr. Graham became the possessor.

By the end of September, Walker was back again in London ; and about the middle of October paid the visit to Freshwater, which Mrs. Richmond Ritchie mentions on page 96. Before leaving town, he completed the wood drawing for her story *From an Island*, which appeared in the November number of the *Cornhill*. This, and an illustration to a story by another hand, in the March number, represented his work on wood for the year.

Two days after his arrival at Freshwater, Walker wrote to his mother, October 15 :—

"I hope you received the telegram, and that it didn't alarm you. The fact is we all went yesterday for a picnic to Carisbrooke Castle, and I was in hopes of being back in time to write, but it was not to be. The day was a tremendous success, every one jolly ; one of those things done on the spur of the moment. I got here at about 10.30 on Tuesday night, after a detestable drive in the cold from Ryde. I had to change horses at Newport, or I don't think I'd have got here at all. . . . Miss Thackeray is going to take me to-morrow morning to see Tennyson. The day is lowering, and now it's beginning to rain ; but we all went this morning to the beacon on the glorious blowy downs."

*October* 16 :—"I shall perhaps stay until Monday morning, as to-morrow I shall be able to do a rose tree in Graham's water colour, from Tennyson's garden. We have all been to see him, and he has been most kind. I am very comfortable and well, but have had no *letters* as yet."

The water colour referred to was *Lilies*; which by this time had been bought by Mr. Graham.

*October* 18 :—"The letters this morning came all of a heap, and made me almost feel that I had been doing wrong ; first in coming here, and secondly in staying so long. Indeed, for a time, I heartily wished I had gone on Friday, and I should perhaps have escaped some of the prickings of conscience which I have felt, and which this morning's letters did not tend to allay. However, I start to-morrow early enough, and shall for some time do my best, I suppose either in ' pot boilers,' or something else. Meanwhile I must be content with the powers that have been given me to work as much as I can, and when I cannot feel equal to work, I must still make up my mind to rest, debts or no debts. One thing I am sure of ; that my work is not likely to suffer in point of refinement, from what I have experienced in my idleness here."

From Freshwater, Walker went direct to Crowcombe. He wrote from Taunton, October 19 :—

" While I'm waiting for the Crowcombe train, I write this, as I find I shall not have time when I get there. It's now 5, and the post leaves Halsway at 6. . . . Yesterday was horribly cold at Freshwater, but bright. I walked to the celebrated beacon, and made a sketch for a drawing for the story, as I find Miss Thackeray is obliged to carry it to another number of the magazine, if not two numbers, and of course I shall be asked to make more drawings. Tennyson was very jolly. We had tea there, and next day he came to see Miss Thackeray and me, and saw my water colour, &c., then we went for another walk. . . . I'm afraid my letter wasn't written in the best of spirits yesterday, and I was rather annoyed at having to break off, but the man goes to the post earlier on Sundays, or some such rubbish."

The story, *From an Island*, was carried to the December number of the *Cornhill*, but appeared without an illustration.

October 20, from Halsway Court :—

" Here I am again, as though I'd never been away, and have laid out everything for the battle, though actual work we haven't done to-day, either of us. I telegraphed from Salisbury yesterday to old North, who was waiting with the vehicle at the station. . . . The day here has been most lovely, nothing has changed yet. The trees for the most part are green and thick, and plenty of roses are out ; altogether it's more like spring than anything. We went to look at my background this morning, and I am delighted with it, and eager for the fray. I've written to that Eatwell for another canvas, more colours, &c., meanwhile I must do my best to finish off Graham's water colour, and send the little mushroom study to Agnew. . . . You must not mind if I stay here a longish time, for the work I intend doing is no joke, and if you feel at all uncomfortable at being alone, you *must come to me*, that's all."

October 21, to his sister Fanny :—

" . . . I'm waiting for another canvas and some colours, and am looking forward to the new picture with much pleasure, and it's not the one I spoke of, though I mean to do that too, but it's more truly original, I think, and the background is *splendid.* . . . . I don't know about doing another *Cornhill;* I don't see how I'm to do it here at all. . . . . Everything is lovely about here. As I was going to my work, I started a fine cock-pheasant quite close to me ; it reminded me of the black game we saw coming home on the coach. My best love to dear Mummy. I quite know all the old dear feels for me while I'm away, and hope I appreciate it."

To make clear the above allusion to " the new picture," it must be explained that, though not completed till the spring of 1870, *The Plough* was thus early in Walker's thoughts, and was the picture referred to. For the background of this picture, the hut, shortly to be mentioned, was put up. " The one I spoke of" was *The Old Gate*, exhibited at the Royal Academy in 1869.

October 22, to his mother :—

" Fan's letter was just too late for the post. North and I ran down to meet the mail cart, and half way down the lane, we heard him pass on

*The Evening's Excitement at Halsway. " Yes—No—can it be? Yes, it is the Mail Cart !"*

the main road at the bottom.  We ran like mad, and whistled ditto, but he never stopped, and in a ' winded ' condition, we heard the sound of wheels die away."

*October* 25 :—". . . I've all but finished the mushroom study—made a very different thing of it ; enlarged it, and introduced some very good bits, and North thinks it a great success.  The water colour of Graham's that gave me such trouble, I've done all but the figure, and I've taken out the lower part of it, for it was strained, and not up to the rest of the figure.  I've rubbed in an oil background, which promises everything, and old North seems to be astonished at my going ahead so."

*October* 27 :—". . . I won't tell you the subject of my work just now, dear.  I fancy that the picture loses some of its freshness with me, when I have been trying to describe it much."

*October* 28 :—" No news, all right and jolly, work going on well. Send us a something to read. . . . We went for a tremendous walk last evening.  Went to the sea, and back over the hill tops in the moonlight, and got home late, and pretty well tired."

*October* 29 :—". . . I ought to have sent off my mushrooms before this ; it is all but ready, but I've been too much engrossed with the other.  I wish Fan would let me have the skirt and petticoat I used for the girl in the garden.  A filthy nuisance, but I am glad I took it out, for I should never have been comfortable otherwise.  I shall be truly glad when I get it away ; must turn to it in a few days.  The other work goes on as well as possible."

*November* 1 :—". . . I have been trying to-day to finish the study, and shall send it off, I hope, to-morrow evening, and shall be glad enough to be rid of it.  Shall send it to our winter Exhibition. . . . A shock of earthquake was reported to be felt here Friday night, 10.30, though N. and I, who were sitting up, never felt it, but Mrs. Thorne says she did, and I believe it's rubbish.  We have a chirping mouse running about the place, who performs ' like a bird ' every evening.  North and I rush out for a rapid walk usually after breakfast, and also after dinner ; otherwise I believe we should swell up with eating, drinking, and work."

*November* 2 :—" I write a line now, as North and I are going at four o'clock to Taunton, for one or two things.  I shall try to get some red fire to burn on the top of the hill behind this.  We take down to the station at the same time the mushroom study, &c. ;  I'm going to offer it to Agnew. . . . The slight shock of earthquake, which North and I did *not* feel, appears to have been noticed everywhere.  How we missed feeling it I don't know, as we were sitting up, smoking and reading. . . . It's very windy here to-day, and impossible to do anything outside on a canvas.  Wish little Martin were here, and I'd finish Graham's water colour at once.   Well, I've no news.   Everything here is showing signs of the coming winter, and I shall have to work away."

*November* 5 :—" All right.   I don't mean to blow myself up with rockets, though we begin directly, for we've just had dinner. . . . I'm making arrangements to have a sort of shed or hut, built of boards, for the background of my great go.   This will keep me dry, and from the wind ; and as it's in a field, I can easily get the owner's permission, who is 'only too proud.'   No dear, you are mistaken.   Up to this time, Minerva has been the only 'attraction' here ; and I have often wished that there were some other, and less stern goddess, to worship.   The day has been fine, but cold ; and my work chiefly indoors, finishing Graham's water colour.   Do not blame me for carrying it as far as I can.   Work carried to the furthest, must always tell to the credit of the doer.   We went last night to a village near this, called Bicknoller, where live some decent people of Mrs. Thorne's connection, and made them happy by sitting and smoking by their fireside.   They have come up this evening to witness the fireworks, such as they are. . . .   I plucked these violets in our garden, an hour or so ago, in the most beautiful amber and grey evening.   The sun always sets more or less opposite the old place, and the effect generally, in this fine pure air, is such as to be seen, not described. I don't think you're well, or you would have written more, or given a reason for not doing so ; but of course it's only to be expected that we should fidget about each other while we're apart."

At the Exhibition of the Manchester Royal Institution this year, there was a £50 prize offered for the best oil picture ; and after consultation with Mr. Agnew, Walker's *Vagrants* had been sent.   The picture, however, failed to secure the prize, which was awarded to Mason's *Evening Hymn*.   On receiving news of this decision Walker wrote to his mother :—

*November* 13 :—" The enclosed will better explain itself.   Cannot be helped I suppose, and I cannot feel angry, for the picture it mentions I have the most unbounded admiration for.   I did not know it was at Manchester.   Two days, and no letter from home ! . . . To-day is very still, and a dark grey.   Yes, I must ask Graham for more money, or give him the option of having something else.   I shall hear from him, I expect, to-morrow or next day ; but he will see at once how different it is.   Poor old North sits and stares at it. . . .   The carpenter came yesterday about my wood hut, and I shall be in it directly it's ready."

*November* 15 :—" Just come in from a smart walk to Woolstone Moor, where my " [sketch of hut] " is going to be placed ; it's in hand now, and meanwhile I go on with my other work.   I had a nice little letter from Graham yesterday, saying by all means exhibit his water colour.   He will be in town in a fortnight, 'and can see it then.'   I feel half inclined to come up for a day or so, if only to meet him.   To-

morrow the water colour goes off to the Gallery, and Agnew and Gambart have promised to send my others down to the same place, properly framed, &c., so you see I need not be in town to superintend everything. Still very cold here, though bright, and I suppose healthy ; but the wind will keep in the one [infernal] quarter, and rob everything of half its lovely colour."

*November* 20 :—" Will you send me the volumes of ' The Ladies' Monthly Magazine ' ? I want to look at some of the dresses. Send 'em at once. Have had to work indoors to-day ; a shocking day, cheerless and altogether abominable ; but I don't mind as I am getting on with work. . . . I wish I'd got some more music. I'd give anything to be getting up ' Don Giovanni ' for instance. You see I've only my exercises, and I'm heartily sick of 'em. I never told you what a comfort the tobacco pouch was, and is. Before that I used to have miserable screws in paper, for of course I forgot my pouch in my hurry. We are going to-night to have a pipe with a nice old farmer, who has been much in America, &c. He has a great coarse white beard, and staring little bloodshot eyes, and always rides a thundering good horse, and altogether looks like a backwoodsman. Tell us what you think of my work at the Gallery, and what's said—whether it *looks* well, &c. I mean to astonish 'em before long, I can tell you."

Walker's exhibits at the Old Water Colour Society consisted of *Lilies*, *The Gondola*, and *Mushrooms and Fungi*, and were a decided success. It will suffice to quote from one writer, who found that : " Mr. Walker's compositions produce that unmistakable impression, and take that strong hold on the memory, which are reserved for work revealing the indescribable quality which, for want of a better word, is called ' genius.' " Of the two first-named drawings, the same writer said : " It is impossible to convey in words the charm of either of these drawings, but a man must be strangely insensible to grace, beauty, and truth, who does not feel their delightfulness."

It may be mentioned that at the sale of Mr. Graham's collection, *Lilies*—12¾ in. by 17½ in.—sold for £1,365.

*November* 22 :—" Just a line to say how glad I am that my things at the Gallery looked a success. I wish when you write you'd tell me if you noticed the little ticket ' sold ' in the corner of each. I recollected yesterday to my great alarm, that I omitted to write ' sold ' on the papers of the Society, and of course could only expect that they would be regarded by Thomas as for sale. I only thought of it at one o'clock yesterday, and immediately telegraphed to Thomas. I expect it hadn't arrived at the Gallery when you were there, and if the tickets were on them I shall know that it was taken for granted that they were already sold. It might lead to no end of bother, any one having, as he thought, bought one of

'em, and insist upon sticking to it.　Yesterday the wind changed at last.
It was warm and beautiful, but it has brought up deluges of rain to-day.
North and I have been down to the station for the books ; they had
arrived all safe.　Many thanks to Fan for doing 'em up so nicely, and
many thanks for the 'Illustrated' and 'Punch.'　I think you will see me
towards the end of the week, if but for a couple of days.　I suppose I
shall hear more about yesterday ; shall be glad to know of any critique
that appears.　We have just had tea, and of course I am up a tree with
my letters.　There never seems any time for anything with me.　I have
worked as usual to-day, and am only too savage that the daylight is so
short."

November 24, to his sister Fanny :—

" I've just struck work, and as old North hasn't yet come in [he's
working on the hills], I've had the lamp brought in, and so can finish off

" *The Hon. Member.*"

your letter before dinner.　I shall certainly be home by Saturday, though
I fear I shall not be up in time to go to the meeting at our Gallery, but
cannot tell until I see the time table.　If I am in time, I shall certainly

go, so you'll have to ' excuse me ' for an hour or two. I mean work now, and nothing but it. As for the Gallery, I rather expected the *Lilies* would come out strong in a way, and I am anxious to see it and the buyer. All right about the ticket 'sold' on the things. I'm sure that Foster having conferred with Thomas, meant that they were regarded as sold, and that the tickets were on them, but it gave me quite a turn when I thought of it, and five minutes after, Mrs. Thorne's son was galloping down to the station with my telegram. You see I did not like a crew of dealers and buyers to think that I'd sent three unsold things to our Gallery, even for five minutes. The Bee-hives, Agnew could not let me have. . . . I said in my letter to Foster, that I could answer for myself, that it was a pleasure to think of going to him at any season, &c., but that as far as you were concerned I could not say positively, as I knew you'd like to be with my mother ; meaning that if you or I go, the Missus goes with us. I think, with you, we must be together ; but I do not see why we should invite melancholy for our guest, by staying at the Burgh. . . . The last day or two here have been beautiful ; the colour most refined, and more sweet than words or brush can express, and the young moon already makes after dinner walking a pleasure. Old North came in perished. At my advice he has left a water colour that has nearly worn him out, and begun another for the time. Well, I've nothing more to say. Nothing takes place here, and there's no variety, scarcely, after work hours. . . . North and I are very glad Graham's in ; our politics go as far as that ! "

A day or so after this, Walker went to town for a week, and on his return wrote the letter to his mother now about to be given. This letter is printed only after much consideration, arising from a fear lest it should be strained in support of inferences at variance with the truth. Its suppression, however, would not only be inconsistent with the spirit in which this work has been undertaken, but would deprive the reader of assistance in forming his estimate of Walker's character. Nor, if taken in good faith, is there any reason why it should be suppressed. Of at least two members of the household, it is true that their nervously susceptible temperaments did act and react on one another in a detrimental manner ; but it would be most untrue to infer that they lived a life of strife in consequence. Far from this having been the case, their affection for one another increased as the years went by. In looking back, it seems to me that much to which Walker alludes is traceable to the effect of his brother John's death. That this deepened the shadows in his mother's life there is no doubt—my memory recalls no other change.

As the omission of any part of the letter might give rise to misconstruction, it is here given at full length :—

"HALSWAY, *Sunday, December* 6, '68.

"MY DEAREST MUMMY,—I half expected to find a line from you on the breakfast table—I don't know why, but I thought from the rather gloomy departure that a line would follow. I should have sent one from

Taunton while waiting for the Stogumber train, but that it would not reach you sooner than this. It strikes me that we are a lot of *sillies*, and don't know when we're well off—wanting everything at once—part of the general temperament, I fear. I was soon comfortable in the train, and by the time we were passing Goring, the sky was beautiful, and a sort of golden promise about everything. At Taunton, old North was on the platform looking out for me ; he'd taken the opportunity of going to buy a macintosh, a revolver, &c., and was evidently glad to see my 'mug' again. It was starlight and fine, and the drive from the station helped to make me enjoy the warm fire and hot supper waiting for us. I soon went to bed, for I felt very sleepy, slept till nearly ten, and came down to breakfast fresh and quite rested. North and I were soon deep in work when we met, and he urges me not to let my 'great go' get stale by leaving it entirely alone—work the smaller picture for the R. Academy, he says, by all means, but lay in foundation for the large one, and keep the mind well on it. The wood house is ready for me, and I shall take his advice. The smaller picture looks promising in its state, and to-morrow I bang away at it. It's a pouring wet day, but with our waterproofs on we're going out directly to look at some material [for my present picture] which North thinks better than some which I have been making do. We've had a *consultation* over the picture, and I do not see why it should not be a great success. I must ask you to send the big canvas at once ; it is much better I find than the one I have here. Let any carpenter put a light lid to the case ; explain to him that there must be room enough to enable me to carry the picture *wet*, that is with corks at the corners. Better not employ R——, he's such a fool ; let whoever does it take it to Paddington.

"We have been for our walk, and had tea. We made a long round of it, and went to see the beautiful background for the large picture. The wood house is not on the ground yet, but I expect the carpenter has it ready to put together. The air is fresh and fine, and in spite of the splashing rain, I have enjoyed to-day. It does not rain now, and I only hope to-morrow will be pretty dry.

"As for yesterday, and indeed other times, I more and more think that being too much together is bad for such nervous tempers as ours. The uncontrollable irritability at trifles often strikes me as startling, on my first going home after a long stay with people, where such a thing cannot be indulged in, for if it were, one would either quickly be put down, or looked upon as *mad*. It is terribly infectious, and to one like myself, such infection is unnecessary, for I am worse than any one, Heaven knows. For the rest, I think with you, that it is our *duty* to look forward, and that only. Fan will tell you that I have already (in what perhaps to her appeared a brutal way) urged the necessity of *only* looking forward ; for with our tempers any reflection or brooding means at once sinking into a slough of misery. Exertion of any kind, but especially away from the house, is the best antidote. One of the worst things is to regard any particular time or occasion as necessarily doleful, for any *special reason*—you quite know what I mean—for doing so means unfitting ourselves for the very work in hand, and we all have *plenty* to do, if we care to do it. This reads very like sermonising, I expect, but you know, dear, that I am preaching to *myself* almost entirely in writing this, and will indeed try to carry out the advice in your letter this morning. I will write, if all's well, to Fan to-morrow. At present there's scarcely time to get this posted, so I must break off. Best love to both, from their own,

"FRED."

The letter to his sister was written on December 8th. After speaking of her visiting various friends, Walker continues :—

"Only *leave them early*; I don't think you're up to that sort of thing quite enough. I recollect some one says, that at any 'evening out,' there is a kind of culminating moment, and happy the he or she who leaves then. By that you may understand a thousand things ; for instance, just as you've made a good impression, or crushed an enemy publicly, or feel that you're looking least tired, &c., &c. 'Going out' is frightfully hard work at any time, especially for one who hasn't £20,000, or who isn't an accomplished Adonis. This is horrible, but true. I shall be with you soon, and there's a long season to come. I don't think you keep or make *friends* enough ; pray what constant bosom friend have you ? It seems to me that you don't take pains enough, and are not tolerant of other people's faults—bothering, galling faults I mean, and every one has them. How is it you never called on Mrs. —, and only know that she's in town through me ? Or ——, or any of those who seem to have been kindly disposed towards you. This may seem like a 'nagging' lesson perhaps, but I know from hard experience, that people don't give something for nothing ; and to be courted, or anything more than just tolerated, one must be either clever, or have great taste, or something that shall make the sight of one's face a pleasure. Any one who hasn't a constant friend, is always liable to hours, evenings, afternoons, of ennui —that is if one is not content with the most neutral domestic kind of enjoyment, and must 'go out' for pleasure."

With reference to the mention of the large canvas, in the letter of December 6th, it may be said that the canvas on which *The Old Gate* had been begun was not that on which it was completed. It had been begun on a smaller canvas, and this canvas, Mr. North tells me, Walker took with him on one of his journeys to town. While there, he copied some of the work on to a larger canvas, which may very well be that referred to in the letter. Mr. North considers that portions of the original— noticeably some of the ivy, which had been painted direct from nature —are better than in the completed picture. The original canvas was in an advanced stage ; five out of the eight figures (though differently placed) being much more than indicated. This canvas, measuring 36 by 50 ins., against 54 by 66 of the finished picture, was among the works sold at

Christie's, after Walker's death, and has lately found a home in the City of Birmingham Museum and Art Gallery.

*December* 10 :—" . . . Enclosed is a sketch of one of the hand-maidens. She has a strange waddle, which I fancy I've managed, and always seems to come into the room headforemost. No news ; work going on well in spite of the high wind."

*" The young 'ooman who broke my flute—and said she didn't."*

On the same date, to myself :—

" . . . I've had to send my flute up to town to be mended ; one of the springs broken (servant, of course), but I shall have it to-morrow I expect. I am improving, I think, especially in tone ; while here, I seldom practise anything but exercises. We are going to spend the Christmas at Birket Foster's, as perhaps you know. I am not quite certain about the Mamma, though I want her to go very much ; there'll be so much going on, that she won't have time to be desponding. I'm working away on my oil picture ; I have not even divulged the subject yet. It's not a large one, and not much subject, but I hope to make it worthy. I am about to begin a six-footer though, that I hope to have in hand during the most of next year. Do you ever have time to look into our Gallery ? I can always give you admission, you know, and catalogue, if that's any inducement. I hear tremendous accounts of the new Academy—one room 80 feet long, and all large—twelve of them.

The 'line' done away with ; I mean its exclusiveness ; each picture, whether by R. A. or not, to be hung according to its merit. Floors of parquetry, flowers up the staircase, &c., &c. I made a descent upon the clique the other day when I went up to town. Your brother was working hard at his frieze for the new theatre, and seemed very cheery, so did the others. North here is doing capital work (water colour), he is most sincere over it, each inch wrought with gem-like care. I hope he'll get into our Society this time ; if his health is spared, I believe he'll do important things. Well, I've no news, you may be sure. One day here is very like another ; the place is full of beauties, but we never go for walks (except on Sundays) until it's dark, for the working hours are short enough just now. The place agrees with me, and so, between ourselves, do the regular hours and simple fare."

December 11, to his mother :—

"All right about the revolver ; be sure my eyes and hands are as valuable to *me* as to any one. My reason for sending for it is, that it may *not* be (to me) dangerous, *i.e.*, that I may know how to use it. We had some practice with it this morning, and it seemed a success. . . . . We went last night in the starlight, and had a look at my grand " (sketch of hut). "I am longing to begin, and have to-day, after lunch, prepared the large canvas with a fine foundation of white. . . . I should like to give a supper to the farm people, before I leave for Christmas ; could it be done with reason, do you think ? Could a basket of things be sent ? I mean things we don't get here, including some bottled beer, and *not* fowls, rabbits, or bacon."

*December* 13 :—" . . . I am very disgusted with the weather of the last two days ; yesterday was odious ; the work I did was indoors ; did not go out at all, and to-day is as bad. Added to this, the railway ruffians are detaining my flute somewhere. It was sent from Boosey's on Friday evening ; North and I are going down to slang them. They have a knack of leaving the things at Crowcombe Heathfield station, although they have long known better ; there it waits until one of the brutes feels inclined to bring it, and charge for bringing it, and the fools here pay of course. I think I shall take a return ticket and come up on Wednesday. I have been feeling rather bored, and impatient with everything. People I write to don't answer—John, for instance, though I merely wrote for the name of a song. People are quick enough in applying for anything *they* may want. As for the supper, think no more about it, a supply of drink which can be got here would be more welcome, I fancy. The other they would not appreciate, and so North thinks. . . . I should think from the character of the *day* here, that with you it was scarcely to be dignified by the name. Impossible not to be influenced by it."

*December* 15 :—" I shall leave this to-morrow by same train as last, taking a return ticket most likely. . . . The picture looks capital, and I am in good spirits once more. All news when you see me."

Here, with his spirits recovered for a time, the letters of 1868 come to an end, and this chapter can be closed. The year had been a memorable one in several ways. It had brought his brother's death, the visit to Venice, and the first of those sojournings in Somersetshire, which were to be continued at intervals till the spring of 1875.

## CHAPTER X.

### 1869.

THE opening of the new year found Walker at the house of Mr. Sartoris, Titchfield, Hants, on his way to Halsway, where Mrs. Thorne's tenancy was now coming to an end. He reached Halsway on January 5, and was soon at work again on *The Old Gate*. On January 7, he wrote to his mother :—

"No news to-day, save that work is going on capitally. . . . The weather is splendid for work, calm and grey ; and so warm that a great coat is scarcely necessary. I am delighted with my visit to the Sartoris's —sent a little note to Mrs. S. last evening, to tell her of my safe arrival, &c. . . . Mrs. Thorne does not leave this until Monday, instead of Friday, so I have a chance of doing most of my work on the background before the man comes in. . . . I have worked like an engine to-day, so want a walk."

Both Walker and Mr. North intended following Mrs. Thorne to her new home ; but the bustle of moving was not at all to Walker's liking, and on January 11, he was back again in London.

January 12, to his sister Fanny at Brighton :—

" . . . The train I was to have come by yesterday was the express, reaching town at six. But the Stogumber train ran off the line, to my great fright. Fortunately we were going slowly up an incline rather, but were dragged with a broken wheel half-a-mile. I had to assist certain ladies and children, and while the precious engine had gone for assistance, we all had to get on in the cold as best we could. Eventually we were carried to Taunton in a truck, luggage and all, and by that time, the express had long since left Taunton ; so instead of six, I did not get here till past ten. I shall go back on Thursday I expect, and the address will then be : Woolstone Moor, Williton, W. Somerset ; so we saw the last of Halsway, as a home, yesterday."

The house at Woolstone Moor may still be seen, though it too is altered. It is the first on the left-hand side as you enter the village after crossing the railway bridge in coming from Halsway. In Walker's time it was a long, low, stone house with a thatched roof. Since then, the walls have been heightened, a double gabled roof and bow-window added, and the front enclosed with iron pailings. It was from this house Walker went out to his work on *The Old Gate*, *The Plough*, *Mushroom Gatherers*, and *The Right of Way*. Here he waited for news from home, eagerly scanned the weather, blew at his flute, communed with his friend, and generally lived the quiet life he so well describes. The following interesting note supplied by Mr. North is a fitting introduction to these times :—

"Walker painted direct from nature, not from sketches. His ideal appeared to be to have suggestiveness in his work ; not by leaving out, but by painting in, detail, and then partly erasing it. This was especially noticeable in his water colour landscape work, which frequently passed through a stage of extreme elaboration of drawing, to be afterwards carefully worn away, so that a suggestiveness and softness resulted—not emptiness, but veiled detail. His knowledge of nature was sufficient to disgust him with the ordinary conventions which do duty for grass, leaves, and boughs ; and there is scarcely an inch of his work that has not been at one time a careful, loving study of fact. Every conscientious landscape painter will recognise in all Walker's landscape the clear evidence of direct work from nature. No trouble was excessive, no distance too great, if through trouble and travel some part of the picture might be better done. He never thought 'he could do better without nature,' or that 'nature put him out.'

"Pictorial art is a translation of a poem in the language of nature, which cannot be written in words. A delight in this unwritten language must belong to every fine painter—

> To hear with eyes belongs to love's fine wit.

"It was rarely that a title for his picture pleased him ; in consequence his titles are of the simplest—*Spring*, *Autumn*, *Bathers*, *The Plough*, *A Fishmonger's Shop*. One exception, and that a very happy one, is *The Harbour of Refuge*, a title suggested by Mr. Clayton.

"Perhaps the ambitious determination to excel in art was excessive in Walker, perhaps he had some intuition of the short time granted him, and so was impatient of partial failure. Certainly he was not content with his work unless it had suggestiveness, finish, and an appearance of ease ; and to the latter I sorrowfully feel that he gave rather too much weight, destroying many a lovely piece of earnest, sweetest work, because it did not appear to have been done without labour. Probably this excessive sensitiveness (to what is after all of minor importance) may have been due to a reaction from the somewhat unnatural clearness of definition in the early pictures of the Pre-Raphaelite Brotherhood.

"Walker could use, and did use, his left hand equally with the right, and often worked with both hands on a picture at the same moment ; as a rule, the left hand (which was the stronger) held a knife or razor, the right the brush. I think he would have missed his knife or razor more than his brush, had he lost either. The uncertain character of the paper led Walker into excessive use of Chinese white in his earlier water colours. This use of white he gradually diminished, until in some of his later work in water colours there is scarcely a trace, and that trace only existing because of some defect in the paper.

" In his oil pictures he used benzine or turpentine very freely, except with colours or mediums. He was not fastidious as to appliances ; anything would do for an easel, and for maulstick a rough stick of timber about 8 feet long, weighing about 20 lbs., was used, resting one end on the ground, the other on the top of the canvas. This answered two purposes ; its weight steadying the canvas, and its firmness giving real support to the wrist when (rarely indeed) Walker felt the need of such help. Painting in this rough and ready way, with no protection from wind, it was often more easy to work on a large canvas with it lying flat on the ground, and much of *The Plough* and other big pictures, was painted in this way.

" With a dark sealskin cap ; a thick woollen comforter—his mother's or sister's work ; a thick, dark overcoat ; long, yellow washleather leggings ; very neat, thick, Bond Street shooting boots ; painting cloths sticking out of pockets ; two or three pet brushes and a great oval wooden palette in one hand, and a common labourer's rush basket with colours and bottles, brushes and razors, tumbled in indiscriminately, in the other ; ' little Mr. Walker,' as the country people called him, was a type of energy. Sometimes I have known him manage to carry his large canvas on his head at the same time that his hands were employed as described, on occasion when, after having been kept indoors by the weather until quite late in the afternoon, his usual attendant help chanced to be momentarily absent."

Many were the letters that were to be written from Woolstone Moor. The first is to his mother, then at Brighton.

*January* 17 :—" All right, dearest ; got here safely, and am quite rested to-day. The place is most lovely ; far, far finer than Halsway, and the background for my big picture has been looking prime. What a day it has been too ! The primroses are out here, and the birds have been singing just as they do in summer. Great daisies turn their faces to the sun, and as we stood at dusk, a great beetle ' winged his drony flight ' past us. Fancy, January 17 ! North was, as you may be sure, very glad to see my face. We both go up to Halsway to our respective work to-morrow morning, and I hope to finish there this next week, and much of the picture I can do here—some trees, &c., are even better."

*January* 18 :—" . . . Yesterday was so balmy, and everything so lovely, I made sure you must all be enjoying it. . . . I found the picture looking all right, and have done well on it to-day. . . . Oh this place! as North and I saw it last evening ; *most* lovely."

*January* 20 :—" . . . I find myself so easily bored here to-day and yesterday ; am almost tired of North's blameless company even. Would like to get on a horse, and ride to the devil—so you see the kind of mind I'm in at this moment. Suppose you are well as can be expected, and suppose they are all enjoying themselves or trying to. Lovely weather here still, or I should go up to town for the figures of my picture. Shall be going for our evening's walk, so no more at present."

Same date, later :—"All right, old lady ; am comfortable again. Been for a long walk in the jolly moonlight. All's going on well, I think, though I am feeling very much away from every one. Shall try hard again to-morrow, for there's nothing like it. Hope from my heart that you are made pretty comfortable. There's much to be thankful for, and not the least [for me] that I am feeling healthily tired, and ready for sound sleep."

*January* 22 :—" Your note and Fan's, also the music, just arrived. The latter, I fear, would be of more use to Fan than to me, I forgot there is no one who could help me through some of the duets ; and I think that not being able to hear or play over the things helps to make me feel this solitude rather the more. Well, perhaps I shall look back on this healthy, simple way of living with gratitude, for healthful it is ; I was only just saying so to North. . . . We drive [usually] after break- fast to Halsway in a gig, with sandwiches and small flask of sherry in pocket ; am always ready for the sandwiches [which in town I could not eat] by one o'clock, take half the sherry, get a cup of tea at a cottage close by, at two, then at it again till five, when North makes his appear- ance. I then pack up, finish the sherry, and we perhaps walk home—did yesterday—or drive back in the dusk. Kind old Mrs. Thorne waits on us at dinner, and we wait for the letters, which come, if at all, about six. . . . . Do not mind an occasional *growl* from me, dear. I am lucky in having you to growl to, let alone everything else ; and in all other moments I know a *blessing* will follow me and my endeavours, if I ' keep my chin up,' and do my best. . . . This morning I had a letter from a Miss ——, with many crests and apologies, asking me if I'd teach her to paint ; that she'd give me no trouble, &c., would be content to watch me at it, &c. ! ! ! "

*January* 24 :—" . . . I shall finish at Halsway to-morrow, then go on hereabouts till the end of the week. I bought last evening a beautiful electrical machine, of an idiot at Williton, who is a cabinetmaker, and was going to cut up the case in which it stands. It is a disc machine, and is worth, I should say, £15 or more. I gave 37*s.* for it. So one of the youthful ambitions has been realised ! The case is the height of a table. Very cold, but bright to-day. The poor primroses will all be killed, I fear."

January 30, to his youngest sister :—

"I just take the opportunity of sending a line, while I'm eating my sandwiches in a cottage belonging to a nice old woman. I bring myself in when the wind's too abominable, and my fingers too numbed. She makes me a cup of tea, and I sit and drink it over her wood fire, and it's heavenly, not the finest wine can equal it. I bring my tea and sugar in my pocket, in the morning when I drive down [fancy me driving a shaggy horse and gig], and leave it in screws of paper on the table, if she's out in the fields. Poor old woman, deserted years ago by a brute of a husband, living alone now with her cat —a subdued kind of animal, who is bothering me now for a bit of bread or ham. The old woman can sometimes earn the noble sum of 8*d.* a day, by driving in hurdles, &c. She asked me if I'd got an old great coat I could spare her, and I think I have. I leave my picture in her cottage, for it's about three miles from Woolstone ; but I finish work here to-day, I think. On Monday, I try to work from a very beautiful tree at Woolstone ; and, please Heaven, on Tuesday, I go up to town, to whack into the figures. There are strawberry blossoms under the hedges already, and any number of primroses ; and some days so warm, that it's difficult to believe that it's this miserable month. Yesterday was too much though, and I gave it up at 3. I thought my arrangement of thatched hurdles, in which I work, would have gone to smithereens with me and the picture, although it's rather a knowing contrivance, and not only protects me from the wind, but makes it impossible for any idiot to come and bother me. . . . There's an awfully jolly little book, that you can put down or take up at any time—*lovely* writing—by Holmes, an American [strangely]. It's called 'The Autocrat of the Breakfast-table,' you get it ; it reminds faintly of Charles Lamb. I was one day telling old Mrs. Thorne that I felt 'low,' and she said, 'Why don't you take a little red lavender, sir ?' On inquiring what she meant, it appears to be an old receipt for the blues, and for disorders of the stomach. Mrs. T. said that her grandame had an affection of the stomach, always in pain, and took it daily ; could never bear herself until she had taken her daily dose—so many drops on lumps of sugar. I dare say any doctor would sneer at it, but I wonder if it would do the Missus good. Well, dear, I have filled the paper, and finished my tea, and must out again and at it."

February 1, to his sister Fanny :—

"Yours has just come—the only letter this evening, to my surprise— so I write to you, and no one else, though I've little to say, more than that I cannot get away to-morrow as I thought, and perhaps not on Wednesday, though I shall try hard, but I find my precious picture wants this, that, and t'other. To-day, or rather this afternoon (for the morning was pouring wet, and I only worked a little indoors) I have been putting in a most beautifully graceful tree, one of the most beautiful in line I ever saw, though of course, as usual, it seems to look nothing on canvas. I had all 'they' hurdles, as folks here call 'em, brought away in a cart from Halsway on Saturday evening, and put up again to-day in a meadow. With them was my picture, and you may guess I felt nervous; for a cart without springs, driven by a rough rustic, is not the most delicate mode of transit. But it was all right, and if I can only finish it in time for the R. A., I know it will be a success. . . . It has been terribly showery, and with lots of lightning and thunder. I have had to be content to work with my canvas covered with rain drops."

The next letter is to his mother, in reply to one from her, giving the result of the election of two Associates to the Royal Academy, which took place at this time ; Mr. E. J. Poynter and Mr. Geo. Mason being the successful candidates.

*February* 3 :—" . . . I cannot leave this until the day after to-morrow, or possibly Saturday. I am working as hard as I can, and as well, and one gets out of one's calculations. This I know ; I'll put my foot through my present work, before I let it go for less than a big sum. I do not intend working at high pressure for nothing now, and if the result does not come to me in one shape, by Heaven it shall in another, and I've said it. Your news was just as I expected—as I told North, in fact, and as I told you. Still it was *news*, and I've just written a hot and furious letter to ——, for it is rather too bad that all my friends should be such cowards, as to be unable to give me particulars of that which concerns me so much ; by this I mean, if I went to the ballot, how many votes, &c. Pray never sympathise with me on that which must inevitably form part of my life's struggles. That I am too young, I know well enough ; and time will only show if I grow ever old enough. Only by a strong hand, and as a matter of course, shall I ever obtain anything ; for well enough I know that great luck will never be mine. The day has been sublime, capital for work, so I am proportionately tired."

After this, Walker went to town to work on the figures of the picture. He returned to Woolstone on March 15, for a final struggle—and struggle it indeed proved to be.

*March* 16 :—" All right, and well. Got here at about 6.30, had dinner, took a walk, and to bed 10.30. This morning had a long consultation with North over the picture, and it is already much better. Shall stick to it hard."

*March* 19 :—" Work going on all right. Have found good models too, and am very hopeful of getting it done. Have a good struggle with it every day till dusk, and feel that it's gradually getting 'the thing.' . . . Don't expect much writing from me ; am tired now having just left off. Have been working on the man in the corner. Wind due W., and very gusty."

*March* 21 :—" All right. Don't expect much writing from me ; I am trying to give all my energies to this picture, and it's a great struggle. . . . The wind has changed again, I regret to say."

*March* 24 :—" All right ; work going on slowly, but well, in spite of cold. Have no news. North goes up to town to-morrow, so I shall be alone for the rest of the time. . . . When *will* this detestable wind change ? "

*March* 25 :—" . . . . North went up this morning, and I have continued the battle since, with all my might. Detachments of models present themselves for my inspection, and if this dreadful wind would but change, I should ' run in ' at a canter. As it is, I hope all will be well ; there's yet time to ' run a coup.' I am quite well, dear, and hope you two are bobbish. I *must* be home by about this day week. Am writing this and eating dinner same time, in order to catch the mail cart."

March 28, to Mr. North :—

" The weather . . . . seems to be reaching a sort of climax, for just now [at dusk] it was *snowing hard*, and so I hope for a change, but if it does not come, I'm dished—I never can do it. Haven't been to Halsway yet ; think of going to-morrow. Can you do me a service by going to the London Stereoscope Co. [Regent St. for instance] near the Quadrant, and get me a photo or two of dogs, such as might help me with the one I'm painting. They publish some very fine things in the way of dogs, and it is the one thing I might be helped in by a photo. My own people should do it, but they don't know my idea of the animal as you do."

Same date, to his eldest sister :—

" . . . . The weather's as bad as can be, and seems to have come to a climax. It's snowing hard, and I feel there must be a change, and if so, I shall be all right ; but I fear that if there be no change, I never can do enough to warrant sending. . . . I go on doing my best in the bitter weather, day by day, and really do not know if I am making a fool of myself or no. Sometimes I am in despair, and could weep with wretchedness, but never do, and then, generally, towards evening, I feel comforted. . . . This will just be in time for the mail cart."

March 29, to his mother :—

" Just to say I'm still keeping up, though almost disheartened. Cannot possibly say if it will be finished [it can never be *finished*] in time, but may be just passable. I am weary of *hearing* the cutting wind, and looking out on the dirty drifting clouds. I woke at dawn, hoping for a change, but saw from my bed the clouds going in the one eternal direction. Have had a bad headache all day, but have worked [indoors] pretty well. Do not possibly see how I can be home by Thursday, though may possibly by a later train on Friday."

*March* 31:—"I'm just off to Halsway, and as I don't return until dusk, send off a line now. I am still hopeful, though unable to say how things are going on. North came back last night—sent on a letter to say he should, as he fancied he might be of use to me, and I'm not sorry. I shall not be up before Friday night, perhaps come by the night mail due at Paddington 4 in the morning. Must be up on Saturday for the Water Colour election, so it will be a broken day, and should do no work at all in that case. The things go to the Academy on Tuesday evening next" [April 6], "not a fortnight hence as you suppose."

*April* 1: —"Send to Briggs, pay him his bill, £1, and get another female lay figure, full size. If he hasn't one, Newman's, 23, Soho Square, might let you have one, or tell you where. Let the lay figure be draped in black, ready for me. I leave this to-morrow afternoon at about 4, and shall be at Paddington at 11 something, and shall be ' out of town ' to every one save Millais, Graham, and Agnew. There's just a chance for me I think. Send for Dick Turley—they will give you their present address at the old one, 154, Seymour St., Euston Square—telegraph to him to come on Sunday morning, and write to Emily Hayward, tell her to come on Sunday morning to arrange with me. Her address is in the red book. I've nothing more to say, I think."

And so, by a supreme effort, *The Old Gate* was despatched to the Royal Academy. It is perhaps to be regretted that Walker was so often behind time in his preparation for the Academy. To say nothing of the effect of such a strain on himself, one is led to wonder whether work so hurried had always reached that stage of development to which he might possibly have brought it. On the other hand, however, had there been no need to work against time, it is possible that some of the pictures we know might have gone to swell the list of unfinished canvases. The reader will learn without surprise, that Walker was again at work on *The Old Gate* in the autumn.

Mr. North gives an old farmer's reminiscence of this picture as follows:—"I remember Mr. Walker when he was down here with you doing the old gate. What a way he was in if any one passed and tried to look. Why he made nothing of taking up his picture and running into the house with it. You know he got my missus to stand a bit, but she nor I nor none of us never got a chance of a look at what he was a drawing."

At the Old Water Colour election, Mr. North was again unsuccessful, and on April 16, Walker wrote to him as follows :—

"I fear you'll be wondering I never wrote. I began a little letter one night, but was literally too tired to go on. Well, the hanging is done, and a nice week's work it has been. I was at the Gallery yesterday, and the men all came in, but didn't knock me down and stamp on me, from which I 'opine' that we did our duty. I'm going on Monday morning with Graham's brother to some lovely trout fishing of his, in Hants; not so good I daresay, as Sir A. Hood's, but still about the best in England with that exception. We go for two or three days. We three dined together last night, the M.P. having 'paired' [whatever that may mean], and left 'the House' till 10, on purpose. I spent the Wednesday evening with them at Grosvenor Place, and they were all very nice, especially the girls. This evening I go to B. Foster's, till to-morrow night—went last Saturday—he wants me to do a water colour for him. I hear my picture was 'admired extremely' by the Council, according to Leighton, who sent me a nice little note to say so. He failed, however, to get me more than the one varnishing day, which was what I desired. Graham said at dinner last night, that the prospect of seeing the water colours I had been helping to hang, was quite marred by the thought that you were not to be seen there, and spoke in a very jolly way of you. I never told you that at the election, you had far more 'scratches' [before the balloting came on] than any one. . . . How about that scarf, and my cup and ball? You can send 'em if you like, and anything else I may have forgotten. They are rejecting tons of pictures at the R. A., I hear—I mean thousands—including all of ——'s. I decided upon not sending anything to our Gallery, and yesterday I told every one I was sorry; I did not say whether for them, or for myself."

The above mention of his cup and ball will recall to some readers the scene in Mr. du Maurier's world-famous *Trilby*, where Walker is represented as playing the game with Little Billee. Among some of the members of the Clique at this time, there was quite a mania for cup and ball, and Walker had taken the fever. It was held [with more or less gravity] that in acquiring the dexterity necessary to bring the ball on the pointed end of the stick, a delicacy of touch was gained, which was invaluable to the painter!

Though unsuccessful at the Water Colour Society election, Mr. North's works were fully appreciated by the Royal Academy, as the following letter to him, dated April 25, will show :—

"I suppose you received my telegram of last evening. I did not write, as I never heard of it till 7, and knowing you were anxious, I at once took a cab to Paddington, and the particulars are these. I called at Little Holland House, and while sitting with Watts, who was full of the Academy, he said, *à propos* of the water colours in the Exhibition, 'Do you know a Mr. North?' Of course I at once told him how much I knew of you and your work, and of the recent disgusting business at the

W. Colour Gallery.   He said, 'Then I beg you'll tell him, that we, the Council, President, and hangers, were *unanimously* charmed with his work, and that they each are not only hung, but well hung.'   He added that he only wished he'd told me sooner, if you were anxious, for I was with them at L. H. House a few evenings before.   So that's all right, stick to it !  I think I would as soon be appreciated by the Academy in its present healthy tone, as by the W. Colour Society.   The day before yesterday, I had to dance attendance at the Gallery 'in order to receive some of the Royal Family.'  By dancing attendance, I mean that, through some hideous stupidity of ——'s, I was at the Gallery by 11—when the Royal Family usually make their appearance—and they were, in this case, not expected till 3, when they came—Duchess of Cambridge, Prince and Princess Teck and suite.   The Princess is very jolly, and I had her a good deal to myself !   Both she and the Duchess asked if I'd been *idling*, observing 'I'd nothing there.'   I said 'No, I'd been working for the Academy ' ; this too with F. Tayler, Callow, &c. standing near !   The fishing of Graham's was delightful, and he was full of invitations to me for the ensuing Scotch season.   None of the fish ran large, but they were in beautiful condition, and gave lots of sport.   One day I took five brace. When I saw the water, I expected to do very little, as it was all running through chalk, and clear as crystal, requiring the very finest throwing and tackle, a fly scarcely to be seen, and always fishing up stream, which is no easy thing.   The varnishing day at the R. A. is next Thursday.   Watts says that two full lengths of Archbishops have been kicked out with ignominy, and that the slaughter generally has been frightful.   I scarcely think I ought to have written this, though, as it was perhaps the least bit in confidence.   Altogether, I don't think the number of pictures exhibited will be much in excess of last year, and that speaks volumes.   Watts says you ought to be working in oils."

The Exhibition of the Royal Academy of this year was, as will have been inferred, the first held in the present quarters at Burlington House. *The Old Gate* was hung in Room 7.   Though, as a matter of course, opinions differed somewhat as to its merit, the criticism of Mr. Tom Taylor in the *Times*, from which I quote, expresses with sufficient accuracy the verdict of the press.   Mr. Taylor says :—

" The first thing that strikes one in connection with it, is the power of arresting attention, and the art it shows, not of telling a story, which is common enough, but of setting those who study it to make a story for themselves, which is far rarer. . . . The composition is scattered, and the figures are too few for the space they are set in ; and, finally, parts of the picture, as the boy's figure behind the labourer, are manifestly unfinished. In spite of these drawbacks, the picture remains one of the few deeply impressed on the memory after leaving the Exhibition."   It was, I think, a not inapt remark of another critic, that the picture reminded him of a novel by Nathaniel Hawthorne.

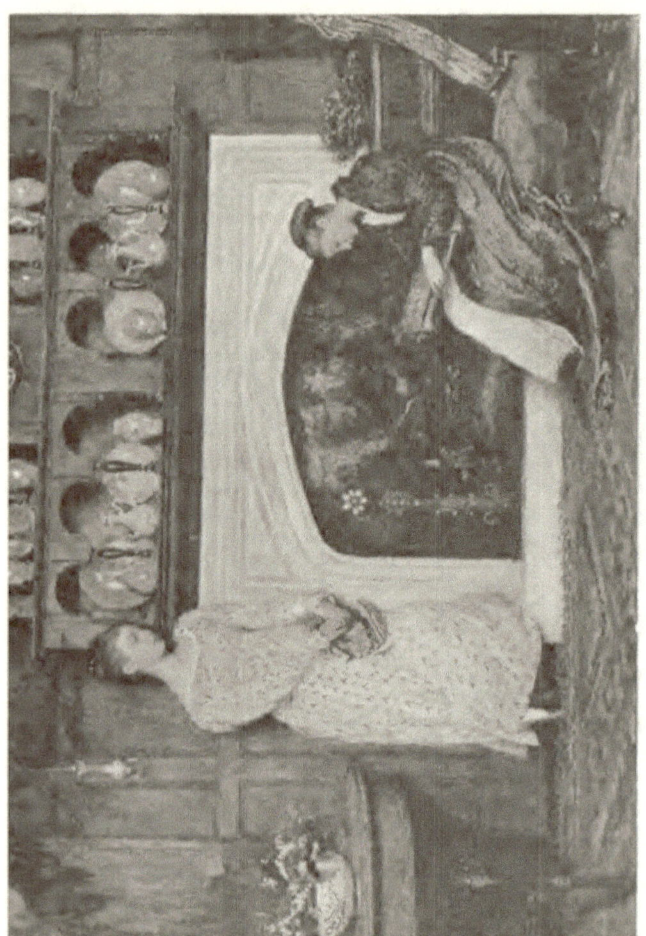

Two Girls at a Fireside.

*The Old Gate* has been etched by Professor H. Herkomer, R.A., and is now in the possession of A. E. Street, Esq.

Walker appears to have spent the months of May and June in town, and there are consequently no letters to give a clue to the work on which he was engaged. From other sources, however, I gather that it was about this time he produced the water colour of *Two Girls at a Fireside*, painted at Witley from the daughters of Mr. Birket Foster, and the pen and ink *Vagrants*, shown at the Winter Exhibition of the Old Water Colour Society in 1870. The illustration to Miss Thackeray's story, *Sola*, in the *Cornhill* for July, would also have been prepared in June. This illustration was the last for Miss Thackeray's writings, and also for the magazines. Its subject was subsequently reproduced in a charming little water colour, now in the possession of Mr. John Aird, M.P. Early in June, too, there is a suggestion from Mr. Agnew, that Walker should paint a water colour of *Wayfarers*; and as the drawing appears to have been finished by the middle of August, he would have been at work on it during this summer.

By the kindness of Mr. Swain, I am enabled to give in facsimile a letter referring to the illustration to *Sola*.

Early in July, Walker went to Maidenhead on a visit to Mr. Leslie. The following, dated July 12, is to Mr. North :—

" . . . . At present I am up the Thames—have been there all last week, and am going back to-night, with the intention of working next week at Bray, I think. I want you to send my sketching umbrella and the easel, directed to 6, Causeway Cottages, Maidenhead Bridge. I have been fishing last week, and had very good sport altogether, but I took no trout, which was my ambition, though I raised a very large one in a weir. The heat here to-day is almost too much of a good thing, and because it's blowing from the east, I fancy. I do not go to Scotland, I think, until next month, and meanwhile I shall be glad of intelligence from you, and let us know how your new ' material ' is getting on. Remember me to the good folk."

July 19, from Maidenhead, to his mother :—

" Just a line to say how much we enjoy the claret and chutnee. As for the sweet little bouquet, it is Bayswater all over, and ten times more precious than any made of Maidenhead blossom. The mignonette was hanging its head, but the jasmine and the carnation all right, and to-day they are all fresh as when picked. . . . This morning was grey and cool, but it has since cleared up, and blazing hot again. Mr. Fletcher and a nephew of Leslie's came last evening. The nephew is a middy, and had only arrived from foreign parts on Saturday. We went with them to the station to see them off, and moralised on all the Skindle folks, of whom there were plenty yesterday. We enjoy them very much—the conceit and general feeling that they are so splendid as to be beyond criticism. Well, there's a rod in pickle for one part of the business, and I am

Dear Mr Swain   I was on the
point of going out when the proof came
yesterday & therefore could give it more of
the attention it deserved — first let
me say I am delighted with it as
a piece of Engraving — it is easy to
see that very great care has been
given it —   I think that the only
part for a little careful Touching
is perhaps the girls face, & that is
I think rather too definite
as to her frown, so I think
that the little line
between the Eyebrows might
be almost taken away or
dotted as I have served it here
Then there is a little line which forms
the tip of the nose which may be
removed, likewise another little line
which conceals the nose with the
upper lip —  For so small a face

these things are too evident & indeed had better be taken away entirely, if it can be done judiciously & after all it is but a mere touch — & a mere touch might be given to the top corner of the Tall man's moustache : it rises rather too high into his cheek & in the proof gives him rather a smile which he should not have —

The foot of the girl is rather too square at the part where I have drawn the dotted line — it has too much this appearance —

I make these suggestions

in this way as I am sure that the slight touches
on the proof would be very little guide—

I am sorry the photo. is so unsatisfactory— let
Miss Thackeray have a proof if you can
spare one & believe me

Dear Mr Swain

Yours very truly    Fred^k Walker.

June 17 69

eagerly awaiting a letter from the Punch people.  Work goes on rather
slowly, the heat and blazing light being against it, but I am enjoying
myself very much, and getting as brown as a berry.  Farewell, my
dear, I am off; we are going down to Monkey Island to see what we
can do."

CAPTAIN JINKS OF THE "SELFISH" AND HIS FRIENDS ENJOYING THEMSELVES
ON THE RIVER.

The "rod in pickle" was the wood drawing which has already been
mentioned as appearing in *Punch* on August 21, 1869.  Of the circumstances under which this drawing was produced, and of the visit to
Maidenhead generally, Mr. Leslie has given the following interesting
account in *Our River* :—

"Walker spent three or four weeks with me at Mrs. Copeland's ; we
usually punted down each day to Monkey Island, where there was the
great attraction to him of two or three trout to be seen ; he never
succeeded in taking any of these, though he caught many large chub.
There was one large trout seen daily, turning over and over just off the
shoal at the top of the island, and here Walker had his punt moored, and
commenced a very beautiful oil picture of a boy fishing.  It was never
finished, and at his death I became the possessor of it ; though unfinished,
it is truth itself in the rendering of river effect.  The clay cliff, with its
rat holes, is perfect, and the shimmer of moving water finely expressed ;
there is something quite pathetic, too, in the little phantom of a boy, so
like in some way to poor Walker himself, casting his line with much

grace and eagerness. I remember well how uncomfortably he worked on this picture, which was propped up very insecurely in the boat, his tubes of colour, rags, and benzine bottle, all contained in a punt scoop ; and as he had forgotten his palette, he used a small bit of varnished wood, which belonged as a backboard to my punt. He had his rod and line beside him, stopping work many times to cast over the large trout's nose ; his boy Collins waited on him as his slave, and had to stand barefoot in the water whenever Walker wished.

"He had with him at that same time a large canvas with a commencement of a Thames bank on it, done, I believe, at Streatley. On this bank was a group of boys fishing ; the method with which this picture was begun was very curious, and was one he was fond of at that period ; the whole effect was laid in with the strongest yellow pigments—aureoline, cadmium, lemon-yellow, and burnt sienna.[1] So rich was the effect, or 'fat' as he called it, that a touch of black and white on it looked quite blue by the contrast. On this picture he worked a little furtively, in a small creek just below Monkey Island, putting in a lot of beautifully-touched forget-me-nots and other bank flowers; it was never finished, and the canvas remained for some time at Mrs. Copeland's.

*     *     *     *

"In these days he would break off work continually to fish, and kept his slave boy always ready to punt him about for that purpose. I altered our dinner hour from seven to eight to suit his convenience ; but even then he came home still later, and so we at length called it supper, and had a cold repast instead of a hot one. He generally had caught two or three large chub ; at supper, I remember working on his feelings about the cruelty of fishing, which he defended very well indeed by the usual arguments, but afterwards, he and I used to take a lantern, and go and let all his fish have their liberty ; it was rather fun, as it is one thing to hold a fish straight off the hook in an exhausted and drowning condition, and quite another to catch him in your hands, when he has recovered his strength, in the well of a punt.

*     *     *     *

"Walker, as a fisherman, had the greatest dislike to the steam launches, which at this time were becoming a rising nuisance, and it was whilst with me that, stung with anger, he made his clever drawing for 'Punch,' entitled 'Captain Jinks of the "Selfish," and his friends, enjoying themselves on the River.' He was most fastidious about this work, rehearsing it many times before he was satisfied ; sometimes it would look to him as though he had taken too much pains with it, and he carefully endeavoured to give it an air of ease and carelessness. Then all the ugliest and most disagreeable points about the affair had to be emphasised : the boiler extra large and clumsy, the smoke, the swell, the black-faced engineer, and the guests on board, with their backs to the

---

[1] (?) Raw sienna.

view, entirely wrapt up in their cigars and brandies and sodas.  In rendering the distant landscape, the work becomes entirely tender and finished
—it is a beautiful little bit of Bray, with the church and poplars drawn
direct from nature ; a bridge is introduced, to prevent the scene being too
easily recognised.  On the opposite bank is a portrait of myself, with
easel and picture upset by the steamer's swell ; this mishap had actually
occurred to me one day at Monkey Island.  Walker watched daily the
embarkation of the boat he had selected for his satire, and I recollect him
lying on the till of my punt, taking keen mental notes of the appearance
of the captain of the craft ; it reminded me forcibly of a cat watching a
bird hopping about in unconscious ignorance.  I was told that three copies
of ' Punch ' were sent to the steam-launch proprietor on the day of publication ; the likeness was very good, and indeed, every one up and down the
river knew it in a moment.  This clever bit of satire had no effect, however, in abating the nuisance in any way, and must have fallen like water
on a duck's back."

DESIGN FOR "CAPTAIN JINKS."

At the time of first writing the above, Mr. Leslie had thought that
the Thames bank canvas with the group of boys had been painted over ;
but in a footnote he says he has since found that the picture is in
existence, and is that which has been entitled *The Peaceful Thames*.
His surmise that the picture was begun at Streatley is, I believe,
correct ; and if so, it may be assumed that the sketch for a large oil picture,

mentioned on page 145, as having been made in June, 1868, was for this subject. The picture is well known from the etching by Mr. Waltner. After Walker's death, it came into the possession of Mr. Graham, and was sold, with the rest of his collection, in 1886, realising the sum of £1,218. It was stated from the rostrum, at the time of the sale, that the picture had been worked on by Mr. North in water colour ; and this is one of the instances where Walker's unfinished work has been added to in an honourable and open manner.

To return to the letters. The last few days of this river trip Walker spent at Monkey Island, and wrote from there on July 26 :—

"All right and jolly; just had supper. George has a bed here on the island, anyhow for to-night. I don't know about to-morrow night though, as perhaps I shall let him go to Maidenhead, and then he can call for any possible letters at Mrs. Copeland's, in the morning. I did very little work when I got here ; it was getting late, and got dark very soon. I thought we were going to have a pelting night of it, but it passed off with a few drops. I regret to say I lost another large fish, and there was no mistake about its being a trout. I thought I'd have an hour's fishing at seven, and we went steadily down for some time, till at last we saw a great fellow tumble about like a salmon. We went down cautiously, and I cast about the place where he rose, and about six yards lower down he came at the fly and I hooked him ; but after a tremendous flounder, showing his great yellow sides, he was off— unhooked himself in fact—rather too bad when I try so carefully. I shall do my hardest on my picture for the next three or four days. I find they have to send over to Bray for letters, but you can, if you like, direct to me here, as they are sure to be sending."

Walker's efforts to secure that coveted prize, a Thames trout, eventually met with success, as he took a beautifully shaped fish of 4½ lbs., the following year, under Bisham woods. Of this fish, he had a cast taken, which he intended to colour to the life ; but either the colour has faded, or he never carried it beyond the preliminary stage. In connection with this trout, Mr. Orchardson tells me that, in 1870, when Walker came to stay with him in Venice, he remembers meeting Walker, and steadying him as he stepped into the gondola, and how Walker, without a "How are you ?" or a word of greeting, clutched his hand, and said, "I've caught a 4 lb. trout !" As at that time Mr. Orchardson was not a fisherman, he was all the more impressed by Walker's enthusiasm.

*July* 29 :—" . . . The rain yesterday, and the high wind of to-day, have put me back, though I have been getting forward with work, thank Heaven. I have been dining with Calderon, Leslie, and Talfourd, at Skindle's, at C.'s invitation, and they walked back with me, all very jolly. Your letter came this morning all right. No news here of course. The place looks very charming, and one feels almost sorry to think of moving, but the comfort is that at least I shall work while in the North. The wind continues to rise, making me think of you all, for it seems to come from your quarter, and you must be getting it pretty rough. Late last night, George and the people here were out on the opposite bank, digging for bait for barbel fishing, with lanthorns, by the light of the moon. I pulled across after them, it was so picturesque. George appears to have caught two fine barbel this evening, while I was away ; so that's the best of the news. This morning was fresh and most lovely, before the wind rose   with a light golden mist."

The work Walker intended doing in the North was the water colour of *A Lady in a Garden, Perthshire*, painted, as already mentioned, at Stobhall— at that time rented by Mr. Graham. He did not, however, go there direct, and the first letter, after leaving town, is dated from Drumour Lodge, Dunkeld, August 5 :

" All right, and very comfortable, save that I know you'll have been looking for a letter, long before you get this ; but the post leaves this at 8 in the morning, and afterwards, unless some one goes on purpose to Dunkeld, it's all up. This is four miles from Dunkeld, all up hill. Mrs. Graham's brother [Mr. Lowndes] was waiting for me at the station with two spanking horses, and we drove away jolly. He was at the station yesterday, too, for the letters don't get here until 1 o'clock, so Mr. Graham didn't know until then that I was delayed. I'm sorry to say that there hasn't been enough rain to swell the river here, so there's not much chance of a salmon until it comes. The keeper sent up a grilse of about 4 lbs., that they'd taken with the fly to-day ; but until we have a day and night's rain, the fish will be at the river's mouth below Perth, and nothing will bring 'em up. So I think that next week I shall go up to the Ansdell's. Graham and I have this afternoon been fishing in a stream that runs below this, something in the same way as the Spean below Corrichoillie, only that it's smaller, though the hills on the opposite side are grand and melancholy. We had very poor sport, and to-morrow we are going up to the loch that feeds this stream, which is called the Braan, and only contains trout. We three are the only swells here  stuck up on a great wooded height, in a pretty ivy-grown house with a pinnacled tower, and a verandah running all along the front, supported by tree trunks with the rough knobs left. I got to Perth at about 12 last night, and tumbled into bed at the hotel, tired enough. Three old chaps got in at Preston, previous to which I had been alone with the Times, Saturday Review, and Punch. The old chaps were very jolly, and offered me big purple grapes and peaches ; but I'd been eating your little grapes, and didn't feel much inclined for theirs. This place is very beautiful ; the sweet banks with the long grass that's not yet quite ripe—I mean no hay cut yet—and the dear old grey rocks, and old blue hills with clouds half way up them, and the same sound of the stream (like Corrichoillie again) that one hears from one's bedroom window. As we were coming from the fishing, we espied a lot of mushrooms, like

great pearls on the sloping bank. We gathered a lot, and they made
one of the dishes at dinner. I wish you were both up North here. I
thought of you, and as I passed the great iron furnaces as you near
Glasgow, I declare it seemed but yesterday that I was telling you to look
out for them. The man has ransacked my portmanteau, and put
everything neatly into drawers and things, as though I were to stay here

" *The Member's Brother.* "

a month. I left it open (after locking cheque-book and other things
into the hat-box), for I thought it nice, and even felt a pride that
my portmanteau was filled with such good things. Well, dear, I must
break off. W. Graham has not left town yet, I find, though I expect
he will be at Urrard by Sunday if I go over, as I think of doing. Good
night to both."

*August* 8 :—" I may as well begin a line or two for you now,
before lunch, though the letters have not come in yet. Mr.
Lowndes [Mrs. Graham's brother] has driven to Dunkeld to church,
and will bring them. Mr. Graham and I have been for a longish walk
in the fine fresh air. We went to look at some falls, very good,
reminded me of the Cour that runs into the Spean. To-morrow we go

down to the Tay to do our best, and early on Tuesday morning, I go first up to Urrard [Mrs. W. Graham is there with the girls, though Mr. W. is not] on my way to the Ansdell's, which I hope to reach by the coach from Kingussie, on Tuesday evening. The work which I propose doing, I shall do when I leave the Ansdell's; this for many reasons, but chiefly because Mr. W. Graham will be here by that time, and can make it comfortable for me if he chooses—he might give me room at Stobhall— and then I expect the Tay will be in better condition for fishing. . . . . It is very peaceful and lovely up here, but I think a little hard work in the way of clambering about the Tay rocks, or down the Spean all day, will not come ill."

*August* 9 :—" I leave this to-morrow morning for Corrichoillie; I secured a letter from Mrs. A., at Dunkeld, as we were coming up from the fishing. She has room for me, and the weather there appears to be good for fishing. We had no sport to-day. I rose three fish, and lost a fourth after a minute's play, and only succeeded in taking a good sea trout. Mr. Graham did nothing. I made a point of going over the garden at Stobhall, and it was very lovely, and I fully intend going at it after a stay at the A.'s. . . . I have this subject, and another which I can commence at the Ansdell's. . . . Mr. G. here, and Mr. Lowndes, advise me to write to W. Graham in time for him to make arrangements for the Stobhall picture for me, and this I intend doing."

August 11, from Corrichoillie :—

" Here safe and sound, and enjoying self. Been out, took one salmon, and lost another. Ansdell took one, and lost three. Shall be on a very good beat to-morrow, and expect sport. All here very kind, and just the same. I did not come up to the house until about 11 last night instead of 7.30. The coach broke down, and it's a wonder some of us weren't smashed. The axle broke, providentially in the middle; had it broken close to the wheel, we should have overturned. As it was, we were kept on the road till five in the evening, to my great disgust. However, I was none the worse for it this morning. I shall commence a water colour on Saturday, I think, and anyhow shall work at it on Sunday. Everything looks lovely here, though it's chilly, and plenty of snow on Ben Nevis, and some on another mountain."

August 18, to his sister Fanny :—

" The salmon, which I suppose has reached you by this, was one of three which I took the day before yesterday; that sent to you was 14½, the other two, 21 and 8. Yesterday I lost a tremendous fellow; he broke the hook [in his jawbone we think] after a violent fight. To-day I am not fishing. Lord Abinger has the best beat, and I want to get on with my work. I do not think I shall be here for more than a week—I may leave on Monday next, even. I had another letter from W. Graham last evening ; he can, he thinks, arrange for my stay for two or three days at Stobhall."

August 29, from Urrard, Pitlochrie, to his mother :—

" Here I am, and very comfortable. I left the A.'s on Friday morning, early as usual, and got here at about 3. To my delight, there was at the station Miss Graham, seeing off some friends who had been staying here, and she told me that her father had been expecting me for the whole week ; so, of course, there was some stupid mistake about the letters, for, goodness knows, I should have been glad enough to come a week ago. There are some nice people here. Two daughters of Kinnaird the M.P., a Mr. Hardy, son of Gathorne Hardy the M.P., &c. I think I shall go to Stobhall to-morrow, and shall probably think of going homewards in about a week from this. The letters had better be directed to Stobhall, Stanley, Perthshire ; for though I may possibly be staying at a ferryhouse belonging to one of the river keepers, where I can get better food and drink than up at Stobhall, yet I shall be there each day. No chance of more fishing ; the glass is high as ever, and the river nowhere. . . . Graham has the ' Vagrants ' and the ' Lilies ' here ; he seems to be unable to leave them behind him. He's very jolly."

September 1, from Stobhall, to his sister Fanny :—

" Just before getting to work, I send off to you a few lines, as I owe them, for the last you had from me was short indeed. The easel, &c., I found at Stanley station all right, and yesterday I got to work. I am not staying here exactly, but at a little ferryhouse near, because I can get better served than here ; but I am here all day, and Graham and his friend Hardy arrived last evening from Urrard, to shoot partridges to-day. So I dined with them here last evening, and as Graham proposed fishing the only place on the river worth fishing, early this morning, I have break-fasted here with them. They have gone out, and I can hear their guns banging away, so I suppose they are having sport. I left Urrard, Monday afternoon. I was sorry to leave, but one cannot stick in one place for ever ; besides, I shall get into a mess about work if I don't mind. . . . You'd revel in this place. It has queer old turrets, and carved coronets and dates on the arches, and the garden is the very perfection of peace and loveliness. I hope I'll soon get forward with work, for I am rather want-ing to get back to the ' nest ' again, I confess. I said I should start in about a week, I thought, but I really cannot tell for certain. As for the fishing, until there's rain, and plenty of it, it's all up. We didn't have a rise, though *we rose* before six, and were quite disgusted ; so we took to fishing for Tay pearls, opening the fresh water mussels as we waded, but our luck was not great. Graham got rather a large one, and I enclose my spoils—we might have got more, but had to go in to breakfast. . . . It's very fresh and cold here, mornings and evenings ; a hard frost on Sunday night, killing off all dahlias, nasturtiums, and potato plants. I

never saw such a wreck as at Urrard on Monday morning ; yet on Saturday, the heat was so great at mid-day, that a great mastiff, kept at the
coach houses, was found dead, as is supposed from sunstroke. . . . I often
think it seems rather a shame that you and the Missus cannot see these jolly
places, because it certainly means *change*, if not happiness.  As for the
latter, I think that a certain medium supply of it is 'served out' to every
one, in a way, if one can only see it ; that hunting for it brings it no
nearer.  [Moral mem.]"

September 2, to his mother :—

"  . . . You ask if I am well, &c.  Of course i am, and never
better than when here in the North.  I only wish I could afford to loaf
about here three months every year.  Graham had a hamper containing
wine and good things prepared for me while I am here, and like a brick,
left a brace of partridges yesterday ; and with trout and all, you see I
am living on the fat o' the land.  They make me a jolly cup of tea up
at the Hall, and a supply of sherry and biscuits is always at my command there.  I am better here, than if I were altogether at the Hall,
because the people there are not exactly servants.  The factor, or
manager, of the estate lives there ; and I fancy they do not care to
lodge any one but just Graham himself, though they are very obliging,
and I had a letter from the said factor, hoping I would command him

and the place in any way, &c.   Here, the ferryman generally begins the day by, ' Eh, Sirr, ye have anither lovely marrning for that laborious fishing,' or some joke of that kind, as he brings in my bath.   The gude-wife cooks admirably.   After this, I am going to write a line to Mrs. Gray, saying I am here, and that I will pass next Sunday at Perth, if they can have me."

*September* 4 :—" I find, to my great disgust, that no letters are to be had to-day, not even by sending up to the Post Office, so I must be content to wait until to-morrow at noon, when I have them sent up to Stobhall by a lad.   I am getting on pretty well with work, thank goodness ; I mean that I am satisfied with it so far.   It will be a com-panion to the ' Lilies,' and Graham asked me to let him see it, if possible, before any one else.   I said I would, at the same time mentioning that Agnew, &c., had asked me specially for a subject of the kind.   I think I shall be quite finished by Wednesday evening, so I think you may look for me by Thursday night, unless anything unforeseen should happen—rain, for instance, enough to prevent work, and raise the river. I understand there was a heavy shower early this morning, before I was awake ; everything seems very fresh in consequence. . . . I am going to spend the afternoon at Perth.   I had a letter from young Gray, saying how pleased his mother would be to see me, if I would excuse an empty house, all the rest being away at St. Andrews. . . . The sprigs of jasmine I put in the glass containing my paint water, and lo, they partly revived and are opening, and give forth perfume more precious than all the Stobhall flowers put together."

*September* 7 :—" I found on Sunday, that no letters would be leaving Stanley, so I took yours into Perth with me, but was too late for the post, so then I knew you would not get it till to-day.   Most annoying. Thomas the ferryman here, like a true Scot, said something about the ' seventh day ' being a ' great blessing,' or something of the kind, and I was nearly saying that, when away from every one, getting one's letters on the ' Sawbath ' was also a great blessing ; but he would only have thought I meant to be disagreeable.   The fact is, I am beginning to find this solitude oppressive, and shall not be sorry to leave, as there's still no fishing to be done ; but I think you must make up your mind to do without me till Saturday, as I have rather a wish to spend a day at St. Andrews [which is on the coast, you know], where the Grays and Millais are."

September 9, from St. Andrews :—

" All right.   Have just arrived here, and just had lunch.   They are all most kind, and they want me to stay over to-morrow, and I feel half inclined to do so.   You'll say it's weak-minded, perhaps.   There's a Ball to-night, and they've taken a ticket for me ; and altogether I should, I confess, like to stay a day or two here.   So don't expect me on Saturday night, dear. I fear you'll be disappointed, but a day or two more won't matter—I shall work all the better for it."

As Walker spent the next three weeks in town, there is no record of the work [if any] on which he was engaged. Neither, in the absence of any mention of the subject of the drawing begun at Corrichoillie, can it be ascertained if this work was ever completed. The Stobhall drawing necessitated another visit to Perthshire ; and on October 3, Walker was again at Perth, on his way to Stanley. On October 4, he wrote from Stobhall :—

" The four fish I sent off just before dinner, went just sooner than I expected, and so this letter, which I hoped to send with them, is of no use—that is, I intended just suggesting that the fish should go to folks in your name or mine, as trifling compliments. . . . The two large ones are not in such good condition as I could wish ; indeed it's getting late, and the fishing, you know, ends on Saturday. But the larger of the two small ones is just fresh from the sea, and looked like ivory, as he jumped and rushed. I hooked him from a rather difficult bank, after just losing one which I played until he was spent, and then he got off, because both the keepers were round the river bank in the boat, out of sight, and I could not make them hear—most provoking. Altogether I must have lost half a dozen fish to-day. The river is simply splendid—a sight for ' sore eyes,' I can tell you—as much as the two men could do, both rowing hard, to keep the boat stationary. The day has been glorious, and yesterday was jolly too ; the dear solemn garden here, scarcely changed since I left it. Here there is a man who waits on me—a lean old chap with grey whiskers—he plays the violin, and fell in love with my flute, at once. I heard him just now, after dinner, playing a reel in the distance ; and on complimenting him when he came up with some seltzer just now, he ' ventured to ask me for A or B flat ' ! which I gave him, and of course, he gave me the reel again on the spot. Altogether I am very glad I came. After to-morrow, I shall do the final work to my ' Perthshire Garden,' and make it much better, I'm sure. . . . God bless all at home. I am sure I was right in coming here now ; the work will lose nothing by it, I feel sure."

From this point, to the end of the year, there are, unfortunately, many letters missing. Walker was at Woolstone Moor in November, but for how long, and whether his stay extended into December, cannot now be ascertained. In all probability, he was there the greater part of both months ; for *The Plough* was the next important work on hand, and would have taxed all his energies. It is interesting to find from a letter of Mrs. Walker's, in December, that Walker was at that time attuning his mind to the subject, by reading Thomson's *Seasons* and Bloomfield's *Farmer's Boy* ; and one letter, fortunately preserved, shows in a striking manner, how much his thoughts were concentrated on the picture. Of the other work of this year, little more remains to be said. If the year

1868 had been the most prolific in exhibited work, the present year was one of the most barren ; for the Stobhall drawing at the Winter Exhibition of the Old Water Colour Society, and *The Old Gate* at the Royal Academy, were the only two exhibits in 1869. The Stobhall drawing was exhibited under the title already given—viz. *A Lady in a Garden, Perthshire ;* and the fact that at the sale of the Graham collection it was catalogued as *Stobhall Garden,* has led at least one critic into the error of supposing there were two distinct drawings. Though painted as a companion to *Lilies,* this drawing was appraised at the sale at the sum of £567, against the £1,365 of the former. I believe, however, there were special reasons for the high price given for *Lilies.*

A short letter, dated from Woolstone, November 11, and evidently not the first of a series, is only of interest as showing that Walker had already been in Somersetshire for some little time. The next letter— that referred to as having been fortunately preserved—is dated November 17, and addressed to his sister Mary :—

" I rather expected to have another line from you, and you know your little handwriting has always been welcome to me—trebly so in this place, where one *waits* for the letters—but as you won't, or, dear, as you *can't,* and I know you must be busy at the new home, I scrawl a line to you over my pipe, and a glass of ' summat to drink,' while old North and fat old Mrs. Thorne [Mrs. Poyser she always seems like to me] are playing at all fours, or some such dreadful game. I must tell you that I go up to town for a week or so on Saturday, to see about the Stobhall picture, and the Water Colour Exhibition, &c., and to make a study or two for the picture I have commenced here ; and since you ask what it's all about, I'll tell you, but I think I must have already done so, for you know I intended doing it last year, and had the little wood house made, opposite the field of action, where it stood through all the summer, and got so warped that it had to be covered all over with a kind of felting stuff ; and to-day a little stove was rigged up in it, with the chimney coming out of the roof thus " (a slight sketch) : " looking absurd enough. However, it helps to make it snug, and I intend making tea there—when the fire's lighted, it roars again. Well, this is opposite a grand old stone quarry, that is wonderful in the evening light, with trees and a fringe of green on the top, but all crags and like a cliff ; and descending from it, fields with good undulating line, and the place suggests something quite wild, and far away from every one. At mid-distance, I intend having a little line of figures—field labourers, seen in profile, as they often are, and sometimes they compose most beautifully—all in different action. Then nearer still, a large spread of bloomy, newly-ploughed earth, purple you know, and sparkling, and still in rather a wavy sort of line ; and right in front, THE PLOUGH, in full action, guided by a strong man. The near horse, *white* in tone rather, with yellowish mane and tail, telling against the dense earth just ploughed up ; and guiding the horses, with long reins, a boy, active and graceful, if I can do him ; and *indigo*

rooks circling about—at least with rather blue lights on them—one just
poised, before he drops on a furrow.   Some teasels and large weeds, right
in the foreground, such as keep their form through the ploughing months ;
the dress of the figures not suggesting any particular time—not the present,
that is—if I can only do it.   The subject is a good one, as you'd say if
you saw the place lit up with the evening glow from the front ; anyhow,
I intend doing all I can with it.   The plough is really very graceful in line ;
some of them a faded vermilion colour.   So now I think I've told you the
subject for my ' next.'   The Missus tells me you are likely to be comfortable, she thinks, where you are ;   more so indeed than at the place you've
left.   She says that you will be able to receive a poor tootler sometimes,
who'll only be too happy, dear, as you know.   I've just been religiously
going through the new trio I mentioned to you—for conscience' sake—
though it's a bother having to practise among folks who don't know or
care a bit about it.   This place is full of geese and chickens ; the former
are rampant.   The moor or green is opposite this, and the railway cuts off
a corner of it.   The geese somehow get on the line, and hiss at the train,
I hear, getting smashed of course while they're about it.   There's a dog
here too, a sandy one, who took to me at first, and now goes down with
me to the wood house.   He is fond of nuts, and cracks them himself,
like a Christian.   North and I generally keep to our practice of taking a
long walk at night, before going to bed ; it's the best thing we can do,
and makes one sleep ; though he, poor fellow, has been tortured with
neuralgia for the last day or two, but is all right now.   I've just received
a kind letter from B. Foster ; he wishes I'll go there when I leave this. .
. . I'm afraid I shall not see so much of you this winter as I could wish,
as this picture must of necessity keep me here a great deal.   My comfort
must be that it's the best way I know of doing it, that's all."

# CHAPTER XI

WALKER spent Christmas at Mr. Birket Foster's. By the middle of January, he was again at Woolstone, at work on *The Plough*. On January 16, he wrote from there :—

"I am all the better for coming down, and I find my work in so good a state, that I shall stick hard at it ; have indeed worked at it to-day, and feel sanguine as to the eventual result. The day has been most sweet and balmy ; blackbirds, &c., singing away, and the colour of everything quite splendid. I telegraphed to North from Bristol, so he was at the station last night. I reached this at about nine, and was very tired, and after supper and a glass, was glad enough to turn in. . . . And now there's another thing which I would like sent, and it is some trifle for the woman in whose field my wood house is ; not too swell—Fan or Poll might hit upon something. She is middle-aged and unmarried, and I think poor enough. I quite forgot to see about it as I meant to. . . . Meanwhile I shall go on with the little water colours. Ask Fan to send me that proof [never mind the tracing, I can do it] and ask her to find the number of the Cornhill containing the cut [which she must tear out and send] of Reine and her spinning wheel, and a fellow kissing her hand ; I think it is the next number to the one she found for me, which was October '66 I think."

The above reference to small work is somewhat puzzling. I do not know of any completed water colour of *Dick and Reine*—"Reine and her spinning wheel, and a fellow kissing her hand "—while the illustration for October 1866, which is mentioned as if it had been lately made use of, is, *Let us Drink to the Health of the Absent*, a subject already noticed as having been painted in 1866 though not exhibited till this year. There is ample evidence that in 1866 Walker was really engaged on a water colour reproduction of this illustration, which appears to have been completed ; but, on the other hand, in a memorandum of money received this year, there is mention [without particulars] of a drawing from *The Village on the Cliff*, which could not have been *Dick and Reine*, if that subject were never carried out, and may possibly have been a duplicate of *Let us Drink to the Health of the Absent.* If this is so, it would have been the second drawing of the subject, and not that painted in 1866, which was exhibited this year.

"That proof" may refer to the illustration to *Sola—Cornhill,* July 1869—as the water colour of this subject was painted about this time, and disposed of to Mr. Gambart early in February.

For some time past, Walker had had the pictures of *Wayfarers,* and *The Old Gate,* at St. Petersburgh Place for further work, and in view of an approaching election at the Royal Academy, it was considered advisable to invite some influential painters to come and see them. This is the explanation of the references to Sir Edwin Landseer in the following extracts.

*January* 18 :—" . . . All jolly here, and work going on very well indeed. . . . Thank dear Fan for the tracing, it will do very well. I hope my telegram was not too late, but it cannot be helped if it was. She would have done well in writing to Millais or Sir Edwin ; of course it is rather an important matter. . . . Wind is E. here, and much colder, but my picture looks very well. I am feeling ditto."

*January* 20 :—" . . . I have worked altogether indoors to-day ; the wind has been cutting, and the day miserable. I have often thought of you all there together, knowing that if it's gloomy here, it must be truly wretched with you. As for Sir Edwin and the pictures, if he does not call to-morrow, it would be better to send them home, I think. Of course he hasn't been—I feel as if he hadn't—and that no good of any kind will come while this unfortunate wind lasts. There's nothing fresh to tell. Our life here is so quiet, that the idea of news seems rich. North is eagerly devouring the daily paper, which he gets just before dinner ; fat Mrs. Thorne is patiently knitting stockings near him. She has lately taken to it, as not requiring eyesight. . . N. and I took a stroll in the gloaming, just before dinner, in search of a young tree of peculiar shape for my picture. We caused quite a panic among the birds, especially blackbirds, of which there seem to be any number : they evidently felt aggrieved, by the noise they made. N. picked up a young thrush, that we both thought a hawk had injured, as we saw one circling about overhead. North seems to think my picture a success so far as it goes, and he stares at it a deal."

January 21, to his sister Fanny :—

"I think you have done everything regarding the pictures most capitally ; in fact, have done all that possibly could be done. The rest must be left to fortune, I suppose. Meanwhile, all that you have done, pleases me very much. I fear that talking to Ansdell or the others, confidentially, would do but little good. I may possibly send a line to A., between this and the eventful day. The letter for the Missus that will reach same time, I wrote last night ; but of course the sleepy boy was only in time to see the mail-cart lights flash round the corner, on the opposite side of the moor. We are at dinner while I write this, and by the way, I have taken to cider [doing in Rome as Romans do], as I find it does not disagree with me as it used. We have not been out at all to-day—it has been too dreadful—have done more work indoors I'm sure, than if we'd braved the bitter air. Dull lead clouds from the E. all day, and slight drizzling snow. The other night some men and boys came 'wassailing'; we heard singing in almost every key, and when they came to the house, we could hear words about 'keeping him warm, and a little more cider won't do us no harm,' which seems to be the usual form of 'wassailing' in these parts, and of course they had more cider in the kitchen. I have in hand a sort of coloured sketch from that story, 'Mrs. Archie,' you know, the introduction scene—does well as a fill-gap, and will, I hope, be finished in a few days, without interfering with the big picture. As for wishing you were here, you'd find it slow enough I'm sure, just now; better perhaps when the spring has fairly burst out, just before the sending in. Plenty of time to think of it then, for a few days perhaps, but then you know so much can then be done if there's but the money when the time comes, and the only thought now should be *sticking to it*, each in our own way just now, and bearing our troubles in silence. We do down here, as you'd say if you could follow us through the dark and mud, scarcely saying anything, and coming home tired out, as we generally do. I sincerely wish the days were longer, and a little less miserable, making work so difficult. Last Monday, just before the wind changed, it was divine—a still grey day, warm, and the clouds high; the sort of day I meant in the 'Old Gate.' Of course I did lots of work. . . . The reason I had no letter yesterday, was because it was sent to Wellington first, instead of Williton. You'd all better make the fellows ashamed of themselves, by writing Williton about three times the usual size, and underlining it. I am going to write to Paddington about it. . . I don't know what to ask you to get for poor Miss Blake, the woman whose field I have. It ought to be some little matter that only London can very well supply; they think more of it, I fancy."

January 23, to his mother :—

". . . No news here; have done no work to-day. Wind still cold and cheerless; can only hope for a change soon. Will return as soon as I possibly can, meanwhile all love to my dear Missus, from her own loving F."

*January* 24 :—". . . The scraps of news are of course most welcome, and though Fan sends plenty, I answer to you, because I've only time to write a short one. I am fully prepared about the election; I mean that the last ray of hope is extinguished by what Ansdell tells Fan. I feel sure he's right. . . . The weather here is so bad that I have not touched the big picture to-day, but content myself with touching on the little water colour 'Mrs. Archie.' It is slight, and I shall send it to Fan, and

see how she can do battle with young Deschamps over it.   She had better
ask him what he thinks can be given for it, if she is uncertain in her mind.
As I say, it will be very slight, and done quite without models, which I
fear will be evident enough.   I have to-day arranged with a farmer about
the horses and everything, even to their standing on ploughed ground
while I work from them.   I made a slight sketch before from a plough,
&c., of his, but now it will be the serious business.   He [the farmer] is a
good old fellow, and anxious to please—he came here and discussed it, over
the inevitable glass of something warm.   So I shall at least have a tussle
with this part of the business before I go to town ; when I shall bring it
with me, I think, for a few days."

The coloured sketch from *Mrs. Archie—Cornhill*, August, 1863—
remained in Walker's hands ; and after his death was sold at Christie's
with the rest of his effects.   It was shown at the exhibition of 1876.

*January* 26 :—" No letters this evening.   Suppose we shall hear who
is the lucky man to-morrow.   I am quite reconciled, I can assure you.
Have done a capital day's work, and had a good dinner.   We are going
for a walk, so no more. . . .   Glorious day here, but very cold ; snug
however in my wood house, and self quite well."

*January* 28 :—" The lucky man appears to be Vicat Cole ; I had a
bet on with North that it would be he. . . .   Well, one can but do one's
best, and that I am fully prepared to do.   It would have been very sweet
though, just now, would it not ?   I expect that at last, if I live long
enough, it will come to me because it will be too clearly my right, to be
withheld from me any longer.   I wish I had a little more the knack of
making myself agreeable as a *business*, and in the right quarters.   I don't
see why you should have been tramping to the R. Academy, when the
question sent to the Ansdells would have been answered by means of a
note.   However, it matters little enough now.   I have been working very
hard on the picture, and it is developing rapidly ; have worked entirely at
it, doing nothing more to the small water colour matter. . . .   The
weather here has changed, being no longer frosty ; but yesterday and day
before, it was lovely here in spite of the cold, for one didn't feel it, being
very dry."

*January* 31 :—" . . . The wind has changed, and a glorious day it
has been here—splendid colour above and below, and soft gusts of wind,
instead of the cutting N.E., so of course I can discard my grievances like
a great coat.   N. and I walked about on the moor after leaving work, and
just before dinner, to see the last glories in the way of colour.   I thought
of you all, and sincerely hoped that, towards the west, you could see from
the window some of the beauties we saw.   The picture gives me a great
deal of worry.   Sometimes I think it will be very much of a success, and
then again I don't know what to think.   I wrote to those Punch people

last night, and shall still strive to go on with the small work ; and so, I hope, we shall get through somehow. I don't much like the idea of leaving this before making some more money, however. Well, I've nothing more to say. Yes, I did get Punch yesterday, and Fun and Tomahawk on another morning ; and thought the two latter so bad that I hope you won't send them again. North says he hasn't yet recovered from them. This beastly month will be over by the time you get this. It's astonishing how we all wish the cold cheerless weather over, and yet how precious it is. . . . There's a lot of ploughing going on, and I am in the thick of it. More about my coming up, later in the week ; meanwhile give me all the news as usual."

Walker went up to town for a few days, and was back again on February 7. On February 8 he wrote :—

"Here quite punctually last night, and very comfortable. . . . Feel much better for the little change, in fact, very well indeed. Got on capitally with work to-day, and have found a fresh place for the foreground, quite near this house, and very secluded, being at the bottom of a beautiful orchard belonging to the woman in whose field my hut is. The little stream winds by, and altogether the discovery is a very great one, I think, because I was always uneasy about this part of the picture. We found it this morning—so much for the after breakfast stroll. I have worked there all day, and a very lovely one it has been. . . . Last night was very jolly and bright, to-day altogether exquisite. Have very little fear for the picture if it only keep like this for a fortnight. . . . I'm going in for another pot-boiler ; shall try to do it in the evenings."

The introduction of the stream into the foreground of *The Plough* was the chief departure from Walker's conception of the picture, as given in the concluding letter of the last chapter. It was, moreover, the cause of what might have been a serious accident to the picture itself. In an article on *The Harbour of Refuge*, in the *Magazine of Art* for November 1893, Mr. North casually mentions this incident as follows :—

"Walker did not invent out-of-door painting, but no man more honestly worked in open air, more determinedly, more appreciatively. I have known him working under circumstances of physical discomfort which would have made painting impossible to most men. On *The Plough*, for instance, he worked some windy days with the canvas lying on the uneven earth, with great stones and lumps of wood on its corners to keep it steady. Once it was carried into the stream which is its foreground, by an extra strong blast, and floated down some way—luckily, face up. This he took very calmly, saying, ' I have noticed that unfinished pictures never come to harm from accidents.' "

*February* 11 :—" I have been making a mistake. I fancied that this was Thursday, instead of Friday—a day out of my reckoning, confound it.

I am jealous of every day now, and have been kept from painting to-day, on account of shifting my canvas to another stretcher, and altering its shape by some inches. Fan will say this is *usual*, and so it is ; but I could never have finished it with comfort as it was, for a lovely tree, &c., which I believe to be almost essential, I must have left out. But the nuisance is, that most beautiful rosy clouds on russet sky trooped up just at sunset, and I could do no more than just make a note of them. The cold here is something tremendous ; my moustache was frozen to a stick last night. We walked home from our long walk, in the bright moon-light, and enjoyed it very much, though North is not a very rapid walker as a rule. Please send me some thick [leather] gloves ; I think driving gloves with wool inside would be best, and will last me a long time. You see I have to carry my big canvas on my head, from the scene of action, Mrs. Thorne's son being away for a time, helping some one through the lambing time. He generally does this, and my poor hands suffer in such weather. . . I expect the ice bears ; I tried some on the moor, just before dinner, and it was like a rock. I hope you are all comfortable in this bitter cold. I am very well and comfortable here, and only thinking how I may best get forward with the picture. Am in rather a fever to see it get on now."

The above-mentioned alteration in the size of the canvas of *The Plough* was, Mr. North tells me, brought about by the help of the village dressmaker, who sewed on the additional piece ! Mr. North also says :—

" His energy when engaged in work was most extraordinary. He would never hesitate to put on his head his large canvas—for instance, that on which *The Plough* was painted—and for a five or ten minutes' rapid work, rush off with it a distance of nearly a quarter of a mile, should the man who was usually waiting for the purpose be absent at the moment."

*February* 13 :—" The gloves, I am sorry to say, are too large to wear. I know there is a difficulty in getting them small enough, but these are useless, and I return them. I expect I am too imaginative, for I fancied such things might occasionally be worn by youths, and by women, and that they would be made for that purpose. The day is detestable ; I am quite tired of it. . . . The afternoon is too awful, or I should go for a long walk by myself. Of course, my work is much interfered with, and I cannot help feeling very anxious about it. The light, too, for indoor work, is very bad, especially as this picture is rather deep in tone. I can only hope that it will alter soon, or I must come up again. . . . It is quite dry, and with that gritty dust that is said to be so valuable at this time. The chimneys smoke here, now and then, and no wonder ; it's blowing a gale. I should say you cannot do better than keep well indoors."

*February* 14 :—" . . . I have another pot-boiler half done, which I have been working on to-day, the light being too bad for the big picture. This will be ready for Fan and Deschamps during the week. The subject is from 'Philip'—they are outside a sick man's chamber door, and there is a woman reading a Bible. I have just commenced another, where Philip reads out his letter of appointment to Charlotte, the little children standing on the landing behind them. I regret to say that, in spite of all care, a dreadful cold is the result of all this infernal weather—almost as bad, I think it is, as the one I had while in town. It is only to be expected, I suppose. It is heartrending to see the poor birds quite tame with distress. A dreadful kind of snow has been falling all day—when I say falling, I mean driving from the moor almost parallel with the road. . . . I am going to have the case for my picture prepared at once, for if this is to last, I may as well get to town, and try to work from the model. . . . I don't ask you to send my skates, because I am resolved to do nothing of the kind during daylight, and the moon is already at the full. The blacksmith's lad here has broken his arm ; did it yesterday, on some ice that North and I had an hour's sliding on in the moonlight, Friday night. All up with the picture, if it had been *my* arm."

Of the two water colours spoken of above, *At the Sick Man's Door—Cornhill*, February, 1862,—was, I believe, the only one completed. I am, however, unable to speak with certainty, having never seen either drawing.

*February* 15 :—" Much better, and done a *splendid* day's work on the big picture. North said, ' Well, I suppose you've made your £100 to-day.' He was looking at the picture a long time. I feel much more hopeful, I need not say. The cold has seen its worst I think."

*February* 18 :—" I just scrawl a few lines, that the boy takes to the post—this instead of waiting until after dinner, and sending it by the mail-cart as it passes, which I usually do ; but it has come on so dark, that I have just given over work. The days are just as bad as they can be—quite enough to wear one out, no matter how stout-hearted one is disposed to be. To-day it has been much as I should fancy you have it—a sluggish whitey brown day, and a fine raw wind, but not freezing I think. I have done some good to the picture, which is all I can say. In Fan's letter she says, if I pump myself out with pot-boilers, I cannot get on with the big picture, and she asks me to keep her letter by me while answering it ; which offers me a splendid chance of *snubbing*, for if she'd done so by mine, she would have seen that I said I found it rather hard to take to pot-boilers after working at the big picture, as I have every day almost. As for its being of all importance, I know that only too well, and chafe enough under the accumulation of cold and darkness ; but then I suppose the pot *must* be kept warm, if not boiling, by some one. I shall probably bring myself and picture up on Wednesday next. I have to see about the frame, &c., &c., and this will be a good opportunity, especially if the weather keeps as it is."

February 19, to his sister Mary :—

" The valentine from the little one came at dinner time, and is quite appreciated. Tell her I think it very nice, and it is the only one I have had this year. I am glad she likes the sketch. I write this to-night [though you cannot get it till Monday] because I have a few moments just nice and handy to write to my Poll in. Old North is not ready to go out yet—is reading the paper, and so is stout Mrs. Thorne near the fire, and with a candle to herself, which she holds close to the paper, and which gives her quite a Rembrandtish effect of light and shade. Tell little Poll that the birds about here are all building nests, at least I have seen plenty fly away with long straws from their bills. There is one poor bird that we feed with sop outside the window—a big bird he is, a thrush—and he poor thing cannot carry straws in his mouth, because his bill is broken, or deformed. We first saw him at the side of the window, trying in vain to pick off some red berries that grow in clusters all up the front of this house, and give much food to the poor birds in winter. Well, it was evident that he could never get one off, and he seemed quite bold and desperate with hunger ; so we threw out some bread, and had the pleasure of seeing him, shortly afterwards, gulp two or three great pieces down. And we mean to feed him every day, so long as we see him come for food. We have a sandy-coloured dog here too [tell her], that always walks in at meal-times, and rests his chin on one's knee, with his eyes turned up and showing their whites, looking quite loving, as if he were not thinking a bit about the good things on the table, though we know he is, and always give him some. He likes us, I know, and generally endeavours to go out with us for a long walk in the evenings, though often it is so dark that we cannot see him, and I generally, when it is a *very* dark night, carry a little lanthorn fastened to my waist. I hope, dear, this vile weather does not depress you very much. Two or three times to-day I have had to leave off work on account of the darkness, but I keep to it, and when I find it impossible, I turn to the little water colour I have in hand, and which I am half in hopes of finishing to-morrow. Everything is very backward here, and the violets that were coming out so nicely before the frost, are all nipped up and dead. A few snowdrops just show their heads ; well, it must shortly be better in spite of itself, so that's a comfort. A nice prosy note this, but there's little to write about here."

February 20, to his mother :—

"I don't at all know about going up on Wednesday. The wind has changed, and the first blue sky for a week past shows such messes and botches, I don't know how I am to leave work until the end of the week, at least. I am quite disheartened with the look of my picture to-day, and must work like a slave. The enclosed from Millais, which came this morning, in answer to one I wrote, will show the time I have ; which is, as I feared, earlier than usual. To-morrow and next day will show me more clearly when I can leave this ; I feel that when I do, I ought to remain to work the figures, &c., up to a certain point, before coming back. . . . The water colour I thought to finish to-day, but have done but little to it, not feeling quite up to it in fact, and we have been strolling about all the afternoon, and part of the morning. It will be finished by Tuesday or Wednesday, I think. Fan will be best able to judge of its value ; I fancy it ought to be 60, because it is rather carefully treated in the way of *painting*. After this, I shall think of nothing but the big picture. The suspense and worry of the last week, and having to make shift with work indoors, I find to be far more wearing than the very hardest work, with things favourable, and the result is that I feel a little depressed and seedy to-day. The wind is N.W. or thereabouts, and though the sky at once showed the change, the air is cold, and the meadows still looking wretched with patches of rotten ice. I wrote a little note to Poll last night, chiefly for the little one's benefit. No news beyond this."

*February* 22 :—" To-day glorious, and the picture going on *very well indeed.* I am quite jolly about it once more, and feel quite a new creature. Shall not come up for a week I expect now. . . . The water colour will be done, perhaps, to-morrow or next day. . . . I am all agog for work, I can tell you."

*February* 23 :—" Just a line ; am too tired to write more ; at work until I could see no longer. . . . You can do nothing in the way of sending models, &c., down here, but can, if you know how, ascertain where a white horse and his harness are to be hired—a cart horse or brewer's horse. Also go to Charing Cross, and look into such shops there [if any] that contain photographs ; ask if they can tell you if a photo of Charles First's statue there has been published. I think the horse rather fine, and want to crib from it."

*February* 24 :—" I really have not had time to finish the water colour, though I just touch on it each day, generally at luncheon time. All my energies seem spent on the big picture, which has all the excite- ment of perhaps not being done ; though yesterday and to-day lessen *that* excitement somewhat. I do not know how to be thankful enough for such days as these two ; have worked till past six—that is, just after six, coming in at once to dinner. . . . To-morrow or next day will finish the little water colour, and then Fan must do her best. . . . Don't expect much writing now, as daylight lasts till six and past. Shall be home, you know, in a week."

*February* 27 :—" By this evening's post, I send the water colour, directed to Fan. I have been working hard at it all day in order to send it off. Fan had better write or telegraph to Deschamps on receipt of it, telling him to come in the afternoon ; I may then perhaps be able to hear about it, Tuesday morning. I am anxious to realise on it as quickly as possible. Fan need do nothing more than just touch the corners with a little gum, and put it flat in the middle of a card—not rub the paint round the edge—I rather fancy G. likes every sign of its having come direct from the painter. Tell Deschamps I think it would look best in a *gold* mount. I shall do no more of such work now, and it has been some strain doing these, and the other as well. You will see me at the end of the week. . . . I cannot tell anything about the big picture. I have worked hard each day, since it has been fine, and have not so much as looked at it to-day."

*February* 28 :—" I just have a minute before dinner to send you a word or two. Yours and Fan's just this instant come. Am always glad to see your dear old handwriting, and Fan's too. One feels one's not an exile at letter time. Yesterday was a lovely day here too, but chilly towards evening ; and I did not go out till then, because of the water colour, the fate of which I shall be glad to learn. To-day has been soft and sweet, thank Heaven. I do, I may truly say, for it. There are all signs of things beginning to give signs of life—little fluffy pods on the bushes, all swelling, and tender green points just peeping through the ground. As for the birds, they are rampant. The poor beakless one has disappeared ; is dead I fear, or else finds food elsewhere. I have been working to-day by the side of the little trout stream, and heard them rising very often, reminding me of past pleasures a long way from this— pleasures still to come perhaps. As for these latter, I think if work goes on well, we ought, we three, to organise a trip after the sending in ; where, we will not decide now."

*March* 2 :—" I write a line in haste, with my mouth full, I was going to say, of marmalade tart and cream, which we often have, Mrs. T. being rather famous for it, and the cream literally ' standing up,' so rich is it. At dusk [which is now just dinner time], there is a general relaxation or undoing, which begins with a glass of sherry, and the heavy boots being taken off ; North, as a rule, opening the paper, which an afternoon train *drops* on to the bank as it passes the moor ; and a little later, just as Mrs. T. is carving the joint, fowl, or what not, at the end of the table, the boy comes from Sampford with the evening letter, or without one, as the case may be. By that time, Mrs. T. has settled down to her knitting, having done all the serving, and now and then volunteers some observation to North [as she did just now], to which there is generally the short answer from North, poring over his paper. Prosy enough you'll say, but I know you like to have the ' situation ' put before you accurately. This even-ing, we are going for our walk, to Stogumber, to look at an old chair, similar to one here, which is mine, and which will soon figure at No. 3, St. P. Pl., and then I shall ask you to make a cushion for it. The chair we are going to see is much the same, we hear—of oak, with flat carved back, &c., very quaint ; and if better than the one here, *I* have it, if not, N. does ! By this you understand [if indeed you can follow this scrawl], that North insists upon my having the better of the two chairs, he having a desire to possess one of them."

*March* 3 :—" I fear *it's a case.* Wind suddenly gone round to E., and as nasty as can be. Shall be home on Saturday, for certainty. Ask Fan to write Unwin the model, to call at Bayswater, Sunday, at one or at two, about sittings—she'll find his address in the red book, I think. Have not done much good to picture to-day I fear ; this change quite enough to account for it."

*March* 4 :—" I reach Paddington by the 2.45 train ; shall be with you about 3.30 I suppose. I have told the framemaker to meet me at Paddington, as he will have a van, and my picture is too big for a cab ; so I shall probably arrive with him."

The remaining work on the picture was done at St. Petersburgh Place. A suitable cart horse was found, and stood in the little garden, as a model for the plough horses.

It is interesting to notice the points of difference between Walker's description of the picture and the completed work. The introduction of the stream has been already mentioned. The "tree of peculiar shape" is also an introduction, while the little line of figures in the mid-distance was to disappear, to give place to the figure of the farmer on horseback. Otherwise the picture remains as described, even to the rook "just poised, before he drops on a furrow."

Of the farmer on horseback, Mr. Orchardson tells me that, when he first saw this figure in the picture, he exclaimed, "Ah—Colleoni!" referring to the well-known statue in Venice. "Do you recognise him?" said Walker, "Isn't it splendid?"

The reader may be interested in knowing, that a view of the quarry can be obtained from the Minehead Branch of the Great Western Railway, on the right-hand side going from Taunton, a few minutes before reaching Williton station. The railway and a road run between the quarry, and the field where Walker's hut stood, but it is hardly necessary to say they found no place in the picture.

Contrary to Walker's custom, *The Plough* was exhibited with a quotation in addition to the title ; the quotation—"Man goeth forth unto his work and to his labour until the evening" [Psalm civ. 23]—having been suggested by Mr. W. Graham.

It may be said without exaggeration, that on its appearance at the Royal Academy, the picture was received with something akin to enthusiasm. A few extracts from the press criticisms of the time must suffice to show this.

The *Times* said :—"This is a common English landscape transfigured by the moment and the light, and made poetic from commonplace, which common-place treatment would have left it. And this we feel to be the noblest and most fruitful function of art, to elevate nature by means which nature supplies."

*Pall Mall Gazette :*—"In the way in which this scene is realised there is a rare and almost epic grandeur ; it rouses the imagination like a poem, with its impassioned richness of colour, its combined fire and dignity of action."

*Athenæum :*—"The colour of this picture is powerful and true, the drawing, not alone of the figures but of the trees, in every branch, and the herbage in each leaf, is exquisite ; the whole is as solid and brilliant as possible. It is a poem on canvas."

*Saturday Review :*—"The great colour-picture of the year comes from Mr. Walker. . . . The figures in their dramatic action, the landscape in its veiled splendour, are not unworthy Giorgione."

The picture was bought from Mr. Agnew by his Excellency the Marquis

The Plough.

By permission of Messrs. Thos. Agnew & Sons Proprietors of the Copyright.

de Misa, Count de Bayona, in whose possession it remains, and by whom it has been several times lent for exhibition. Mr. Macbeth's fine etching is known to many.

At the Summer Exhibition of the Old Water Colour Society, Walker had but one drawing—the water colour reproduction of *Wayfarers.*

The two following letters are to Mr. North, on the rejection of his oil pictures by the Royal Academy.

*April* 28 :—" I purposely deferred writing until *yesterday*, for then I hoped to have been able to write in a very different strain, and now I hardly know what to say, for in truth I am far too disgusted to say much ; far more disgusted than astonished, though of course this was my first feeling yesterday at the ' varnishing.' I cannot blind myself to the fact of this being a very unfortunate thing, and were you less certain of eventual success, I would counsel resentment—that is, the only form of resentment that you and I can show—but then cool perseverance, and reserving these very things for them when they will be of another way of thinking, is far more of a winning game. Upon my soul, when I saw some of the men that both you and I know, airing themselves yesterday, and knowing too the extent of their aims [as I do fully], I was half inclined to give way. You've no idea how much contempt I felt for most of the stuff there. Write me a line to say you don't take this much to heart. I have been away until yesterday at Foster's, and am feeling less pumped out than when I saw you. I have both your letters. Do as you think best as regards Miss Blake. Mrs. Thorne had best give her to understand that nothing unreasonable will be paid by me ; I can assure her that. Perhaps it had better be put to arbitration ; I am tired of people trying to get the best of one."

Miss Blake's idea of reasonable compensation for allowing the wood hut to stand on her field, worked out, Mr. North says, at something like £1,500 per acre per annum !

*April* 30 :—" By all means send the pictures here, I would have written for them had you told me where they now are. Agnew will probably be calling here next week. Your framemaker will bring them here from the Academy, if they have not already been removed. I saw Graham at the private view yesterday, and was speaking about this matter. He seemed rather nicer, I thought, than usual. Don't be put down, for goodness sake, by this. . . . Mine is in the exact spot that I had last year."

Walker's labours on *The Plough* had left him in a low state of health ; and certainly, the way in which he worked in the open air in all weathers, was calculated to try a much stronger man. After spending a short time on the Thames, he determined again to visit Venice, where Mr. Orchardson was then staying. The following letter, dated

May 11, was addressed to Mrs. [now Lady Constance] Leslie, by whose kindness I am enabled to print it :—

"I have to acknowledge the receipt of your letter, and to return you my hearty thanks for your kindness in sending it. I assure you I have a very keen desire for such spontaneous praise, especially from those whose taste I know to be good and pure. I can only say I am *sincerely glad* that you admire my picture. I think I am going away—to Venice, I think—next week. I have had a succession of colds, and feel that complete change is the best cure. Moreover I have plans for working while there—or at least of commencing some work, and perhaps of returning to it next autumn."

This mention of plans for work is worthy of notice. When the time comes to speak of *The Harbour of Refuge*, it will be seen that an idea was already in Walker's brain, from which that picture was to be evolved. Any interest this second visit to Venice may have, is due chiefly to that fact.

On this occasion, Walker decided on going overland by easy stages. He left London for Dover, on May 30, and in a short letter from the "Lord Warden," says :—" I was sorry to leave both of you, I can assure you ; and if all does not go quite smooth, shall turn back at any point."

May 31, Brussels :—

" All right, and feeling pretty jolly, though rather tired, as it's been a long day of it. Met B." [Mr. H. Blackburn] "all right, and we decided on crossing to Calais only, instead of Ostend ; glad we did, as it was very rough. We have had a stroll through this splendid city. . . . I find B. has written to Murch, the artist, at Munich, to say we shall be there."

June 2 :— On the railway between Coblentz and Würzburg :—

" We made a slight alteration in our journey yesterday, went on to Coblentz, instead of stopping at Cologne. . . . Am feeling all right now, but rather seedy this morning. I think it's all right, however. The 'bruisey' feeling I mentioned, seems more muscular than anything, I fancy, and that tightness relieves itself. Altogether I think and hope it the fag end of the colds I've had, and must be more careful in future [please God]. . . . Blackburn is a very good companion, and saves me a world of trouble. I wish he were going the whole way, but once at Verona, I am all right. I think I shall telegraph to Orchardson from Munich, and not leave Blackburn and Murch, till I get an answer."

June 4 :—Hotel of the Four Seasons, Munich :—

" I have just been out to get Fan's short letter, and have telegraphed to Orchardson to say I shall be with him on Wednesday. By this you will see that I have all along insisted on doing the journey by easy stages, rather to Blackburn's astonishment sometimes ; nor am I sparing expense, so far as comfort goes. I have decided on not going to this Passion play, as I heard from Murch [who met us at the station on our arrival last night] that the journey is a bothering one, that the whole thing is very fatiguing, though beautiful, and that one is by no means sure of getting lodging. This last decided me, and Blackburn will probably, on Monday, go a short part of the journey with me, to a place he wishes to see, leaving the Passion play until to-morrow week. . . . Würzburg, that we left yesterday, was a wonderful old place, with a nice river [the Maine] running through an old bridge with statues on it. We loafed about, and watched the cigar-smoking officers saluting each other. We went up to the citadel, with its ramparts frowning over the town ; we were escorted by a handsome trooper with a bronzed face. He noticed **B.** picking a wild flower for his button-hole, and just fancy, he stooped and plucked the enclosed, and handed them to me, gracefully too—Fan would have been charmed with the simplicity of the act. Now my route on leaving this on Monday, will be as follows : on Monday night I reach Innsbruck, . . . . Tuesday night I reach Verona, . . . . and Wednesday evening, please Heaven, I reach Venice."

June 5, from same address :—

"As it's a rainy and miserable day, I cannot do better than just write a line or two, for we neither of us feel the least desire to go out ; and for myself, I only know I feel low-spirited, if only to think that after coming so far, it should be as chilly and uncomfortable as when I started. I dare say it will be all right by to-morrow night, and better still when I get t'other side of the mountains, the day after. I had an answer from Orchardson last night. . . . . Of course I am often wishing we three were together, roaming about, as you may be sure ; especially when one sees glimpses of beauty of a kind not to be seen at home. This precious place stands something like two or three thousand feet above the level of the sea, so no wonder it is not particularly hot. If I return overland, I shall do it by the more direct route, I think, the one I already know. I leave this by 10 o'clock to-morrow, and hear that the view from the line across the mountains is, in parts, magnificent."

June 9, from San Gregorio, 351 Calle Barbero, Venice :—

"Here I am, and feeling well and jolly. Got here yesterday about 5, Quiller, and the faithful Antonio, meeting me at the station. I left Innsbruck at 9 in the morning the day before yesterday, getting to Verona at 9 in the evening, having crossed the Alps at the Brenner pass, and a most wonderful day it was, the mountains and snow looking terrific. Then as we got down nearer Verona, getting more like Scotland, only ten times grander, and finally into the loveliest valley I ever saw, I think. At Verona, there was a letter from Quiller, to say he had

got a comfortable room here for me, &c.   It is almost difficult to believe
that two years have passed, and more, since I was here ; it seems but
yesterday. . . . Well, it's beautiful here—just nice and warm, not hot—and
Quiller says it has been wretchedly cold, and that I am fortunate in not
coming earlier ; so you see it is all for the best. . . . We strolled about last
evening, in the Square of St. Mark, dear old place ; and I wished very
much that you and Fan were here, and Quiller agreed with me that it
had been jolly enough.   I need not say how often I think of you both,
and hope you are comfortable ; believe me, I am now, this place is so
resting and fresh.   You would be surprised at my comfortable bedroom,
and I have a sitting room adjoining, where we take our coffee and rolls,
first thing."

Mr. Orchardson remembers Walker's pleasurable excitement at
finding himself again in Venice.   How, on the morning after his arrival,
he was continually running from the breakfast table to the window
to look at the scene below, till Mr. Orchardson thought the breakfast
would never be finished.   Another little incident Mr. Orchardson calls
to mind is that one day Walker, fancying his bitten finger-nails were
attracting attention, drew in his hand, saying : "Don't look at my poor
fingers.   I've done everything I can to cure myself.   I've rubbed my
fingers with bitter aloes, till I *love* bitter aloes."

*June* 10 :—"Before turning in, I begin a line or two, to say yours
and Fan's came to hand this afternoon, and glad enough I was to have
them.   I had sent Antonio the faithful, once to the Europa, but the
manager was out and the porter couldn't tell him anything about any
letter ; and while Quiller and I were afterwards standing on a bridge,
watching the goings on, Fan's well-known hand was suddenly put before
me from behind—the faithful one had been again, and had followed us
with it somehow.   Well, it's just lovely here, and I am quite well again ;
my appetite returned, and thoughts of work coming upon me.   But we
have been idling to-day most perfectly ; strolling through the little quaint
streets, and seeing the sort of daily life that the ordinary visitor never has
time to see, for he is *doing* the regular thing, and cannot afford to study
back streets, I suppose.   There is a good deal of lightning to-night, and
we have this evening been mingling with a sort of flotilla of boats that
gathered to hear the music on the Grand Canal, given by a kind of choir
of men and boys, composed, Antonio says, of ' gondolieri and men who
paint houses.'   Any number of coloured lamps, and the whole thing
moving slowly along on the water, like something unreal ; people burning
coloured fires as they went.   On our way home, we stopped for some of
the famous beer at Bauer's—Fan has often heard the Fosters speak of it—
and we of course drank to the absent ones.   It's just warm enough to sit
with comfort in the open air after sunset, without risk, as we did, for
instance, last night ; and I must tell you we had a little surprise yesterday
—we met no less a person than Barlow the engraver [of Kensington], and

with him Eli Lees the Lancashire mill-owner, and another who was taking care of both. We were coming through the Square of St. Mark, when I heard my name called from a café table, where they were taking coffee. Of course they were delighted, and we joined them—they were making the usual hurried visit, and were off again this morning. *Saturday morning.* . . . You surely must have decent weather for the little garden slip, by this time. It pleases me much to think of the little balcony and the place generally looking pretty. I shall be glad enough to return to it, when the day comes."

The balcony with its verandah, and the boxes and hanging baskets of bright flowers, which Mrs. Walker tended with such care, has disappeared ; and a bow-window has taken the place of the French window which led on to it.

*June* 16 :—" Yours, and Fan's enclosed, came yesterday while I was out, and glad enough I was. I had called at the Europa as usual ; indeed Orchardson chaffs me about my anxiety for letters, or at least affects to ; but one's being away from everything makes one very much interested as to the time the letters arrive. . . . I have been put off the sketch I was beginning at St. Mark's, by a precious festival, which will bring many people into the church for two or three days, and so interfere with me, for one cannot very well work among the worshippers. The ringing of bells to-day has been a complete nuisance, seeming never to cease. I intended going to Mestre by train to-day, but the sun has been so powerful that I am sure I should have done no good. I did not sleep at all well last night, for some reason or other, and feel rather stupid to-day in consequence. We went to the Lido before lunch, and had a pretty long walk along the shore. There was a cool breeze, and the sea was deliciously limpid. Since we returned I have been inquiring at the agent's of Burns & MacIver, as to the prospects for the remainder of the month, &c., and find they rather tally with the arrangements mentioned in their letter to me. There is a vessel of theirs now at Trieste, which will probably be here in four or five days, and remain [to take in her freight] for a week. This vessel is the ' Morocco,' which left Liverpool at the beginning of last month, and it just occurred to me that if I find myself not getting on with work, or if the weather changes disagreeably, &c., I might possibly take passage by her. . . . Orchardson is rather staggered, I fancy, at my already mention-ing any arrangements for departure ; but he himself will not remain, should it turn very hot, or mosquitos become rampagious. . . . Yes, as you say, the journey, or at least the latter part of it, was glorious. At Verona [I quite forgot to tell you], at the Hotel, while I was looking over a balcony, a gentleman asked me—seeing that I was English, I suppose—if I could tell him anything about the amphitheatre [there is an ancient one there in wonderful preservation]. I told him all I could, and said I half thought of going to have a look at it again. We went together, and I found he was a great fisherman—knew all about the Spean [a Scotchman, I think]—and was going to some stunning trout fishing of his own in Germany ; and before we parted, invited me to go with him—would provide me with a rod, &c. I should have gone if I hadn't made my plans, I think. I foolishly forgot to ask him his name. . . . That's capital about the roses—due, I expect, solely to your own tender care, my dear. . . . *Friday*, 2.30 : I broke off last night to go to dinner, and finish here at the place we take lunch—Bauer's. . . . We are going to take a stroll in the narrow busy little streets ; they are so narrow as to be shady and cool, compared with the open places. You will judge by this that work is not progressing very fast ; but perhaps it is, after all, not unwise to take that part of the matter coolly just now. I hope my dears are enjoying themselves, as I am. Quiller sends his kindest regards. He chaffs me about this—says I must have posted you up to all the latest news on this page, if I have not dived into futurity even."

*June* 22 :—"The 'Morocco' is here ; she arrived in the night, and I have just been on board, and seen Captain Leitch, who tells me she will leave this on Saturday he thinks, though he will have to stop at Malamocco, a port about ten miles from this, either to take in, or discharge, part of the cargo, and so not leave finally, until Monday or Tuesday. I don't know if I go on board on Saturday, or at what time in fact ; anyhow I think I shall take passage by her, so of course you will not write to me on receipt of this. She seems a fine vessel, and Leitch seems a fine fellow, something like Captain Muir, and brown as an Indian. He tells me he has rather a nice party of passengers—four or five, I think he said. The route he takes is down the Adriatic [of course] stopping a day at Corfu, then straight to Malta, and from Malta right away home, not stopping, he thinks, at Gibraltar ; the whole passage being about fifteen days more or less, but this I suppose, under favourable circumstances. So you see it will be quite a voyage, and Quiller says he truly envies me, and I think would gladly go with me, but is such a wretched sailor, that he dare not."

*June* 25 :—" . . . We had a tremendous thunderstorm last night ; began while I was out at dinner [Quiller kept indoors the whole day]. I never saw such splendid lightning—literally in streams it was, goodness knows how many at a time—the thunder, at one time, never leaving off at all. I watched it from one of the arches of the Piazza, and could see every line of the 'Morocco,' lying right out in the distance among the others. It appears she will not be able to leave this to-day, at least there's some talk of it, the tide or something preventing. I shall ascertain, this morning, before posting this note. If it were not so truly a good thing to return by her—I mean so beneficial—I think I would return the other way, as being shorter, especially as you say 'come home' ; but so far as one's poor calculation goes, I'm sure it's best I should wind up my wanderings in this way. I can see Quiller is strongly tempted to risk continued sea-sickness, and everything else—he was

much fetched by the trim, fine, character of the vessel, I could see too. Yes, I will return by her, and you must not mind the rather long gap in all this letter writing ; for you see, as yet, there's no invention for sending letters out to meet vessels at sea ! . . . . *Saty. aftn.* Just time to post this. The ' Morocco ' goes to-morrow, and I go aboard on Monday morning, all being well. Quiller will go with me to Malamocco."

*June* 27 :—" I'm just off. We go in the gondola to Malamocco, with two additional rowers. Am all serene. If any letters come here, Quiller will send them home. A fine bright morning, and I am looking forward to the voyage with pleasure. The ' Morocco ' leaves Malamocco at about four this afternoon."

Scraps from Corfu, Malta, and Gibraltar close this series of letters, and Walker reached Liverpool on July 13. The only work he appears to have completed on this occasion, was a slight sketch of the house where he stayed. It will be noticed that again there is no mention of any visit to the pictures.

On July 29, Walker wrote to a friend—Mr. Alex. S. Stevenson—as follows :—

" Just a line to say that I go on Monday up the Thames, with my mother and sister, for a little while ; and should anything occur in the matter of the election of my friend Phillips—I mean should you be in town, and anything take place—of course I will come up directly. My mother has taken some little lodgings just above Gt. Marlow. The address, in case you think it well to write me, is Mrs. Harding's [near the Turnpike Gate], Bisham, Berks. Of course too, if you are in that neighbourhood, I hope you won't forget to let me know it."

One result of this stay at Bisham was the water colour of *The Ferry*, of which a brother artist declared at the time, it was " simply the finest drawing that had been done in the century." An examination of dates in Walker's papers would seem to show that *An Amateur*—a coachman in a garden, about to cut a cabbage—was also produced at Bisham, but of this I cannot speak with certainty. An unfinished study for *The Ferry* was included in the sale of Walker's works at Christie's, and shown at the exhibition of 1876. From this study [which I am informed remains in the state in which Walker left it], an exceedingly poor and worthless etching has been concocted—a contrast to Mr. Macbeth's etching of the finished drawing.

It so happened that one of my brothers, two friends, and I, were up the river in August of this year, sleeping in our boats ; and I have a pleasant recollection of Walker, his mother, and sister, accepting our limited hospitality at our halting place for the day, at the lower end of the Bisham woods.

Walker stayed at Bisham till about the middle of September, and on the 13th, wrote from there to Mr. Stevenson :—

"On chance of this reaching you, I send a line to say I hope to go to some friends in Perthshire shortly, and could join you *en route* for a day or two, if you are at Barresford and could receive me. This is supposing that you are at the fishing—that there is yet any fishing—but do not hesitate to tell me if you cannot see me. I wrote you some time ago, telling you of my movements, &c., directed to the Langham ; have been doing some work here, and shall go to town on Monday next. I remember your saying you thought to be in Northumberland at about this time, but of course shall [if I do not hear from you] conclude that you have been obliged to alter your plans. I wish I could have seen you here—the very finest part of the Thames to my thinking."

The following letter to Mr. Stevenson, from London, though undated, belongs to this month :—

"You'll be thinking it very strange that I haven't answered your kind letters, but the fact is, I have been unable to say anything definite about getting away ; there is some work I *must* finish before anything, and I've sometimes felt that I have no right to leave at all, after my many wanderings, but the chance of going to you, and possibly getting a fish, I do not like to let slip. I understand you to say you are not at home after the end of the month, and I suppose the fishing too must be drawing to a close ; the Tay goes on during part of next month. Tell me if a day or two next week would be soon enough. I am ashamed to be so vague, but until to-morrow night, or the day after, I am in a state of dreadful muddle ; but if on Monday morning I have a line from you saying that you can receive me any time next week, I can telegraph to you. Excuse all this haste—just saving post, and off to that Orchardson, who has come back, instead of dying elegantly at the seat of war. I am going to *snub* him for not writing lately."

The work which had to be finished was probably *An Amateur*, as the drawing was in Mr. Agnew's hands early in October. In explanation of the reference to Mr. Orchardson, it may be said that Mr. Orchardson, on leaving Venice, had come back through France, then in the throes of the Franco-German war.

September 29, to Mr. Stevenson :—

"All being well, I purpose leaving for Tynemouth to-morrow at 10. Should anything prevent me I will telegraph. . . . I am not feeling very well, and fear I shall not be able to take part in the festivities to-morrow, even if I am in time. I was looking over the costume you mentioned, and find it scarcely wearable. A day or two rod in hand, will get me right, I am sure."

September 30, to his mother, from Newcastle station :—

"Just arrived here, quite jolly, and feeling comfortable. It has been a

positive *rest*, and I have had a nap.   There will not be time to write from
Tynemouth, so I send this scrawl.   Hope my dears are all right, now
their grizzling worry is on the move.   Will write all news when I have
it to tell."

October 2, from Tynemouth, to his sister Fanny :—

" . . . . I cannot help feeling great sorrow for the gloom I have
had such difficulty with lately, and will do my best to discard it at once and
for ever.   I am feeling well enough now, and grieve to hear of your
attack, though I scarcely wonder at it.   Give my best love to dear
Mummy.   I hope she will have a quiet day to-morrow, and free from
worry.   I will soon return ; had best go on to Perth though, for a day
or so."

October 4, to his mother :—

" Just one line to say I am about leaving this, and think, under all
circumstances, I may as well go on to Perth, if only for a day.   We are
first going to Durham [Stevenson and I], as he thinks I ought not to miss
seeing so beautiful a place, and I am very anxious, too, having heard a
great deal of it.   So I shall take leave of him this afternoon ; he has been
kindness itself, and I am sorry to leave him."

October 7, from Perth :—

" I shall be home to-morrow night, all being well.   Did think of
starting this morning, as I had a restless night ; but having to call here
for flute and things, I could not get back in time, so went on with breakfast, and shall take it easy for the remainder of the day.   They are all
very kind here, and I am all the better for the trip I think, but getting
uneasy about work, so must get back, and really buckle to.   Can go to
see Agnew perhaps, when the time comes. . . . Rather disagreeable
weather, and *no fishing*."

When the time arrived, Walker found himself able to leave his work,
and pay a visit to Manchester ; and by the kindness of Sir Wm. Agnew,
I am enabled to give the following interesting account of what happened
on the occasion.   Sir Wm. Agnew says :—

" In October 1870, Fred Walker visited me at Summer Hill, Pendleton.   Mr. G. D. Leslie, the late J. E. Hodgson, and your brother Henry,
were of the party, and a jolly time we had.   I had, in the early part of
that year, built a fine room, in which the billiard-table was placed.   My
family was then all about me, and young, and my wife and I had
established a rule not to have it used on Sundays.   My brother, John
Henry, was of the party, and on a certain Sunday, he took my artist
friends to make some calls, and dinner was fixed for 5 o'clock.   When it
was suggested that they should play pool after dinner, I told them we
did not use the table on Sundays, and I retired to the library, having to

write some letters. I was absent from my friends for an hour, and on rejoining them, was surprised to see my children burning corks to make charcoal, and my butler sharpen-

ing billiard chalk. Fred, stand-ing on a chair, burnt cork and billiard chalk in hand, was at work on one of the loveliest designs he ever made, on the angle wall of a large recessed window. This subject—a mer-maid, her face in profile, her long hair streaming in the water, holding out her arms to a little baby merman, who had been pricked by the shells at the bottom of the sea, and whose face expressed fear of the mother. [Linley Sambourne made a copy of this, and I think it appeared in *Punch*, when there was an article on the visit of the *Punch* staff to Manchester, on the occasion of my eldest son's majority.] Leslie was at work on the end wall, upon a Thames subject; your brother on another wall, drawing myself and Fred playing at billiards, inimitably clever —game forty-nine all. I lean on my cue, my ball is just over the pocket. Fred is striking; his trousers raised show his pretty foot and a striped stocking; as he leans over the table, his hair falls, and he is about to pot me! Walker touched on the figures. Over this, your brother drew my coat of arms [according-to Marks], with motto in scroll, 'Ecce Agnew Dei'!! Hodgson monopolised a wall, and he drew the base line of a Highland landscape, half way up it. Then Marks drew the waters under the earth, with Marksian fishes—the Tobacco-pipianus, &c., &c. Fred claimed the wall *vis à vis* to the mermaid, and drew a lovely girl, garlanded with jasmine, and holding in both hands a basket of flowers, exquisitely drawn, suggested by my daughter's face, figure, and passion for flowers. She was greatly loved by my guests, and by every one who was pri-vileged to know her. They worked till midnight. Next morning, full of enthusiasm, they sent into the City for some sticks of charcoal, and Italian chalk—would not leave the work—and when I returned home for dinner at 7, I found them all working in their shirt sleeves, happy as larks. George Leslie's subject developed, and all four had a hand in it. The scene represents a backwater in the upper Thames. In the foreground a lovely girl is feeding poultry, another girl sits on the parapet of a terrace—birch trees—these beautifully drawn by Hodgson, the poultry by your brother, swans in the river, and the water lilies, by Fred. At the left corner, on a pedestal, appear the initials, G.D.L., F.W., J.E.H., H.S.M., Oct. 1870. This work covers the whole wall. It was retouched by Leslie, in 1887. Fred's work has been glazed these twenty years past. He drew also the portrait of a friend being hanged—a caricature of my brother—and other grotesques. These are covered now by tapestries. The walls being new—at least not being a year old—were lined with what paper-hangers call a 'lining-paper.' A decorative paper had been ordered from Paris ; need I say it was countermanded ? Hundreds of persons have asked to see this room. They were never denied the opportunity. Students of Fred Walker's work, and lovers of his genius, cannot fail to find delight in the spontaneous expression of his power, recorded on these walls."

On November 22, Walker wrote to Mr. North :—

"Just a line, and with apologies for not writing earlier. I've very little to say. Am in the last agonies of a drawing for the forthcoming Exhibition ; the sending in day was yesterday, and I have it back again, to work on up to the last moment. I called at the Gallery to-day, and all three hangers came out. I fancy they rather like what I've sent. One or two of the better men have been asking if it's your intention to try again. I said I didn't know—rather *thought not*, &c. ; but, between ourselves, fancy you'd have a very good chance, if you care for the nuisance and risk, once more. You, of course, know best, but I can't help thinking, that such as that waterfall would have weight. I told Agnew you hadn't finished it, and his answer was—he'd be glad to see it, whenever it was finished."

At this Winter Exhibition of the Old Water Colour Society, Walker's drawings were :—*The Ferry* [sent in without title], *An Amateur*, pen and ink drawing of *Vagrants*, and *Let us Drink to the Health of the Absent*. The following criticism of *The Ferry* is taken from the *Athenæum* for December 3, 1870 :—

" Mr. Walker's anonymous drawing, No. 334, has, with abundance of incident, nothing but beauty in nature for a subject. . . . This is a gem of exquisite execution, the result of intense feeling for nature and perfect taste. Stothard might have designed the elegant figures, but he would not have wrought them out so thoroughly as Mr. Walker has done ; several of them have the grace of the antique with the verisimilitude of modern *genre* at its best. . . . The charm of this picture is completed by the richness and sobriety of its colouring, the faithful rendering of the varied textures of the objects represented, the unity of its chiaroscuro, and the breadth of its effect."

Of *Let us Drink to the Health of the Absent*, the same writer said :—

"It is wrought as perfectly as a picture by M. Meissonier, and has a wealth of grace that the Frenchman never rendered ; above all, pathos and a beauty of homeliness such as never appear in him."

I also find the following, in a letter from Mr. J. R. Clayton [Messrs. Clayton & Bell] :—"Your drawing of *The Ferry* is enough to drive artists to despair. I agree with the French painters now over here, who are saying that, in its direction, art cannot further go."

In addition to the unexhibited work of this year, already mentioned, Walker completed a water colour drawing of the standing woman from *Vagrants*, which was first seen in public at the exhibition of 1876.

The last letter of the year, addressed to a near neighbour, calls to mind Leech's sufferings from the organ-grinding fraternity. As the letter remains among Walker's papers, it may possibly not have been sent.

*November* 25 :—"I much regret having again to call your attention to this matter, but I find the cries of the bird in your garden so intolerable a nuisance, that I am compelled to speak of the matter in all seriousness. I have been much away this year, and although my mother and sister both complain of their comfort having been affected by it [especially when warm weather rendered open windows necessary], I am fully aware that this is a trifling matter, where a pet of any kind is the cause. But now I am compelled to protest once and for all against it, as materially interfering with my daily work—at all times of a difficult kind, and requiring, if success is to be looked for, absolute quiet—and for this reason, as I think I once explained to you, I had my painting room built where it is. I can say with pride, that as a rule, those with whom I have to deal, ever show a readiness to aid me in my work, or at least to remove any obstacle to it where possible ; and I cannot, as yet, in this case imagine, that it is being purposely interfered with. Surely I am not asking too much, in suggesting that if it be necessary for the bird to have air, that in front of your house is not less fresh than at the back. In conclusion, I beg to say, I am sure you *cannot* have any idea of the trouble this has already given me."

# CHAPTER XII.

## 1871.

WALKER's next Academy picture—*At the Bar*—was painted at St. Petersburgh Place, and there are therefore no home letters in which he relates the progress of the work.   In the second week in January, he was thinking of and arranging the picture, being at the same time engaged on

the small version of *The Plough*.[1]   A letter to Mr. Agnew, dated
February 16, refers to the latter picture as follows :—

" A smaller—or rather, I should say, the original—edition of the
' Plough ' will be finished to-morrow.   I mention this, as I spoke to you
some time ago about it, and indeed think you saw it at an early stage.
I have up to this time refrained from showing it elsewhere, and have
worked on it very carefully, and consider it has all the material of the
larger picture, indeed would be preferred by many who have not space
for a large work."

Notwithstanding the above, it was nearly the middle of April before
the picture was finished.   It was first publicly seen at the exhibition of
1876.   Another unexhibited work, painted early in this year, was *A Girl
Reading*—a girl holding a book, seated by a table on which are some
flowers.   In February, Walker designed the last of his invitation cards
for the Moray Minstrels, for which he was awarded a unanimous vote of
thanks, and elected an Honorary Member of that body.

The great event of the year to him, was, however, his election as
Associate of the Royal Academy on January 26, my brother being
elected at the same time.   On the evening of the eventful day, his sister
Fanny wrote as follows :—

" Wall " (a model) " brought the news on a card of Orchardson's,
with Marks's and Wynfield's names on it.   .   .   .   Fred and Mr. Mills
were playing a flute duet in the study, Mrs. Mills and I had just gone

" *Kuhlau*."

[1] In possession of Humphrey Roberts, Esq.

down to them. My dear mother was in the house, when Eliza came down to the study, and said *Mrs.* Wall was at the door, and wanted to see him. Dear Fred looked at me with a half-awed, peculiar, earnest, look ; then left the studio. I stayed a minute to explain to the Millses how I must leave them, but didn't tell them why, or what was vaguely in my thoughts. Then I saw dear Fred on the stairs ; he simply said ' I am an A.R.A.,' and we kissed one another, feeling acutely. . . . Fred went down to see Marks, with whom it was an old promise it should be so on this night."

As a matter of course, letters of congratulation came flowing in. What was not so much a matter of course, was the affectionate tone of many of them, and the reiterated assertion that in honouring Walker, the Academy had done honour to itself.

Walker's election to the Academy was followed, on February 4, by his election as Honorary Member of the Belgian Society of Water Colour Painters, by unanimous vote.

The customary visits to Academicians, consequent on his election, rather interfered with work on *At the Bar*, but in a few days, Walker was again engaged on the picture. His chief difficulty was, naturally, with the woman's face ; his idea being that its expression should leave unsolved the question of her guilt or innocence. Another difficulty was in finding a suitable dock. In his search for one, he visited Salisbury and other places. The Old Bailey seems best to have answered his purpose, as he went there several times and made sketches. After all, he does not appear to have been altogether satisfied with the material for this part of the picture, as only a few days before sending in, his sister Fanny made a journey to Beaconsfield to look at a dock, which, however, turned out to be of no use. As usual, the members of his family freely gave their services. His sister Mary stood for the face and figure of the woman, and his mother roamed about London, to find a hanging lamp of the kind he required. Their interest in the picture was, in fact, remarkable. It was almost as if the poor hunted creature portrayed on the canvas, stood before them in very truth. At night, the forlorn woman in the deserted studio, was spoken of by them in tones subdued by sympathy. To those who only saw the picture in the glare of the Academy, this may seem like exaggeration, but it is not. I was privileged to see it on the easel, and found nothing strange in the effect the picture produced on them.

Walker's aversion to show unfinished work had increased very much of late years, and in the case of *At the Bar*, it was most marked. His eldest sister wrote that all the week before the picture was sent in, she had had to receive people, and tell them it could not be seen. It was very backward, and Walker was dismayed. On March 25, he wrote to Mr. North :—

"I'm in an awful state about my work, and would like to fly to you for a day or two, if you are still there after the 1st, which is my day for sending in to the R.A."

Again, on April 4 :—

" Well, the precious picture went in somehow, all its sins upon its

Sitting for At the Bar (water colour)

head. No one saw it, literally no one, save C. Collins and Lord A. Campbell—not one buyer. Graham and others came, but I was locked up."

April 12, to Mr. Agnew :—

" . . . . *No one* saw my picture. I was hard at it up to the last minute, and shall be at it again the moment I can get into the Academy, for some of the important parts are unfinished; and in any case it is my intention to work at it again when it leaves the R. Academy. The subject, which is no secret, I will tell you; it is simply a figure of a woman at a bar of justice, a dim suggestion of another figure—male, of the *usher* kind—being introduced below. The size is rather smaller than my last year's, so the figure comes rather large; and the interest, I suppose, centres inself in the woman's face, which is turned towards the spectator, and looking, somewhat upward. As I say, no one has seen it, for I insisted on not being disturbed. The picture is altogether" [? low] "in *tone*, the shape of course upright; and the dim head and shoulders of the man below leaning on the edge of the dock, the woman's dress below the bar, being shown. Title, ' The Prisoner at the Bar.' "

On the very day the picture went in, Walker was working from a model, on the head of the usher, and the clock from which he painted, was procured for him by his mother, the same afternoon.

At the Academy, the hangers had great difficulty with the picture. It was so low in tone that, as was said, "it looked like a hole in the wall." After being tried in several rooms, it was eventually placed in the Lecture Room. On the first varnishing day, Walker came home from the Academy dreadfully depressed, wishing he could take the picture away. It was the one picture, with the exception of *The Lost Path*, that was returned to him unsold.

In spite of those shortcomings of which Walker was conscious, the high qualities of the picture were fully recognised. The *Times*, in concluding its first notice of the Academy, said :—" We cannot pass from the room even now, without a word of recognition for Walker's *At the Bar*, a wretched wasted woman who has had to ' hold up her hand ' at the Old Bailey on a charge of life and death, and who, after the agony of the day's trial, now, as the evening shadows gather dark about her, turns her wasted face and wild eyes to the door by which the jury enter with their verdict. One hand is clutched in the agony of suspense; the other plays nervously with a sprig of the rue which it has been the custom to place on the ledge of the prisoner's dock at Newgate, ever since the gaol fever decimated Bench, gaol and jury-box."

The *Athenæum*, after having in two previous notices, referred to the picture as " heartrending and intensely powerful," and " noble and almost awful," says of it :—" One of the grandest pictures in this exhibition— certainly the most intense of all in its tragical expressiveness— is Mr. F. Walker's life-sized figure of a woman, *At the Bar* [1168] : she is dressed in a modern costume, and has her hair dishevelled; she looks forward eagerly, yet with a half-vacant look that is deeply moving and profoundly pitiable : the expression is supported by the attitude of the body and the action of the hands, which are held in front. The largeness of style displayed in this work is honourable in the highest degree to a painter who hitherto has exclusively used a small scale for his figures ; its gravity and intensity of tone must be admired on the same ground.  We do not understand the extraordinary gloominess of the effect selected by the artist.  The picture is so badly placed that half its fine qualities are certain to be overlooked by the casual passer-by.  We recommend a careful study of it."

It will be convenient to give here the further history of the picture. After it had been received from the Academy, Walker wrote to Mr. North—on August 4 : —

" I promised to write you on receiving 'the Prisoner at the Bar,' but really have been so *put down* by it, that I scarcely like to ask you to see it.  I feel that it must, in effect, be *done over again*."

His sister Mary, on going into the studio one day, found Walker on his knees, with the picture on the floor, rubbing down parts of the woman's face and neck with pumice stone preparatory to repainting them. This he never did, and the picture remained in the state here shown, at the time of his death.  It must be said, however, that the photograph from which this illustration is taken gives no idea of what the face originally was.  On looking closely at the face on the canvas itself, it was still possible to discern traces of what it had been, but these the photograph has failed to reproduce.  Possibly the depth of tone of the picture, which had if anything increased in the eighteen years that had passed before the photograph was taken, may have been the cause of this.

When, after Walker's death, the time came to make a selection of his remaining works for sale at Christie's, it was at once decided that this picture could not be sent,  It was accordingly warehoused, and was after-wards at the private house of my co-trustee, Mr. G. G. Treherne, for some years.  Here it remained until he could no longer give it house-room, and some decision respecting it became absolutely necessary.  No course was free from difficulty.  The trustees had no power to present it to the nation [even supposing it would have been accepted] ; to let it leave their hands in its then state, was probably to expose it to unfair treat-ment ; and the least objectionable course appeared to be to entrust the restoration of the head to some well-known painter, preparatory to a sale by auction.  The question then arose, who would be best fitted to undertake the invidious task.  Acting under the advice of a small number of artists, Mr. Macbeth, who by his numerous etchings had been so closely connected with Walker's work, was applied to.  He most generously responded to the request, and I have learnt with great regret, that his action in so doing has exposed him to censure from some, who surely could not have been in possession of all the facts of the case.  His labour was entirely one of love, and undertaken at the earnest request of the trustees.  He stipulated that he should have by him at the time the

AT THE BAR.

small picture of the same subject, and the kindness of the owner of the picture enabled the trustees to comply with this condition. Mr Macbeth carried out the restoration, and the picture was sold at Christie's on May 4, 1889. The fact of the head having been restored, with the small picture as a guide, was set forth in the catalogue, and was also mentioned from the rostrum.

I conclude this account of the picture, with the following extract from Mr. J. Comyns Carr's *Essays on Art* :—" In his treatment of the face, Walker here gave evidence of a power of passionate expression that is not revealed in any other of his works ; and for this reason the experiment, although not entirely successful, must be regarded as of the highest interest, as an indication of the probable development of his talent. Its imperfections were solely due to his inability to adapt himself at once to so large a scale of execution, and not at all to any defect of imaginative resource. . . But those who remember the picture as it was first exhibited, and who can recall the desperate and hunted aspect of the woman's face, and her expressive attitude in the dock, will certainly admit that a painter who could command such intensity of human feeling, and who could also present the careless beauty of such a subject as *The Bathers*, must have been possessed of gifts that had not yet seen their full development."

The letter of March 25, quoted from, above, was written to Mr. North on his long delayed election to the Old Water Colour Society. It began as follows :—

"I can't help sending you just a line, to say how jubilant I feel at this afternoon's work. By a strange fluke, you were elected *twice*, by some mistake in the order of balloting ; and I am delighted to say that the second time, you came in *unanimously*, the first time nearly so. With you, came in Macbeth [who has sent stunning things], Houghton, Hale, and Goodwin ; the two last being landscape. H. S. Marks is also elected 'on his known reputation,' that is, without sending the three works."

A further extract from the letter of April 4, is here given :—

"I think you are an ungrateful wretch. I believe you are rather sorry, if anything, that you were elected into 'the Society,' from the tone of your letter. The Woolstone drawing is stunning, and with one or two little things, may be all you desire. I think the clouds a leetle *patchy* —you know what I mean—rather abrupt, and in isolated forms : not quite delicate enough. The notion of the figures is excellent, especially the woman throwing up her arm ; and now, as I write this, it seems to me that the clouds I mention, are in the other drawing, with the hill in the background. But it is a trifling fault I have noticed before ; in your picture of the Turf-cutter, for instance. Your Blue-coat boy, I thought most charming, and only marred by one little thing—the little girl with him was not as *pretty* as she might have been. I do not see how I can get to Woolstone this week ; the fact is, I am in a fright about the Society—nothing ready, and the sending in is on the 10th. I may commence something, with the idea of working on it, after going in."

Walker gave up the idea of doing anything for this Summer Exhibition of the Old Water Colour Society, and was unrepresented there.

Owing to the fact that he was working at home for some months, both at the beginning and end of 1871, there are fewer letters in this year than usual. It so happens, too, that in those he wrote, there is less that would be thought worth quoting.

During this summer, he spent a couple of months or so, on the Thames, at Spade Oak Ferry, below Marlow. On May 14, he wrote :—

" . . . . Have made one or two preliminaries as to work, and commence in grim earnest to-morrow. . . . Everything is looking beautiful, and most promising for work. If the wind would but change, all would be well. My cold has almost left me, and I am all right."

*May* 16 :—". . . Have been hard at the thorn bush, which is just at its prime. . . . I have just sketched in a water colour for Deschamps' people. Shall go on with it I think—just a slight thing with a lilac bush, which is not yet faded. . . . Don't put A.R.A. on letters."

The mention of the thorn bush [evidently not the first time it had been spoken of] would seem to show that Walker's thoughts were dwelling on *The Harbour of Refuge* ; this, as far as I am aware, being the only picture of this period, in which a thorn appears. It is true, the one in the picture is a tree, but in the case of a thorn, the terms might easily have been used indifferently. Moreover, the thorn would not have been in bloom the next year, until after the time at which the picture was sent to the Royal Academy. In any case this would only have been a preliminary study, as the background of the picture was not painted here, but [as is well known] at Bray.

The drawing with the lilac bush was to develop into *The Old Farm Garden*, an important, though unexhibited work. Walker's mention of it as "just a slight thing" is another instance of the way in which his subjects grew under his hand.

*May* 22 :—"Just a line to say I'm all right, going on comfortably with work, &c. . . . The wind has gone round to the E., but it is bright and not cold, but rather blustering. Yesterday was rather too hot, and plenty of confounded people on the river and the banks."

THE OLD FARM GARDEN.

June 5, to his sister Fanny :—

". . . Am not getting on quite so well with the drawing, partly through this truly infernal weather. Have just been out with it, returned with my hands quite nipped with cold. . . . I should be getting on tremendously, I know, if it were really warm and still. It quite wears me out, watching day after day for a change. I don't know who is worthy of the R.A. in the forthcoming election—must think over it. . . . Shall be up as soon as this drawing will let me."

June 8, also to his sister :—

"I fear that you and the dear Missus were looking out for me last night, and consequently uncomfortable at my non-appearance. I am getting on rather better to-day, but the mess I got the thing into, was really disheartening. I attribute it wholly to the vile weather. . . . You and she will be getting weary of all this, but I do not feel disposed to come up before I have got the better of the thing, and would fain do the other too, before making my appearance. In any case, I must come back for the oil picture, and please Heaven, the weather will then get less wintry."

June 11, to his sister Mary :—

"I want you to help me again. I came up last night, bringing with me a water colour with a figure in it, of a woman knitting— nearly back view, *black frock* with white spots [or rather little circles] all over it, the frock quite plain in make—that is, plain gathers or plaits up to the waist—and the sleeves like ordinary coat sleeves, rather full at the shoulder, with large white collar. This is my idea of the figure, which is only just put in, there being no suitable shemales down thar. Now could you, without *much* inconvenience, come to-morrow morning and stand for it? I say ' much inconvenience,' dear, for I know it will bother you, but then I know that you have offered to help me whenever you can, and I want to get this off my hands soon as possible. This drawing isn't anything much ; merely a bit of garden belonging to a farm, with tulips and beehives."

A word may be added to Walker's description of *The Old Farm Garden*. The girl as she walks has dropped her ball of worsted, upon which a cat is about to spring ; a row of the beautiful old florists' tulips, which the whirligig of fashion is again bringing into vogue, borders the path ; there are farm buildings in the background. The drawing was bought by Mr. Frederick Lehmann, by whom it was lent to the exhibition of 1876. Here it was seen by Mr. Ruskin, who said of it :—" No drawing in the room is more delicately completed than this unpretending subject, and the flower painting in it, for instantaneous grace of creative touch, cannot be rivalled ; it is worth all the Dutch flower pieces in the world."

A GIRL AT A STILE.

Early in July, Walker was again at Spade Oak, engaged on the water colour of *A Girl at a Stile*, probably "the other" drawing mentioned in the letter of June 8.   On July 7, he speaks of going over to Bray, to "see how things are there," which may possibly mean that, by this time, he had discovered the almshouses as a background for *The Harbour of Refuge*.   In another letter, he says he is "making something of the big canvas after all."   This would, I believe, apply not to *The Harbour of Refuge*, but to the picture which has been entitled *The Peaceful Thames*. He certainly had this picture with him at Spade Oak, as well as at other places ; and though it was never finished, he would take it up now and again.

About the end of July, Walker returned to London and painted the water colour of *The Housewife*—a woman in a court-yard, shelling peas— the background of which was taken from the house of his friend, Mr. Charles Collins.   He subsequently began an etching of this subject, not, however, carrying it very far.   I well remember his showing me the water colour at St. Petersburgh Place.   After putting it into my hands, he stood by silent while I pored over it ; and when at length I spoke in terms of admiration, his tongue was loosed.   He was always simply and unaffectedly pleased when he saw the pleasure his work could give.   I recall the words : "You know, John, I meant her to be a little *creamy* sort of woman."

THE HOUSEWIFE.

On September 6, Walker wrote to Mr. Hooper:—

"I write to ask you to help me in a certain little matter. Mr. Wilkie Collins is [as certain advertisements show] about to have produced on the stage, 'The Woman in White,' and there has been a little discussion on the subject of a good *poster* ; the result being that I made at the house of his brother, Mr. C. Collins, where I write this, a sketch of the said 'Woman in White,' and it is thought to be in some degree suitable, so I propose trying my hand at the thing itself—a dashing attempt in black and white. The figure ought not to be less than 4 ft. 6, or 5 ft. in height ; and to my way of thinking a vigorous *wood-cut* would be the thing, on a sheet of [pear?] wood the size of a door. Will you help me with your counsel and graver, or I might say chisel."

In another letter [now unfortunately lost], Walker wrote to Mr. Hooper :—

"I am bent on doing all I can with a first attempt at what I consider *might develop into a most important branch of art.*" This extract is given in an article on *The Streets as Art-Galleries*, in *The Magazine of Art*, for May 1881.

September 11, to Mr. North :—

"Pardon me for not answering sooner. I am alone in town, my folks being *pro tem.* at Eastbourne. . . . I'm going North, and they [if they've the strength enough for the villainous journey] will follow. . . . Am just about knocked up trying to do a poster for Wilkie Collins —his 'Woman in White,' about to be produced in the theatre—but the poster not a bad idea, if I can do it. A figure in white, cut out of a black ground, and Hooper, the engraver, rather enters into it."

The same date, to his mother :- -

"Your two letters received this morning, also a very charming one from Wilkie Collins, thanking me warmly for helping 'The Woman in White' by my poster. I am going on with it, and do not think I shall commence anything else before going away."

*September* 13 : "I think from the tone of yours this morning, that you're not quite comfortable, and it's a shame. Come home rather than that ; but if you'd rather stay for a few days longer, turn out of your present lodgings on receipt of this and get into better—go to the 'Sussex' or the other—you *must not* be annoyed if you can help it.—I fully intend that you go North as soon as you're a bit braced up for it. The poster is going on beautifully, and I'm expecting C. Collins every minute."

September 14, to Mr. Hooper :—

"Wilkie Collins has just been, and expresses himself *delighted* with what I've done.  I have got it on to the big paper, but not on to the blocks.  These I have had fastened together by a carpenter, and I don't quite know whether you'd say they fit close enough.  I don't like to ask you to come round again, but you could tell in an instant whether they'll do to proceed upon. . . I have got more 'go' and purpose in the figure, and it strikes me we shall make a good thing of it."

As far as I am aware, this poster was the first thing of the kind done in England by an artist of Walker's eminence.  It represents the back view of a life-sized figure of a woman, a shawl partly over her head, her face seen in profile as she looks back ; one hand raised with finger to her lips, the other holding the door by which she passes out into the starry night.  The drawing was first made on paper, in chalk and charcoal ; the outlines were pricked through for transfer on the wood, and the design then drawn by Walker on the wood itself.  The original drawing was exhibited at the Dudley Gallery in 1872, and again at the exhibition of 1876, when, Mr. Hooper tells me, the holes made for the transfer were still distinctly visible.

September 15, to his mother :—

" . . . Had a very bad night, and feel rather seedy to-day. Have not slept well at all lately. Don't care how soon I get away. . . This morning a German band, long before I was up ; [really it must be seen to] yesterday a lot of sheep [same time]. Eel-eye walked off with a grouse to-day, just laid for my lunch. The wretch has been asleep ever since."

Eel-eye, often mentioned in the letters, and introduced here under such unpromising circumstances, was a favourite black cat, with something of a halo of art about him, inasmuch as he had been the model for the kitten on the cradle, in Sir John Millais's picture of *A Flood*. He survived the household of St. Petersburgh Place, and ended his days in my house.

Before going to Scotland, Walker spent a few days in Derbyshire. On September 23 he wrote to his mother from the Peacock Hotel, Rowsley :—

" . . . I've been out exploring, and the place seems very stunning ; not so rocky or wild as at Bakewell, if I remember rightly. I took my tackle, and though I only caught a couple of grayling [something like a mixture of a dace and a trout], I could see that it's a capital stream, and is rather Scotch [the midges bit a little]. I shall get on better on Monday, and for a day or two shall think of nothing but resting myself."

September 28, to Mr. Hooper :—

" Here I am, and have already shaken off all little ailments and restlessness. Have had one or two days' fishing for trout and grayling, there being a couple of good streams in the neighbourhood. I cannot resist asking after the small engraving of the ' Woman in White,' though I fear that you will have left town before this reaches it. Was the photograph satisfactory ? Pardon a natural curiosity I feel in the welfare of the poor woman, and give me a line to say how all has gone off."

From Rowsley, Walker went on to Perth, where his mother and sister were to join him, on their way to Mr. Ansdell's house by Loch Laggan. From there he wrote to Mr. North, October 15 :—

" Just a line to tell you I am in the land of the living ; shall return to town at the end of this week. The sport on the whole has been better than I expected, because all accounts were of the gloomiest description. I had first of all some good trout and grayling fishing ; then had a line from Graham asking me to go on to him, then another telling me he had to rush off to his ridiculous constituents, but offering me a chance on the Tay. On getting there from Perth, I found the head keeper with a long face. I hadn't seen the river, but soon found it was rather like coffee, so I had to go back again. This was because the river rose immediately after Graham had written. However, he like a great brick, gave me next day and another. Two of the fish I took were 25 lbs. each, and all in prime condition for the time of year. Have taken a few trout here, but it's getting too late ; that on the Tay closed on the 10th. Meanwhile I had to meet my folks, and we're all here together. I've done no work since I left ; the poster appears to be a success. I have here a photo of it ; will send one of 'em to you if I can get one. There are some horrible small copies made of it I hear—lithographs—enough to make one's hair stand up."

October 21, to Mr. Hooper :—

" I returned from the North yesterday morning, and your letter and the small copy of the poster followed me this morning. Of course I am much disgusted with some one [whoever it may be] for so treating me. Nothing would have been easier than to copy on to the wood a photo, which I am sure you would not have refused to cut. It has taken from me all the interest and pleasure I felt in the thing. . . . I am almost inclined to send in a surprising bill for the big poster ; seeing now that they forget I made it quite a labour of love."

October 24, to Mr. Hooper :—

" I should be glad if you could procure for me one or two copies of the big poster. You'd be surprised to hear that the theatre people have been *too busy* even to have the courtesy to send me one. I hear that the play will be produced at Paris, where also the poster will perhaps be seen. I suppose the lettering could easily be altered. If it goes to Paris, I hope and think it will meet with better treatment than it has here. Let me cordially thank you for so *splendidly* cutting it. I'm just off to see Miss Thackeray. She has begged me to resume work with her, and I am going to see about it. Would like to have your services, if possible."

The negotiations respecting further illustrations for the *Cornhill* came to nothing ; not, it is hardly necessary to say, on account of any difference between those immediately concerned. In a subsequent letter to Mr. Hooper, Walker gives the reason of the failure as follows :—

" As for the Cornhill business, I fear it's all over. I have been able to come to no arrangement regarding a certain question of copyright, which I think I have every reason to *insist* upon, and without which I will never again put pencil to wood."

With regard to this mention of copyright, it may be said that among Walker's papers is a list of oil pictures and water colour drawings which he had registered at Stationers' Hall as artist's copyright, evidently under the impression that by so doing he had secured the copyright to himself.

The mere registration was not, of course, sufficient to effect his purpose, and the subject is hardly worth referring to, except as illustrating the apathy in such matters prevalent among artists as a body. It seems strange that a member of the two great representative societies in oil and water colour, anxious to retain the copyright of his works, should be left in ignorance of the means whereby he could attain his object. One would have supposed that every member of either society would, on his election, be furnished with plain and simple rules, founded on the best legal opinion, for his guidance in so important a matter.

THE RAINY DAY.

Of Walker's exhibited works this year there were but three examples : *At the Bar*, at the Royal Academy ; and *A Girl at a Stile*, and *The Housewife*, at the Winter Exhibition of the Old Water Colour Society. He had, however, not been idle. In addition to the unexhibited works already noticed, there are yet to mention *The Evening Walk*, and *The Rainy Day*. Of the former I can say nothing, never having seen the drawing. *The Rainy Day*, though no mention of it appears in the letters, was, I believe, painted at Bisham, which place is within easy access of Spade Oak. It is now to be seen in the South Kensington Museum, and has been etched by Mr. Macbeth.

# CHAPTER XIII.

## 1872.

THE year 1872 will ever remain memorable in Walker's life, as that in which he produced *The Harbour of Refuge*; now, by the munificence of Sir William Agnew, in the National Gallery, and widely known by means of Mr. Macbeth's etching. Whether or not this picture be regarded as Walker's masterpiece, comparison in this respect must be made with what had gone before, as no subsequent work of his hand was destined to dispute the title. Let it not be supposed from this, however, that his powers had reached their highest development—the whole character of the man is against such supposition. Still, as this was the last exhibited oil picture in which his full strength was shown, one could have wished Walker's own words respecting it were more numerous than is the case. It is possible some letters are missing; but I believe [the place being easily reached from town] he made no long stay at Bray, while painting the background of the picture, and that the absence of letters is thus to be accounted for. However this may be, the reader will bear in mind that, for the first three months of the year, Walker was engaged on this picture.

The first letter I have is dated January 30, and addressed to Mr. North :—

" I've rather been looking for a line from you, but suppose it has been *work* and nothing but it. You'll be glad to hear about last night's election at the R.A., where two men were to come on to the Associate list ; but as one of them, it was generally known, must be an architect or engraver, I was chiefly interested in the election of the other—the painter—and John Gilbert [Sir John !] came in after a somewhat exciting scratch ; the highest besides him being Hodgson, Prinsep, Peter Graham, &c., Marcus Stone not being well to the fore. There were others of course, having their one, two, and three scratches, but I'm bound to say I was quite constant to Sir John, for I consider that he has, on the whole, been a most useful man, one that a beastly public has long known, without being aware of it—you know what I mean. How many a good thing of his, you and I have seen in print, recognising the man. How he has worked ! It is not because he is the President of our Society, or because, as a 'sop,' he has a miserable knighthood, he shouldn't be A.R.A.; although [you'll scarce believe it] as a reason against his election, it was urged that *as* a Knight, and the equal with the R.A. President, he, Gilbert, *must* at once be put over the Associates' heads, and be made a full member. If so, all the better, I say. . . . I was anxious to be off with the news for Gilbert, and rushed past Wall & Co. who were to be seen wistfully standing by the railings in Trafalgar Square, to the Garrick. Well, so much for that. Now let me know what you are about, and how it is with you there. I don't know whether I'm on head or heels, but go at it more or less every day."

March 6, to Mr. North :—

"May I ask you to help me in a little matter? I want you to try and obtain for me a *scythe*, of the make peculiar to your part of the country ; one with good 'line,' and with the ornament [cane is it ?] on the handle. It is for my present picture [I have a reaper in full action], which I think goes on as well as can be expected. I have been at it deuced hard, and I think that, for me, it will be a success. These beautiful days make me remember those that are gone—that I passed with you. Tell me how you go on—I mean as to work—just now. Of course we are all slaving away. Well, it will be over all too soon ; and *for me*, I think that I may possibly desire a little fishing, when this is finished. What were you saying about that stream, the Exe, isn't it ? Would it be worth my while going in for it ? Can you furnish me any more information? I half think of going to Derbyshire ; but then the place you named winds through fresh fields and pastures new."

March 13, to Mr. North :—

" The scythe and the flowers both to hand safely ; and a thousand thanks for so kindly helping me. I was intending to write you before post time yesterday, but found self too pumped out at 6. Picture going on all right I think ; wish you could see it before it goes in on the 6th of next month. Can I do anything for you ? . . . The scythe's stunning, but I shall not use the cane-work. I think it'll be a success—it's the quadrangle of an almshouse."

Although there is an absence of letters bearing on the progress of *The Harbour of Refuge*, it is possible, by means of information supplied by Mr. Orchardson, to follow with interest the development of its subject. Mr. Orchardson tells me that in the spring of 1870, when staying at Witley, he and Mr. Birket Foster saw one Sunday in church, a group of old, bent labourers on a long bench in front of the pulpit, reposing in the gleams of sunlight that lightened the gloom of the place. It occurred to them that here was a scene in which Walker would delight. They accordingly sent for him, he came, the scene took

The Harbour of Refuge.—The Original Design (*Water Colour*).

hold of him, and he said he would paint it. From this starting point, by tortuous paths, *The Harbour of Refuge* was to be arrived at.

When, later in the year, Walker joined Mr. Orchardson in Venice, he was still full of the subject—the letter will be remembered in which he speaks of having plans for work in Venice. It seems strange that a painter so essentially English as Walker, should have thought of transplanting to Italy an idea born of his native soil, but so it was. "Might they," he one day suddenly asked Mr. Orchardson, "be Roman Catholics?"—and many hours were spent in a vain endeavour to find a setting for the group of figures among the splendours of St. Mark's. Again he asked, "Might they be resting under the vines?" Mr. Orchardson saw no objection, and lent Walker his gondola for a visit to the mainland. After a day spent at Mestre, Mr. Orchardson met him on his return. His expression of despair showed at once that the vines had been a failure. Soon after this, Walker left Venice ; for no other reason, Mr. Orchardson believes, than that he failed to realise his subject. When next Mr. Orchardson heard of the picture, Walker had found the almshouses at Bray.

Mr. Orchardson's account receives striking corroboration from the position of the group of old men in the original sketch for the picture, which, by the kindness of Sir William Agnew, is here reproduced. It may, too, have been noticed that the letters from Venice in 1870 speak of Walker making sketches in St. Mark's, and also of his intention to go to Mestre.

In comparing the original design with the finished picture, it is noticeable how little the old men have lost by their change of position. Their personality and importance have been preserved in a manner wholly consistent with the account of the growth of the picture out of the simple scene at Witley. These figures were very real to Walker. In the little man waiting to burst in with a flood of talk on any pause in the reading, he took quite an amused interest. Mr. North says, in the article in *The Magazine of Art*, already quoted from :—" The little man in black with his hands on his knees pleased the painter much ; he had a whimsical notion that he might himself become just such a little figure in old age." To me Walker said of him :—" He's the sort of little man who'd talk a donkey's leg off."

After he had decided to move the old men further into the picture, Walker was possessed by the idea that there ought to be a statue of the founder, and wandered about London in search of one. Meeting Mr. Birket Foster one day, he said in his excited manner, "I've got a founder." "Where?" said Mr. Foster. "In Soho Square." Mr. Macbeth remembers being in Newman's, when Walker hurried in, borrowed a brush and some colours, and made a sketch on the spot.

It may interest the reader to know that the statue, though no longer in Soho Square, is still in existence. When the Square was made into a public garden, the statue came into the possession of Mr. Thomas Blackwell, who had contributed largely to the expense of the altera-

tion. By him it was given to Mr. F. Goodall, the Academician, who set it up in some ornamental water in the grounds of Grim's Dyke, Harrow Weald, now the property of Mr. W. S. Gilbert, where it still remains. It is supposed to represent Charles II., and is in the dress of the period.

Walker appears to have materially modified his first idea of the statue. In a notice of the picture in the *Athenæum* for May 4, 1872, the statue is described as " in a bag-wig, knee-breeches, buckles, and a coat with wide lapels " ; a description fairly accurate as regards that of Soho Square, but in no way applying to the statue in the picture. The writer also refers to the picture as *The Old Almshouses*, a title by which it is altogether unknown. The explanation of these discrepancies is, I believe, that the exigencies of the press had required the critique to be prepared in advance. In that case the writer would have relied on notes taken before the picture left the studio ; and as he would certainly not have imagined such a figure as he describes, the statue, as he speaks of it, must either have been on the canvas at the time his notes were taken, or Walker must have told him his then intentions concerning it. In the final rendering, little more than the pose of the Soho statue is retained.

Until the evening of the day on which the picture was sent in, the title had not been determined on. Mr. J. R. Clayton, to whose happy suggestion the naming of the picture was due, gives the following account of the incident :—" I called on Walker in St. Petersburgh Place to see the completion of his picture for the R. A., and nearly missed my object, for the work was on the point of delivery to the carman who was to take it to Burlington House. I found Walker in front of the work, to which he was giving slight touchings ; meanwhile he was in sore perplexity as to the title it should bear in the catalogue. He had tried all kinds of names, but was satisfied with none. While I stood admiring the work he kept calling out excitedly, ' Clayton, there's a trump, do give it a title for me, now do ! ' On the spur of the moment, I suggested ' The Harbour of Refuge.' At this the effect on Walker was electrical. He at once danced about in the studio, snapping his fingers and exclaiming, ' That's it, you can't better that.' I pleaded for second thoughts, and the chance of thinking of something better ; but Walker repudiated all attempt at amendment, and thus the work obtained its name."

In the year 1884, there was still an old man at Bray—" waiting," as he said, " for the end "—who remembered Walker, and pointed out the window from which the background of the picture was painted. This was one of the upper windows, on the left-hand side of the entrance to the quadrangle.

Although certain details of the picture gave rise to some difference of opinion amongst the critics, they practically agreed in their verdict on it as a whole. The *Times* spoke of it as " most exquisite and complete," the *Pall Mall Gazette* saw in it a " powerful and elevated piece of colour and design," the *Saturday Review* pronounced it " after its kind a masterwork," and the *Athenæum* affirmed that "Mr. F. Walker's success almost amounts to a triumph."

After the picture was sent in to the Royal Academy, Walker went for a few days to Farningham, and while there began the water colour of *The Village*. On April 12, he wrote to his mother from the Lion Hotel :—

"Your telegram reached me just as I was going to buy one or two flies suitable for this little stream. It's a success, my coming here for a day or two. . . . The stream here is quite small, and although it passes in front of the house [I can see it coming through the bridge under the road as I write], one has to get to some meadows in order to reach the fishing belonging to the hotel. I left at about 11 this morning, and got a brace of very pretty trout. . . . The day is lovely. This is a small village, nearly, but not quite, like other places—you know what I mean. Every place has a sort of individuality, but there's nothing to *describe* here. Some miller's men come and stand on the bridge and smoke, the rooks 'caw' from some big trees, and I bought some flies at a little chemist's. Am quite comfortable and *quiet*—shall just go on like this until the varnishing days at the R. A. May do a little bit of water colour from this window, on the Sawbath : the bridge, church, &c., come rather well. Hope you'll both do your best to make yourselves happy."

The same date, to Mr. North :—

"There's a rumour that my 'Harbour of Refuge' is snugly placed in the *big room* at the R. A. My folks leave 3 St. Petersburgh for Brighton this afternoon. I want to shake down comfortably at Dulverton as soon as possible ; that is if I can get lodging. . . . Could only get one picture for the Gallery."

Walker's one picture at the Summer Exhibition of the Old Water Colour Society this year was *The Escape*, completed in January. It was the reproduction of an illustration to a story in *Once a Week* for March 2, 1861, entitled *The Magnolia for London with Cotton*, to which reference has already been made.

April 16, from London to his mother :—

"Just a line to say I've got back, and find all right, and everything to be desired, save the well known faces to welcome one. The apple blossom is out next garden, and our own looks neat and jolly. Poor dear Eel-eye has already welcomed me."

April 21, from the Luttrell Arms, Dunster :—

". . . North came to lunch, and I decided with him which way I'd best come ; in the evening went off to Willis's rooms, and heard a good deal that was satisfactory about the picture—for instance, the exact position—which is at the end of the large room, in an admirable place. Perhaps you remember Millais' picture of 'Moses' which was in the

THE ESCAPE.

centre. Well, in that place there is, this year, his picture of three girls playing whist ; on either side are two somewhat unimportant pictures, portraits I think ; beyond these, and on the 'line,' come Calderon's picture and my own, balancing each other as it were. And the council were unanimous in their praise of mine, the President especially ; and last but not least, Frith, who is one of the 'hangers,' has become a convert and a believer in your son's work, and speaks very enthusiastically of the picture. I mention it because I have known that, although he has liked me personally I fancy, he has been an opponent in *effect*, and always regarded my election as premature. I refrain from repeating all I heard he had said, but it was very complimentary. I'll tell you when we meet. Well, on getting down here, of course I inquired about the fishing, and made all arrangements to get over to Dulverton on Friday, 17 miles, but a drive through very beautiful country, and half of it by the banks of the charming little Exe. Enjoyed the drive immensely, and my hopes ran high of a little really nice fishing ; but on getting to Dulverton, I found the best inn a beast of a place, squalid, no one to receive an arrival, except a beery ostler brute who sauntered up ; added to all this, any amount of hammering and painting—the flooring even being up—a pretty prospect for a poor devil in search of peace ; the excuse being that the place was 'changing hands.' I found the only other place a mere pot-house, no lodgings to be had ; so after an hour or so, to rest the horses, some nasty cold meat for self, took my departure, and hope I shall never see Dulverton again. The driver knew of a little inn, about half way back, he said, at a village not much out of the way; so I tried it, but found it a wretched little cold hole, suggestive of despair and suicide. Heaven knows how I should have passed to-day in either place—it's actually *snowing* again, and as there are here and there roses out, you may guess how welcome it seems. . . . . The waiter has just told me that there's no soup ready, because you see, 'we so seldom have visitors in the *winter*.' This makes me feel that your notion of the climate really being unlike that which we had when you were a girl, has something in it; and yet, as I say, there are roses that the last week brought out, and the enclosed bit of hawthorn blossom, which I picked yesterday from a tree as big as that in my picture, and full of blossom, makes it, after all, quite a riddle. If it's like this to-morrow, of course I shall think of going home again."

The same date, to Mr. North :—

" I intended sending a line by last evening's post, but being out, overshot the hour. You'll be surprised to see that I'm still here ; but I must tell you that Dulverton was such a hideous failure that I simply came back as I went. Tried a little village called Winsford, but saw so little chance of comfort that I preferred doing the daily drive, if it so happened that I stayed here at all ; and as there is a return of good old Christmas weather and plenty of snow, I may prefer getting back to the delights of town. Shall see to-morrow, however. This inn is satisfactory, but I can only say that my heart sank as I was set down at the *best* Dulverton Hotel. Heavens! what a place, not even clean, although the beastly house-painters and hammerers were all over the place, flooring up in the basement, &c. Was quite glad to get out of the place again. The second best inn was only a little pot-house, and no lodgings to be had. I drove back again, and as the distance to Dulverton is seventeen miles from this, I felt quite tired of it. The only excuse at Dulverton was that the place was 'changing hands.' There are two places I mean never to see again if I can help it ; that place and Chard."

April 23, to his mother :—

"Only just to say that as it's so unsettled here, I think it best to be back, even if I go away again for a few days up Thames or somewhere, after the varnishing. Much warmer, that's one comfort—so far from the fishing too, and the fishing not so wonderful after all. Have in hand the wee water colour I began at Farningham."

April 26, from London :—

"Just back from the R.A., and it's a *complete success ;* it's *done* this time I think ; congratulations all round, &c., &c. Holds its own wonderfully. No need, dear, to come home until next week ; things seem to be going on so well, that you are better breathing that fresh pure air."

April 29th, to his sister Fanny :—

"Just off to the Academy, and send a line as I may not be back before 5. . . . Get whatever you want to make yourself comfortable as to dress, for the private view, but be sure that whatever you wear is quiet and ladylike. Not a *tinge* of eccentricity, mind ; I've got to loathe it."

Walker appears to have spent the next few weeks in town, and part of the time was engaged on a black and white drawing for the frontispiece of Mr. William Black's *A Daughter of Heth*. Towards the end of May, he was again at Spade Oak.

June 2, to his mother :—

"The telegram confirming last evening's matter came this morning, being, I suppose, too late for the easy-going rustics of these parts ; besides it involved a quarter of an hour's walk in the dark, and the delicate feet of the corduroy-clad messenger might have become damp, and himself bedewed. So your telegram read rather funnily, this being Sunday morning. Very showery, but a sweet soft wind. Have rested at home all the morning, just looking at my colours, and beginning a hint of something tiny, that I'm not sure of going on with to-morrow."

As Walker was constantly going up to town from Spade Oak, the

letters at this time are intermittent, and the references to work are few.
He speaks of "touching on the little Prisoner at the Bar," "cleaning up
a little of the small Prisoner at the Bar"—the picture which was exhibited

Frontispiece to A DAUGHTER OF HETH.

at the Dudley Gallery in the autumn of this year—but beyond this, and
a mention of the "big canvas," presumably *The Peaceful Thames*,
nothing is to be gathered as to the work on which he was occupied.

June 25, to his sister Fanny :—

". . . I cannot refrain from telling you how annoyed I feel at the slightly
impertinent way even —— has of wanting to know more of my whereabouts than you choose to tell. Why, good Heaven, if I told *all* folks of
my work and whereabouts, I should have some of my ' friends and admirers'
sitting down to paint this very hill, *in front of me*. The next person who
asks, answer by saying I'm in Ireland, or dead, whichever you like. I
intend to make a point of preserving as much mystery as *I* like ; tell
people flatly that I intend to keep my movements [whenever I have work
with me] a matter only known to ourselves—they may guess afterwards,
and crib my work after it's exhibited, as much as they choose ; that I
cannot help. . . I have been asked by Stevenson to go to him after the

5th of next month, and think I shall do so, and shall see if it cannot be arranged for you and the Missus to go later, with some comfort to yourselves. I am preparing another drawing for 'Punch,' of these infernal steamers—fifty must have passed this yesterday."

The above extract is worthy of notice, as supplying a reason for that secrecy about his work, which with Walker had grown almost to a passion. Rightly or wrongly, he believed, that in certain quarters, admiration for his works passed legitimate bounds, and manifested itself in a manner calculated to do him harm. It was a subject on which he felt very strongly. His family in this, as in all else, loyally supported him, and were ever on their guard to preserve the secrecy he desired. And thus, in all connected with the scenes and subjects of his pictures, a circle was drawn round the three at St. Petersburgh Place, which few were allowed to enter. The contemplated *Punch* drawing referred to, was not carried out.

July 7, to his mother :—

"Almost too hot to write ; altogether a dreadful day. . . . The picture's certainly going on, and I shall resume it directly I come back from the North, but not *stay* here, that is, I shall have a few days at it, coming down in the morning and returning each evening. It will be quite up to my mark I think."

July 11, from Oban :—

"Just a line to let you know I'm here ; shall stay until Monday morning I think, as I fancy there are some good walks round the coast, and some sea fishing not bad. Who should be here, going on to the Hebrides, but Mr. Black, 'Daughter of Heth,' you know."

*July* 14 :—" . . . And now I'll tell you what I think of this place, and begin by saying that I'm glad I'm going away. The place is lovely enough—you and Fan must remember the kind of scenery—but it's spoiled by a most insufferable kind of tourist, prig, monied, respectable, parsonic, clement—people who stare as they pass you—a set, too, who *dress* for the place, although it's no more than a village. And don't they gorge themselves at the table d'hôte dinner. There was a stout, big-nosed, reverend gent last evening, who told anecdotes that one was *compelled* to hear, so loud was his manner. He drank a deal of wine, and a little later, having to go into the coffee-room to speak to a waiter, I saw this abled-bodied parson at a *meat tea*, provided for those who come afterwards by steamer, &c. The favourite topic is the different routes ; one gets sick of the names 'Glencoe,' 'Fort William,' &c. Yesterday there was a steamer going out from this to Staffa, to a place called Fingal's Cave, and I am glad to say that as it blew fresh all day, and as it was necessary to go right out to sea, some of them did not come into dinner last evening ; but the aforesaid parson was as good as a dozen. . . . That Eel-eye must be shot or pizened ; he'll he having the blackbird next. Or stay, instead of pizening him, he shall be muzzled as dangerous. But are you sure it was a robin, and that he did not *find* it dead? . . . I hope it will be a success, this visit, and that there will be something like sport. I took some little cod, whiting, &c., on Friday, and went out again yesterday, but, as I said, it blew rather fresh, and I did nothing. I did not want to begin with a Sunday at Stevenson's, or should have gone yesterday."

July 17, from Auchineilan, Lochgilphead :—

" . . . I must tell you all about this place in my next ; suffice it now to say that it's a dear little place, *lovely* in fact, overlooking a small loch. The fishing promises to be *pretty* good only, nothing like some that we know of. However, for a few days, it will be to me a perfect rest I'm sure."

*July* 18 :—" . . . You have not received anything like a description of this place, which is really very beautiful, overlooking a small loch, and having solemn-looking hills on the other side ; the coach road running past down below, very much like the road below Corrichoillie. There is a larger loch a little way off—Loch Awe—thirty miles long, and wider than Loch Laggan, and Stevenson has a small screw steamer which is being prepared for use on the loch. To-day, we are going the whole way along to the other end, by a steamer which goes backwards and forwards daily. We are going to the river Awe, which leaves the loch at the other end, and which has good salmon fishing I hear. . . . I am feeling capitally well, and feel that this trip is doing me all the good in the world."

July 19, from Taynuilt Hotel, Bonawe :—

" . . . We came by the loch steamer down Loch Awe, and the river Awe is the stream that runs from it to the sea, and this hotel is situate about midway down, and the keeper of the hotel has the right of fishing one side. It's very like the Spean in parts, and the fishing is good in April, and lasts till October, so altogether it's a ' find.' We're going out again, S. and I, at 5, and I hope I shall have better luck ; but it quite cheers me to think that, at a future time, I can get good fishing so easily. . . . We go back to Auchineilan to-morrow, in time to see Stevenson's own steamer put in the water. . . . I'm awfully well, and shall return like a giant refreshed."

*July* 20 :—" I'm writing this on board the little steamer which carries us back over Loch Awe to Auchineilan. I've just heard that unless I do this, it will not reach you for ever so long. . . . Well, I did nothing last evening, but I am fully resolved to go back again next week. I'm most impressed with the wildness and beauty of that river. They have been catching three and four salmon a day, in some parts, and it's full of sea trout besides. This neighbourhood suits me wonderfully."

*July* 21 :—" I intended writing a whole chapter this evening, and now the stupid time has gone by, and your old boy feels tired after this prosy day. Not that there's any news. I've taken no salmon, only a trout or two : my bad luck quite astonishes S., he never knew the like he says. We're going up the hills to-morrow—just he and I—to some loch fishing there, and perhaps on Wednesday I go back to the Awe for a day or two, and then may perhaps think of going S. to my dearest Mum. Bless you and dear Fan a thousand times. Your loving care at home, and the feeling I have, in consequence of knowing that you are both there, and that two on whom I may most fully rely, will, please God, still be there when I return, is by no means the least of your boy's comfort in closing this and his eyes to-night."

*July* 22 :—" Just one line, my dearest. Been out all day, and very sleepy now. Been up among the hills with Stevenson, to some little lochs there. Took six dozen small trout. . . . To-morrow shall be on the loch here. There's to be some netting of the fish, and I'm anxious to see the result."

*July* 23 :—" . . . Some fishing with the net done in the loch to-day, showing what glorious trout it really contains, and I must say I was astonished. You see I've done nothing here as yet : no luck, no breeze, and yet it has not been very hot."

July 26, from Taynuilt Hotel, Bonawe :—

" . . . I'm quite disgusted with the fishing ; my luck has been so bad, I am quite demoralised by it. All this morning I fished without getting a single rise, except that of trout. I shall go out again in a little while, but don't expect to do anything, there's been so much lightning. Why, I'm told that at 1 o'clock this morning it was terrible, but confess I was fast asleep. I know that a perfect storm of wind and rain raged here

when I arrived, and to-day it's half a gale, making it most difficult to keep the fly on the water. . . . I'm sorry to have had such bad luck, but the change has been a very good one, and I mustn't grumble. Well, I suppose I sha'n't write again before leaving. I get back to Auchineilan to-morrow. . . . 9.30 p.m. *Just taken a salmon;* a handsome little fellow of 10 or 11 lbs., lovely in shape, shall take it to Stevenson to-morrow—only just time to say this. Raised two others—shall come here again if I'm spared."

August 4, to Mr. North :—

" . . . I've just come back from some fishing in Scotland, and am in for some work here for some weeks. Tell me if you're coming up or going down, or what."

After his return to London, Walker was engaged on the drawing begun at Farningham—*The Village*—completing it about the end of August. Already he had decided on reproducing *The Harbour of Refuge* in water colour, and had the oil picture in his studio for a fortnight during this month. He does not, however, appear to have made much progress with the reproduction this year. Other work was probably the Spade Oak subject, as he had had the canvas sent up to town.

September 7, to Mr. North :—

" . . . I am still at work here, both in oil and water, in hopes of making a decent show next year, and this winter. I want to get away though, and contemplate a dash of a few days to the North before settling down. The afternoon before last, I went to Brighton, having on me a sudden impulse to see the Aquarium there, and certainly it is very wonderful ; in some respects, far beyond that at Sydenham, although very incomplete as yet. I left yesterday morning by coach, and arrived in town with some of the vapours blown from me. Let me know when you contemplate coming up, and what work you have been about."

From his boyish days, Walker had always been fond of an aquarium. Not very long after this, he had quite a large one, with a slate bed, put up in the studio. It was never stocked ; nor, indeed, altogether completed at the time of his death.

September 14, from the Peacock Hotel, Rowsley, to his mother :—

" . . . Well, I've had no sport ; the fish aren't rising at all, though each day may bring a change. But I've half a mind not to stay very long, but push forward N. Of this I'll give you notice either by telegram or letter. To-morrow I shall do a little bit of work, I hope, that I mentioned before starting. . . . This place has some very good bits about it ; but has the same objection to it that I found at Oban, viz. a tendency to be bothered by amiable, monied, and highly respectable tourists—people who go to Haddon and to Chatsworth, and who

THE VILLAGE.

just now seem to affect fiery-red shawls, and a loud gossiping way of talk, and who stare besides—the females these, the men one needn't mention. Of course I may go on to Graham if I get so far as Kelso ; will see. But meanwhile, know ye both that I am well and happy, and at this moment tired with tramping about in long grass in my ' waders ' all day. . . . I truly hope you will both make yourselves as comfortable as possible, so far as the resources of the little place permit."

*September* 18 :—" . . . I am getting sick of having no sport. I've just telegraphed both to Graham, and to the people at Taynuilt. Of course it's probable that both the Tay and the Awe are not in good order, and in that case I shall come straight home. You ought both to go somewhere ; you'd have nothing to do here, unless it were wading through wet grass. It's blowing a bit, too, now ; and I can only say that if it weren't that I don't think I've quite set myself up for the next six months' work, I should come home to-morrow. I'm quite well, though ; I mean feeling an absence of all *seediness* that I've so often complained of lately."

*September* 20 :—" Your letter at any rate makes me decide upon remaining here until Monday. Whether I then go North, or return home, will depend a little on a letter that I shall expect from Graham by Monday. You see I don't like spending more money than I can help ; but, as you say, I had better do all I now can, to help me to the hard work I must go in for when I get back."

*September* 22 :—" Just a few lines to tell you of my movements—my ' autumn manœuvres'. . . . You had better send a telegram to Pople's Hotel, Perth, to-morrow, so that I shall get it on my arrival to-morrow night. A telegram from Graham came last evening while I was at dinner, offering me one of the beats on the Tay for Tuesday, the only day available for that particular beat. . . . I only took one trout again yesterday ; should have done well, I think, for the fish were rising, when a sudden storm came on. A flash of lightning went off close to me, like a gun, then an awful peal of thunder. It was so close that I fairly bolted, putting my fishing things under a bush. . . . I've begun a bit of work that'll pay expenses, I fancy."

Of the subject of the " bit of work " referred to, there is no record.

On his return to town, after only a few days in Scotland, Walker began the drawing of *A Fishmonger's Shop*, considered by many to be his highest achievement in water colour dealing with an original subject. On October 29, he wrote to Mr. North :—

" I'm working hard at a fishmonger's shop, with a great slab of fish, and a fair buyer ! "

In making sketches of the shop, he worked from the inside of a

four-wheeled vehicle—cab or brougham—and again found a model for
the female figure, in his sister Mary. Accounts differ as to the locality
of the shop. The drawing was subsequently etched by Mr. Macbeth,
and in the circular announcing the etching, it was positively stated that
the shop was situate in Arabella Row, near Buckingham Palace ; but on
what authority, I am unable to ascertain. No single site, however,
furnished all the material which Walker required. My own impression
[confirmed by Mr. North] is that the slab of fish was taken from a shop
in Bond Street. Mr. North also tells me that a shop at Hampton
Court suggested the cornice and balustraded entablature.

At the Winter Exhibition of the Old Water Colour Society, the
drawing was well received. The *Saturday Review*, after taking exception
to the subject as " unsavoury," said :—" No display is less agreeable to
the senses than a shop-front full of fish, and yet by skilful art treatment,
dependent on a harmony of colour, on balance of composition, on
illusive realism, and on cunning dexterity of pencil, a perfect triumph is
gained." *Athenæum* :—" The showboard is loaded with superbly painted
fish of all kinds, of all degrees of lustre and colour, an aggregate of gems,
the splendour of which has rarely been approached. . . . This is a little
masterpiece of colour, both local and general." The criticism of the
*Times*, was so appreciative, that, at the risk of wearying the reader, it is
here given in full. " If we want a contrast with Sir John Gilbert in
every point of character and power, we may find it in Mr. F. Walker,
another Associate of the Academy, who ranks as high in water colour
as in oil. In him exquisiteness of finish, the subtlest pictorial feeling,
and the most delicate sentiment of grace and refinement, replace the
facility of conception and arrangement, the dash and vigour of execution,
and the enjoying sense of the picturesque, which carry us over much
that is commonplace and careless in the work of Sir John Gilbert. Mr.
Walker's power is of that fine order which can find food in any subject,
however, at first blush, unpromising for refined treatment. Thus he has
here made a perfectly delightful drawing [330] out of an old-fashioned
fishmonger's stall, such as may still be found in many a London suburb.
By throwing his figures into the costume of sixty years ago he escapes
from the familiarity which often jars with artistic association, besides
getting an opportunity for showing his peculiar secret of grace in the
figure of a lady and boy in the fashion of 1810, the unbecoming nature
of which, in the lady's case at least, the painter's exquisite feeling has
completely overcome, and, indeed, converted into an attraction. The
boy pauses, hoop in hand, to look at the eels in their large earthen pot ;
the smiling old fishmonger is leaning forward to verify his customer's
choice. The long and low-browed front of the shop is painted a
weather-beaten green, on the ledge of which stands a row of red flower
pots, with creeping plants. This combination of reds and greens,
charming in its subtleties and refinements of colour, serves as the frame,
within which, relieved against the dark back-ground of the ill-lighted
interior, is displayed the rich lading of the great wooden slab, with the

metallic green of mackerel, the silver of salmon, the shot sheen of
herring, the rose of red-mullet, and all the intermingling russet and
golden browns and purples of gurnets and plaice and perch, and other
fresh and salt-water fish, flashing and playing into one another with a
splendour due to nature, but a subtle harmony of arrangement due to the
painter.   This splendour of colour is concentrated by the mellow green
of the painted woodwork, and supported by the piles of baskets, of
whose rich browns the painter has made the most artful use, while the
great earthenware eel-pot, catching the full light, gives the key-note to
the highest passages of colour.   We can remember nothing of the
painter's more strikingly showing his artistic instinct than this drawing,
or more worthy of close study by those who wish for an illustration of
the wealth of pictorial subject-matter lying unused and unsuspected
around them.   The grace of the woman and boy is so much thrown
in by the painter beyond the suggestions of the fishmonger's shop, and
is just what we should not have had in a Dutch version of such a
subject."

The drawing—$14\frac{1}{2}$ by $22\frac{3}{4}$ inches—was purchased from the easel by
Mr. Frederick Lehmann, for the sum of 600 guineas.

December 5, to Mr. Stevenson :—

" . . . The Fosters intend to have another jollification at Xmas, and,
*entre nous*, something on a complete scale in the *theatrical* line is contemplated, into which your humble servant is drifting.   The accompanying
wood-cut and sketch require some explanation.   The wood-cut—but per-

haps you may have seen it before—was a caricature of a certain offensive person on the Thames, whose vile steamer was the detestation of everybody, and whom I christened Capt. Jinks. I have often spoken strongly of steamers on the Thames, where they are utterly out of place ; but the sketch, which is a caricature of my caricature, was sent to me by some one I suspect to live not 100 miles from Witley, after I had been *in your yacht on Loch Awe*—too cruel, was it not ? Your steamer is quite in keeping on a vast lake ; but our friend Jinks is the leader of a thing that will eventually be the ruin of our sweet Thames."

The Christmas merry-makings at Mr. Birket Foster's hospitable house had always been thoroughly enjoyed by Walker, and he probably drifted into the theatricals without reluctance. From a programme before me, I learn that the pieces played were *The Birthplace of Podgers*, and *Fish out of Water*; Walker taking the part of "Mr. Erasmus Maresnest [a Literary Enthusiast]," in the first piece. How he acquitted himself I do not know ; but Mr. Orchardson tells me that at these gatherings Walker would sometimes show great power of assuming and sustaining a character by himself, and with but little aid from "make up." On one occasion, he came into the room as "Major Walker," with whitened hair and eyebrows, and a high collar, and deceived every one. At such times, with the throwing off of his own character, his natural shyness and nervousness would disappear.

The scene for the second piece—a library—was painted by Walker. A year or so ago, it was disposed of at public auction, together with other scenery which was painted by Mr. Birket Foster.

# CHAPTER XIV

1873

THERE were doubtless times during the gaieties at Witley, when Walker's thoughts turned to his plans for serious work. In a letter from his mother, dated from Milford on the first day of the New Year, there is evidence that the picture to which a peculiar and pathetic interest attaches, had been by this time determined on—the unfinished picture which has been named *The Unknown Land*. So great an interest indeed, does this "glorious subject," as Walker calls it, possess in itself, that there is no need to endeavour to enhance it by reading a special meaning into the title, or by supposing the picture to have been conceived at a time when he felt that his health was failing. The title was, after all, merely suggested as a probable one ; while he worked a great deal on the picture before his health had unmistakably begun to fail. At what period his family were first seriously anxious about him, I never knew. On such a subject they were silent, as if in dread lest the utterance of their fears should bring about a confirmation of them. Not for some time to come was there any outward sign of change ; and if here and there in this year's letters there seems a plaintive tone, subdued, sad, and of an added gentleness, solicitude for his mother may have been the cause. However this may be, she was with him now, to send him New Year's greeting in these words :—

"My dearest Son, I cannot but think of you, since you left, your continual patience and never failing kindness to me, and so many others have come to my mind in full force. May God bless you and return it tenfold, this is no hackneyed sentence, my dear, but in the fulness of my heart I mean it. . . . I will go home strong to help you, my Fred, in all I can, you will I know say how, frankly as to a dear friend and grateful Mother."

Walker's efforts in the histrionic line had left him rather overdone. On January 2, he wrote to his mother :—

". . . Am feeling the result of the last week a good deal to-day, slightly languid and low—shall be all right in a day or so, but wonder that I feel so well, considering how little rest I had—won't do it again in a hurry."

And on January 4, to Mr. Hooper :—

". . . I have just returned in a perfectly *battered* condition, from a terrible bout of private theatricals and scene painting, and find your letter looking me reproachfully in the face, from the table where I left it in the hurry of my departure."

The tone of a letter to his mother on the same date is, however, more promising as regards work :—

"No news, and no letters. Am getting into harness again, thank goodness. Dined at Garrick Club last night, and was asking an old member about Dawlish, Teignmouth, &c., and fancy from what he said, I shall have to go perhaps to Plymouth, or even to Cornwall. Am not sorry to be on dry land during this rough weather. Shall give up the idea of a voyage to Canaries ; it would take a week each way at least, which I cannot afford. May go again to Canterbury too, and use my old subject of the little pale boy watching near a grave. Shall alter it to an old woman busy with some bright flowers on a green mound—the boy there, as in my first notion. A beautiful bit there is at a corner of Canterbury Cathedral. Am going to work very hard."

Though again in Walker's thoughts, the old subject of the boy near a grave was not to be taken up. More pressing work lay before him in *The Unknown Land*, the picture indicated by the reference to Dawlish and Teignmouth in the foregoing letter. The subject of this picture—mariners, after a long voyage, arriving at an unknown shore, and beaching their boat with feverish eagerness—was itself a development of an old idea. In the illustration to *The Settlers of Long Arrow*, in *Once a Week* for October 12, 1861,[1] the sweep of the bay, the position of the boat, and the figure of a boy coming up the beach, are clearly the forerunners of the water colour studies for the picture ; and, as has already been mentioned, the illustration was in Walker's studio at the time of his death. For the carrying out of the subject, a sojourn at the coast was necessary ; hence the inquiries of which Walker speaks. Further inquiry, however, seemed

See page 29.

S

to point to Lulworth as more likely to suit his purpose, and to this place he went on January 12.

January 13, Cove Hotel, Lulworth, to his mother :—

"By this you'll have received my scrawl of yesterday at the station at Wareham, and I found that it was a ten mile drive here, so I did not arrive until after dark, rather tired, but none the worse, and took a little stroll to the Cove which looked in the moonlight very good, but not answering every expectation, and I'm afraid I shall have to go on further for some of the 'material.' However, the water looked limpid and clear, as it broke on the little beach that glistened in the moonlight. Later, the wind seemed to get up, and during the night seemed to reach a gale, with rain. This morning is rough, and with a grey sky, and I haven't yet gone out, for if it must be confessed, I was troubled in the night with a very unromantic pain in my foot, . . . I am forced to think that it is a touch of *gout*. This is a very quiet village of a few houses, and this 'Hotel' isn't *palatial*, but isn't uncomfortable. . . . I sha'n't think of leaving this until I've *done something*, if only a sketch, although I may find it possible to work most of it here ; but the *shipping element* is quite wanting, only a few small fishing boats being visible, and those hauled up from the water while it's so rough."

*January* 14 :—"I have just come in from making some little mems. and sketches, and shall begin a design from them directly I send this off. . . . I have been hobbling about and getting a notion of the place — feel that I shall make something of it, and am eager for the fray. I fancy that this precious foot is all produced by that hard work and anxiety at Xmas, and it will be a lesson. . . . When the wind blows from the N., I am told that this little Cove is like a millpond ; and with a good blue sky overhead, it must look very lovely. A beautiful little brook of crystal water runs into it, which of course I mean to paint."

*January* 15 :—"The easel has arrived, the foot is almost well, and I have decided on staying, and going at it here as hard as possible. I've been this morning for a walk to a place where there are some fine rocks standing by themselves in the sea ; and altogether I feel that there is, or ought to be, quite enough to work from, here, and I'm just going to undo the canvas and put it together. . . . I shall be able to work partly in a boat house on the beach, belonging to the coast guard. Don't tell any one where I am, North excepted, and ask him from me not to mention it."

*January* 18 :—" . . . By this post I have sent a letter to Newman's in Soho Square, directing them to prepare immediately a stretcher for my picture, 6 ft. by 4 ft., which is a little bigger than the one I brought down, but not too big for the canvas I have begun on. The reason I mention this is, that I have in my letter to them requested that they

DESIGN FOR THE UNKNOWN LAND—(*water colour*).

would immediately let you or Fan know the exact hour when it will be finished, that you may either call or send for it, taking it on to Waterloo, thus losing no time ; besides I want you or Fan to write the address label, which may be tied on at Waterloo. You know there won't be any mistake then, besides I don't want the ' A.R.A.' to be scrawled all over it. . . . To-day is bright, and if the wind would but go down, I should at once try to make a study of the sea. Shall have to press into my service the coast guard men and their boat, indeed they seem about the only folks about [thank goodness], and I've already permission to work from their boat house. I had to engage their services in a manner that made me feel like a fool. My macintosh blew into the sea while I was making a little sketch, and I was powerless to rescue it, with my game foot, and saw it being carried right out ; so had to limp up to the little row of houses where they live, and ask their help, and they went off in a boat for it, to the tune of a ' bob ' each."

January 18, Saturday night :—" It's a pouring, dreadful, night here ; goodness knows how long this is to last. I'm getting sick of this rough weather, and begin to long for a little quiet, though it might be colder. I cannot help thinking of the poor souls out at sea. I don't get on quite so well in the evening, as I could wish, with my work, because there doesn't seem to be even an oil lamp in the house ; two candles don't give me light enough, and I think you'd better send one of those reading lamps, if you can spare it. . . . Shall make something of this picture, I hope, but am fidgeting at not getting on quicker. . . . I feel as if I'd been away a month. Shall not be sorry to get this picture into such a state as will bring me back to work in the barn. . . . Pouring cats and dogs. *Sunday morning.* Yours enclosing ——'s just come. . . . You see by his letter *he's a gossip,* and I'd very much rather have no one coming down here, through being told by him, *I'm* here. One of my ' followers' that he speaks of I mean, and there's plenty of time for any one who hasn't anything particular to keep him in town, to *come down here for a subject.* It has been an awful night, and this morning is dark and wet. I can see the ' white horses' tearing into the entrance of the Cove. . . . Your little line of this morning gives me the idea of being written in low spirits. Keep up, my dear, as well as possible, for the sake of your loving F."

January 20, Weymouth : —" Such a beast of a cold blustering day, I thought I'd come over here to have a look at the ships, of which there are plenty in Portland Bay. . . . I've been thinking of introducing in my picture some shrubs or trees, just seen in the foreground ; and directly I get back [next Monday], I think of going to the Botanical Gardens, Regent's Park, to see if there are any *orange trees,* aloes, or palms ; in fact anything that I might ' go in ' for, that is to be found in a hot-house, and there is a splendid one at the Botanical Gardens. If Fan can spare the time, . . . she might even go to the Gardens for an hour, perhaps

with Poll, and report to me whether there *are* any good orange trees, &c.
. . . I only wish the weather would get calm. There was a little snow
in the night, which isn't all melted in the hollows and in the shade. You
know I hate snow, and I get sick of hearing the wind. It seems clearing
up a bit now ; shall venture forth."

January 21, Lulworth :—" The stretcher, &c., and letters and paper,
arrived safely this morning, and a thousand thanks. Am hard at work ;
have stretched the canvas, and will not let anything interrupt me. . . .
Wind changed, and shall hope for smooth water now. Yes, send the
lamp, as I must work at certain sketches at night. . . . My only chance
is in working hard—getting to bed pretty early, which I do here."

*January* 23 :—" Box arrived safely at noon. All right, nothing
broken, thousand thanks, no time for more, best love, F."

*January* 24 :—" All right ; *am hard at it*, and feeling more hopeful
about it. . . . Don't think I shall come up till Tuesday—no need to—
and every hour here is of importance. There's a train reaches Waterloo
at 5.30, which will be time enough I think for the meeting, which is at
7.30. The lamp is a great comfort."

The meeting which brought Walker to town was for the purpose of
electing three Associates to the Royal Academy. Walker was not one to
shirk the duties which his connection with the Academy and the Old
Water Colour Society imposed on him. He returned to Lulworth the
day after the election.

*January* 30 :—" A *beast* of a day this, snow that just now doesn't
stay, but I know that as soon as the evening comes on, it will get colder,
and I'm afraid that we shall have it pretty deep to-morrow. I've plenty
to do indoors, and I certainly shall make a movement in a day or two, to
see first what Beer is like ; and I have come across a photo, among those I
brought down, of Anstey's Cove, and I can plainly see that in some
respects it will suit me better than this, so I shall probably go on to Torre
or Torquay, whichever is most suitable, and probably hire a *bathing
machine* to work in. Shall *go at it hard* any way ; *won't* give up if I can
help it. . . . Am quite well, and more hopeful about my work."

*January* 31 :—"Shall leave to-morrow at 11, for either Beer or
Torquay [I think the latter]—can't make anything more of this Cove,
and am sick of the discomfort and bother of the little place. May
possibly come back for the little stream, but shall be able to tell later."

February 2, Torquay :—" I reached this at about 6 last night, feeling
tired and disgusted with the journey, which was a very tiresome one, because there were so many changes—besides one long coach drive, two
ditto omnibus [from station to station], making the journey infinitely

more wearing, and longer in *time*, than if I'd come from Bayswater—and all this to find it cold, pouring wet, and a tearing wind from the E. I took a walk last night, and thought a great deal about the position of affairs ; and having been to-day to see Anstey's Cove, I have come to the conclusion that I cannot do better than *take my own time* over this glorious subject, and give up the idea of having it in *this* Academy Exhibition. I do not think I should be doing myself justice in going on with it against time ; and when I remember what may be made by a combination of Lulworth and Anstey's Coves in *warm still weather*, compared with the almost overwhelming difficulties of rough dark weather and bitter cold wind, I'm sure all sensible men would say I'm a fool to persevere. The landscape and sea I might get through with, but I am desirous of making the figures all important, and have a scheme in connection with it, that I cannot carry out now. The pluckier course in short, is to make it as fine as my powers will allow me.

"At this moment I am undecided whether to stay on to make one or two studies that will help me at home, or to come up on Tuesday ; in any case, I would like to fix on one or two little matters to-morrow at the cove, there's a sort of wood house down on the lovely beach, for instance, where I might work, and to-day being Sunday, could find no one there. The beach and the headlands are far finer than Lulworth I think, but then the cove has not the beautiful circular sweep that the water at Lulworth takes, nor the stream of fresh water, but between the two, I know I can make it all I want. The sea to-day, instead of having a gentle ripple on to the beach, was thundering in in a manner quite frightful, and clay-coloured, instead of green and limpid. . . . You mustn't imagine that I've given up any idea of sending at all to the Academy—there's yet time for me to go on with what I intended doing, but I am confident that this is the best course to pursue with regard to this big one, and a big one it shall be before I've done with it.

"I naturally felt a little dispirited as I walked about in this place, last evening especially, but am not sorry I came. I thought of bygone times with a feeling that, all things considered, what was done here *was certainly for the best*—a sad time enough for you both."

Walker left Torquay on February 5, and spent the next four weeks in London. This prolonged stay in town, at a season when his plans for the Academy would seem to have necessitated work in the open, may possibly have been due to the occurrence at this time of a "break down in the spring," mentioned in a subsequent letter. At the beginning of March, he went once more to Woolstone.

Of the work, if any, on which he was engaged while in town, there is no record. I believe the words "what I intended doing" referred to *The Peaceful Thames*, as he certainly made an effort to send this picture to the Academy, and may have worked on it during his stay in London. The first letters from Woolstone, however, do not apparently relate to this picture, but to the large canvas intended for *Mushroom Gatherers*—pre-

Design for The Unknown Land—(*water colour*).

sumably the " Grand Landscape, painted in Somersetshire," now in Mr.
Leslie's possession, of which he speaks in *Our River*. It would almost seem
as if, after laying aside the Torquay canvas, Walker had a little lost
heart ; and though he worked on both *Mushroom Gatherers* and *The
Peaceful Thames*, it was apparently without any very sanguine expectation
of having either ready in time for the Academy. In addition to these
two oil pictures, he had with him at Woolstone the *Fishmonger's Shop*,
received from the Old Water Colour Society for further work, and was
also engaged on the small version of the same subject.

March 5, Woolstone :—" All right, as you may guess ; got here at
9 last night, and found North waiting at the station. Hope you had my
telegram from Taunton. To-day has been most lovely, and I have fairly
got to work, and only left off at dusk."

March 6, to his sister Fanny :—

". . . The place is just the same here as usual—the gentle meadows,
the birds singing like mad, and the same knowing old dog who gave me
a cordial welcome. Mrs. Thorne too, just as if I'd never left the place.
Well, it's a *rest* certainly, only I hope it isn't selfish to leave home cares
behind me."

March 9, to his mother :—

". . . Have been working at the 'Fishmonger' to-day, and part of
yesterday, as some of the big picture is wet, and I cannot go on as I wish
until it's quite hard, which will be to-morrow I think. Weather warm
but showery, nothing to complain of ; shall be able to tell you more of the
picture to-morrow or next day. . . . I'm quite well and jolly. Of course
I wish I could tell you more about the picture, but we agreed that it
would be of no use to *worry* one's self about it. As you say, I ought to
make the most of this truly beautiful fresh air, and I do."

*March* 10 :—" . . . Have been finishing up the 'Fishmonger.'
Weather here very windy and showery, so have not been working out of
doors ; besides a lot of paint on my canvas I am awaiting to get dry.
Self and North all right. Have done a lot to the 'Fishmonger' to-day,
and have told Lehmann that he'll see a great improvement."

*March* 11 :—" I have been getting at the big picture again, although
I have not taken it out of doors—there has been half a gale blowing, and
I had a lot to go on with. Altogether, I cannot say I am as hopeful as
I ought to be about it. You see I've not had a good chance yet out of
doors ; but if to-morrow is fine and pretty calm, shall go at it all day,
for it is at length in a good state for taking out."

At this time, Mrs. Walker was far from well, and the next letter is to
his sister Fanny.

*March* 16 :—"I don't know what to say about leaving this, but expect it will be on Tuesday. . . . I hope you had my telegram last night. We walked to Williton and I sent it about 20 or half past 7. What a night it was! It seemed too bitter even for snow ; but before we went to bed it had begun to fall, and it's coming down quite thick, all to-day, and there seems to be a tendency in the snow to come from the W., so perhaps we shall have another change. I haven't done all I want here, but it would be silly to remain if the weather keeps bad ; can easily take it to Marlow for a day or two at the end of the time, returning to town in the evening. Been wondering so much how my dearest Missus is to-day, hope she will go on as we expect she will."

Same date, to his sister Mary :—

" . . . Well, I've worked very hard here, and persistently too ; but to-day makes me think that it's all up with any more open air work for the present. Must show it to you directly I get back ; want your help with a dress of a girl in the Mushroom picture. It's snowing hard enough now, and I only fear it may interfere with the mail cart to Taunton."

On March 18, Walker went up to town, taking the picture with him.

March 19, to Mr. North :—

" According to our arrangement, I write to tell you how I have gone on, and how the Mushroom picture looks. You'll understand when I say that I have used nothing but *benzine and rag* this morning, on the right-hand side, both above and below the ' broom ' bush, and it looks all the better for it already ; altogether it looks about as satisfactory as I expected. I am by no means sure that I can finish in time ; shall go on quietly. It was a great mistake to deepen that side of the picture so much ; quite destroyed the look of reflected light that it ought to have. Am still greatly pleased with what I did on the ' Fishmonger's Shop ' while with you. . . . A beast of a day this ; shocking bad light, and a devilish N.E. wind that moans and groans. Am pestered to death with models who want the sitting at the R. Academy. My Mother is by no means so improved as I could wish—she seems very prostrate, and my sister looking anxious and harassed."

March 24, to Mr. North :—

" . . . You will like to hear of my progress with the picture ; and although I have kept to it most constantly, I fear I must say that I begin to give up all hopes of doing enough to it to warrant me in sending it to the Exhibition. It's useless to shut one's eyes to what may be done at a time when one hasn't to battle with *everything*—want of light, want of nature to work from, want of everything save hurry and worry. God help me, there's enough of that ; the wretched models even are all engaged by Jones and Smith, although they can find time to literally haunt the place in quest of this Academy sitting. I don't feel that I am doing myself justice in going on in this delirious fashion, though I don't for a moment regret having carried it as far as I could under these circumstances. Yesterday I went so far as to think I'd not go to the meeting at Pall Mall to-day, but my good sister persuaded me to give up at 2 o'clock, and go to the 'election of Associates,' and there *wasn't* one ! Understand that there was *no one* elected. I do consider it a bad sign, going into that gallery and not being able to feel comfort in looking at the precious things extending right round the walls of the gallery. The most powerful of the contributions were by the *rising* school ; you know already the names I could mention—a brother of some one already in the Society, and two men who seemed to copy the faults of others, again in the Society—so who can be blamed for thinking that we have enough of it without bringing them in? There was the usual stuff, so bad that one could even smile at it ; but it was not a flattering or comforting thing for the Society."

Walker returned to Woolstone on Saturday, March 29, having only a week in which to finish anything he intended sending to the Royal Academy.

*March* 30 :—"On reaching Taunton, I couldn't help sending the telegram, which I hope was received before you had 'retired.' I felt very tired and very low-spirited during the whole journey, but, thank God, I had a thoroughly good night's rest, and this morning had a sensation of renewed hope about this picture ; but I shall not *think* even about Saturday, shall go at it each day early and late, and I know that I can thoroughly rely on North's opinion as to sending, when the last moment arrives, if I am then undecided. The young girl he mentioned will do very capitally, and is each day at my service, thanks to North's arrangement. The rain came on to-day, while I was attempting a short sitting from her in the orchard at the back of this house, and I have since worked indoors. Am quite thankful to have been away from all the bothering 'callers' to-day. I hope and pray, my dearest Mother, you will keep getting better ; the one and only thing for you is quiet, and no anxiety about others : you at any rate have the knowledge that I at least am in the right place, and am feeling much more myself than I did all last week."

*April* 1 :—"All right, just come in, and can scarcely see. I want Fan to go to Spooner's, corner of Wellington Street and Strand, and ask for some photos of sheep and lambs, and send them on at once. Have worked like a nigger, and am hopeful. The 'Telegraph' can say what it likes, but I don't happen to be painting 'Mushroom Gatherers'—by this you'll see I have altered my subject, and have still the Mushrooms for another time. Mail-cart's due. No more save love."

This change of subject, so late in the day, would seem to show that Walker could have had but faint hopes of sending anything to the

Academy. It is curious, too, as bearing on his frame of mind at the time, that though he speaks of having given up the *Mushroom Gatherers*, he still asks for photographs of sheep and lambs, which were undoubtedly to be used for that picture. It was, however, really laid aside, and the few remaining days were devoted to his other subject, *The Peaceful Thames.*

*April* 3 :—" All right, *shall finish*, and if I don't write again, expect me by the train that reaches Paddington at six o'clock on Saturday. Have done a month's work to-day."

April 6, from London, to Mr. North :—

"You will learn with perhaps some surprise, and *at first* perhaps a little disgust, that the picture did not leave this house last night. I came to the conclusion—and my folks here to-day agree with me most fully in the course I have taken—that it is a far more creditable and right course to pursue, to *go on with it* rather than let it be seen in its present state. The best part of what I have done is utterly lost and put down by that which I have commenced on the canvas, without being able to carry through ; but you know so thoroughly, that I need not even speak to you of the great effort it cost me last night to make this decision. I am *convinced*, however, that it is a good and *dignified* one, if I may say so, and I feel that I shall not think otherwise in time to come. Probably I shall take it down to you again ; but meanwhile shall work on the hill up Thames, sending it down to-morrow perhaps, while I finish the ' Fish-monger's Shop.' Understand plainly that I think there is very little really *lost* work, but it requires to be developed, and the subject to be carried more to the foreground—more of this anon. I am a little fatigued to-day, and fear that I interrupted your work yesterday. . . . Tell us if there is anything we can procure for you, or send you, in the way of dress or ' properties,' or indeed anything that may help you in working the water colours."

The same date, to Mr. Agnew :—

"Your letter was forwarded to me by my sister, and I am sure you will quite understand my not having replied to you, or indeed having written to any one or seen any one, when I tell you that I again took my work to Somersetshire, and on returning to town last night, after a week of most severe work, came to the conclusion that the more dignified course with regard to my picture would be to go on with it, rather than allow it to be seen in its present state—this conclusion I came to on seeing in my own room, how much more might be made of a subject and kind of work that ought at least to have the very utmost care that I am able to give it."

And so the picture was left unfinished. Whether Walker worked on it again I do not know ; but if so, he probably took from, rather than added to it, as the idea he undoubtedly had at one time, of sending the picture to that Academy Exhibition, hardly seems compatible with the state in which it remained at the time of his death.

Though unnecessary for the artist reader, it may be well to state that the alterations Walker so frequently made in his pictures were not caused by any inability to overcome technical difficulties, but were due to a recognition—intuitive, Mr. North thinks—of the necessity of bringing all the component parts of the picture into harmony with the dominant theme.

At the Summer Exhibition of the Old Water Colour Society, Walker's only contribution was *The Village*, already mentioned as having been painted in the preceding year. This drawing has been etched by Mr. C. Waltner.

After a month or so in town, Walker was planning another fishing excursion. On May 16, he wrote to Mr. Stevenson :—

" . . . Now you must, like a good fellow, let me know on what day you reach Auchineilan. Goodness knows I am anxious enough to get away, but a beastly east wind is blowing hard, giving me the blues, for I know there's no enjoyment to be had while it lasts. I dream of fishing every night—crystal streams of immense depth, and fish of monstrous size.

Will tell you in good time of my departure, and meantime shall anxiously look for a line from you telling that all is well."

May 25, from Dunoon, to his mother : —

" Just a line to say I am all right, and feeling much revived already by this glorious change, and am looking forward to joining Stevenson to-morrow. Will tell you all about this beautiful place in my next. . . . Hope you are both better than when your *poor old worry* was with you. Shall return quite another creature, I am sure."

May 26, Auchincilan :—"Got here in safety, and have been out with Stevenson and his friend Mr. Watts, fishing on the loch. Very late, and self very tired."

The Mr. Watts here mentioned, is Mr. H. E. Watts, the well-known author of the *Life of Cervantes* and other works.

*May* 29 :—"Just returned from Taynuilt, that's to say, the yacht reached this end of the loch at about ¼ past 10, and as I was up at 5 this morning, am pretty tired, for I fished until this afternoon most carefully. I got up early, because the only chance of a salmon just now, is either very early morning, or late in evening, and I lost my one chance by the hook breaking, in striking a fine fish which I raised soon after I began. The others did nothing ; we only took trout, but had good sport with them. Found all the letters and papers on getting back, and can only say God bless you both for giving me all news, while I am ' loafing ' in this beautiful place. *Am perfectly well*, only rather red with the air, and sun which has been deliciously warm. My old dear will be tired of these scraps instead of letters, but the only chance of a line is now in my room after getting home so late ; I can scarcely keep my eyes open, with that delicious sense of comfortable fatigue, that one never gets except under these circumstances."

May 30, to his sister Fanny :—

" Just a few lines before starting to one of the lochs among the hills—we may not be back till late, and it gives me no chance of letter

*" Curious appearance presented by A . . . . S . . . . n Esq., when going to fish in the Hill-Lochs.*
*May* 30, 1873."

writing. . . . I am feeling so much better, that it's difficult to imagine
myself the same worn-out nervous creature.  It seems to me that air and
exercise alone will keep me well and happy, and here I get both ; must
have walked many miles yesterday, a long day it was. . . . Returned
late, my dear, and very little to add save that we had a lovely afternoon,
too lovely indeed for sport, took very few, but rode over wonderful
hills, on horses, to the beautiful desolate lake."

June 1, to his sister Mary :—

"  . . . Thank you, my Poll, for your little letter.  I have been
enjoying myself prodigious, though there's been but poor sport, the
streams all too low and bright, the weather far too beautiful.  We got
some good trout, but no salmon, the only chance being very early in the
morning, and late at night.  This was at the Awe, on the other end
of the loch, 30 miles away, to which we went in Stevenson's little
steam yacht.  I got up before 5, and got to the water before the sun
was on it, and hooked a fine salmon, and with most awful bad luck,
the hook *broke in his mouth !*  After that there was no chance except for
trout ; we got plenty of them, and had a jolly day—indeed all the days
have been delightful.  I made a riddle while we were resting and refreshing ourselves.  I asked, ' Why would any one seeing us there, say at once
that Stevenson was a better educated man than any of us ? '—the answer,
' Because he was the Senior [Wr]angler.' . . . I shall be sorry to leave
this beautiful place, but there's a subject I'm thinking of, that I can
get material for at this Iron place, and I have promised to go."

The same date, to his mother :—

" I have received a very satisfactory letter from T. Hugh Bell, saying
that the strike is ended ; and I propose leaving this on Tuesday morning.
. . . Shall stay with Bell until the end of the week I expect, then get on
to town, but there's plenty of time to let you know of my movements.
Am *awfully well*, and beginning to want to get to serious work again.  It
has been a glorious little holiday here, and so I don't so much mind the
want of sport."

From Scotland, Walker went to stay for a few days with Mr. Bell, at
Coatham, Redcar ; his object being to procure material for the projected
picture to which he alludes above.  This subject was never carried out—
I do not find that it was ever begun—but the fact that Walker had in his
mind another picture, the theme of which was labour, is worthy of
notice.

June 17, to Mr. North :—

" You must excuse me for seeming to neglect answering yours ; have
been fully occupied since my return from the North, and yet have done
nothing.  This glorious weather makes me think of you, and what you're
doing.  I am alone in town, my people being at Milford in Surrey,

and I appear to be *sticking* regularly with work, am so brim-full of subjects I suppose [!] ; anyhow I've enough of them. The one I think of going at in the North, is a *whacker*—wish I could see you for a while, fear I can't get to you just now, but would like to very much. When do you return ? Have heard what you suggested about the disastrous canvas I worked on so hard in the spring, but I don't think it will do. I hate the very sight of it—would far rather begin on anything fresh."

June 21, to Mr. North :—

" I have just come up from Milford, Surrey, from my Mother and sister, and find your letter and the easel, &c., many thanks. I am rather depressed and worried ; my Mother is not so well as I could wish, I return to her again to-day until Monday morning. My work does not progress ; have been trying to get on with a water colour from the ' Harbour,' but cannot somehow—it is stale and flat. I am bilious, and enjoy nothing, and your remarks about my work, and time going on, are too true, I fear. Have been waiting for a man to come to town with whom I was staying in the North of England, a great ironmaster. I think of going to his district with reference to a picture, and he tells me that there's material that he thinks will suit me in S. Wales, near Cardiff. What I have seen already in the N., scarcely will do, and he proposes taking me, later in the season, to some *old* works of theirs near Durham, that are more what I want ; and, without going into detail, more *varied*, as are those in South Wales he says, and some connections of theirs will show me all I want. I could explain the subject more fully to you if I saw you, which I would very much like to do. I am sick of this series of failures or half failures, and shall not be myself until I am right into a big and successful thing. How could I get to Cardiff from your part, would you like to go with me ? I might combine some of the material that I find in S. Wales, with that of the North ; and for more reasons than one, would prefer to work with or near you, if possible. . . . I am rather out of sorts, as I said before, and the break down in the spring seems to have rather un-nerved me—I am dissatisfied with everything. Am truly glad you are getting on so well in the quiet, away from all this sickening cackle about Shahs and shows—every one seems to have run mad here.'

June 30, to Mr. North :—

" Your letter ought to have been answered sooner, but I have been away to Milford, Surrey, for some days, with my Mother and sister, and we returned on Saturday, when I expected to meet here the man with whom I stayed in the North, and whose relations live in S. Wales. Had I seen him, I should have heard more about his return to Durham ; but, unfortunately, while I was out for half an hour, he came. I think from all I hear, that the part I have yet to visit in Durham, will suit me better than S. Wales ; so if I go to you, it will be more with an eye to the *Mushroom picture*, which I am still bent on doing : indeed, I was at work on a bit of background that I think might do, while I was at Milford. My stay there, though only for a few days, did me much good ; I got over some of the terrible depression that I've been feeling of late. I am finishing one little bit of water colour that has hung about for a long while ; and in spite of want of light, I find myself to-day working very fairly, therefore I think you must not expect to see me just yet. I should like to go back to Durham with this man if I can, for his influence there will procure for me unlimited civility and attention from the natives, instead of 'half a brick' at my head, which I rather think a possibility from the glimpse I have had already of those parts. Some of the old workings up there are far better, I hear, than any I've yet seen—more picturesque, I mean."

The water colour referred to above was, I believe, the small *Fishmonger's Shop*, which was completed shortly after the date of the foregoing letter. The other work on which Walker was engaged at the time was the large water colour of *The Harbour of Refuge*.

July 28, to Mr. North :—

" . . . I'm kept here on account of the schools at the Academy, that produce each day in me a state of irritation bordering on madness. I feel inclined to box the ears of the ' students ' all round."

August 2, to Mr. Agnew :—

" . . . There were several small matters I would have liked to discuss, but they will keep until I see you. I wanted to point out one or two things in the large ' Harbour,' that might with advantage be done. If you are going away, perhaps I might retain the picture for the present —until we meet, in fact. I wanted also to show you the water colour, which I fancy will give you *much satisfaction*. I shall only be away for a short time if I go away on Tuesday, it is to get through some open-air work that is now at its prime. I can resume the water colour immediately on my return."

A few days after this, Walker left London for Torquay, to ascertain if further inspection of the material to be found there would confirm the opinion he formed in the spring of its suitability for the background of *The Unknown Land*. As will be seen from the next letter, the result was satisfactory. He at once gave instructions for the canvas to be sent to him, together with his copy of Victor Hugo's *Toilers of the Sea*.

August 7, Torquay :—" It's all right, I think. I've laid everything in train for *most successful work* between this and Anstey's Cove. Took a long walk soon after getting here yesterday, and felt convinced at once that it would be all right. It looked simply *glorious*, and I have arranged with a man to have my canvas kept under lock and key on the very beach itself, and also to have a boat to take it across to the other side of the cove that not only gives me the best view, but cuts me off from the tourist beast. I also took a boat this morning from the harbour, in order to see two very splendid rocks, one called ' London Bridge,' and forming a natural arch ; I only knew it from the photo, before this, and that was from the *wrong side* for the picture ; but on getting to the *other* side, I found it if anything better, and another detached rock there is, of the *exact shape, &c., I have already made a sketch of*, and altogether, I feel most *hopeful* and *well*—the weather glorious, and very few people about, the fools seem to shirk the place, and goodness knows why. You will, by this, have received my telegram, telling you I have found lodgings near to the cove. The address is :—2, Wellswood Park. Why ' Park,' I don't know, except that there's some garden place behind the row of houses—however, it's perfectly quiet, not dear, and not too far from the shops, although near the scene of action."

*August* 8 :—" . . . A glorious day, but it would be too hot I fear for you, yet I would like to know of you both going away somewhere for another change. Only tell me *where* you might be thinking of going, and *when*. Am gently settling down to work, and have determined not to leave until I've *done it*, if it occupies me a month. . . . The colour of the sea at the cove is quite like the Mediterranean."

*August* 10 :—" . . . It's a somewhat gloomy day, but I have worked pretty well, because I could manage it from the boat-house on the beach, and the doors being kept nearly closed, screened me from bathers and other intruders. I think I shall be able to do all I want from the said boat-house, which will make it unnecessary for me to use a boat, which I should never in any case do save in calm weather, so be quite easy in your mind on that subject. . . . It's rained once or twice, but as I'm under cover, it don't matter—all the better in fact, as it will keep intruders away."

August 13, to his sister Fanny :—

" . . . Am getting on capitally with work ; so well that I half think of taking a holiday to-morrow, by going to Totnes, which I have long wanted to see. There aren't many people here, thank goodness, but what there are, you'd be disgusted with ; vile excursionists and semi-plebeians. I shut myself up in my boat-house, tying the door with a rope, and leaving space enough to give me light, and a view of the glorious cove, and the terrific ridge of rocks. There is any amount of wild clematis, that climbs among the trees and bushes, and if I can, I shall go at it before I leave this."

August 16, to his mother :—

" . . . My work has gone on rather slowly this last day or two. I

T

am much bothered by the *secret* way I am obliged to keep myself shut up in that boat-house, because the folks about the beach are of that kind, that, once known I am there, I should have no peace, and I have therefore to be constantly on the look-out, getting a bit of work by snatches. However, it goes on, and I am very well indeed, and shall work like a nigger at it in a good light at home, after all this experience."

*August* 20:—" . . . Pouring with rain here, but I am just going out. . . . Have arranged with a man to get my canvas up to some foliage, &c., near the cove, where the wild clematis, &c. is very fine."

*August* 22:—" All right, and working very hard. *Work much improved to-day*, just going back to it, self perfectly well. . . . Shall remain here until I feel *quite* satisfied that I've done enough. Weather perfectly lovely."

*August* 23:—" Just the usual line to say I'm all serene, and work going on well. Weather lovely, and only the brutal people that infest the place, to complain of. . . . Work is beginning to show up well now, but I shall be another week or more at it, I expect."

*August* 26:—" . . . Last night there was a storm as severe as the one you describe ; it was coming on while I was in my wood house on the beach, just as it began to grow dark, and the lightning was splendid. I get on very well down there ; have contrived a way of having the doors nearly closed, and tied together with rope, and some planking at the lower part, so that no one can see in. Sometimes, if it isn't a very bright day, I have to open the doors wider ; and then, any one with sharp eyes might see the doors mysteriously and slowly close on the approach of footsteps, or when I hear voices. One man did make a dash at the place so quickly, that I was taken by surprise. It came on to rain suddenly, and I did not hear him, so he saw what I was at ; so I made the best of a bad job by turning my work to the wall, inviting him in, and asking him not to tell any one what he had seen, telling him the reason why. . . . I am determined to do the leafage, &c., while the green trees here are in their prime. I know what it will be if I shirk it ; shall be *going mad* next spring, before any leaves have come out. Shall be glad to see my old Missus again, but it's best not to hurry back to town before the change can have done good to any of us, or before I can have carried out what I came to do."

August 28, to his sister Fanny:—

" . . . I think my work promises to be a complete success. Have yet to do the foliage, which is the toughest part ; that done, I can return for any other part of the background, between this and spring, if necessary. Am now going to rush to Paignton, where I saw a little stream dashing under the road, to the sea, and which I think might be useful."

September 2, to his mother:—

" Your letter of this morning reads as if you were a little depressed when you wrote it. I expect you are wanting to get back to the 'Burgh, and to the little comforts that you can, after all, get there. We shall have much to talk about, you and I, when we meet ; I confess that I begrudge each precious day now, and wish I could stay through next week or part of it, for I feel that the things I can see here, I cannot meet with elsewhere this season. I am loth to leave the place before I am absolutely finished, for I managed most carefully in the first place, and could not get the convenience for work anywhere, that I secured here. The people of the house imagine that I am—like every one else—doing nothing ; not being aware of a certain large case that was taken down to the cove. They little imagine that when I come in at dusk, I am fagged, not with doing nothing, but with pretty hard work—my materials, of course, I keep down there, and secrete the key on leaving. I pay half a crown a week rent ! On Sunday, I took a glorious walk to a place where I found all the green things that I would like to introduce, and to-morrow I shall spend the whole day there, making sketches. The place suits me, I think ; anyhow, I have been very well here, and have generally slept well, and had a good appetite. Have just been into the town, to the Post Office, for some colours I sent for to Roberson's. I don't choose to have 'em sent here, with their ' A.R.A's.' "

*September* 5 :—" . . . The weather here is cool and bright, with an occasional shower. Shall be glad to see my work at home, and shall have to go at it like mad, and the water colour of the ' Harbour ' as well."

*September* 7 :—" . . . It has been beastly weather here, cold and wet ; the people on the beach, too, have been a great nuisance. One ' artist ' took up his quarters sketching, just outside my house, quite blockading me, and little thinking there was a *sketch* of considerable size within a few yards of him. The rain, later in the day, drove him off ; but he was there yesterday afternoon, and I saw him as I was getting down on to the beach ; so I made some memoranda elsewhere, and he was gone when I returned. It has been very wet, but turning out a fine evening. I shall be off now, and you will, I expect, not hear from me, but see me, on Tuesday."

September 11, from London, to Mr. North :—

" I've just returned with some work that *will do*, I think, and am now hard at it here. This is just to ask if you are at Woolstone, and how you get on, when you come to town, &c., are there any mushrooms in your neighbourhood, would it do [in case I find I can manage it] to make a dash into your neighbourhood for a day or two, before the month is quite over, and the above articles all gone? Are you alone? A letter this morning, tempting me sorely to go salmoning at the end of the month, but I must try to resist the temptation."

September 27, to Mr. North :—

" . . . I am finishing a very careful and elaborate water colour of the 'Harbour of Refuge'; been at it ever since I came from Devonshire, and it's almost been the death of me, especially as I had to refuse that invitation to the salmon and the North. I suppose I shall have my reward some day. The water colour is 3 feet long, the most important I've yet done, I think—shall have it at our forthcoming Exhibition at Pall Mall. Do you know I've a notion of yet going on with the Mushroomers, on the canvas I had at Woolstone, with about 18 inches taken off the left side. I've taken out those precious lambs &c., and I find there is so much careful work, that it would be a shame to lose it. I have another stretcher that will just suit it. Shall take out a lot of that bramble stuff in front, and make it more like the original design—no hill at the back, but trees appearing above the hill side on the left, &c. What think you? I ought, in that case, to have a week with you before the trees get bare. I should like you to see what I have brought from Devonshire."

October 1, to Mr. North :—

" Thanks for your letter. You know how glad I shall be to see you, but I fear you will be disappointed with what work I can show you, and I feel disturbed at the notion of this being one of the reasons for your coming to town. However, you will, I am sure, be able to give me some suggestions as to the big picture. Of course, there's not a vestige of a figure, it is just as I brought it from Devon, for I have been hard at the water colour, which has been indeed hard work, because it has not the interest of being new, and yet requires great care."

October 6, to Mr. North :—

" I said something about writing a line to-day, but I find I've very little to say. I've been pounding away at the water colour 'Harbour,' and I think it looks *much* better since yesterday. I shall let you know more about the time you may expect me ; meanwhile, if you should happen to see any stuff that may suit the big canvas, perhaps you'll kindly make a note of it. It strikes me that poor Pinwell must have thought me full of talk last night, but I confess I felt anxious to place ' furren parts' before him in as good a light as is warranted by the limited experience of yours sincerely, F. W."

It may be said in passing that, though their names are often coupled, there was very little intimacy between Walker and Pinwell. Mr.

26 lb
caught at Inverness
THE TEMPTATION OF ST ANTHONY WALKER   SEP. 73

North remembers this visit. He was going to see Pinwell, who was ill at the time, and induced Walker to accompany him. It was, he believes, the only occasion on which Walker was in Pinwell's house.

October 9, to Mr. North :—

"I am looking for a line from you. How about the trees? Would it be possible for me to take a complete little holiday next week—for a week say, or ten days—and yet return and find things possible in your neighbourhood? I have been going at the water colour so hard—at the mower for instance—and it looks so much better than when you saw it. I almost think I ought to have a change; I want it very much."

A week later Walker went to Ludlow.

October 17, to his mother :—

"I'm much better already, and I think I shall stay on, at any rate for a day or two. . . . The place is surprisingly *good*, now I come to see it in a better light and with refreshed eyes; I can fancy it being quite a place to come to, if one can only do so without being followed or badgered. . . . I can imagine *lots* of work being done here; it is rather unlike any town I ever saw—which is saying much—moreover, I find that the fishing is not so difficult to get as I imagined. . . . I had a little fishing this morning—had some sport—quite as much as I expected, the place being new. I am quite well and in better spirits than when I left town."

*October* 23 :—" . . . This morning I seriously thought of returning ; there has been a complete change in the weather, all the streams being flooded, and fishing put a stop to for a day or two. This afternoon turned out so glorious that I took a long ramble, ferreting among the queer streets and buildings of this wonderful old place, and seeing many a bit that I hope to remember in case of need. Afterwards I went for a stretch away from the town, returning by some fine rocky hills that overlook the stream, near the town. . . . I must have a day or two's work on my return, and then shall, I think, go off to Wool-stone. *Am quite well* and comfortable ; the change has been most beneficial."

*October* 26 :—" I've just returned from a long walk, some 10 or 11 miles. . . . The walk has been a glorious one, but very wild, to a great stony hill that one sees from every part near this, called the Titterstone. I lost my way, which made the walk longer ; and was precious glad at length to find a little alehouse, that I ought to have passed an hour before, where I had some beer, and oh such bread and cheese ! The bread smelt of wheat, and some butter I had with it, of cows and cream. I could have eaten all before me ; and, for the few pence I paid, had more good, I think, than many a big dinner has given me. . . . Shall be in capital trim for work, after this holiday, I hope."

October 31, from London, to Mr. North :—

" I've just returned [the night before last] from Shropshire, where I was idle the whole time, so feel proportionately ashamed of myself. Got some grayling fishing, and self into rather better tone. I wanted the holiday very badly, or I should have gone on to you first. ' Fresh fields and pastures new ' I have seen, and want to tell you all about it. I am doing my best to finish the water colour ' Harbour,' which I could take with me if I joined you. Am wavering between the one canvas and the other ; I fear that the leafage being so entirely gone, will render it useless to take the large canvas to Woolstone ; but the other and older subject, I still cling to, but fear I can never make it right on the old original canvas, moreover, I do not think it need be so large. . . . . They are both beautiful subjects ; but the old one I have in my mind so thoroughly, and as you know, have already done so much towards it, that I could, I think, quietly and at Woolstone, go at it successfully, even though the warm weather is past. Give me your sentiments, and tell me whether you think it would be worth while joining you before you come up to town."

November 3, to Mr. North :—

" Since writing to you, there has developed on me a frightful cold in the head and throat, such as I have scarcely ever had before ; making immediate action in the shape of a journey quite out of the question. Had it not been so, I couldn't have left before the end of the week ; besides, the hot water cure and the gruel would be losing their effect, so I must hope to see you here, and you know how gladly I'll go to see this formidable amount of work at your rooms. Come and see me as soon as you can ; there are things I want to talk to you about."

November 13, to Mr. North :—

" I would like to see you so soon as is convenient to you on getting to town ; something concerning *work* I want particularly to discuss with you. . . . I am writing this in a putty-coloured light—the nearest comparison I can make—and in a marrow-chilling atmosphere. I begin to think it is useless going on in this way ; you'll hear what I propose doing. . . . I went last evening to Croydon, and conducted a grand display of fireworks, to the delight of a tribe of nephews ! It recalled to my mind our performance on the hill behind Halsway."

November 20, to Mr. Agnew :—

." There has been no daylight for the last week, until this morning ;

and that only for an hour or two here. I wish you could call on me, I am anxious to consult you about something. The water colour [which you'll say looks very 'prime'] is all but done ; it goes to the Gallery on Saturday afternoon, but I think I might have it out perhaps for a couple of days, after Monday."

November 27, to Mr. North :—

" . . . My water colour 'Harbour' is here until noon to-morrow, and I'm *tired out*."

The question of wintering abroad was the subject Walker was anxious to discuss with Mr. North. He anticipated that not only would the change to a warm climate be of benefit to his health, but that he might meet with the tropical vegetation he was in search of for the picture of *The Unknown Land*. His first idea was to visit the Azores, and he obtained letters of introduction to some of the residents in the principal islands. Eventually, however, Algiers was decided on, Mr. North, who was not in good health at the time, arranging to accompany him. The farewell dinner to the Clique, already mentioned, took place on December 8 ; and on December 18, the travellers left London for Dover, crossing the next day, and staying two nights in Paris.

December 22, Marseilles :—" Safely arrived so far you see. . . . We've arranged to be off by the steamer to-morrow afternoon at 5 ; so, my dear, you must not expect another letter for a day or two, the passage across taking from 35 to 40 hours—by no means too long for me as you know, it is a *rest* and a change, seeing that I am not sea-sick. The weather is calm, and certainly warmer than in Paris, and we have to-day gone through some most glorious scenery ; places that both North and I thought, if we live, we might some day make profitable, and to a considerable extent too. . . . Don't forget the children with your usual tip ; though I'm ashamed of myself for the suggestion, you aren't likely to forget anything of that kind."

December 26, Algiers :—" I hope that by this you have the telegram I sent this afternoon, announcing my safe arrival yesterday morning ; we got into port at about 7 o'clock. . . . I saw that it would be all right, from the lovely green and wooded character of the hills seen from the vessel, and I can only say that we are astounded at the fresh and lovely beauty, the thick leafage, &c., and profusion of flowers ; the roses are in full bloom, and the oranges ripe, there are already wild flowers in abundance, and every day will increase them, a glorious sun striking fresh life into one, and the whole affair a *complete success* ; butterflies, buttercups and daisies, climbing plants—the enclosed is a sort of clematis blossom— the green grass and weeds, rival that of Devon in the summer. The Bells have been truly kind ; and the best news is, that we have, through them, secured a small house almost within a stone's throw—can be seen from the windows of this charming place, which has a beautiful court, and my bedroom has a cupola or dome, Moorish fashion, with pretty casements and tiles. I only wish from my heart that my two dears were here to share it, and if we are spared for another time, I shall not come, I know, without you. The house we go into to-morrow, and the expense is not greater, or so much, as if we were in the town, which stretches out at our feet, and the harbour too in the distance, the wonderful ultramarine sea beyond, and the Atlas mountains [some with their everlasting snow] at our right. . . . North is utterly collapsed ; and I confess I had no idea we were coming to such a wonderful place. . . . Please God, you'll see me and my work in a different state from that in which I left you both. *I am quite well and myself again.* . . . I can only add, that I have, I think, all the material for my picture here, besides that for a wee water colour or two at the same time ; the plants and trees in Bell's garden, and ours across the road, are all sufficient . . . . we have [only fancy] luscious oranges in our own garden. I can only *thank God* for having allowed me to come here, and God bless you both."

Mr. North well remembers Walker's delight as they approached Algiers. He says :—"Our great dread had been, that of finding our destination a country arid and rocky, as the neighbourhood of Marseilles, or as the photographs of the Holy Land suggest that region to be ; but as we came into smooth water, in the early morning, he looked from the porthole, and with delight said, ' All right, beautiful, green as an English summer ' ; and so it was."

December 29, Campagne Cousin, Mustapha Supérieur :—

" You see by the above that we have shifted our quarters from over the way. . . . I am writing this at the open window, in the warm sun. . . . It seems so odd to look out of window on to the road, and see dusty-looking Arabs tramping along, or balanced on their donkeys ; and the women we have seen when we went into the town, all have their faces covered except the eyes, and wonderful eyes they often seem. Then, on the distant road looking down the slope of the hill, towards the sea, one can see the camels going along in a sort of procession, looking as if they had come from the desert, as I dare say they really have. . . . It's turning out a glorious day, the sky of that deep blue only seen during summer in England. Heavens ! how I wish you and Fan were here ; but for the long and fatiguing journey, I would suggest your following us, but suppose it had better not be thought of this time. Still, could you be here, it *must* do you so much good, my dear, I can only say that it is worth going through the journey. There is a gardener attached to this house, included, and whom we have not to pay—he sent us up a fine great bunch of roses, and one or two carnations—fancy, at the end of

December !   I shall go down when I have closed this, and see if any oranges have dropped off the trees.   There are small Mandarin oranges, rather bigger than Tangerines, that grow here, and are very delicious, and the blossom having a rich perfume.   But above all, the great charm to North and myself is in some of the bits, and the line of hills and trees, looking for all the world *English* ; only here and there an aloe or ' prickly pear ' reminding one that we're so far away."

# CHAPTER XV

IF in certain letters in the last chapter the reader has discerned signs
of coming trouble, he has read them rightly. Were it not that the
narrative of Walker's life would be incomplete without his record of
these closing months, I could wish to pass lightly over the events of this
year and hasten to the end. If I refrain from so doing, it is from no
wish to dwell on what is painful.

The first letter of the year is to his sister Fanny, dated January 2 :—

" I write a few lines to you this time, although I know it's just the
same whether to you or my darling Missus. . . . To-day has been
rather windy and not quite so nice, but the full moon to-night is wonderful.
I only hope you are both getting along pretty well—not one word have
I had about poor old Eel-eye. . . . What would I not give to be able
to have five minutes with you both just now ; but there, it will make my
return, please God, all the sweeter. *Keep your peckers up.* We are
getting on very well here, and gradually settling down both to work, and
to the daily life of the place, getting to bed earlier than *I* have been
used to of late, 10 to 10.30 being the usual hour, but alas, we have
been led into a little gaiety these last few evenings. The Bells have
trotted us out, making calls &c., under the pretence of taking us for
drives ; and the result is that we found ourselves doing the fashionable ;
and we last night, for instance, witnessed *private theatricals* at the
Consul's, meeting there the whole of the English element. . . . I wish
you could have seen the private theatricals, my dear, so completely the
fixed standard of imbecility ; the men being, as usual, worse than the
' lady actors '—we, as before, under the wing of the Bells, having dined
with them, and driven with them to the Consul's. There also dined
with us at the Bells' two Misses Cobden, daughters of the great Richard
. . . . we called on them with the Bells last Sunday, and on others,
winding up with a visit to the Jardin d'Essai, a most wonderful place,
where they try, or essay, all manner of experiments in acclimatising
tropical and other vegetation, the result being something beyond
description ; from the most splendid date-palms [that grow naturally

here and bear fruit] to the groves of bamboo, the leaves of which, rustling in the breeze, while they form a thick and grateful shade, give a sound like a stream of water, reminding me of Scotland. India-rubber trees seem to grow in all the gardens here ; I couldn't help thinking [as I looked at some very full splendid trees glittering in the sunshine] of the poor plant at home, kept going only by your and the Missus's loving care—and I love the *care-takers* a million times more than any one or anything I can ever see here. I have fixed upon a wild and very beautiful corner of Bell's garden for much of my work. The wind got up suddenly this morning, bringing in the ' white horses ' from the Mediterranean, making it useless to have my canvas outdoors. I've fixed upon a bit in a lane too, near this, which I think I'll make into a water colour."

January 5, to his mother :—

" Your two letters came to-day, just as we were finishing *déjeuner*, during which I was anxiously waiting, as I knew it to be about letter time. . . . Well, I can only say that the letters did me more good than I can tell, for I was beginning to get a little anxious, it being just a week since your last found me at Bell's. . . . Since Saturday, there has been a great change in the weather, which, although warm, is very wet—heavy drenching showers like April at home—and which is doing good beyond calculation to the country [although for the time rather annoying to us], and which will make the myriads of flowers spring into blossom like magic. . . . We went again yesterday, to the Jardin d'Essai, and I found a sweet and lovely bit that I *must* do ; there is a lemon tree in fruit, with some cypress trees, and a stone water tank, &c., &c., all snug and in a corner, waiting to be put on a little panel in water colour. Have been to-day working on a little bit from a window overlooking the house top —a view of the harbour and sea, some of the town, &c.—it was too wet to think of working on the big canvas. . . . I only wish my dears were here, even if my Mammy seldom or never left the house, but sat near this fragrant wood fire, and in a cane arm-chair that I generally use, away from any draught, and in which I can smoke, write letters, and enjoy myself generally. Well, we shall be able I hope to talk about it, and possibly make arrangement for another time."

*January* 9 :—" . . . We did not work outdoors yesterday, beautiful as it was, as we are warned against doing so immediately after rain, even though the sun is hot . . . . and we intend to be very careful both in this, and not standing about after getting heated. We mean, for instance, to always drive to any place we may want to work at, [any distance off, walking back. . . . We're both going on *very* well, gradually getting acclimatised."

*January* 17 :—" . . . Work is going on all right I think. Yesterday was wonderfully fine, but it has changed in the night, and there's a regular tropical downpour just now. . . . I did hope to send you a nice long letter this time, but North says I must pull up. . . . We are both quite well, thank goodness."

*January* 18 :—" . . . I wish I could describe the feeling of satisfaction that a letter from home gives me—there's nothing like it. . . . The place is still to my mind a success, a wonderful spot, when one thinks of those frosts and fogs. It's been wet though, and now that a few days have elapsed since the event, and you won't think that at any moment the place may be swallowed up, I perhaps may tell you that nearly a week ago there was a slight shock of earthquake here, *very* slight, and one of those that are not at all unusual. It rather amused us because we could *really* call it an earthquake. North and I have our bedrooms opening one into another, but separated by a little room we use for washing and dressing in ; we usually have the doors open, so that we can talk to each other. We had both got into bed, and were both reading—I know I was—when a curious rumbling sort of shake took place, a trembling, and a looking-glass on the wall of my room gave a loud crack. North called out, ' That's an earthquake '—he said his bed felt as if it were moved slightly towards my room. It was not more than a passing waggon might have done, but yet it was somehow different. We agreed to inquire about it next morning [we slept soundly], and found it had been generally felt, so there ! That's our experience of an earthquake. I'm sorry, of course, I cannot tell you of gaping fissures in the walls, and terror-stricken inhabitants [North and self]. . . . Our grand salon has divans or couches round it, and pillars nearer the centre, supporting arches, and a cupola or dome of the true Moorish shape, with tiny little stained glass windows near the top of the said cupola. . . . *Tuesday morning.* The above was written rather late on Sunday night, and I broke off, as I was rather tired. We had been for a long walk on Sunday afternoon, first to the Jardin d'Essai, then we went into Algiers, and wandered about in the queer old streets and market-place—a regular scene from the ' Arabian Nights,' such as I never saw painted, or really described in any book. We watched the different scenes until dusk, the mixture of lamplight and daylight adding to the effect. . . . No, my dear, you must not think I am sad because I only sent a scrap of a note. I never send so long a letter as I'd like to ; even now I feel I must be getting to work."

January 27, to his sister Fanny :—

" . . . To-night we are going to dine with Madame Bodichon and Miss Jekyll. I haven't mentioned Madame B. before, because she has been away on some trip with Miss J., but they came back, and I had immediately a little letter from Miss J., asking if I'd go to their house, which I did for an hour. They can get us models I think. . . . We went into Algiers on Sunday, and indulged in an afternoon's Arabian Nights sort of sight seeing—*très* wonderful this glimpse of another sort of world. We went into those parts where I suppose the usual English don't go—queer, narrow, winding streets, up and downhill, thronged with busy folks, a Babel of tongues, dignified old bent men that one would like to shake hands with, and oh, such fine-looking young ones sometimes. We got separated once, where a lot of business in fish was going on, fish with queer shapes and lovely colour, fresh from the Mediterranean. Not once have we met with anything like rudeness or an approach to it : you know what some of *them* would have to put up with in London—the impudent stare, and disgusting laugh ! No drunkenness, and no *policemen* here. I assure you I have seen faces and features here, that have seemed they *must* belong to those capable of the highest and finest achievements ; and yet, poor souls, perhaps wanting for a penny."

January 31, to his mother :—

" Just a few lines so as not to miss the post. Another glorious morning, and I shall get to work directly this goes off. Should have written last night, but we went again to Madame Bodichon to dinner, and afterwards to her sister's, with the Miss Jekyll I mentioned, where I did some tootling. . . . Work is going on, rather slowly perhaps, but *well.* . . . Shall soon be able to tell you how long I think of remaining here."

*February* 2 : —" . . . I fear that you, my dear, have been less well than I had supposed, but can only hope you will get through this time without much of a breakdown : from what you say, it is enough to try any one. It has been chilly and showery here ; I have not been working outdoors. . . . We have been calculating as to how soon we may look towards returning, I know *I* should like to directly it's possible. This living ' en garçon ' is all very well, but very tiresome sometimes from its sheer monotony ; so different from being a week or fortnight with a fellow, and within a day's journey of town. The little accounts as they come in are a bore to us—true, North does it mostly—but *you* know what they are, and the beastly little attempts to overcharge are most irritating. I am of opinion that I can get away by the end of the month, but this is only a haphazard guess, and if I do, I must rely on being able to work like steam at the figures after I get back, in order to finish at all. Must hope to be able to work well here for the remainder of the time. . . . Had a long walk into the country yesterday afternoon, with Bell ; glorious as ever the place seemed, but if one is feeling at all the fact of being away from all one cares for, the loveliest place must seem wanting in something—this was my case a wee bit." [Next day.] " All right my dearest, and jolly—a fine sunny day, and I've been at it outdoors a bit. Shall work indoors this afternoon, as there's a breeze getting up."

*February* 5 :—" I shall just begin a few lines before going to bed.

I haven't been getting on so quickly with work the last few days ; . . . shall get on well enough I hope, my Missus, but I don't care what people *expect* of me, so that's flat ; they'll get what I choose, and if that happens to be *nothing*, they'll have to wait till it's something. My reputation is dearer to me than it has ever been, and I shall now try to do only that which you, and Fan, and I consider the right sort of thing, and with this nice *conceited* sentiment, I shall retire to ruggins." [Next day.] " Have been working better to-day, the sun gloriously warm and comforting. Shall endeavour to go on and not worry myself by thinking of other men's work, or what is expected of me ; shall finish if I can, and if I cannot, I hope that in the end I shall be none the worse. You ask, my dearest, how I *look*, and how I *am*. Well, I expect I look rather a bear, for I haven't shaved since I've been away, and shall not until I'm obliged ; with this exception, I suppose the same old fright—no fatter I expect, but no thinner, but as you say, you'll have to judge for yourself. I feel all right, my dear. . . Shall work away as well as I can, my dears, to get back as soon as possible ; glad enough I shall be, you may be sure. Still think I can do all I want here, by the end of the month."

*February* 9 :—". . . I am getting on better with work I think ; am beginning at length to ' knock it into shape,' but I don't like to think of how much I've done, or how much I have to do. Have been a great deal bothered about the disposition of the figures, and find I must make the subject a good deal *simpler*, in order to tell its story at once, which is of the very first importance. The colour, as North says, is pretty pure, thank goodness, and will tell I hope in the end ; I have worked indoors to-day, having plenty to do, besides it was showery and squally. The light, of course, is good every day ; and as I read your letter, I felt at least that I must be thankful for daylight, and indeed it helps to reconcile one to this banishment, of which I am beginning to get heartily sick. Mrs. Bell last night accused me of being homesick, and I boldly avowed that I *was !* . . . Madame Bodichon and Miss Jekyll are leaving for England on the 24th, and I have a vague hope that I may finish enough here, to be able to take their suggestion and travel with them. I don't think North will be able to finish in time to join us, if *I* can manage it ; I don't know yet, but shall try very hard—it would relieve me of a lot of travelling worry, for *they* would take care of *me*, both being very good travellers, especially Miss Jekyll, who is I hear quite a ' courier.' . . . I have been getting very uneasy about *you*, my dear, hearing that you kept being unwell, but am reassured by to-day's letters. Don't go out more than you can help : keep to the chair, with a good warm wrap about your dear shoulders, and let everything go hang—a fine thing it is, your talking of being ' of use ' and ' doing things,' in a time like this ; why the only thing you can do is to keep as well as possible by giving your body every possible rest and comfort—time enough to think of *doing* anything when the trees begin to look green again, and the

lilies of the valley are in bloom. Our Fan has pluck enough, and I hope
strength enough, to be commander-in-chief. I know she has goodness
enough, and does not forget that each act of management and economy
carried out, is a direct benefit to *me*, as much as if she were using my
paint brush for me. I don't often express myself in this way, for it
isn't necessary, to *my* Mother and sister. I shall be glad enough to
return to the little home, with all its cold weather, and what seemed such
drawbacks sometimes, while I was there—they ought not to be drawbacks—God knows they seem little enough as I try to remember them.
The loveliest place on earth is not like home; a difficult thing to im-
press on those who've never left it, and haven't felt the intense yearning
and sense of being *far away*."

*February* 14 :—" Just a line to say all's right, and self well, work
going on steadily. . . . Weather, the last day or two, beautiful ; quiet
and warm, but before that, rainy and windy. Will tell you in my next
if any preparations can be made as to models for my return. Thanks
to both my dears for their loving care."

*February* 16 :—" Yours and Fan's and the Punch, received this
evening, after having for once taken a holiday. We arranged with
Madame Bodichon and Miss Jekyll, to start this morning to a place
along the coast [they driving us in Madame B.'s carriage] where there
are some fine rocks, &c., and to which place I must go with my work,
one day at least before leaving this. A glorious day it has been ; just
a summer's day, with a delicious air, and gentle light clouds—a day to
remember indeed—certainly the most pleasant since we have been here.
For we made it a little pic-nic, and the society of two good clever women
made it none the less pleasant. We got home here at about 6.30. We
did a lot of walking, in various ways, and finally left them at their door,
after a day that had more enjoyment and less petty worries in it, than
most holidays. There was just a gentle wave on the exquisitely clear
sea, and from the rocks we looked down into the green pools and their
waving seaweed. And where we had our luncheon [and I was preciously
hungry], there was a little curving beach of pretty stones, and detached
rocks outside the tiny bay, just such as will help me with what I have
had to *alter* in getting on with work. We returned by another route,
inland. . . ." [Next day.] " I am sure I cannot leave quite so soon as I
hoped ; not by the 24th, for instance. Of course I am anxious to get
back to my old dears, but it would be madness to leave this before I'm
quite finished here. No getting out with work to-day, for it's blowing
half a gale, though bright and sunny."

February 20, to his sister Fanny :—

" . . . By this time you'll know I can't get away so soon as I expected ; as for leaving with Madame B. and Miss J., it's out of the
question. We've had a vile succession of squally and rainy days, very
treacherous I should think, and I have declined to work outdoors on a

flapping canvas. All this has retarded work you may guess, although I have found plenty to do indoors, and we both think that what I must do, will be all the more easily got for this indoor treatment. Still it is very riling ; for, with all the cold, and everything else, I want to get back very much—am getting sick of the beautiful place, and yearn for my native pavement. I am sure it will be a week later than I hoped, before I can get away—it would be madness to leave what I came for, before really getting it, and although the weather has been bad, each day advances matters here [new flowers, &c.], and of course I leave all open air work on this canvas, if I am to finish at all this spring, so soon as I leave this place. We are going, after dinner, up to Madame B. ; they will be sorry to know I can't leave with them. I have had some more fluting, and did the little Mozart Andante before a very ' select audience,' the other night. . . . The crocus was all right, and *licks into fits* anything here, the enclosed being the nearest approach to it."

February 25, to his mother :—

" On board the steamer. . . . You'll be surprised, and I hope glad, to learn that I left with Madame Bodichon and Miss Jekyll yesterday, by this steamer. I came to the conclusion that it would be best. I wasn't getting on with work, was thoroughly homesick and with no appetite, my throat, too, was irritable, and altogether I felt I was doing no good there ; so at the last minute I got my things packed, my place taken on board the boat, and here I am. It's glorious weather, quite calm as yet, though we're nearer Marseilles than Algiers ; from which place I am very glad to have started. I don't think it suited me in every way, all small reasons no doubt, but quite sufficient to make up the sum—will tell you all about it when we meet. No place like home : I am worn with the eternal gabble of a foreign tongue—with *everything* that is foreign—and long to get back to the simple fare, and the *little fight* that awaits me. If it is bitter cold, so much the worse ; I cannot help it, but am heartily sick of being away. Old North was sorry enough you may be sure, but thought I was acting for the best ; should not have stayed so long but for *work's sake* I can assure you. This will reach the Burgh as quickly as if posted yesterday in Algiers. We get to Marseilles to-morrow morning early, and go on to Avignon I think, on the way to Paris, and I expect to reach the Burgh either on Sunday night, or some time on Monday—most likely the latter —but will contrive to let you know meanwhile, either by telegram or letter. Slept last night with scarcely a break, from 8 till 8 this morning, for I felt awfully tired in mind and body. Quite well to-day, and have fed capitally. We passed, about two hours ago, the steamer from Marseilles that contains any letters I ought to receive at Algiers to-morrow, and which will simply have to be packed back again to the Burgh. By coming now, I escape the rough weather that is sometimes felt here during the next month ; and although I have not done so much on my canvas as I hoped, I do hope and trust that I shall be able to go on with it on

getting back, with renewed spirit.   Anyhow, I am sure I was receiving
no benefit from being away."

To the kindness of Miss Jekyll I am indebted for the following :—

" I cannot remember when or where I first made Mr. Walker's acquaintance, but I knew very little of him personally till the winter of
1873—4 when I passed some months at Algiers with my friend Madame
Bodichon.   I think it must have been about Christmas that we heard
that Mr. Walker had come out with Mr. J. W. North.   It was a particularly dull and dark winter in London, and he was impatient of the
annoyance and hindrance the want of light was to his work.   Also he
thought of making studies for the landscape accessories of a large
picture [*The Unknown Land*] which he brought out with him.

" On first arriving he seemed in good spirits, cheered by the brilliant
light and many new impressions, but as these faded he became gloomy
and wretched, and seemed to take a horror of the place and a special
dislike to everything French.   It was only occasionally that one saw a
gleam of his fine artistic sense ; and the personal qualities that had made
him dear to many friends, were to us unknown.   One of my pleasantest
recollections of him was when standing one bright afternoon on the
rocky coast, looking westwards at a distant low mountain that bounded
the view and showed between sea and sky ; a sort of lowering frown
that seemed habitual to his face, replaced for the moment by a bright
smile ; he kept repeating to himself : ' Pure ultramarine — pure
ultramarine ! '

" He took a particular dislike to the aloes and prickly pears so
abundant in the district, calling them respectively plants made of zinc
and putty.

" The whitewashed walls of one sitting-room in the house where he
lived were covered with funny little pencil drawings.   Neither he nor
his friend could speak French, and the French woman who cooked for
the little *ménage* took her orders for dinner, before going to market, by
means of these hieroglyphs.   I remember a drawing of a duck and green
peas, cauliflowers, &c., &c.

" He had a nervous dislike of his picture, then in an early state,
being seen by visitors ; I remember having to take some pains, when he
asked me to come to explain to a carpenter about making a case, to keep
well out of view of the face of the large canvas.

" I do not know if it was the only time he had been abroad, but he
gave me the impression of a man who had lived very much in one set of
people : his surprise seemed unbounded that everybody did not know
all about him ; not, as it appeared to us, from any sort of undue vanity,
but from simply never having occasion to realise that there was any world
but just the one in which he had lived.   We may have been in error,
but this was the idea it gave.

" As time went on, his bodily and nervous condition became evidently worse, and he seemed to think he should not get home alive.   In addition to serious bodily discomfort, he was desperately homesick.   Over and over he repeated, in a way that was very piteous : ' I shall never see a hansom cab again.'

" Mr North was not returning to England, Mr. Walker's whole long-ing was to get home, but he felt utterly helpless and unable to organise his journey ; and when Madame Bodichon said we were going home shortly and would take care of him if he liked to come with us, he eagerly accepted.

" He seemed very ill and out of spirits the day we embarked, but we were much relieved by finding him much better next morning ; he walked briskly up and down the deck, and seemed cheered by being really on the way home.   At Marseilles he seemed much tired, and was irritated by the sound of French.   There was some trouble about his picture, as the Custom House required the case to be opened ; this I undertook to see done without looking at the picture ; they made difficulties about taking so large a case by the passenger train, but this was happily got over.

" My friend remained in Paris, her servant and I went on with the invalid, and that evening I had the satisfaction of seeing that at any rate his fancy of dying before he again saw the land of hansom cabs was not realised.   We said good-bye at Charing Cross, and I never saw him again."

Walker returned to London without having derived benefit from the change, and with much careful work effaced from his canvas.   Mr. North tells me that, to the elaborately painted rocks and cliffs of Anstey's Cove, Walker added, while in Algiers, a quantity of hanging leafage and trees in the foreground, his aim being to show a wealth of tropical vegetation extending to the very margin of the sea.   He painted up the sea and shore, and in the foreground placed groups of figures, suggested, Mr. North thinks, by the Elgin marbles.   The picture had been arranged, and was apparently going on towards completion, when one day Mr. North found Walker had destroyed the Anstey's Cove rocks, having painted them over with patches of grey colour.   The line of the horizon had all along been too high for the figures, and much was lost in the endeavour to improve the picture in this respect.   There is nothing to show that the canvas was worked on after Walker reached London : at the time of his death it remained but a shadow of its former self.   It was bought at the sale at Christie's by Sir Lowthian Bell, for whom, indeed, it had been originally intended.

One other result of the visit to Algiers was a water colour, the subject of which, if I remember rightly, was a boy in picturesque costume, tending some goats, on a grassy slope overlooking the sea.   As far as I am aware, this drawing has never been exhibited.

Soon after his return, Walker's illness took a more acute form. Added to this, the state of his mother's health was causing him great

The Unknown Land. (*The Unfinished Canvas.*)

anxiety. Indeed, the further history of the year is little more than a chronicle of endurance. Let the story be told in his own words.

March 24, to Sir John Millais [1] :—

"Your kind letter came last night—most *acceptable* and *comforting*, believe me, and pray accept my warmest thanks. Of course I feel my present position very acutely—a sad conclusion to months of effort, and I fear that folks will judge me harshly ; but as you say, I must hope to have the ' more next year.' I came back from Algiers thoroughly upset, my stomach and liver appear to have been nowhere : the place seemed never to agree with me, and this bronchitis completes matters. I haven't seen any one, for I haven't been allowed to talk, and the doctor says I must take every care of myself for the next two months ; but that once well, I shall be better than I have been for a long time, Be sure I'll gladly accept your invitation to see the pictures—will hope to call on one afternoon this week."

April 5, to Mr. Agnew :—

"Your kind letter received yesterday, for which pray accept my warm thanks. I have indeed been passing through a dreadful time of it as you may guess, and I feel my position very acutely as to work. I should have been glad to see you just now, had you been in town. I am allowed to see friends for a short time. They seem to think I am going on quite satisfactorily, but my spirits sink to that low ebb that I find it hard to believe anything good. Let me have a line saying when you return. My Mother is seriously ill here, and so my poor sister is hard driven, I need not say."

May 20, to Mr. North :—

"Your letter came to hand last night, and I write a few lines in hopes they will reach you before you leave Algiers. It is just possible that I may not be here when you arrive, for it is intended that I get away as soon as the *weather* permit. I must tell you that I have had a fearful time of it, and am terribly pulled down and shaky. . . . It has been altogether a very serious matter for me, and it will require a great deal of W. wind and all favourable circumstances to bring me up again. The Dr. has done all he can ; and, poor man, is only able to beg me to make the best of it, hoping each day will bring a change, that being the one and only thing required to bring me round, so of course this month has been such as for cruel virulence doesn't often occur even here. I was to have gone [and suppose I still shall go] to Tunbridge or Sevenoaks, on the way to St. Leonards or some such place, and a friend has offered a house in Cornwall, which later, perhaps, we may avail ourselves of,

---

[1] As these sheets are under revision, the world is the poorer by the loss of him to whom this letter was addressed ; and who said of Walker, " He was the greatest painter of the century."

but at present the journey would be far too long. What I have suffered this month, it would be difficult to tell—the 'hope deferred,' the weariness and each day's sameness, the sun often glaring into the house quite hot, but the air outside just poisonous to my irritable throat. To-day is quite the same as any other, parched and with that beastly look of *dirt* in the air, and looking as if it might very well continue for another month. Could we have foreseen all this, the Dr. says he would have advised me to make a voyage to Madeira or some place, and would suggest it now, but that we still hope that this cannot last. . . . *Thursday* 21*st*. I conclude this rather gloomy epistle. The weather is just the same, worse if possible, being warm and 'muggy,' except I suppose in the wind. It seems that such a May has not occurred for 50 years ; so be thankful that whatever annoyances you have had, you've been out of it. . . . My Mother has been quite laid up, and scarcely leaves her room yet, so you may guess what a time my dear sister has had of it ; the whole real work falling upon her, and most nobly performed. I sincerely hope that the venture has been, with you, a success generally. You must have become acclimatised. . . . My sister heard from a friend this morning, that the barometer was falling ; blessed news if true, but it scarcely looks like it. Shall see your work in due time if all goes well, and expect it will be a *good jump forward*."

At the end of May, Walker was able to make a move to Sevenoaks, his sister accompanying him. On June 18, he wrote to Mr. Agnew, from the White Hart Hotel :—

" Your letter forwarded has reached me here, for which many thanks. We came away so suddenly, that I am sure you will excuse my sister's not writing. This is more than a fortnight since, and only three or four *good* days have we had here. Those days we took advantage of by getting what the Dr. considers the first necessary thing for me now—air and exercise—and the result was such that I began to look upon my troubles as past ; but these most cruel winds have the effect of keeping me indoors, and depressing me in a way I cannot describe ; the Dr. only wonders that I have borne it so well. Altogether, last month and this have been as bad for me as possible ; despite all this, I am slowly gaining strength, and hope there may yet be warm sun and west wind before the summer months are gone. Am most truly glad Mr. Street has the ' Old Gate,' and through you. I had heard that it was to be sold. As regards your proffered help, my dear Agnew, I scarcely know what to say. I *do* want help, and a great deal too ; it harasses me beyond measure now, when I most require peace. I had better write to you on the subject in a few days I think. It is quite uncertain how long we remain here—may move any day or hour *seaward*, according to wind and Dr.'s orders."

June 24, to his mother :—

" . . . I think it will be jolly for us all to be at Folkestone, and

Fan must fetch you, . . . there will be more *resource* there for me I am sure, or at any rate I'm getting tired of this place after all the filthy E. wind. . . . Am certainly considerably stronger, and the improvement only shows me that I should have been a very different creature by this time, if I had but been able to get W. wind and good daily walks. . . . I shall be going out sea-fishing I expect, at Folkestone, since I can't do trout or salmon, though perhaps I may yet hope to get to Alec. Stevenson's as the season gets old."

July 3, from Folkestone :—

" . . . You will like to hear from myself, dear, something *about* myself, and it is not easy to give an account, for I do vary so in my sensations, and sometimes feel so much better than at others—so well sometimes as to feel anxious to get back and to work, . . . the long and short of it being that a little more patience and some decent weather, with *good daily hot sun*, is what I really want."

July 18, to Mr. North :—

" I'm sure you'll begin to think I have forgotten my promise to write, but believe me I have not been unmindful, and I remember that you had news from my Mater of me, before we came here ; and really up to that time, a little more than a fortnight since, the whole thing was a matter of such complete endurance, owing to the beastly weather, that there was nothing to write about. I was entirely debarred from getting any exercise, and at one time we thought we must give it up as a failure, and return to town. Since coming here, there certainly have been some good days, but others—the last three or four for instance—are too like those of May and June : cold E. wind and bright sun, no *real comfort* in being out. The place is the usual sea-side stuccoed affair—parade, overdressed people, bad music, and shell-fish. . . . *Work* quite out of the question. I don't think I ever was in a more impossible hole : stucco everywhere, right away to dusty, melancholy-looking potato and corn fields, with the well-known chalk downs of the S. coast in the distance. I gave up all notion of work a week ago, up to which time I did really think I'd find something, for I am getting impatient to begin again. Am strong enough, thank God, to once more return to it I believe, though they have, perhaps very wisely, urged me to refrain from it as long as possible. . . . It has altogether been a *pretty time* since the winter, has it not? I think I have gone through every phase of misery and apprehension. Do let me know how *you* are, my dear fellow, and how your work goes. We shall be here for at least another week ; then perhaps to Surrey, in the Godalming neighbourhood, or perhaps up Thames ; but really we are in a state of indecision. Back to town is of course out of the question just now, and if I am to begin, it ought to be gently, on a wee water colour I think—something to commence setting the *pot simmering* once more. My dear sister has been constantly with me, and will be I hope. My Mother is with my married sister at Croydon at present. Whether she joins me or not, will depend upon where I am, that is, if not too far away for her."

In his *History of the Old Water Colour Society*, Mr. J. L. Roget gives the following letter, dated from Folkestone, July 23, 1874, and addressed to Mr. S. P. Jackson :—

"I fear I must give up the notion of being at the Thames side this season, for since I wrote to Leslie on the subject I have had a letter from my doctor, who thinks I ought for this season to avoid the Thames as 'lowering' and 'relaxing,' compared with certain spots I have mentioned to him as being good from an artistic point of view—and as there is some chance of my going to Scotland a little later, perhaps it is better for me to give up the notion."

On leaving Folkestone, Walker and his sister were for a short time at the house of Mr. J. P. Heseltine, at Chiddingfold. From there they went to Mr. Birket Foster's, and eventually found lodgings at Brook Farm, Brook, near Godalming.

August 24, from Brook Farm, to Mr. North :—

"I ought to have written a long time since, if only to report progress, but somehow I seem to have lately but little comfort in writing, for I have so little good news, and indeed so little to write about. And now, although I am going on well—*was* going on admirably in every way —I am in trouble about both my Mother and sister ; they are both here and seriously ill. My sister was suddenly taken ill, in something of the same manner as two or three years ago . . . and a bad relapse taking place last Sunday night week, I really thought we should have lost her.

My poor Mother [who joined us here after we were fairly settled on coming from Folkestone] attempted too much in the way of nursing, and has utterly broken down, her state at one time being thought quite critical ; so I am in a nice plight. Providence seems latterly to have forsaken me. This is about the very worst state of things that could have come about, just as, feeling myself again, I thought to commence work once more. The place is very lovely, crammed full of stuff for work, but I am quite unmanned. I must not leave the place, although I can do no good, and I am almost at my wits' end. I wish you were here—I seem to need help and advice. The friends hereabouts are truly kind, but I feel helpless and *alone*. The beauty of the place almost seems to mock me, for I get on—not at all. We came for this month . . . but how we are to move, I know not. I would willingly pass next month here, would have been glad enough to stay even longer, for as I say, it is lovely ; and only something like peace of mind wanted to make work and enjoyment once more possible. This farm is at the commencement of a little sort of village, with its Inn, &c. ; and by the way, although humble enough, the woman at the Inn said she *might* have a bedroom ready. This is in case you should be able to come down— *this* place is full, and like a hospital."

August 29, to Mr. North :—

" A few lines just to acknowledge yours received this morning. I am thankful to say they are both going on as well as can be expected, but I do not think I ought to leave this place at present, though I might join you later. I should be very glad to do so if all goes well, but perhaps had best not speak with certainty. My Mother must be got to town so soon as she can be moved, which may be perhaps in a week's time ; but my sister will have to remain here, I think. I ought not to leave her in that case, but meantime I will write you again. I am more cheerful about them and myself too, than when I wrote. . . . Do not then, my dear fellow, contemplate so long a journey, as I must make up my mind to stay here just now—could not in any case go back with you next week."

September 15, to Mr. North :—

" Just a few lines to say that we hope to get to town to-morrow, although it will be a rather severe trial for the invalids, especially my poor Mother. What I have gone through in this place I cannot tell you. I shall have to take a thorough change, with or without work ; do you happen to be coming to town ? I should be very glad to have a talk with you, I seem to need counsel, and yearn to be away from doctors, &c. Have done little or no work ; my constant state of anxiety making it impossible. Should like to get away for a little while with you, to Devonshire, for instance, when they are once fairly settled at Bayswater, and have half a mind to telegraph to you, for goodnes only knows when this will reach you. I hate and detest this little place in a way I can't describe ; am sure I could not endure it many days longer, my nerves are utterly upset. I want your advice, and would above all like a little holiday with you, if you could but spare the time."

September 19, from London to Mr. North :

" I think that if all's going on well here, I had better leave on Monday by the 11.45 from Paddington, and if you send me a line to-morrow, I shall know on Monday morning whether you would join me at Taunton or Exeter. . . . I am feeling the reaction after this dreadful time, and the Dr. says I certainly ought to go, and at once. My Mother is very ill, and I scarcely like to leave my sister, but can do no good here if I stay."

September 20, to Mr. Agnew :—

" Your letter was forwarded to me in Surrey, where I have been staying since my sister and I left Folkestone. I have been going on very well, and had commenced work again ; but you will, I know, be sorry to learn that I have had a time of the very greatest anxiety and trouble, on account firstly of my sister falling seriously ill, and my poor Mother, in an attempt to nurse her, utterly broke down, and is now, I fear, in quite a critical state. We got to town on Wednesday, my Mother having to be carried to and from the train. I cannot tell you of all that I have gone through since the beginning of August, but I am quite upset, and the Doctor says I must get away as soon as I can, for I am useless here and doing myself positive harm. I have commenced some water colour work which I hope to show you in due time, but I assure you that work was quite out of the question for any one in my position—we were at a farm away from the help and comforts that invalids expect. I have arranged to leave town to-morrow and join North ; taking what I have commenced to Devonshire, where we shall spend a short and I hope peaceful time. I should have had some work finished by this time, but for this terrible business. A better time is I hope coming now, for it has been a dreadful year to me."

The work begun at Brook was that to which Walker presently refers as the " corner cupboard " subject, afterwards to be altered to *The Rainbow*. Trite as the conceit may be, his use of the sign of promise under such circumstances is not without its pathos.

From this point, unless otherwise mentioned, the letters are to his sister Fanny. When Walker left London, he had seen his mother for the last time.

September 22, from Torquay :—

" You had my telegram last evening I hope, saying that we had arrived, &c. North was at Taunton, and from that, the journey to this

was short. He thought me looking better than he expected, knowing
what worry there's been. I only hope that my poor dear is not too
worried, that I am *right* in coming. North thinks I am, and that I
ought to pass at least a week in doing nothing but gentle exercise ; then
I propose going on to Woolstone, where I hope to go on with the water
colour work. . . . We went this morning to Anstey's Cove, and North
was very pleased with the part, as I knew he would be ; but is still of
opinion that it is too much to *begin* upon now, that for my own sake
I'd better not begin at once to cope with so big a canvas. I cannot tell
you all he says, or the argument, but it is I think full of sound sense,
and is *one* reason why I wanted to come here with him. . . . North
thinks I ought to go on with and finish both the little garden subject
and the ' corner cupboard ' at Woolstone. . . . As for my Missus, I can
only send her my fondest love and duty, and hope she will take it as
easy as possible, as the surest way to getting about again."

The " little garden subject " was also, I believe, begun at Brook,
but was never carried very far.

*September* 30 :—" Just a line, my own Fan, to acknowledge your
telegram, which made me feel much easier than when I had your letter.
Shall not leave this until Saturday I think, as I have got through some
work here, and can very well remain until then. It is quiet, and is
suiting me I think. . . . My poor dear Missus ! It worries me to
think she is not better ; you have but to tell me, my dear, whether
you would like me to come back. Give her all my love, and tell her that I
will of course be back by the next train if it would comfort her, or
rather, if there is anything I can do."

On the envelope containing the above letter, the following message
from his mother is written in pencil in his sister's handwriting :—" Her
kindest love and your coming would unsettle us all, all you have to do
is to keep well for all sakes."

*October* 1 :—" Shall leave this to-morrow. . . . The weather here
has changed—not nearly so nice—so think it best to go to-morrow
instead of on Saturday. Shall perhaps return here later, if I decide upon
any work I might get on with, but meanwhile shall do all I can at
Woolstone. Shall hope for favourable news of my dearest Missus
to-morrow."

October 4, from Woolstone :—

" . . . It's very quiet and peaceful here, and I am glad to get back :
scarcely a leaf is turned, but I fear this high cold wind will do much harm.
We went for a walk this morning, and made notes of the well-known
spots. . . . Sunday here is like Sunday *elsewhere*, somewhat *prosy* ; I
hope you have been managing it pretty well. My tenderest love to my

Missus ; I don't write to her because I'm not going to bother her with letters till she's stronger."

*October* 5 :—" Just a few lines, my own Fan, to acknowledge yours of yesterday, which I received a little while ago, while returning from a walk to Williton. The boy with the pony cart caught me up—he had been for letters, &c., to Williton—so I read it as I walked along. Tell my dearest Missus, in answer to her message, that ' a beast walks on *four* legs,' and that soon, I hope, with Heaven's blessing, she will again be quietly using her *two*. It has been a nice day here, and I felt this afternoon inclined for a bit of a stretch, so left off work and went out by myself, for poor North was very ' down ' about his work, and was trying to make an alteration that I had suggested. I am feeling ' quite myself ' to-day. . . . I am perfectly safe in Mrs. Thorne's hands, I can tell you ; her good old motherly ways would gladden the heart of our dear Missus. . . . . The little corner cupboard subject is getting near completion, a girl comes to-morrow to stand. I have slightly altered the intention of the two figures : have made them looking at a rainbow that is seen through the window—do you not remember my calling you to see one at Brook ?. . . And now, dear, I want you to hand this letter to our Poll when next she comes, for I want her to do a little matter, that she will gladly, I am sure, and I don't want you to be bothered by it, and insist upon your not having a hand in the matter. I want the canvas that has the beginning of the ' Mushroom Gatherers ' sent here. . . . I hope I am not making a bother dear, in wanting this done, but I must say I'd like it down here, if only to alter the shape, and work at *indoors*. I mean to be very careful about working outdoors, and in fact have made up my mind not to do so unless it happen to be both dry and warm. . . . Well, dear, I intended this to be a little gossiping letter, but it's all taken up with the above ; I know you won't mind. It's a sad time for you, my Fan—your life would be a happy one if my wishes could bring it about. It's post time now, and the boy is waiting."

October 7, to Mr. Agnew :—

". . . In a day or two, . . . thank Heaven, I hope to complete the first water colour painting since my illness, and which I propose placing at your service. It has been a frightful year for me up to this time, but I am now able to enjoy my work, and hope to continue to do so either in town or hereabouts, during the winter. My Mother is, I am grieved to say, in a very precarious state. I have news of her daily, but her condition causes me the greatest anxiety ; they think it best for me however, not to be in town just now, both for my own and my work's sake, as I can do but little good in a sick house, and can only say I am now recovering from the frightful anxiety I endured in Surrey. Any work that I send to you, of course I should like to have for exhibition ; this water colour for instance, I wish to send to our forthcoming winter Exhibition in Pall Mall."

*The Rainbow*—Walker's last water colour of an original subject—duly appeared. . It was his sole exhibit this year.

*October* 8 :—" All right, and work going on well. . . . It is quiet and peaceful here. I only wish you could participate in it, and perhaps you will, my dear, when things are less gloomy. Keep up, dear, you have my love and sympathy, be sure. I continually think of you, and especially in the evenings."

*October* 12 :—" I have just received our Poll's letter. I *quite under-stand* its contents, and fully agree with you both that it is best for me not to go to you now. My tender love to my Missus, and if there is anything I can do, mind and let me know. . . . I am sure that the only thing I can do just now, is work here ; the weather keeps fine and much dryer."

*October* 18 :—" . . . We went for a long walk this morning, going up one of the Quantock hills ; a very lovely day it is, though autumnal, but very enjoyable for walking. . . . Have been turning my attention to the Mushroom canvas, and think I shall carry it through *this* time ; there is already a whole lot of work on it, and North seems to think I ought to find it pretty straightforward work. However, I must get that little water colour off to Agnew, but it seemed to ' hang fire ' a bit ; have not been able to get quite the models I want. . . . I suppose I am best here, my dear, but often wish I could be a little comfort to you just now—had half an idea of running up, if only to see —— to know if he thinks I'm strong enough for the work I want to go in for ; but then I pretty well seem to know what he'd say, and as I feel so much my old self again, I shrink from more doctoring. Must simply take every care of myself, and use my own judgment ; besides, I feel that if I went to the Burgh just now, it would perhaps only unsettle and excite the dear Missus."

*October* 21 :—" . . . I wish you were less harassed, my Fan ; I'd give a deal, I know, to have you passing quiet days here, if you did not get sick of the sameness, of a different kind from yours. I couldn't stand it this morning, and walked round by Williton a long way, and this afternoon went to Stogumber. Had a fling at the Mushroom canvas *outdoors* yesterday, it was mild and quiet, and I left off at 3, none the worse. The man who went up with me to carry the canvas, I made stay there ; he lay on the grass as if it had been a sofa, happy creature ! To-day is awful, only fit for walking ; the wind enough to tear up the trees. My poor dear Missus, what can I do—can only feel miserable to know what she and you go through. God bless you both. Do not forget, my Fan, how much real work you are doing, and how perhaps the folks that you mention as looking happy, are none the more so because their lives are less useful."

*October* 25 :—" . . . Keep up, dear Fan, as well as you can ; *command* me, your own devoted Fred, in anything you think I can do. You know I am forgetful and all that, but I hope not wanting in the right love for you, and the sense of what you and my poor Missus are both going through."

*November* 1 :—" . . . Of course, dear, I am dreadfully worried about the dearest Missus, but quite understand about not going to you ; but if she expresses any wish to see me, I am sure you will let me know. . . . God bless you, my Fan. He does in one sense, by giving you the power to help and comfort those who need it ; the *happiest* life is that which is most unselfish, and therefore containing least reason for self-reproach."

*November* 4 :—" I know you'll like a few words, my Fan, if only to say all's well here. No news ; we're both pretty comfortable, the weather good, but rather cold this morning. We play at dominoes before going to bed. You'll say we are old fogies, and so we are. My tender love to my poor dear, and to yourself."

*November* 5 :—" Do not be under any apprehension that I do not fully realise the state of my poor darling. I know it too well, and have been quite prepared for the worst since I have been here. I am perfectly certain that all that could be done, has been, and am sure you may rest all confidence in —— ; he thought matters very grave when he was called down to Brook. I had his letter this morning, and one almost entirely on the subject, a short time since. He says [in that of this morning] that I may *rest assured* everything possible is being done. It can only render matters more sad, to have any misgivings now. I have none ; my only fear is that it is too much for you, my Fan. There *can* be no room for regrets ; certainly none in your case, and your love must be now tempered with resignation. I am best here, I am sure of that, for I should only be in the way. Am anxious enough here, but am at least doing *some* work, which would probably not be the case in town ; so do not think about me, my Fan, and do not write more than you think necessary. Have been at a standstill rather with the two little figures in the wee 'rainbow' subject, but a woman stood a short time to-day, and I think I have managed that. It is warm and gentle here —we went for a little walk last night, and saw some glowworms. Shall have our mild game of dominoes I suppose, when we have done writing."

*November* 6 :—" . . . A most splendid day it has been. We went for the usual little stroll after breakfast, and the air was so sweet and fresh, we walked to Watchet to have a look at the sea, and home over the hillside. Were out all the morning, for we could not resist it, and I am sure the time was well spent. How often I thought of you and my poor dear ! "

*November* 8 :—" . . . I did hope to have told you that one of the water colours was finished by this, but it still wants a day or two's careful work. Shall send it directly on to Agnew ; you'll see it later no doubt."

*November* 11 :—" It has been a miserable day here, with a fierce N. wind, heavy clouds, and showers of rain and hail. . . . I have been at work upon the little water colour ; it's nearly finished now, and I am getting quite pleased with it, for I have made more out of it than I expected. I am sorry that you should not see it before it goes to Agnew, for I am a little undecided [as usual you'll say] what to ask him for it. I wish my poor darling could see it, and see that at least *one* little bit of good was got out of that miserable Brook."

*November* 12 :—" . . . It has been a fine bright day, but rather a bracing one ; the glass which we have outside our sitting-room window being nearly down to freezing-point this morning ; but we had a bit of a walk before work, and another on leaving off. I keep on touching and touching on the water colour, and feel that it *must* go, so it shall either to-morrow or next day. . . . I wish you could have seen the beautiful evening colour and effect we enjoyed as we walked home this evening ; suggestive of glorious ' old masters ' in front, and great solemn blue hills, with a thin golden young moon in the amber sky, that dipped herself behind the said hills as we came down to the moor. I fear I felt it chiefly that every one could not enjoy the loveliness."

*November* 13 :—" . . . I am quite satisfied since receiving yours and dear Sally's. Am sure I am right in being here, and quite understand how much anguish I am spared."

*November* 17 :—" I expect I shall be with you, my dearest Fan, I don't see how I can remain here. . . . North persuaded me not to go up to-night, when the first telegram came, and he since tells me that he felt sure all was done that could be, indeed that the first telegram was to prepare me. God's will be done, I have been prepared."

Mrs. Walker died on the evening of the 16th at the age of sixty-six. Although she had not been wholly spared the pain of seeing yet another son's declining health, the final sorrow was at least withheld from her. She had lived to see her hopes in this her gifted son fulfilled, her belief in him justified ; she had shared in the triumphs she had helped him to win : her work was done.

It was Walker's wish [as indeed it was the wish of all] that his mother should be buried at Cookham, and on me fell the duty of accompanying her remains by night—the first of three such journeys on a similar errand.

We left London on the evening of November 20. It was a strange journey; the market carts slowly rumbling towards town, their tarpaulins covered with hoar frost; the night house where the carters refreshed themselves; the hushed villages with here and there a light in a window, telling of night watches; the long lines of hedgerows bordering the silent fields. Before reaching Maidenhead, the fog was so thick, that one of the men with a lantern had to lead the horse, and only a whitening of the mist as we neared Cookham showed that the day was breaking. Reverently our burden was laid to well-earned rest.

In the succeeding letters much must be passed over.

*November* 19 :—". . . I have the comfort of telling you that I sent off the water colour to Agnew, registered by post. North went with me, for it was very blustering, and he had enough outdoor work this morning. I had worked and touched upon the water colour a good deal, and of course have not been able to do much just now, and North persuaded me to give it up as impossible to carry it farther."

*November* 20 :—". . . Went for a good walk this afternoon—went through Williton—and having to get stamps, I bought *the* local paper and posted it to you. I only did it because I thought the mixture of conceit and stupidity might amuse you for a minute. Friday evening is always made important to Mrs. Thorne by its arrival; of course every place and person named therein are familiar to her. I took up the everlasting Mushroom canvas again to-day, and suppose that eventually it will come to something. . . . I have found it very difficult to remain here, but have forced myself, knowing that it is best. . . . Keep up your courage, my Fan, and feel the warm comfort of knowing that you have been doing your duty to the utmost, and under overwhelming difficulties."

*November* 22 :—". . . It has been a dull melancholy day here, rather depressing. We went out before dinner; found some wild roses, rather unusual at this time of year—quite a cluster. It sounds bad what you say about the fog yesterday, but perhaps the weather will alter, and so allow me to come up. I confess I would like a little change of some sort. I am feeling pretty well; very well considering. I have *known* all through that it was best for me to remain here, though I felt it cruelly enough."

*November* 25 :—". . . I have been going on with the Mushroom canvas, and begin to see what I can make of it. Can do it all indoors I think, for I intend making slight sketches and memoranda where necessary."

As will have been already gathered, the "Mushroom canvas" was never completed. The nearest approach to a finished picture of the subject which had been so long in Walker's thoughts, is the well-known study, in oil on paper, which has been etched by Mr. Macbeth. The date

X

FREDERICK WALKER

of this study cannot be given with accuracy, probably it was begun as early as 1868. It was among the remaining effects which were sold at Christie's.

At the end of November, Walker went to town for a couple of days. On his return he wrote, December 4 :—

" . . . It has been a jolly day here, mild and quiet. I did a wee bit of work this morning, and this afternoon we went for quite a long walk. We are none the worse for our journey yesterday, and it is pleasant to find it not frosty, and the geese rampant by the brook opposite. Mrs. T. is very glad to get us back again, she says—her occupation is gone when we are away. I brought down a lot of things, including the photo of ' The Old Gate,' and am going to make a small light-coloured replica, if possible in time for the Exhibition. We have just had dinner, and the dog is snoring on the rug, *aldermanically*, and North is scribbling away opposite to me."

The " small light-coloured replica " developed into a most carefully finished reproduction of the oil picture. It was yet another instance of the way in which Walker's conscientiousness urged him to improve upon his original idea.

The remaining letters of the year relate chiefly to another attack of illness from which Walker suffered shortly after his return to Woolstone. It was from the local doctor who was now called in, Mr. North first learnt that Walker's lungs were affected. When in London, it had been arranged that his sister should join him in a few days. Her visit was, however, postponed from time to time in consequence of his illness, as he was unwilling that she should leave London until his health had been so far restored as to allow her to take a much-needed rest. The improvement he looked for was slow in coming, and when, on December 17, she joined him, it was again to minister to his needs.

# CHAPTER XVI

1875 .

By the beginning of February, Walker had fairly recovered from the effects of his late illness.  On February 1, he wrote from Woolstone to Mr. Phillips :—

"  . . . I little knew when I saw you, what I should suffer ; have had a bad illness since. . . . and had to be attended by the local doctor. He . . . says I need thorough change and *peace of mind*, the latter of the utmost importance, and most difficult to get.  Says that's all I want, and that my state otherwise is all right."

A day or two after this, he went to London.  With renewed strength had come the desire for work.  It is possible that while at Woolstone he had further advanced the water colour of *The Old Gate* ; at any rate he was at work on the drawing after his return to London, completing it in time for the Summer Exhibition of the Old Water Colour Society—his last exhibited water colour.

After some six weeks in town, Walker and his sister returned to Woolstone.  The place where he had so often found peace and rest, and for which, as his letters show, he had so great an affection, was to furnish the material for yet another picture—*The Right of Way*.  Whether this, his last oil picture, had been begun before he left Woolstone in February, cannot be ascertained.  Mr. North was not at Woolstone when the picture was painted, and only knew the subject of it after it had been sent in to the Royal Academy.  As the weather so early in the year would have been against out-of-door work for one in Walker's state of health, it is probable it had not.  If he did not begin the picture until after his return to Woolstone, about the middle of March, the fact that it was sufficiently finished to be sent to the Royal Academy early in April  says much for the rapidity with which he could work at times.  It seems somewhat strange that, with *Mushroom Gatherers* and *The Peaceful Thames* so far on their way, these subjects should have been discarded in favour of one of which there is no previous mention.

As *The Right of Way* is no longer in England, having been purchased by the Public Library, Museums, and National Gallery of Victoria, Melbourne, a few words of description may not be out of place.  The

THE RIGHT OF WAY.

scene is a meadow, the time early spring.   Through the meadow, winding
its way into the picture, runs one of those little streams that Walker
loved.   In the foreground, a woman, bare-footed and carrying a basket
of eggs, throws one arm round a little boy who clings to her, frightened
at the approach of an aggressive ewe, which, in defence of her lamb,
disputes the right of way.   The child's fear is echoed in the attitude of a
quaint little dog looking out from behind him.   Some rising ground on
the left beyond the stream, other sheep and lambs in the meadow, farm
buildings in mid-distance, and the tower of Sampford Brett Church on
the right, make up the picture.   As one stands at the point of view from
which the picture was painted, on the right and looking slightly backwards, can be seen the grand old quarry which forms the background of
*The Plough.*

Though unpretentious in subject, and far from finished, there were
not wanting those who recognised the picture's charm.   Let me give
one more quotation from the criticism of the day :—" If one wished to
see how, with the slightest materials, and with no great pretence of
minute accuracy, an artist can transform a landscape into a poem, one has
only to look at Mr. Frederick Walker's *Right of Way* [25].   There are
the yellow stars of the celandine gleaming in the soft green meadows, but
one does not stay to count their petals : there are young lambs playing
about in the grass, but one does not stay to see how their eyes or their
ears are painted ; it is enough that we have before us a vision of the
Spring-time, real enough to recall the Spring-times of our youth, and full of
all the wonder and tender mystery and charm that memory throws around
our recollections of the opening of the year."

One other drawing remains to be mentioned ; the water colour of the
figures on the terrace, from *The Harbour of Refuge.*   This drawing was
among Walker's effects at the time of his death, and was disposed of at
the sale at Christie's.   A letter written shortly afterwards speaks of it
as the last work on which he was engaged.

After sending *The Right of Way* to the Royal Academy, Walker was
for a short time at Brighton, but was in town for the varnishing day and
the private view.   On May 4, he wrote to Mr. H. E. Watts :—

" . . . I have done enough talking and seeing pictures lately, to make
a little holiday up the Thames yesterday very sweet indeed.   When are
you at home ?   I did think of going to Italy, but it is getting so late in
the season as to be too hot I fancy.   Shall be here, I expect, for the next
week, although each day makes me more unsettled, and I want to begin
some work outdoors.   It is *an age* since I saw you ; tell me, if you have
time, how we can meet.   I had a little trout fishing in Surrey the other
day, and want some more."

May 6, also to Mr. Watts :—

" All being well I'll join you at the Savile Club to-morrow for 6.30.

I'd have written before, but thought to call at Pall Mall this afternoon on chance of seeing you   I don't know what to say about Scotland, but we can at any rate talk over possibilities.   That I'd *like* to go, I need not say."

In the end it was arranged that Walker should join Mr. Watts at Perth, on the way to St. Fillans, and he left London on May 10.

On May 12, he wrote to his sister from the Drummond Arms, St. Fillans, Loch Earn :—

"Just a line.   Watts is waiting, and the post here goes at the absurd hour of 3.   Am all right and the weather ditto ; a W. wind, but not much sport as yet.   The air is sweet and with splendid hills all round the loch.   I don't think we shall remain here long unless there's good sport, but get on to Loch Tay or somewhere else."

*May* 14 :—" . . . I am feeling rested, and enjoy the quiet of this place, though the sport is poor. . . . My bedroom looks out on to the lake and to the great frowning hills opposite ; the hills very like those on the Spean, the same beautiful colour with granite peeping through the surface here and there.   The cuckoo's note is to be heard here, only he sounds faint and small compared with what we hear of him southwards. Lots of primroses in the lower ground, and the trees about as forward as when I left town.   Watts is nice to be with, he seems unselfish and gentle. He has told me a great deal about Australian life, and what he experienced on the other side of the globe.   He is sure that if I could afford the time, a twelvemonth spent in a voyage there and back and a holiday at Australia and Tasmania would do me more good, mentally and bodily, than anything.   The climate must indeed, from what he says, be glorious ; he only wishes he were going out again.   November is the best time, and there are splendid *sailing* ships that go round the Cape of Good Hope.   To-day is the gentlest morning we have had, scarcely any wind, indeed the loch looks rather ' ily,' but we're going out some distance."

After Walker left for Scotland his sister came to stay with us at Croydon.   On Whit Monday, May 17, after spending the evening with some friends, we returned home to find a telegram awaiting us saying Walker had been taken seriously ill, and that his sister's presence was necessary.   It was too late for her to start that night.   She left London next morning by the first train, but could not get further that night than Perth, where Mr. Watts met her.   She reached St. Fillans on the Wednesday.

For the following account of what had happened I am indebted to Mr. Watts.   He writes :—

" In the early May of 1875 I planned with Walker a short fishing

trip in the Highlands.  We met at the Savile Club to discuss the project.
He looked to me then very ill—more ill than I had ever seen him—and
I did not think he would be able to come with me.  He seemed, however, very eager for the expedition, to which he looked forward with much
delight.  We parted without any definite promise on his part, but it was
understood that I was to await a telegram from him at Perth before proceeding farther.  On the morning of my arrival at Perth I received, what
I hardly expected, a telegram from Walker, saying that he had made up
his mind to join me, and asking me to meet him at the station that
evening.  He looked very ill on arrival, so much so that I felt some
dismay and compunction at having tempted him from home.  We slept
at Perth, and next morning started for Crieff, whence we took the coach
to St. Fillans, on Loch Earn side.  Walker seemed much better, and was
in his usual high spirits at the prospect of sport.  We fished a little that
afternoon in the loch, and for two or three days after, intending to go
on farther to some salmon fishing which had been promised us on
Loch Tay.  One night we sat up rather late at the inn discussing the
scheme of our journey, of which the next stage was to be Dalmally.  He
talked of his art, and of some projected subjects for painting.  He asked me
to tell him of my experiences in New Zealand, and seemed to be especially
interested in my description of the beautiful island of Kawau in the Bay
of Auckland—the island Eden lately possessed by Sir George Grey.  The
luxuriant vegetation of strange and novel forms, the virgin forests, with
their tangle of lush greenery, the rich colours of the native flora, with the
*rata* blooms throwing a crimson shade over the silver shingle—all these,
the new and unconventional features in the wild landscape, in a land
scarcely touched by the foot of man, seemed to attract very strongly the
imagination of Walker.  He questioned me over and over again minutely
as to the details of the scene, telling me that he had conceived the idea
of a picture to be called *The Unknown Land*, which was to represent a
party of immigrants landing on some shore where all the features of
nature were new and unfamiliar.  We sat up till past 12 o'clock talking
of this subject—Walker full of life and enthusiasm.

    "The next Sunday we spent in rambling about the shores of the
loch, and arranging our tackle.  In the afternoon, in a bright warm sun,
we strolled to the opposite side of the loch, and sat down on the bank
with our pipes.  On getting up to return to the inn, I was in advance.
Nearing the little bridge which crosses the river flowing out of the loch,
I turned and saw that Walker was some distance behind me, walking
very slowly, with a handkerchief to his mouth.  When he came up I
perceived that his handkerchief was stained with blood, Walker looking
very pale and frightened.  I asked him what was the matter, and he
seemed to have a difficulty in speaking, but made light of the blood,
saying that he had been thus seized with a bleeding before.  I led
him to the inn, which fortunately was only a few yards distant, and took
him up-stairs to his bedroom.  I helped to undress him and put him to
bed, not knowing what to do and being more frightened than he was.

During all this time, and especially when he moved or attempted to speak, the hæmorrhage continued. With some difficulty, it being the the Sabbath, I engaged a lad to fetch the local doctor—there was none nearer than at Comrie, which was some six or seven miles distant. The doctor came somewhat late in the evening, and prescribed some simple remedies, in which I could see that poor Walker had no more faith than in their prescriber. All that night I passed, as I did the next night, in Walker's bedroom, being afraid to leave him, though much distrustful of my own qualifications as nurse. The second day I felt that something more had to be done, so with Walker's consent I telegraphed to a friend at Perth to send up at once the best available medical man in that district. There came Dr. Gardiner from Crieff, a very well-known and highly qualified Perthshire physician, who, after a careful examination of Walker, took, as I saw, a very serious view of his condition. A nurse was sent for, to my very great relief, and everything was done which was possible in that remote Highland village to make the patient comfortable, who, all this time, was never able to leave his bed or take any nourishment except milk, any exertion on his part, to talk or to move, bringing on a fresh flow of blood from the lungs. At Dr. Gardiner's instance, Walker's sister was telegraphed for from London, arriving at St. Fillans on Wednesday.

"There is little more to tell of the story, which is one of the saddest in my experience. I had to return to London after some days, but received daily notes of Walker's health from his devoted sister."

The last letter that Walker wrote lies before me. It is written in pencil and speaks for itself :—

"My poor dear, You'll be quite worn out, but Watts will be able to tell you I'm better, and if you take no harm I shall soon be all right with you near me. I did not want to send for you but they seemed to think it best. Watts is waiting. All love to my dear. F."

A fortnight of suspense, relieved occasionally by more hopeful news, followed Fanny Walker's departure from Croydon. The evening of June 3 brought a telegram which prepared us for the worst. Walker died at St. Fillans at half-past five in the morning of Friday, June 4, on the ninth day after the completion of his thirty-fifth year. The entry in the register states the cause of death to have been phthisis.

In the evening of that day, after giving such notice of his death as the limited time allowed, I left London for St. Fillans. On my arrival the next afternoon, his sister took me to the room looking "out on to the lake," where lay the remains of my dear friend, and, as I cannot help thinking, one of the greatest painters England ever produced. His sister had arranged everything, there was nothing left for me to do, and in a couple of hours we began our homeward journey, reaching St. Petersburgh Place on Sunday morning.

The funeral took place at Cookham on Tuesday, June 8, the remains

having been taken down overnight.   A bright fresh morning, contrasting
with the sadness of our errand, ushered in a day such as Walker loved.
The coffin was taken to the little sitting-room in the cottage of one
of his old Cookham friends ; and there later in the day, came those whom
love of him and of his work had brought from town.   But for the short
notice more would have been present at the funeral, though no numbers
could have added to the impressiveness of the scene—impressive from its
absolute simplicity.   As we stood around the open grave and saw the
sheep browsing among the grassy mounds, glimpses here and there of the
river he delighted in, the wealth of early summer lit up by a glorious
sun ; in addition to their affection for the man, none but must have felt
the pity of it that the painter whose figures had found fit setting in such
surroundings, whose insight had revealed to us new meaning in rural
scenes and rustic labour, whose unsullied art had been a brightness in
our lives, should have been taken ere he had reached the fulness
of his prime.   After more than twenty years have passed, one who was
present writes :—"The way in which all gave way to uncontrollable
emotion, which found its vent in tears, was an incident never to
forget."

When all was over, we were told that Mr. H. H. Armstead, then
A.R.A., had offered, as a labour of love, to execute the medallion portrait
now in Cookham Church.

Whatever may be the verdict of posterity on Walker, it is doubtful whether the death of any painter of recent times has evoked from the press a greater unanimity of praise. Much might be quoted in support of this ; the following extracts must, however, suffice :—

The *Times* said :—" To-day will be laid in the secluded churchyard of Cookham, by the side of his mother and one of his brothers, Frederick Walker, A.R.A., a young painter of rare genius, cut off prematurely in the springtide of his powers. At little more than thirty Walker had already made his power felt in three fields of art—as a designer on wood and as a painter in water-colours and in oil—in a way possible only to genius. His later achievements as a painter have gone far to override the recollection of his earlier work as a designer on wood ; but in this character he had the same wide and well-marked influence on his contemporaries and successors as he had already had on the younger generation of our water-colour painters, and as he promised, and had indeed already begun to exert upon the oil painters of his time."

The *Standard* :—" No truer artist in the highest meaning of the term has England ever produced—none who wrought more earnestly and patiently in the lofty and difficult path he had chosen for himself. It is perhaps scarcely just to his memory to say that he was not popular. He had certainly begun to be so even among those who were unskilled in appreciating all the tender grace and the exquisite delicacy and grace of his work. From the date of the first important picture which he exhibited at the Royal Academy, *The Lost Path*, his merits have been recognised by an ever increasing circle of admirers, and they have been those whose admiration passed the bounds of æsthetic sympathy into a feeling of personal love and respect for the artist."

The *Pall Mall Gazette* :—" Among those who care for what is best in English painting there can be but one feeling as to the gravity of the loss. This is not the time to attempt a full or critical estimate of the painter's powers, but it may be safely said that for some years past he has stood in the very front rank of English artists. There was something in the nature of Mr. Walker's talent which compelled the admiration of every school of artistic opinion, and it would be impossible to name any other painter of the time whose merits were so universally and so generously admitted. This is especially true of the praise of brother artists. With the public his fame, although considerable, is still short of its due measure ; for Mr. Walker, although he treated the simplest and commonest themes, had no command over those qualities that claimed for a picture instant and loud applause. But with the more attentive students of contemporary art his extraordinary gifts have long been respectfully and warmly acknowledged. That the works he has produced will survive the praise of the hour, there can, we think, be little doubt ; for joined to a delicate perception of pictorial beauty, Mr. Walker had a stronger hold on reality than almost any of his contemporaries could boast."

The *Examiner :*—" The past week has witnessed the death of one of the truest artists England ever possessed. . . . No painter ever had a more rapid and decisive influence upon his contemporaries. His manner in every branch of his art was of such fascinating originality that others quickly followed in the lines he had laid down. He had formed a school of drawing before he took to painting, and he had attracted followers in water-colour before he was known as a painter in oil. The truth of his art was so undeniable, its imaginative quality so unobtrusively expressed, that it at the same time both compelled and encouraged imitation. Other painters hastened to occupy the new ground that he had made his own, but in spite of all rivalry it remained his own to the last."

On the Friday after the funeral, Mr. Agnew and my eldest brother met me at the studio for the purpose of selecting such of Walker's remaining works as could be sold at Christie's. It was at once decided that *At the Bar* could not be sent. The works selected were : eighty drawings in pen and ink, pencil, and sepia ; thirty-nine sketches in water colour, including two designs for *The Unknown Land*, the original design for *The Harbour of Refuge*, and the drawing of the figures on the terrace, on which Walker had been last engaged. The oil studies were six in number, and included the canvas of *The Unknown Land*, and the landscape and advanced study for *Mushroom Gatherers*. There were also six etched plates, amongst them that which was the forerunner of *Wayfarers*. The sale took place on July 17. There was a large attendance of artists and other admirers, and the prices realised were very high. *The Right of Way*, then in the Royal Academy, was by a misunderstanding included in the catalogue, but was withdrawn at the sale.

In order to give effect to Mr. Armstead's offer to execute the medallion portrait, a meeting was held at the Arts Club on June 17, at which an executive committee, mostly composed of artists, was appointed, and a subscription list opened. Later in the year, the committee issued a circular inviting the loan of Walker's works for exhibition—the exhibition so often referred to as that of 1876—for which Mr. Deschamps kindly placed his Gallery, 168 New Bond Street, at the disposal of the committee. As, towards the end of December, the pictures arrived at the Gallery, the opinion of the committee was I believe unanimous, that Walker stood even higher than they had thought.

The exhibition was opened early in January, and all who had laboured to do honour to Walker's name were amply rewarded by its success : it is still spoken of as something that stands apart in the memory. Even to those who had delighted in his works during the previous twelve years, the exhibition of them collectively came almost as a revelation. The request of the committee had been so generously responded to, that a more complete display of any artist's life's work can have been seldom seen. Of previously exhibited works but eight were absent, while there were many

which were here seen for the first time. The series of exhibited oil
pictures was complete with the exception of *At the Bar ;* and a fully
representative collection of wood drawings showed Walker's progress in
this branch of art. The press was unanimous in its recognition of his
genius. Trying as was the test of such an exhibition, the outcome proved
him, in the opinion of his contemporaries, to be worthy of enduring fame.
And, though this will seem small praise to those who hold that art is a
thing apart from the subjects of which it treats, there was not a line in
the exhibition but spoke of purity of purpose and a refined mind.

The success of the exhibition woke an echo in the old Woolstone
home. Good, motherly Mrs. Thorne wrote :—"There is great praise
and talk about the lovely Pictures down here, I feel so proud to hear it."
"Thank you, Dear Miss Walker, for the Paper ; that part of it about
the Dear young Gentleman's Pictures I have very carefully preserved.
Oh how pleased I am always to hear his great praise ! and what must
*your* joy be ? Dear Soul, he was too clever to live, I fancy—everything
bespoke him."

My story would be incomplete without further mention of the last
survivor of the St. Petersburgh Place household. For a time, the
necessity of attending to her brother's affairs, and later on, the absorbing
interest of the exhibition, acted so far beneficially on Fanny Walker that,
about Christmas, she seemed to be recovering something of her wonted
spirits. It was, however, but for a time. When it came to settling
down to the daily round of life under such altered circumstances, her
strength was unequal to the task. During the following summer, her
mind became unhinged, and an illness similar to that from which she had
previously suffered, brought the end. She died in my house at Croydon
on September 6, 1876, and thus all three passed away in less than two
years. My third night journey to Cookham was to lay her by the side
of those she loved.

If it be asked, how did Walker's personality strike one who knew
him as I did, the answer will, I think, be found in a perusal of the foregoing pages. Any traits of character which the letters seemed to me to
illustrate, I have been careful to give, and where he has so fully spoken
for himself, I can add but little. Much, too, depends upon the point of
view : mine was perhaps too near for me to be altogether impartial.
The reader will form his own estimate of Walker's character, unbiassed
by the opinion of others. Mr. Hodgson, who also knew him, found
him, "often trying," and "not altogether lovable." Trying, yes : it is
a way genius has. Palissy, when he tore up his floor boards for fuel,
must have somewhat interfered with the domestic arrangements, and it
is conceivable that Shakespeare was occasionally irregular at meal times,
and in other ways transgressed the rules of a well-ordered house.
Lovable : he was lovable to those who were nearest to him, he was
certainly lovable to me. Of his faults, if it could not be said with
truth "a friendly eye would never see such faults," to see them rightly
was to recognise that they sprang from that temperament that helped to

make him what he was—an artist to the tips of his " poor nail-less fingers." They were faults of temperament, not of heart. For all its little outbursts of petulance, it was a gentle nature. Few men spoke less evil. Like Charity, he sought not his own, he vaunted not himself, was not puffed up. For ever striving to reach a high ideal, his conception of the possibilities of his art contrasted with his own achievements, and bred in him humility. If ambition, not for personal gain, but to become a worthy labourer in the world of beauty, be a fault, it was his. To Mr. Leslie he said, " My ambition is to be the top of all, and if I live, I will." In his evening walks with Mr. North among the Somersetshire hills, he felt depressed at his dissociation from the star-lit universe above him, and like the lark beating his wings against his prison bars, impatience at the limitation of man's powers.

Let the companion of those walks here give his estimate of his friend.

"Still some few, now very few, of the villagers remember him, describe his rapid movements, his horror of observation, his fiery expostulation at any petty act of cruelty or meanness. In my thought, after all these years, he remains a very clear and noble figure, without a trace of meanness. Hasty, impatient, with a grand contempt for paltry worldliness ; and absolutely, in the truest sense, unselfish."

My task is ended, and these records of a life pass from my keeping —let me trust not altogether to unsympathetic hearts. Have I been faithful to my charge ? Have I, in the choice of his own words, and in what I myself have written, given a true picture of the man as he was ? I cannot tell. I can only say that, with the fullest sense of responsibility upon me, I have striven to do my best. Such as my labours are, I place them as a tribute on his grave.

# LIST OF WALKER'S EXHIBITED WORKS

| Year of Exhibition. | Title. | Where Exhibited. | |
|---|---|---|---|
| 1863 | THE LOST PATH | Royal Academy. | |
| 1864 | SPRING | Old Water Colour Society, Summer Exhibition | |
| | GARDEN SCENE | Ditto | Ditto |
| | REFRESHMENT | Ditto | Ditto |
| | SCENE FROM "PHILIP." (Philip in Church) | Ditto | Ditto |
| | SKETCH. (My Front Garden) | Ditto | Winter Exhibition. |
| | SKETCH FOR DENIS DUVAL. (Denis's Valet) | Ditto | Ditto |
| 1865 | AUTUMN | Ditto | Summer Exhibition. |
| | MOSS BANK NEAR TORQUAY | Ditto | Winter Exhibition. |
| 1866 | THE BOUQUET | Ditto | Summer Exhibition. |
| | No Title. No. 352. (The Introduction) | Ditto | Winter Exhibition. |
| | THE STREET, COOKHAM | Ditto | Ditto |
| | No Title. No. 385. (The Sempstress) | Ditto | Ditto |
| | No Title. No. 413. (The Spring of Life) | Ditto | Ditto |
| | WAYFARERS. (Large oil) | Mr. Gambart's Gallery. | |
| 1867 | BATHERS | Royal Academy. | |
| | FISHERMAN AND BOY | Old Water Colour Society, Summer Exhibition | |
| | A VACARME. (" Village on the Cliff") | Ditto | Ditto |
| | No Title. No. 336. (The Violet Field) | Ditto | Winter Exhibition. |
| 1868 | VAGRANTS. (Large oil) | Royal Academy. | |
| | WELL-SINKERS | Old Water Colour Society, Summer Exhibition. | |
| | No. Title. No. 228. (The First Swallow) | Ditto | Ditto |
| | THE BEDROOM WINDOW | Ditto | Ditto |
| | THE FATES, AND CHAPLAIN'S DAUGHTER | Ditto | Ditto |
| | STREAM IN INVERNESS-SHIRE | Ditto | Ditto |
| | LILIES | Ditto | Winter Exhibition. |
| | THE GONDOLA | Ditto | Ditto |
| | MUSHROOMS AND FUNGI | Ditto | Ditto |
| 1869 | THE OLD GATE. (Large oil) | Royal Academy. | |
| | A LADY IN A GARDEN, PERTHSHIRE | Old Water Colour Society, Winter Exhibition. | |
| 1870 | THE PLOUGH. (Large oil) | Royal Academy. | |
| | WAYFARERS. (Water colour)[1] | Old Water Colour Society, Summer Exhibition. | |
| | No Title. No. 334. The Ferry) | Ditto | Winter Exhibition. |
| | AN AMATEUR | Ditto | Ditto |
| | A Sketch. (Pen-and-ink, Vagrants) | Ditto | Ditto |
| | LET US DRINK TO THE HEALTH OF THE ABSENT. (" Village on the Cliff") | Ditto | Ditto |

[1] In possession of W. Cuthbert Quilter, Esq., M.P.

| Year of Exhibition. | Title | Where Exhibited. |
| --- | --- | --- |
| 1871 | AT THE BAR | Royal Academy. |
| | A GIRL AT A STILE | Old Water Colour Society, Winter Exhibition. |
| | THE HOUSEWIFE | Ditto       Ditto |
| 1872 | THE HARBOUR OF REFUGE. (Large oil) | Royal Academy. |
| | THE ESCAPE | Old Water Colour Society, Summer Exhibition. |
| | A FISHMONGER'S SHOP | Ditto       Winter Exhibition. |
| | AT THE BAR. (Small oil) | Dudley Gallery. |
| | CARTOON. ("Woman in White") | Ditto       Black and White Exhibition. |
| 1873 | THE VILLAGE | Old Water Colour Society, Summer Exhibition |
| | THE HARBOUR OF REFUGE. (Water colour)[1] | Ditto       Winter Exhibition. |
| 1874 | THE RAINBOW | Ditto       Ditto |
| 1875 | THE RIGHT OF WAY | Royal Academy. |
| | THE OLD GATE. (Water colour)[2] | Old Water Colour Society, Summer Exhibition |

*** *Owners, other than those with whom the author has lately been in communication, would greatly oblige by sending him particulars of any water colour drawings by Walker in their possession.*

[1] In possession of Humphrey Roberts, Esq.
[2] In possession of Reginald H. Prance, Esq.

# INDEX

Y